The Webster Chronicle

To Jim & William —

Enjoy!

[signature]

The Webster Chronicle

DANIEL **AKST**

BLUEHEN BOOKS
a member of
Penguin Putnam Inc.
New York

This is a work of fiction. Names, characters, places, and incidents either are the product of the author's imagination or are used fictitiously, and any resemblance to actual persons, living or dead, business establishments, events, or locales is entirely coincidental.

BlueHen Books
a member of
Penguin Putnam Inc.
375 Hudson Street
New York, NY 10014

Library of Congress Cataloging-in-Publication Data

Akst, Daniel.
    The Webster chronicle : a novel / Daniel Akst
        p.   cm.
    ISBN 0-399-14812-4
        1. Newspaper publishing—Fiction. 2. Child sexual abuse—Fiction. 3. Fathers and sons—Fiction. 4. New England—Fiction. 5. Journalists—Fiction. I. Title.
PS3551.K58W4   2001   2001025679
813'.54—dc21

Printed in the United States of America

10   9   8   7   6   5   4   3   2   1

This book is printed on acid-free paper. ∞

Book design by AMANDA DEWEY

Are you sollicitious that their Bodies may be Cloath'd: you should be no more sollicitious that their Souls may not be Naked, or go without the Garments of Righteousness.

— COTTON MATHER,
The Duties of Parents to Their Children

The Webster Chronicle

Anniversaries are important to journalists, and so it was that on this, the fifth anniversary of his less-than-triumphant return to the town of his boyhood, Terry Mathers prepared himself for the ordeal of the night ahead by single-handedly smoking a reefer of Rastafarian proportions and heading hatless out into the night.

His destination filled him with dread. The YM-YWCA in Webster was near the former railroad station and just down from the old post office but distinguished itself from the other two by clinging even more tenaciously to what was left of its tattered dignity. Burdened by its Oz-like yellow brick and gewgaws and its redolently old-fashioned name, so suggestive of salvation and temperance and lye soap, the former Young Men's Christian Association (the words were carved with embarrassing permanence above the lintel) was bent now on rescuing itself from the downtown seediness in which it had joined so many of its counterparts in more significant places. It had workshops for middle-aged women, a support group for gay teenagers, an oral history project for the local seniors, low-impact aerobics for the lunchtime crowd, and even some silent films. "We need to *matter* more," the plump new director had told Terry in an earnest lunch the month before, her ruddy face aglow with hygiene and commitment. Always eager to remain unjaded, Terry had kept indulgence out of his smile and promised to take a closer look. Thus, a short while later, he couldn't wriggle out of an invitation to serve on an evening panel at the Y discussing the great question, "Whither Webster?"

Now that the day had come, he was a wreck. He was conscious of trying to look nonchalant, of keeping up appearances, and he blamed his sudden violent diarrhea on the takeout he'd ordered in from the Middle Eastern place around the corner. The babaghanouz, the lettuce—he thought with a chill of the terrible *E. coli* outbreak he had covered at the county fair during the summer. But he couldn't really fool himself. He always ate vegetarian takeout from the Middle Eastern place. He only got sick when he knew he would have to speak in public.

It was all because he stuttered. Sitting in his drafty, disorderly office earlier in the evening, he closed his eyes and tried to calm himself. It was just another meeting after all. What was one more gathering in such an assembly-minded community? His evenings were filled with board meetings, civic functions, and lectures of every kind; lectures seemed to multiply, in fact, even as the word *lecture* itself had disappeared, its place usurped by *workshop* or *seminar* or *talk*. Lecturing was the terrible thing his stepdaughter, Phoebe, accused him of doing sometimes, the kind of thing that was done in the days when Webster was the home of young Christian men. Yet the men and women of modern-day Webster loved these things, craving them like sunshine. This never-ending round of civic convocation had been a burden at first, unsustainable additional punishment after the Rotary dinners and church potlucks and so forth. He'd sent housewives as stringers, or when his own attendance seemed mandatory photocopied the *New York Tribune* crossword puzzle and kept it shuffled among the agendas, draft resolutions, and other paper effluvium of town government, an amulet from that other world intended to ward off sleep. Nowadays, of course, he was just glad to get out of an evening and sometimes even went to school board meetings, the most dreaded variety of all, where despite the killing piety, the pretty young mothers could divert you from the droning of the trustees.

Terry Mathers liked to think he was appealing to women and, for most of his life, had cultivated a shuffling, boyish persona he felt was in keeping with the speech impediment that often made him feel like a frustrated adolescent anyway. He was a tall man, athletic, with a broad, ingratiating face and wavy dark hair thinning only at the top, too high for most other people to see but sufficient anyway to make him cover it with a baseball cap most of the time. Like many tall men, he slouched and, at Webster's many meetings, often slumped deep into his chair, as if in hiding from some larger earnestness he feared might eclipse his own. Or was this posture a holdover from his school days, when he shrank from the terror of being called upon? As a boy, nothing could render him more completely mute than a sudden, public demand that he speak, and so he had pretended in class not to know the answers, no matter how obvious they might be, for had he been asked his own name he couldn't speak that either. Couldn't speak that especially, for some reason. He was better now and through constant vigilance had achieved an uneasy coexistence with whatever power it was that wanted to chain his tongue, but he never forgot that his mysterious demon stood ready to gag him the minute he let down his guard. Nowadays he succumbed mainly when he was most emotional, another reason he worked so hard to control himself. "It's OK," Abigail would say during their protracted phone conversations when Terry got so worked up. "Just breathe." It was his curse that spontaneity and calm were the only cures and that striving for them only pushed them farther away. To stutter still at forty was humiliating; he was surprised that lately he was finding it more embarrassing rather than less, and whenever possible he avoided speaking in public. When there was no choice, he adopted a regimen of humming, singing, and elaborately prepared remarks (practiced to sound offhand). But the only truly effective remedy he had found over the years was marijuana, or so he had come to believe, and as time went on and stresses mounted, he had come to make a habit of it.

He had the office to himself at this hour. As he smoked, he watched his father on TV. It was a nightly ritual for Terry, this business of witnessing Maury Mathers deliver bite-sized sermons from the pulpit of television, and Terry almost always performed his filial duty with the help of his friend Mary Jane. Tonight, as on most nights, Maury was by turns impassioned and learned, offering a trenchant commentary on the future of NATO. Terry tried to listen but it was hopeless. Probably because of the dope, he usually got caught up instead in the old man's expression and rhythms, the performance aspect of his oratory, the irksome fluency his son could never emulate even if they had so much else in common. Terry and Maury looked alike, people always said, and as Terry got older the resemblance grew more pronounced, even as his father grew more theatrically sagelike in the inflating ether of television.

Terry hated television, hated it even more than he hated driving, and single-handedly persuaded the Webster schools to run an annual week without TV, during which various sporting matches, performances, and other festivities were held in a frantic attempt to make everyone forget their addiction. Afterward, sooner or later, they all drifted back, of course. Even Terry, despite his public loathing, found himself watching mindlessly during his newfound solitude. That his father should forsake the rich world of print for the tawdry evanescence of television was satisfyingly in character, he now felt, as if the elder Mathers had casually turned his back on the word itself and all its manifold offspring. It was like saying *sayonara* to the universe. Like dying. By watching his father pontificate, Terry could feel wholesome, uncompromising, clean.

After Maury's nightly visit, Terry had had to tackle the task of putting together a preliminary story list for the next week's edition, and being stoned helped with this too. It muted the harsh contrast between his father, who appeared twice daily on national television and was watched by President Reagan himself, and Terry, who sat here in Webster, where there was the local kid admitted to Harvard, word that the sewer board would probably approve sixteen new condos on the Talbert tract, and a minor brouhaha over a teacher's smack to the ass of some kid at the Alphabet Soup Preschool. That was funny. Alphabet Soup was hugely popular in Webster; he remembered his own little boy not getting in, not passing his "observed play" test or something. Now the mother of the spanked boy wouldn't leave Terry alone, and so he would get someone to make a couple of calls. Why not? Maybe the place was becoming too high and mighty for its own good. Besides, people always wanted to read about kids and schools. It was like Little League and animal stories—they couldn't get enough.

There was even some sexy investigative reporting skedded: a piece on local firms that did business with the county and gave money to county-wide political campaigns. He could see the subhead: Why Inmates Eat So Much Moussaka (because, as the story explained, the campaign of Mayor Dominic Loquendi for County Commission got $3,000 in donations from the Spartacus Diner in Rockton last year). Normally Terry would swell with pride at such a story, but on this night of nights he was without enthusiasm.

And so off he trudged. The Y was only a few blocks from the *Chronicle,* which clung to a side street like a poor relation to the nearby huddle of civic virtue that included, besides the Y, the town hall, the police station, the public library, and a few other stony buildings from 100 years before, and Terry decided to leave his car at the office, as he customarily did when he walked over to the Y to work out or coach what he still thought of as midget basketball. He liked to save money on gasoline, but like so much else with Terry it was also a matter of principle; he hated what cars had done to the planet and the culture, and he inveighed regularly in print against their poisonous and alienating consequences. Besides, on foot you observed a level of reality that was invisible when the world is seen projected onto the screen of an automobile's windshield, and even though the temperature wasn't much above zero and Webster had embarked on an unusually bad winter, God remained, as ever, in the details. Downtown Webster, despite its great familiarity to him, was a lonely place on a desolate wintry night, overlit here and there thanks to the local congressman's way with federal money, and empty except for Pinot and a couple of the other places that catered to the faculty members and shrinks and investment advisers who helped make the town such a pleasantly hypocritical place to live. Turning a corner onto Main Street, he walked past The Old Bean, brightly lit like some Edward Hopper fern bar, the college students inside all jeans and hiking boots and fishermen's knits, the girls in scarves and earrings sipping lattes behind the steamy windows while the boys, soft-faced, still looked like children. Those windows, which seemed to separate him from the warmth of his own youth, foggily emphasized how cold it was outside, in the here and now. An icy wind off the frozen Vanatee River smote him as it scoured the streets, which except for a few central blocks were still snowy from a recent storm and crunched frigidly under foot.

His pace quickened; his feet already felt frozen and from here on, he knew, things were pretty well buttoned up for the night, except for In Vino Veritas, the tony wine store in the next block. He would look inside and wave when he passed it. Otherwise there were just the two banks, the former Webster Savings & Loan whose recent collapse had cost Uncle Sam such a pretty penny, the beauty parlor favored by the old women, the barber shop favored by the old men and the young of both sexes, the imposing limestone First Presbyterian Church ("Relax!" said the signboard. "God loves you!"), sundry small retailers and service establishments and then finally, when you crossed Baxter, there was Krieger's Department Store: brass polished, windows nicely trimmed, sidewalks shoveled the way Charlie Krieger himself shaved, down almost past the top layer of skin, and coffers no less bare than the pavement so carefully cleared of snow. Having just closed for the evening, they had to unlock the doors to let people out.

Terry reached his destination shivering, his moonish face bright with cold. The Y was humid as a greenhouse and smelled pungently of chlorine from the swimming pool in the basement, and sweat from the locker rooms and basketball courts. You could hear the squeak of sneakers on the hardwood, the occasional shout, and Terry wished he could play rather than work. He struggled to control his breathing as he felt the tension rising in his stomach. A recurring image flashed reassuringly through his mind—of himself open in the corner, calmly bending, leaping, and then firing, the ball inscribing a long, high arc through timeless air until it tore through the net with a slap.

For the umpteenth time, he resolved to consort less frequently with that demon weed marijuana. It was hurting his wind and thus his cherished one-on-one game, but that demon was Terry's best friend in Webster right now, and despite his righteous misgivings they consorted happily as he entered the brightly lit auditorium, late as usual. He could see that the vast majority of the audience were women, and unconsciously he preened for them even as he walked quietly to the front and slipped into the seat at the end of the dais, behind the cardboard sign that said EDITOR, THE WEBSTER CHRONICLE.

"Speak of the devil," he heard Melissa Faircloth say cheerily, and a few claps rose cordially from the assembled gathering. Rangy, red-haired Melissa, at once elegant and ungainly, stood calmly at the podium, her accustomed position as head of the local League of Women Voters. "I was just commenting on the coverage in this week's *Chronicle*," she went on. Her softly wry Southern accent was always a relief from the winters of Webster, and the notion of this modest succor from the tundra outside (amplified by enough cannabis to neutralize a rhino) brought Terry nearly to tears. He swallowed these, belched slightly, and giggled. Melissa, bless her, was undaunted. "I was about to say, when you so conveniently appeared, that the fate of our downtown is inextricably connected to what we as a community decide about Krieger's."

Terry grinned gamely, the savory taste of marijuana reminding him of a small problem with hiccups. The *Webster Chronicle* of November 5, 1985, the very day on which the question "Whither Webster?" was being addressed, brought home the news that Krieger's, a publicly held chain of six small-town department stores based in Webster, was the subject of a hostile takeover bid by Ira Rothwax, a Philadelphia retailing magnate and corporate raider. The *Chronicle*'s publisher had received a heads-up two days earlier that a bid from Rothwax was expected, and Terry had gone all out, in just twenty-four hours junking or holding everything he'd done for the week and remaking the entire edition. It had been like the old days, like working at a real newspaper. Since then he had slept for exactly four hours.

Exhaustion, stage fright, and a fat reefer had taken their toll on his attention. The audience seemed unusually vivid, almost threateningly so, but he barely heard a word any of the other panelists said. When his own turn came, he could sense people holding their breath.

"W-W-W-" he began. "W-W-W-W-" He tried once more and then inhaled sharply. He was shocked to find himself already stuck, unable even to pronounce the name of the place where all of them lived. He pretended to look at his notes and tried to clear his mind.

"Good evening," he said, recovering, and he could feel a sigh of relief as he smiled through his gathering blush. His stuttering, he had come to think, was almost as painful for his listeners as it was for him. But tonight his preparations worked their magic. He tried to speak casually, to forget his audience, and confined himself to some brief generalities.

"W-W-Webster has proven to be everything my f-family and I h-hoped it would be when we moved here," he lied, adding that "the q-q-question of K-Krieger's immediate future is as m-m-much on our m-m-minds as yours. As m-most of you know, they are our b-b-biggest advertiser, and t-t-they anchor a downtown full of the r-rest of our advertisers."

After his initial scare, he quickly settled down, his stoppered words at last tumbling out in a rush, like beer poured rapidly from a long-necked bottle, and before he knew it, he was done. He finished with the same almost delirious sense of relief he felt any time he managed to speak publicly without finding his words chained inside his chest.

The rest of the time passed, Terry wasn't sure how. He spent most of it scouting for women in the audience, coming back to one particular unfamiliar face whenever he dared, a small woman with a taut figure in the front row. She wore a purple suit with a short skirt and seemed dressed up in the charming way of women who do not dress up all the time, her hair opting out of whatever plans she might have made for it and her shoes scuffed with weather. Something about her made it hard to stop looking. He was yanked back to the present during the question-and-answer period, when one of the few men in the audience stood up, and in a loud, almost hectoring voice, asked: "How can you people any longer drag your feet in doing what needs to be done to bring some parking downtown and save the community's biggest private employer? Are you all deaf, dumb, and blind? We're about to lose Krieger's, and you all sit here talking all this planning gobbledygook."

The speaker was Ed Krcyszyki, the wiry, bellicose leader of the union representing workers at Krieger's. Terry was fond of Krcyszyki, who had spent six years putting himself through Web State at night while selling women's shoes by day, and who had risen from his hands and knees to elevate the lives of his many fellow employees. His whole life, in fact, stood as a rebuke to Charles Krieger, the self-absorbed Krieger's heir whose cosseted youth unjustly culminated at the helm of the department store chain, which he ran now largely for his own benefit. *Krcyszyki was right,* Terry thought. *How can we not build the garage? How can we let Krieger's go—and the* Chronicle *potentially with it? Are the people who run this town crazy?* At the back of his throat he could taste the rise of cannabis-inflected bile.

Realizing that the question "Whither Webster?" would become yet another discussion about parking, Terry came so close to weeping that he had to take a deep breath, heaving his chest and surprising himself by rasping. He got this way after a lot of pot, which lately, before an evening like this one, he found more and more reason to administer prophylactically against the misery of participatory democracy, just as travel to some equatorial backwater demanded inoculation against obscure tropical diseases.

The next thing he heard was Melissa's soothing voice. "This is obviously a hot subject here tonight," she said, "just as it was when it was first laid to rest a couple of years ago, and the League will be scheduling a forum on it very soon, I promise you that. So I'm gonna cut off the discussion now before we get going in a direction that keeps us here until morning or a technical knockout, I don't know which."

One or two good-natured titters arose, and Terry wondered why sensible, adept Melissa Faircloth was not queen of the universe. He marveled at her unerring instincts and tried to give her a warm look. Maybe it was time to take the head of the League to lunch.

When Melissa had thanked all the panelists, she firmly told the audience to remain seated. Like all League audiences, this one consisted entirely of gluttons for enlightenment who had no trouble doing so.

"I'm pleased to introduce a special guest this evening," said Melissa, "a newcomer to our community who has a very important message to share with us tonight. I've taken the liberty of inviting her because I thought you'd all want to meet her, and because I think the subject of her professional concern is so important. So without further ado, let's all welcome Diana Shirley, the county's new child sex-abuse specialist, who will say just a few brief words to us. Diana?"

To his horror, the woman Terry had been staring at suddenly rose and was approaching the stage. Frantically, he ignored her, then thought better and flashed a weak smile, but she wasn't looking. He loved the way she moved. Why on earth did the county need an expert on the sexual abuse of children? What jittery times, Terry thought; poor Leon Klinghoffer had only recently been shot and thrown off the deck of the *Achille Lauro* by Palestinian terrorists, and the other day Terry's lifelong dentist confronted him with rubber gloves and a mask. Like everyone else, he was worried about AIDS. Child abuse wouldn't surprise anyone in such a climate. Dimly he recalled something about a grant for this. At least the person they were funding was good-looking.

The room was silent as the speaker, without a shred of nervousness, affirmed how glad she was to be in Webster and how grateful she was to Mayor Loquendi for his help in securing the federal funding that had enabled the county to employ her. Then, knowing she was speaking on what amounted to borrowed time, she quickly described the national problem of incest and child abuse, which only now allowed its name to be spoken. There were an estimated 240,000 cases of child sexual abuse annually in this country, she said with striking matter-of-factness. It was something that happened in every community in America, even in a place as nice as Webster. With confidence, she reported that someone in this room had been the victim of such abuse as a child, and that more than one person knew someone who was an abuser. Terry paid close attention, not just to the words but to the person who spoke them. She was a small, erect woman with a childlike quality about her features, even though she was probably thirty-five, and she had a powerful voice of unusual clarity delivered from a small mouth beneath round, dark eyes and short, curly hair of an oaky blonde color. He thought her supremely sexy.

Fortunately, she continued, community resources were starting to become available for dealing with this most hidden and shameful problem, both for the abuser and his or her victims. Many of those in attendance took notes, as women often did at such gatherings, but Terry didn't notice because he was absorbed by his own note-taking, and by the speaker's unusual ability to compel attention. He was reminded of school-teachers he'd had as a boy, their posture perfect and their voices confident.

"The thing for all of us to remember, in this day when children seem so unfortunately grown up, is that they *are* innocent, they *are* powerless. Children have no lobbyists, they don't get to vote, they don't have lawyers, they can't write letters to the editor. Somebody must speak for the children. And that somebody"—she paused and looked around—"that somebody is us. It's nobody but us. Because if our voices are silent, if your voices are silent, you, as the people of Webster, then these children who are being abused have no other option but to lean their heads against the window pane of the school bus and watch their childhoods slip away.

"OK. So what can I do? How can I make my voice heard? Basic stuff. Badger every legislator, every assemblyman and state senator, call your congressman, get after the press—" did she direct a glance at Terry here? "—because they're the ones who set the agenda. Don't let your writers and editors fall down on the job until the problem is recognized and the problem is solved. There's a shortage of funding, a shortage of training, and most of all, which is why I'm here tonight, a shortage of awareness. There's so much work to be done. So I guess the message I want to leave you with is to remember that you're the only voice of the violated child. If you don't speak, there is silence. I'm not saying it's always going to be easy. But think how much easier it is for you than for that poor child."

Afterward, there was a smattering of heartfelt applause—a smattering not, Terry could see, because the audience wasn't impressed but, on the contrary, because it was deeply so. He was sure a couple of people even wiped tears from their faces. Then the speaker quickly alit the stage and became invisible, engulfed by a bodyguard of women from the audience who rushed up with serious expressions on their faces. They took pamphlets, business cards, added to their already copious notes. He wanted to meet her but hung back, waiting for the crowd to clear and determined not to trample on anything. What would it be like to know this woman, he wondered. What was her story? How had she come to this particular moment in the history of the universe? He tried to play Sherlock Holmes based on her clothing and speech, but his faculties were overwhelmed and it began to dawn that he was thoroughly, vertiginously stoned. *Hold very still,* he told himself, hoping the dizziness would pass. When Diana's other admirers had mostly drifted away, he went up and introduced himself, discovering with relief that his mind and body remained on speaking terms. But something in her tone set him on edge: a hint of officiousness, a little chill, the slightest narrowing of the eyes. Could she tell he was high? He felt baited, jealous of her fluency. If she would adopt that role, he would take the one of insinuating, suspicion-filled reporter. It was a part he knew well.

"So tell me, what's the budget for your office?"

"Well it's really just my salary. I share an assistant."

"OK, what's your salary?"

"I'm not going to tell you that!"

"It's a m-matter of public record."

"Then go look it up!" Diana said, shaking her head at this chutzpah and turning to pack up her things.

"Look, I don't know if you're n-n-new to p-public life, but you're r-really not helping your cause by a-a-alienating the local newspaper."

She whirled on him furiously.

"The problem here is that you can't seem to focus on the issues," she said. Her eyes were huge. "There are children in this community suffering sexual abuse that will leave them scarred for life, and all you want to know is what kind of paltry paycheck I get for this job. This county isn't spending a dime of its taxpayers' money, and even if it were, my pay would be a rounding error in the overall budget. Do you have children, Mr. Mathers?"

"I-I-If I say yes, a-a-am I entitled to an opinion?"

"Any time you want to talk to me about the substance of what I do, give me a call, OK? I've got to go."

"I'd be happy to talk about the substance of what you do," Terry said. *Stop now,* he told himself, knowing that his love of disputation was leading him into ever deeper shit. "But whether there's anything for you to do is part of what I meant to ask you about. Wouldn't we be better off spending this money on shelters in the inner city or training schoolteachers to spot abuse so they could report it to the police?" Diana, packing more rapidly now, looked as if she might respond but then thought better.

"Why," Terry continued, "does Vanatee County need a child sex-abuse expert? I-I mean, with all due respect."

But by that time, she was headed for the door.

"W-W-What kind of response is that?" he called after her back. "I mean, what kind of message is that sending? H-H-How can you change anyone's mind by walking away?"

She kept walking, and he was left to figure out by looking around how embarrassed he needed to be. Not terribly, he assured himself, closing his pad, but just then an older woman brushed past, shaking her head.

"Such a cynic," she tutted.

I'm an idealist, he wanted to say. *A frustrated idealist.* But he couldn't get the words out fast enough to stop her, and so he moved off to take care of business, pretending to be the hearty, loud-laugh sort of fellow the mayor and several others seemed to want him to be, until finally the place was all but empty and he drifted toward the exit.

In the deserted parking lot, he noticed a faded red Saab going nowhere with the engine running. Terry Mathers was a man who believed deep down that the gods looked out for him, and tonight the world again confirmed his grace, having sent him not only Diana but her car troubles. *My cup runneth over,* he thought.

"It's your parking brake," he told her. "They get all slushy and then freeze up as the temperature drops. Better not to use 'em, if you can avoid it. Park in first, cramp your wheels, whatever." He would sound manly, telegraphic. "Here, lemme try something."

He flicked the lighter he carried with him for medicinal purposes (he had used it that very night to light a joint) and slid under the car. He was freezing, but it was hard not to smile. His lighter was much too small to melt what was no doubt under there, in his experience, but it was a marvelous chance to be heroic. And in truth, Terry would have done this for anybody; he loved helping people, even if they always proved insufficiently grateful, and he was glad to have lust in this case to mask the impulse to martyrdom that usually motivated him.

"Can you knock it off with a screwdriver or something?"

No, he wanted to lie, but instead he said, "Do you have one?"

She opened the rear hatch and pointed to a compartment containing a little tool kit complete with a pair of pristine white gloves. He noticed that she also had a large first-aid kit kicking around in back, as well as a beat-up picnic cooler, a snorkel and some flippers, a tangle of bungee cords, a bicycle helmet, a flattened roll of paper towels, and a can of stuff that would supposedly inflate your tire if you had a flat.

"I'm sorry about before," he said emphatically. Sometimes it helped to blurt. "I really wasn't trying to give you a hard time."

"Well, you're doing a good job making up for it."

The heaviest thing available was a kind of wrench in the tool kit, and he used it to knock off the frozen slush and free her emergency brake. He took his time about it, though, wanting it to seem a bigger favor than it was, and in fact it was hard without enough space for a clear swing at the thing.

"God, thanks so much," she said as he climbed stiffly out from under the vehicle. "You must be just frozen under there. You're not even wearing gloves!"

"No big deal," he said. His hands were numb. "Start it up, see if the brake light goes off."

"It worked! Get in and get warm at least," she said, seeming not at all nervous now, and as she cleared the papers and cassette tapes off the seat of her car, its flanks whitened by the snow and salt of the country roads in winter, he felt a little sheepish again, which made him worry about his speech.

"Where's your car?" she said, looking around the lot. "Can I give you a ride somewhere? Or let met buy you some coffee—you look like you need it."

"Well, I'd still like to do a story about you. About your coming here. We could talk about all that."

They drove in silence, out past where Main Street turned into the county road. Webster sprawled haphazardly in this direction, with buildings seeming to be set almost randomly in the former cornfields that were now mainly parking. Not more than a quarter of the spaces were ever filled, and tonight they were almost all empty. There had been a thaw,

melting enough snow to make all the roads wet, but by now everything
was frozen again, and the temperature was dropping fast, making driving
treacherous. Diana drove jerkily, taking too much time to work the shift
so that the car was losing momentum whenever they entered a higher
gear, and he could feel the scantness of their traction sometimes during
these powerless intervals. She must be from someplace warm, he decided.
(Fresno, he would later learn. Her father had been a minister there, and
she inherited his religious impulses. Lacking his faith if not his calling,
she had chosen to save the tenderest souls in her own way.) When they
arrived at Aiello's, an Italian diner on the edge of town, they found the
icy parking lot curtailed by gray banks of frozen snow, the stripes
between spaces invisible and the cars parked in such haphazard array that
they seemed abandoned by their drivers to the winter. They slipped into a
spot hidden like a canyon between four-wheel-drive vehicles, the new
craft of choice even for Webster's vegans.

"Hiya, Chip. Decaf for you?"

"Thanks, Harriet." He blushed at being called by his boyhood nick-
name. "And a piece of something sweet."

"And coffee for you?" Harriet smiled crookedly at his companion,
arching her penciled eyebrows. Her hair was dark brown, but you didn't
have to look too closely to see that she was old. "I'll get you a menu."

"Just decaf for me too," Diana said, removing her coat and jacket. He
noticed that the bottle-green cable-knit sweater that she wore was frayed
slightly, and too long, so that the sleeves covered her knuckles, which
enhanced the impression given by her small size and big eyes that she
might still be a little girl. He groped briefly for a word from a recent
crossword until finally it came to him: *neoteny.* He spotted cat hairs on her
youthful bosom and, eager not to be caught staring again, quickly looked
around the restaurant. Aiello's was off the beaten path, and its patrons at
this hour were mostly strangers to him except for plump old Pearl Gibson, who sat in a corner dunking dog biscuits in her coffee and feeding
them to the cocker spaniel who sat in the booth beside her. Terry
motioned with his chin, and Diana turned to look. When she turned back
she was flushed and smiling, and mentally Terry thanked the old lady for
so thoroughly disarming his guest.

chapter **TWO**

The next day, Abigail Thorndike settled into her office at the *Chronicle* early as usual and did all kinds of busy work until Terry appeared. He got to the office late Thursday mornings, visibly luxuriating in the miracle of the week's edition and the great distance between it and the next one, and it was with an uneasy mixture of affection and resentment that she watched him saunter smugly through the nave-turned-newsroom, his blue woolen New York Yankee cap set at a jaunty angle. She sighed and looked away when he stopped to flirt with Ariadne Tidwell, the prettiest of his young reporters, whom Abigail knew to be a complete incompetent, and when she looked back he was gone, having ducked into his glass-walled office. There he was, on stage as usual in his own little shrine to boyhood, his work space the customary shambles of papers, toys, and other wise-guy paraphernalia. There was a little basketball hoop and a bag of foam balls, so he could shoot a bunch without getting up after each one, and on the corner of his desk there was the skull, which he kept not as a memento mori—God knew Terry had an adolescent's sense of immortality—but rather because he thought it made him seem cool, the way Phoebe had started smoking. Abigail waited a decent interval and then buzzed him on the intercom.

"Come on in, gorgeous," his voice squawked through her speakerphone. She saw him looking across the room at her through the glass of their offices. It was annoying that, in dealing with her after their separation, Terry would use lust to simulate good cheer. "Is it my turn? OK."

She watched him hoist his bulk out of his chair. As he approached, she looked around, as she always did, making sure there was nothing she didn't want him to see, but her desk was immaculate, and the rest of her office was neat if a little formal. It had glass walls, just like Terry's, and a red Persian rug on the corner of which sat the high-heeled pumps (shiny mahogany today) that she still wore to work, even here in Webster, with her silky blouses and pearls.

Abigail and Webster had never been a great fit. She came of what had once been known as good family, at least on her mother's side, which was Canadian, and she was conscious of having inherited some of her mother's irrepressible superiority. Her family had opposed her marriage to Terry, whose destiny even then seemed radically unequal to his father's, and who was Jewish besides, and although they never allowed their opposition to flower into unpleasantness, things were never the same between parents and daughter from the day she told them of her intentions. It was as if they would insulate themselves against the inevitable disappointment the marriage must bring by disinvesting in this perverse child and piling their hopes on her three siblings. On the other hand, Abigail had been a great favorite of Terry's mother, the two of them sitting sometimes in unspoken commiseration over afternoon cocktails, in warm weather watching the sun set over the gentle hills to the west. When Maria died, her daughter-in-law felt the loss as much as Terry did, and it marked the end of Abigail's illusions about her new home.

"Madame Publisher," her husband said in sardonic greeting and barged into the room. As he entered, in his flannel shirt and threadbare khakis, he closed the blinds and settled into one of her two leather-upholstered club chairs, holdovers from the days when their initial financing left money for such things. She walked around to the front of her desk, put her stockinged feet together, and leaned back.

"So Krieger's," she said with a sigh. "You want more space?"

"P-Put your shoes on."

"Terry, be serious."

Six months after their separation, they had fallen into some new, more complicated entanglement. It was exciting. Together they had grown stale and careworn, but apart they were often on fire for each other. They had made love in his horrid little apartment a few nights ago and, spurred by resentment, she had spanked him until her hand hurt.

"Trade. S-S-Shoes on, everything else off. Except the p-pearls."

Abigail twitched impatiently. "I want to talk business, Terry. Krieger's is taking four full pages this week, including the Part I double truck."

"Geez Louise, it's raining money!" he bellowed. It was strange that he never stuttered when he shouted or whispered or sang. "Of course, I'd just as soon give it back."

"Give it back! Are you nuts?"

"It's just a knee-jerk thing. I get worried that it puts unspoken p-pressure on the coverage, or that the sheer volume of advertising would give us an air of bias, or being b-beholden. Whatever. But don't worry, Charlie Krieger doesn't have enough money to get me to like him."

"I don't give a shit about Charles," Abigail said with a sigh. "He just happens to be our biggest advertiser, and it matters to this whole community whether his stores are locally owned or just another asset in the portfolio of some cold-blooded carpetbagger. It also matters that this community have a voice like yours, which it won't if the *Chronicle* goes under." She would appeal to his vanity. One of her new contact lenses hurt—she was trying the soft ones this time—and she put this pain into her voice. "We need Krieger's, Terry, and so does Webster, just as much as it needs you."

"W-Would it be another editorial that you have in mind?"

"What I'm trying to get across to you is that this newspaper is going to play a crucial role in the Krieger's takeover fight. We're shaping public opinion."

"Abby, sweetheart, we can fit an entire press run into half a dozen station wagons. We're not widely read on Wall Street."

"This isn't going to be decided on Wall Street," she said impatiently. "It'll be decided in the legislature, in the communities where Krieger's has stores, and by how the larger media get the story out. And you're the one they'll look to. So can you handle an extra thirty-two columns? We can give some of the big advertisers a freebie if you can't fill."

"No, I'll take all of it, what the hell. We'll do some kind of chronology, run a bunch of stuff I've been holding."

"Thatta boy. I knew you could do it."

"So is there any chance we can p-pay ourselves something soon? I am r-running on empty."

"I can give you a couple hundred."

Terry sighed and rubbed his face in his hands.

"Look, we were lucky to make payroll at all this week," Abigail said. "Terry, I don't know if you have any idea how bad things are around here, but trust me, they're terrible. We're behind with almost all our vendors, neither of us has been paid in more than a month—right now this newspaper just isn't viable, and if it fails, it'll drag us down with it. We're personally on the hook here, remember?" She sighed. "Have you talked to your father yet?"

"As a m-m-matter of fact I have talked to him. Everything is copacetic on that front."

Abigail looked at him, trying to gauge his truthfulness. *Why do I have to be in this position?* she wondered. *Why does he always have to be the wayward son and make me into the nagging mother?*

"You're saying you've come clean with Maury. He knows there's no way we can pay him when the note comes due in something like ninety days."

"Kn-knows all about it."

"Was he upset?"

"Not really."

"So what did you come up with? Some kind of extension?"

"N-n-nothing that formal," Terry said casually. "He's just gonna go along with us for a while. He understands and wants to help. Doesn't have much alternative, really."

"Well see, that wasn't so bad, was it? I wish you'd done that sooner. I'd have felt a lot better about things."

"He's not stupid, Abigail. He knew something was up. We're always late with the interest anyway."

"Meanwhile, we really need to think about letting a couple of people go. Either that or live in a car."

"This whole thing would look a little better if you put those shoes back on," he said, pointing at them. *A little boy,* she thought. *They're all little boys.*

"I'm not sure you're entitled to any milk, if you won't buy the cow." She kicked him playfully.

"I can't buy anything if I can't get some money out of this paper sooner or later," he said. "Listen, I don't mind you plotting with your boyfriend—"

"He's not my boyfriend!"

"—to keep his stores independent, but why are we just soliciting Krieger's? If we really want to make money, we ought to get some of the business Ira Rothwax is laying around, with those big ads in the *Wall Street Journal*. You know what a full page costs in that thing?"

"Good point," she admitted. "I'll call Rothwax, milk him for all he's worth."

"That's the spirit! Why should we arty bohemian types be the only ones who stay poor in this whole business?"

"That reminds me—we've got the open house for Marty's art class coming up. Don't forget. You promised we'd both attend."

"Count on me."

"Mr. Reliable," she said dryly.

As Terry slipped out of her office, she felt a pang of despair. She wanted to grab him, throw something at him, get his attention somehow and make him realize what he was doing, how much she felt. *Stupid!* she wanted to hiss. *Don't you see there's too much history between us?* Abigail had studied history in college, before joining the great herd of humanities graduates stampeding fearfully into the law, and she still read history avidly. Reading and thinking about the past had led her to conclude that a present without context had no meaning, that people who changed their lives like their clothing almost weren't people at all. History was important to her, and history was what she had with her husband. Just think: they had known each other almost half their lives.

That was why she wouldn't tell him about her dinner the night before with Charles Addison Krieger III, during which he explained that he'd hired the small investment banking firm of Flemington Mercer to help him restructure the company. This, Abigail knew, was code for borrowing inordinate sums, selling precious assets, and in general screwing things up so royally that potential bidders are driven off in despair. Kind of like wrecking your house to fend off well-heeled buyers.

"I'll be honest with you," Krieger had said, his eyes dissembling madly. "It was discouraging. The top mergers and acquisitions law firm and two of the top investment banking firms are already on retainer to Rothwax, and we couldn't afford them anyway. The fees these people charge! Abby, I can't believe you threw all that over for life in this modest burg."

"I was a securities lawyer, Charles. An associate, specializing in taxation. I never made that kind of money. I was the sort of people they would hire. I think the guys in M&A saw me as essentially clerical. They knew they could still make me cry."

"Their fees make me cry. This is like my divorce, only worse. I gotta pay through the nose to stay single."

They were at the Saddle & Crop, the best-known restaurant in Webster, but it was a restaurant of a certain type: the entryway was flanked by a lamp crafted from an animal's paws and, on the other side, an elephant leg umbrella stand, while the rest of the place was festooned with stuffed deer, moose, pronghorn antelope, badger, a variety of birds and fish, antique guns, fishing rods, wicker creels, and anything else an animal rights activist might need to conclude he'd been sent to hell for his sins. The menu boasted every conceivable form of game, and you could pick your own filet from a rolling cart glistening with raw flesh.

"See, this is what happens when you go public," she said, allowing herself this little I-told-you-so. "You take other people's money, and you discover that other people have some very different ideas about things than you do." Especially, she might have added, when the company's stock is off 60 percent from the initial public offering price in three years. Krieger's simply wasn't very profitable anymore.

"I know, I know. This is all because of the cousins and nephews and nieces and all the other fucking Kriegers my fecund grandfather spawned. They want to make movies, live in Venice, who knows what. Everyone wanted liquidity. To them, Krieger's is just a giant teat at which they hope to suckle all the livelong day. I can just see them all jostling for a nipple, like little piglets."

Terry is right, Abigail thought, maintaining an expression of rapt interest. *This man is an asshole.* They had been high school rivals of some kind, dueling princes, a pair of young aristocrats in a tiny, charmed kingdom. Now Charles spent part of every day on the racquetball court and kept his graying hair carefully trimmed. Someday, sooner or later, there would no doubt be mottled skin and uneven hair loss, but before that he would enjoy a sleek period as silver-haired aristocrat, ever more at home in his carefully tailored suits and manicured fingernails. But he was the kind of asshole Abigail found herself liking, the kind she had known and come to appreciate in her former life. What she liked about Krieger was his paradoxical authenticity. Even when he was conniving and manipulating, flattering and flirting, always there was the sense of someone real, someone who was never seduced by his own lies. When Krieger gave generously of his shareholders' money to causes like the Police Athletic League, he did so ironically, just as he referred to the company jet in the Krieger's annual report as *The Indefensible.* On his tax return, where it asks for occupation, he always put down "merchant prince." Abigail was reminded of her favorite uncle's cardinal rule about running a business: you kept two sets of books because there was no worse sin than believing what you told everybody else. Unlike the rest of Webster, Charles Krieger had perspective on himself and a sense of humor about things. It was as if he understood, where others didn't, how soon we would all be dead.

The Saddle & Crop was another reason she liked Krieger. It was his favorite restaurant, and they treated him like royalty there. Terry almost never set foot in such a place—she imagined a sign over the door saying, "Vegetarians, abandon all hope ye who enter here"—and after all these years, she was fed up with eggplant and couscous, tofu and miso, mushrooms and brown rice, all the pale and salty substitutes that left you thirsting unquenchably for something you could never quite name after every meal. All that time, she had come to see, what she really wanted was meat.

"Charles. Have you considered the nonfinancial aspects of this whole situation?"

"Of course I have." His blue eyes were hard as gems. "I understand what local ownership in a firm like ours means, what role we play around here, how many families are counting on us, what it would mean for municipal tax rolls if any of our stores closed . . ."

"Yes, but have you considered how you should handle these things? How you should *exploit* them? Public opinion, Charles. Politics. The local courts, with their sympathetic local judges."

"Well, no, not exactly. But I'm all ears." His look suggested otherwise. She had always suspected he nursed a crush.

"It's just that takeover battles for companies like yours are as often won in these arenas as on Wall Street. I mean, let's face it, you've already lost there. A lot of the outstanding shares have already passed into the hands of arbitrageurs, and you'll find them quite a neutral lot emotionally. They just want the highest bid in the shortest time. It's a very clean position, really."

"You know, Abby, with your legal background and your experience in the court of public opinion, you might be able to do us as much good as any of those high-priced shysters back there in the city."

"Well, it's probably true that the media can help, depending on how your story gets told and how the people and the political leadership react to it."

"OK, I'm sold," he said with a smile. "You're hired."

"Hired?"

"As our chief strategist."

"Charles, I already have my hands full with the paper and my family, such as it is."

"But who else can I get? Who has the perspective and experience that you have in these matters? In Webster yet? Who else can I trust? Some hired guns still wet behind the ears from MBA school?"

"You flatter me too much. I've already told you everything I know about the subject, and if I took on one more thing, I think my daughter would strangle me in my sleep."

"A consultant! Better yet! I'll make it worth your while, believe me. I'm planning to issue all kinds of stock options in this crazy restructuring we're about to do, and I've got 10,000 that would look just great with your name on them."

"Look, that's very kind but I'll be happy to do what I can just this way, over dinner or a couple of sandwiches or something. Just let me stick you with the check."

"Fine, we'll haggle over compensation later." Krieger signaled impatiently for their waiter. To Abigail, he said: "Will you join me for some of their really old brandy? This is on the company, remember."

So uneasily, Abigail was engaged. She did not like the idea of conniving with Krieger in this way, or at least this was the story she told herself, but she was determined that the stores should remain independent. The *Chronicle*'s prospects otherwise were dismal. Rothwax owned large outlets in a couple of the giant regional shopping malls, and she felt certain that if he got hold of Krieger's, he would close many of the newly acquired stores in no time, maybe fill the big old spaces with a collection of boutiques that hardly advertised at all, or maybe leave the buildings vacant, for all he cared, until they were filled with university extension courses, Social Security administrators, dropped ceilings, shuffling desperadoes, all the accoutrements of urban abandonment. Cheaply produced flyers would swirl around on the windswept sidewalks outside, and parking would no longer be any problem at all.

Schools always made Terry nervous, even after dark. It was because of school that he still got butterflies in his stomach when the leaves started to turn and the first chill breeze of September reminded him of summer's end, and this vague fearfulness was amplified in visiting his son's elementary school in the dead of winter because it was the same one he himself had attended as a boy. Even now, worrying a million and one things by day, his dreams by night put him back in that institution, where he had forgotten his homework, his classroom, his pants.

As he approached the haughty Gothic schoolhouse, set back in smug indifference to the broken and windy schoolyard out front, he felt like a boy now, a boy scrubbed and slicked into his Sunday best, tie askew and rebellious cowlick doggedly erect. Inside, it was warm, and made him think of summertime family gatherings, station wagons stacked up outside, the mothers and aunts sweating in their dresses and pearls as they beamed at him indulgently. Yet it was such a middle-aged feeling, walking through these spotless corridors with Abigail, who seemed so wifely at this moment, subdued by the idea of school the ways girls always were. They were like the farmers who had used to come on open-school night, callus-handed country folk too shy to talk to each other on this sacred ground where book-learning took place. Abigail adopted the funereal mumble he knew well from visits with her to doctors, marriage counselors, and other places where she felt embarrassed to be or to be overheard, as if upholding one's dignity required ventriloquism. She drove him crazy this way, walking stiffly along like some latter-day Ed Sullivan, her lank hair drawn down around her face. He was fed up with the way his wife hardly gestured, rarely joked, didn't do voices or imitations, couldn't make him laugh. He had married an accountant, a bean counter. Behind him a peal of flirtatious laughter rang out, and he looked longingly in its direction. The floors were so highly polished he wanted to take off his shoes and slide.

Marty was the only one who felt at home here, and he charged forward with the confidence of belonging. They heard the voices of other, heartier parents echoing off the corridors ahead of them and soon found themselves in a large room where the annual first grade art show was being held. The students had been asked to portray the most important issue or event in their lives, however stylized the rendering, and they had done a good job. There were acrylic paintings, works in crayon, sculptures made from wire hangers, starched *Chronicle* newsprint that Terry tried at first to read (hoping to spot something familiar), and an installation about missing children made of empty milk cartons. One or two of the still-married people he and Abigail knew weren't sure what to make of them together, or how to deal with them individually when their friendship had been couple to couple. But there was a complete mixture of parental and spousal arrangements, and most people thought nothing of Marty's separated parents showing up at the art fair together. They were grown-ups, after all, and the child was with them.

Marty was a dark-haired boy, tall and slender for his age, and with characteristic energy he tugged eagerly at each of his parents, anxious to show them his contribution to the exhibit. It was a painting, larger than most, and Abigail saw it first, so that Terry's response was colored by the way her face fell. When he caught up and took her elbow, she covered her mouth with her hand and began to cry.

The paper was covered by grayish teardrops, but through them one could see three figures: a woman, a man with a beard, and a little boy between the two, beseeching them. The man and the woman looked away from each other, and the boy, who looked at them with two faces, was closer to the man than the woman. All their faces were blackened with tears.

Marty looked confused and then sad; surely he had known he'd get a reaction, but he can't have imagined it would be so powerful. Terry sent him off to look at the other drawings and took Abigail out into the corridor, where he tried to calm her. She waved him off, biting her lips, and when he persisted she blew up.

"Look what you've done," she cried. People permitted themselves only the briefest glance and then tried not to look. "Look what you've done to your son, to all of us. I have to explain that Daddy still loves him, it's just me he doesn't love anymore. He doesn't understand, Terry. He doesn't understand why he can only stay with you when I'm not around, or why Phoebe won't visit you at all. I don't understand either. I really don't." He tried to take her in his arms, but she pulled away, her face hot and contorted with pain. "I really, really don't," she cried.

"Ab-Ab-Ab—" He took a deep breath and tried again. "It was something we both wanted. I didn't mean to hurt you."

"Give me your handkerchief."

"I use these now," he said, offering a Kleenex.

"All of a sudden we're strangers."

"I couldn't cope with the laundry. You've changed too. Your clothes, your glasses."

"Girl's got to keep up appearances," she said wearily.

"You look nice."

"Cut the crap. Don't flirt with me—you're my husband." She blew her nose loudly. "Give me another tissue."

"That's all I had," he said.

"Go talk to Marty, then, will you? I need to find a bathroom."

Terry took a deep breath and went back into the classroom, where he looked once again at his son's artwork. Seeing it by himself now was like a spike through his heart, and he wanted more than anything to reassemble the pieces of his family and shower its members with kisses for accepting him back into its bosom. Yet he remained unsure what to do or where his allegiance might lie. It crossed his mind that in order to make their marriage work, he and Abigail ought to consider selling the *Chronicle,* which was like a lead weight dragging down their prospects into the dark and silent depths of the ocean. He could feel them descending with it, feel the waters rushing past his ears.

Looking for his son, he found him finally pouting off in a corner, attended by a teacher.

"I'm sorry for making Mom cry," he said, gasping through his tears. His face was hot and blotchy.

"Marty, it's OK." Terry hugged him. "It's OK."

"She usually likes my drawings."

"Sh-sh-she loves your drawings, pal." Terry sat on his haunches and began wiping at his son's face. "This one was so good that it made her cry, that's all. We're both so proud of you, Marty. You're a real artist! You've used your pain to create beauty, and you did such a remarkable job that Mom just burst into tears. Sh-sh-she didn't mean for you to get upset. She'll be back in a minute, and we'll all go home and have dinner."

That night, as they prepared food, they were all quiet. Marty helped his mother make salad dressing and then played quietly with some little race cars, running them over the table, the chairs, and up his father's arms and shoulders, down his torso and along his thighs and legs, as if in some voodoo ritual to capture the essence of a person who would soon be gone.

"The upstairs toilet is still running," Abigail said as she got leftovers out of the microwave for dinner. "Do you want to look at it or should I get the plumber?"

Terry was disheartened to receive such news about their house in this way, as an outsider, and almost as sad that the family's home was always in such a state of marginal repair. They had bought it in such hopes, their realtor—Melissa Faircloth—presenting it as a fixer-upper full of potential. Now it was clear he and his family would always live in leaky, drafty houses, weighing their discomfort against the cost of a plumber, an electrician, or perhaps more aptly, a bulldozer. He liked doing this work but never seemed to have time. "I'll fix it," he said. "I'll get the parts this week."

"Phoebe, come and eat," Abigail called.

Phoebe, from upstairs, called back something inaudibly sullen.

"Come down and eat!" her mother repeated, looking at the ceiling in appeal.

"I'm not hungry," Phoebe said loudly and then slammed the door to her room.

No one was, as it turned out. Marty insisted that his father cut up his spaghetti and then wouldn't eat and wouldn't say why, until finally he started to cry. His parents decided to wait on their own dinner until they could put him to bed. Terry carried him up and talked about some fun things they might do, and when he and Abigail came back downstairs they skipped eating, instead collapsing on the sofa with their drinks.

"Are you going to take Marty this weekend?" she asked.

"Sure, I'll take him. You have plans?"

"Nothing in particular, I just need to know. He wants to be with you. I don't want him disappointed, that's all."

"The way I've disappointed you."

"Terry, what are we doing here? Do you want a divorce? Is there somebody else? Just tell me."

"Look, maybe this was all a mistake, this whole thing with the *Chronicle.* Maybe—Abby, what if we unload the paper? Get rid of it, take a nice long vacation and try again? You know, a clean slate."

"You don't want to sell the *Chronicle.* Who are you kidding? You love the *Chronicle,* writing your column every week, needling the City Council, stirring up trouble."

"I really don't know anymore," he said truthfully. "I'm so damned tired."

"Besides, what lunatic are you thinking would buy this thing? It doesn't make any money. We're in debt up to our eyeballs. We'd have to give it to our creditors."

"M-m-maybe that's what we should do."

"And just write off everything we own? The children's college money? Tell your father 'sorry, we can't repay you after all'?"

Terry was silent, and Abigail kissed him hard. "I'm not that easy," she said. "Don't you know that by now?" She kissed him again, thrusting her tongue deep into his mouth and clutching at his shirtfront. "Let's go, kiddo. No arguments. You can slink off to your bachelor pad afterward."

chapter THREE

Most people thought Terry Mathers' exile arose from what he liked to call the Great Transgression. He had erred, not so much in fact as in judgment, but so badly that in his own mind he had disgraced himself once and for all in the sacred temple of journalism, soiling his robes before the entire congregation, and it was in this fallen state that he took his father to lunch in New York and told him of the plan to move to Webster.

Walking to the restaurant with the old man on that deceptively cold November day, their clothes pale euphemisms against the freezing truthfulness of the air, he wondered how many people had noticed that Maury Mathers' lifelong swagger was showing just the slightest hint of the totter it would someday inevitably become. The day was sunny but vengefully cold; Terry's ears hurt, and the two men were battered by the currents of a thousand wind tunnels swirling between a thousand tall buildings. On their right they passed Radio City; the hooded and bundled tourists waiting outside danced and stamped their abstract commentary in the chill air, a chorus of mummies bearing mute witness to life's passing tragedies. The wind blew the elder Mathers' white hair around, but he made no effort to suppress this biblical effect, instead simply leaning his massive upper body forward and gliding silently, implacably, toward their destination. He seemed unaffected by the buffeting, yet below the belt his spindly legs looked doubtful, vulnerable even, their outlines embarrassingly plain when the wind plastered his pants up against them like a shroud, the skinny ankles showing with every stride. To his son, the great Maury Mathers looked top-heavy, easy to knock over—Babe Ruth on a bender. He wore the air of seriousness he donned so often now that it had replaced the normal expression of his face in repose, yet he seemed to be decaying, shrinking before Terry's eyes. There was a brown spot on one of his temples, surely an age spot of the kind his son could now search for on the backs of his father's hands, and looking closely, Terry could see that there was nobody to trim the delicate hairs in his father's ears. This forlorn knowledge mitigated the eager anticipation he had been feeling about their lunch, where it would be his solemn duty to deliver to his father a powerful blow. Because it was not intended as such, Terry had felt entitled to the guiltless pleasure of merely doing what he wanted while coincidentally striking for the giant's very heart. Now, with his usual softness, he was not so sure.

"You're leaving the *Tribune*," Maury repeated uncomprehendingly.

It was an act, Terry felt sure. Maury would take at least as much satisfaction as anyone else, and probably a little more, at having his worst suspicions confirmed, but his father also would be hurt to learn that his only son was turning his back on him and his world with what would seem characteristic imprudence, a quality that cannot be reassuring in an offspring when one's ears are full of hair, one's skin begins to spot, and every day the final deadline, the drop-dead date, gets closer.

Maury was no kid, but the truth was that he had been dying all his life. Plagued by illnesses occasionally real but mostly imagined, he was forever consulting doctors, taking medications whose complex interactions were themselves the cause of further ephemeral symptoms, and going on and off eccentric diets, none of which ever seemed to make any difference except briefly, in a period of euphoric placebo that lasted until Maury's faith in this latest regimen began to waver. He often caught cold and, during the winter, was rarely seen without a handkerchief or tissue in his hand. Before lunch, with feigned discretion and a look of great solemnity, he took a series of pills, and he would do likewise afterward, no meal being complete unless this form of pharmacological grace might be pronounced before and after.

Terry had come right to the point. Always impatient, he couldn't stand the small talk, the recitation of the specials, his father's smug banter with his favorite waiters, all this ritualized foreplay followed by some protracted effort to soften the blow before just giving the news and then getting on with the meal. He had tried once before, in his father's office, but found himself humiliatingly unable to say the words. He had ridden the elevator several floors up above the glorious lobby and made his way through the ethereal precincts of the pundits, his footsteps lost in the carpeted hush, but when he arrived the old man was on the phone. Maury waved him in, made a yackety-yak sign with his hand and smoothly worked to wrap up the conversation while Terry sank into a black leather and shiny chrome Le Corbusier armchair. Spying on his father, he could see much of himself in the older man, only refined, squared off, thanks probably to the genetic influence of his mother. Maury looked more like a Marx—the family name before someone changed it—the older he got, his nose and ears enlarging, his chin softening and his white hair beginning to look patriarchal. This was before his latest makeover, before the new haircut and expensive health spa and surgical tightening around the eyes. It was when you could still see Terry's grandfather in Maury, the last in a long line of watery-eyed rabbis, the last man in the family never to own a razor or doubt the existence of God.

"Nervous," Maury said when at last he was off the phone. Terry's heart skipped a beat. Was he really so transparent? But his father meant the secretary of state, with whom he'd been speaking. "He's worried the right-wing parties in Israel will derail the peace talks again. Make the prime minister take a hard line just for electoral reasons." Maury sighed. "He's hoping if I do a commentary it'll help the guy's courage, signal that the Americans are behind him."

Terry just couldn't do it, not there in that office, in that enveloping chair with the windows looking out over New Jersey and the secretary of state calling for reassurance. That was when they had settled on the lunch, where Terry could at last explain his decision to quit.

"But why, Terry? You've got a marvelous career there. Your best work is ahead of you."

Terry's face burned. It was a certain sort of curse to be Maury Mathers' son. Working as a journeyman at the nation's most important newspaper, accomplishment enough for some, was failure if your father had settled down to life as a sage and national shrine after a career as the most decorated journalist of his generation. Since his glorious ascent to the Valhalla of television a generation earlier, surveys showed Maury Mathers to be one of the most trusted figures in America, not far behind Walter Cronkite and the Quaker Oats man. He was a commentator nowadays, breathing the rarefied atmosphere available to the lungs of opinion-makers in posh offices many floors above the shabby streets below, thinking and preaching from facilities that overlooked the decrepit newspaper building not far away where his son had toiled behind stacks of phone books and files in an attempt to carve out a little privacy. Terry had labored in the long, dark shadow of his illustrious father for so long that he was no longer considered to have the complexion for life in the sun. Nothing could be sadder, he thought in those days, than to remain known as the great man's pale and prosaic son even into his own dotage, right on through to the death notices, and so he wanted out. The Great Transgression was a message from God that said, "Run."

"And Abigail? There's not a lot of call for securities lawyers up there, is there?"

"D-D-Dad, I said *we're* buying the *Chronicle.* N-Not just me, us. We'll work together. She can handle the business side of things. She'll be publisher. I'll be editor."

"It'll be good for Phoebe, no?" Maury said without conviction. "A nice place for kids, Webster."

They both understood this as unnecessary self-justification. Terry wasn't mad at his father for having left him there while he moved from story to story, soaking up official lies and trying gamely to purify them through the filter of his own integrity. With the exception of his speech impediment (had it set in right around the time his father moved out, or was this only something he had begun to believe later?), Terry's boyhood had been no more painful than most, and he would yet come to see it, through the clammy fog of old age, as a sunny, youthful idyll.

"We'll be happy, I hope. We'll control our own destiny, we'll be together, a-a-and we'll get off this treadmill we're living on here."

Just then an elegantly turned-out older woman came up and touched Maury on the sleeve. The skin of her face was pulled, as if by some unnatural force, tight against her bones. The effect was somehow piscine.

"Will you pardon me for intruding?" she said, glancing indifferently at Terry. "You're Maury Mathers, aren't you? Oh, I just had to tell you how much I admire you. Your commentaries are a ray of sanity for me. Would you mind giving me your autograph? Right here, sign today's *Tribune,* what could be better?"

"And whom do I have the pleasure of signing for?"

"Sylvia. Just make it to Sylvia. The girls will be green!" To Terry, she added, "I used to read him in the *Tribune,* that's how far back I go."

"Now you read *him* in the *Tribune,*" Maury said, gesturing with his pen after signing with a flourish. "My son. Better writer than I ever was."

"Wonderful! My God, you don't look old enough for such a big boy."

"We try to get out and have a little heart to heart now and then—"

"Ah. Don't say another word, I'll leave you men in peace. Thank you so much, you've made my day!"

Maury smiled at her like a gargoyle until she had slipped out of sight.

"Your mother will be happy," he said at last to Terry. "Have you told her?"

"Not yet. I wanted to tell you first."

The older man smiled tightly and nodded. It was a victory for Maria nonetheless.

"L-L-Let's face it, Dad, for the past couple of years I've been in a kind of limbo here, and after all this time I'm just not motivated to come to work anymore."

"This isn't about that Kelman business, is it? Because nobody holds that against you any longer. Nobody. Believe me."

Terry blushed. His father did not mention, as he had at the time, that he had made a phone call to his great friend the editor in chief, father to father, to keep Terry from being fired. "I'm grateful, Dad, but why are you telling me this?" he'd said at the time. "Because you're not entitled to think otherwise," his father had said. "Because I deserve a little credit. And because I don't like to have secrets from you. Even good secrets. What you don't know can hurt you."

Now Terry only sighed.

"I'm g-g-grateful for what you did, Dad. But maybe that was a sign I should have p-p-p—p-p-p—" Terry took a deep breath and snapped his fingers hard—"paid closer attention to. This j-just isn't for me. This l-l-life isn't for my family."

Their food arrived. It was the expense-account sort of Chinese restaurant where they made the little pancakes for you at your table. Terry felt compelled to thank the waiters at every turn, but Maury ignored them, asking for things without looking at the help and confining his banter to before and after the meal. The food itself he seemed to regard as a matter of right, and Terry, recognizing this, confessed to himself that he envied it.

"Dad," he began, and he could see the old man go on the alert at the sudden upward inflection of his voice. "I h-h-haven't even t-t-t-told you yet what a great opportunity I think we've got here in the *C-C-C-Chronicle.*" He reddened; his stammer was back, just when he most wanted to seem confident, calm. "A c-c-classic n-neglected property, in an upscale community, no r-r-r-real competition. We could d-d-double the circulation and triple advertising. Abigail thinks we could even p-p-p-pull in some national ads if we went about it the right way, maybe distribute f-f-f-free copies at some of the s-s-s-summer festivals, get the c-c-c-city people to notice us."

Maury gave a little shrug. Who knew? It might be possible.

"Dad, we've g-g-gone over this c-c-carefully," Terry said, now paring his words to essentials, as he always did when his stuttering was worst. Immediately he was reduced once again to childhood, stammering as he struggled to explain some breach. "We've g-g-got a good broker h-h-handling it, and I think we kn-kn-know what we're getting i-i-into. What we need to m-m-m-make it happen is an e-e-e-extra $200,000."

"And you want it from me?"

"To b-b-b-borrow it from you. We'll p-p-pay you back in f-f-five years, and your loan will be s-s-secured not just by the paper, but by the b-b-b-building."

"Is that part of the deal? That was the old Congregational church when you were growing up, wasn't it?"

"That's the place. It's that great old p-p-pile downtown, worth half a m-m-m-million at least. We'll have a loan agreement and everything. Dad, we just can't b-borrow any more from the banks. We've got to have more e-equity."

"It's a lot of money."

"I-I-I know it is. I don't take this lightly."

Maury sighed and looked around. Terry started to say something, thinking guiltily of all the loans and grants over the years, the money when he was younger for a new transmission or some uninsured dental work, the gifts of money later on with estate planning in mind, but his father held a hand up, nodding. *Relax,* he said wordlessly. Terry blushed again. He felt emasculated at such times by his speech, an object of pity to his listeners.

"Tell you what. I won't lend you two hundred grand, I'll invest it. You need equity, right? So what good's a loan?"

"T-t-they won't know it's a loan."

"You'll know. You'll be in hock up to your eyeballs. You need equity, my adventurous son, equity, and that's what I'm offering. I'll be an investor, a silent partner. You just got done saying what a great opportunity this is. You can't let me in on it? You'll still have a controlling interest. I won't say a word."

"It's g-generous, Dad, really, and I a-appreciate it. But we want to own this outright. We want it to be just ours. You own the p-p-place I'm leaving. I love you, but I can't have you owning the p-place I'm going."

Maury was silent for an instant. A watch as thin as a coin peeked out from his shirtcuff; it had no numbers and, as far as Terry could tell, no hands.

"You wanna think about it?"

Terry shook his head and then felt it easier to get out the words. "I c-c-can't think about it. I've thought about it all my life."

"All right," Maury said with a sigh. "All right. I'll talk to my accountant—we'll work something out."

"Thanks Dad." Terry was embarrassed. "I g-g-give you my s-s-solemn word, you'll g-g-get back every penny with interest."

"A man is always interested in his children. That's all the interest I need."

"N-n-nevertheless. Principal p-p-plus interest. It's important to me."

Both of them ate a little. His father had sprouted small wattles, Terry noticed. When had this happened? They quivered with the rapid shocks of his jaws working on the food.

"So you're going off to live the quieter life," Maury said pensively, making a sort of transition. He would employ condescension, Terry saw, and then regretted how hard he was on the old man. Chewing mercilessly, Maury continued: "A lot to be said for what you're doing. Community journalism—heart and soul of this racket. This thing of ours." He gave a little laugh. "*La cosa nostra.* I guess I'm taken aback because, you know, I'm just a little bit envious." His eyes flickered at this patent lie. "I sometimes wish I had done the same thing when I was younger. Put family first. My life—all of our lives—would have been very different. I admire you, Terry." He touched his son's arm. "I mean that sincerely."

Thus did the father give his approval as he always had done before, freely and without conviction, flinging the toupee of benediction over the naked scalp of resignation. Terry, struggling not to get upset, tried to see it from his father's perspective. He could tell the old man was already thinking about how all this would play with his fellows at the club, the face he would arrange, the solemn and equally unmeant expressions of admiration they would put forth echoing his own. Terry was already dreading the day when, with Phoebe grown, he would make himself sound enthusiastic about her waiting on tables, failing as an actress, living with a musician. He would be in a locker room full of other *alter kockers,* the scars from their bypass operations lurking like snakes amid the bushy silver hair of their chests, and these men would listen and then patronize him with their foxy grins.

"So you propitiated the gods with an offering of Chinese food," Abigail said later when he got home.

She was circumcising vegetables, loudly chopping the ends off green beans, carrots, asparagus. She and Terry were in the kitchen, where they drank not wine but martinis, a recently acquired taste that made them feel grown up, conspiratorial. Drunk. Abigail, after weeks of abstention, would allow herself just one. Phoebe was at a friend's house and so with unspoken relish they made dinner without her, for Terry a pleasure so great he felt guilty, perhaps especially since she was not his daughter, in any official sense of the term, even if he was compelled to be her father. Terry's was a blended family, as such uneasy cohousing arrangements are known, and sometimes the ingredients clashed. Sometimes, in fact, there was very little blending indeed. All three co-habitants had different last names, and Phoebe spent part of the time, albeit a small part, with her original father, in Los Angeles. She was primarily Abigail's, to the extent she was anybody's, but she struck Terry as someone on her own since who knows when, too smart for her own good and everyone else's too. Most nights she was a radioactive presence at their dinner table, pulsing with mysterious poisons when Terry in particular, lacking the patience of true paternity, wished only to enjoy the bread salted by the sweat of his brow in the company of loving family. *I am innocent,* he wanted to say, *guilty only of believing for a while that I loved your mother so much that I must also love you. Your own sad limbo is not my fault.* He knew that the decision to transport her to Webster, in her mind not unlike being sent in irons to Australia, had only increased her disdain, and so mentally he thanked the Horsleys for taking her off his hands for an evening, and wondered yet again, with a certain longing, what it would be like years later when Phoebe was in college and they were finally free. He honestly had no idea how attached to her he already was.

"He's resigned, I think. Maury is never p-placated, but like most gods he's not very interested in anyone else and can b-b-barely see mere mortals anyway. So yeah, he's okay. He'll make the loan. Our lunch was OK."

"Maybe we can watch our video tonight," Abigail said hopefully. They rented videos for weeks on end, never finding the time to watch, but she persisted in renting new ones. The triumph of hope over experience.

"Which one is it?" Terry asked. "I forget."

"*Triumph of the Will. It's a Wonderful Life.* What's the difference?"

He smiled and took a drink. They would never watch it, certainly not tonight, when they had the apartment to themselves and Friday evening stretched out before them in a gorgeous ribbon of possibility. Roy Orbison's voice climbed into the stratosphere on the stereo, and Abigail's lush figure, ripe with the fetus of their son (their secret for awhile), seemed impossibly sexy. Was this some strange evolutionary miscue? What would be the biological purpose in making a woman so appealing when she is already with child? To keep the child's father interested and on hand? Or was it something more than just his wife's recent fullness and unexpected witticisms? Maybe it was the scent of freedom. After his lunch, Terry had begun to be optimistic once again, excited even, about their move. This was what our lives will be like, he thought: unhurried, voluptuous, free. The prospect was arousing for both of them, and they began making love even while they were cooking. Abigail's neck was irresistible, and he tasted it while she ground herbs, unbuttoning the top of her blouse so he could imbibe her perfumed shoulders. Unbidden, she walked to the hall closet and squeezed into her high heels, and at that point Terry said dinner could wait and she agreed. The image of his wife unclothed except for a pair of shiny pumps would always remain powerfully affecting for him, even when it had become just a fault he could find in others by comparison, and certainly it was affecting on that long-ago night in New York. Abigail was strong, her back broad and her shoulders round with muscle, and she used her strength in making love, leaving no room for ambivalence or laziness. Her lank hair looked tousled and rich at such times, and her pale features flushed. It was a dazzling change. In clothes, she always managed to look oddly dowdy to her husband, like some older sister or aunt, and her dutiful approach to life accentuated this impression, as did the thick glasses she wore. She had trouble with contact lenses, and expensive haircuts seemed wasted on her colorless hair, which hung around her sharply symmetrical features like moss after a rain. Her clothes, no matter how new, never seemed quite to fit or be in fashion. She had no sense of style. Terry relished her undressed not just for the obvious reasons, but for the great transformation that occurred when she was stripped of the disguise he found her clothes to be. She was a brilliant and beautiful woman, and he liked to be reminded of this by having her remove the frumpy trappings of everyday life. Pregnancy helped. Both of them found Abigail's swelling fecundity shockingly erotic, and afterward they ate in the state of delicious anesthesia that often follows hard sex. It was as if Terry had won for them some form of release simply by telling his father they were giving up and moving away.

Escape had been in the air in those days. Everyone they knew, exhausted by striving and terrified by the distant thunder of forty, fantasized aloud over dinner and after tennis about chucking it all and getting away, finding some simpler life, having more time, etc. etc. ad nauseam. None of them had any time for books, but they all pored over *Metropolitan Home, House & Garden,* all the tantalizingly named and country-obsessed shelter magazines as they wolfed their take-out Chinese food, longing to create the kinds of homes and lives these journals of despair portrayed. "When we were young," Terry said to Abigail, "these magazines m-mocked us with the things m-money could buy. Now they mock us with the things it can't."

Among their friends, these discussions of flight were conducted in a kind of code, various assertions of stress standing in for the unspoken troubles in a marriage—troubles that found room even in Terry and Abigail's cramped apartment. There was that strangely irritated feeling of having roommates rather than loved ones. Everybody was simply in everybody else's way, tolerable only as long as each held up his end. Conversations were mostly about who would tell the cleaning lady to do what and what was to be done about dinner. The only topic that ever seemed to ignite any interest anymore was moving.

At some point Terry and Abigail took these discussions beyond the realm of fantasy. Perhaps it was the point at which his career turned to ash, or maybe it was when Abigail acknowledged that unless she sprouted some additional rows of teeth, she would never make partner. This defeat, this slinking off to find some other job among the army of bravely clad rejects turned away from the heights, was not something she looked forward to, any more than Terry looked forward to slogging through years of dutiful penance in the cause of rehabilitating himself at the *Tribune.*

"I hate our life, you know that?" Abigail had said after one of those dispiriting exchanges she and Terry seemed to be having more of as their marriage wore on—a kind of tired sniping that didn't even rise to the level of a fight. "What's the point of all this? Where are we going with it? We work like maniacs just to make enough to live in this crummy apartment and send our daughter to school with those wretched little snobs and we never get to spend any time together. I billed fifty-four hours last week. *Billed,* you understand? So a disgusting little man who inherited all his money could take his restaurant chain public before the fad for eating under a talking marmoset passes. Why?"

Terry looked at her with delight.

"Well, we can make a change," he said. "Everybody's a-a-always talking about this, but we can do it. I don't intend to be a passive actor in my own life. How about you?"

"Look at Phoebe, look how we're raising her. I kept track of our interactions last week"—she had read this in a magazine, Terry knew—"and leaving aside arguments, I talked to her for maybe thirty minutes. In the entire week! All her friends have too much money, most of their parents are divorced, and we're headed the same way if we don't do something."

"I know what we can do," Terry said. "How do you feel about p-p-publishing a newspaper?"

For Terry, this had been an enduring fantasy. It was part of growing up, he had come to think, part of recognizing who he was. He acknowledged now that he had never had the ambition that his father had had, had never been able to shake some essential doubt about the monomania required for greatness in any direction, and in darker moments saw his stutter as a metaphor for some profound indecision. He lacked faith not just in God, whose existence he tossed aside when his youthful prayers for an end to his speech impediment went unanswered, but also, and much more secretly, in life, perhaps for the same reason: an overriding sense of the futility of things. He had been a campus radical when he wasn't playing basketball in college (he missed Vietnam because of a precociously herniated disk), but even then he was fully immersed in neither of these subcultures, straddling them thoughtfully and deriving what fulfillment he could from each. Despite his politics, he was glad to accept a Mustang convertible from his father.

Afterward he bummed around the country, holding a variety of jobs and living for a while in the Haight, where he played pickup some days in sandals, before beginning as a freelance for the alternative press, writing about police malfeasance and tweaking the bigger papers for ignoring stories involving advertisers or the local ghetto. He did this in San Francisco, Los Angeles and, gaining confidence, in national magazines until, surrendering to the inevitable, he cut his hair, shaved, and gave himself up to a career at the *Tribune,* the best he could hope for given that television was foreclosed by his stutter. Besides, television was more than anything else about the people on it. He still burned to advance the cause of justice, to comfort the afflicted and afflict the comfortable, but the more powerful the medium, it seemed, the harder it was to say anything meaningful to anyone, and it was galling that after so many years running from the overwhelming presence of his old man, he was now squarely in his shade. In this sense, his decision to leave was inevitable. His embarrassing misjudgment in the Kelman affair had been a catalyst, but the change had been a long time coming, and he saw buying a paper like the *Chronicle* as an opportunity, at long last, to get out on his own and make his mark in a different way, in a different world from Maury's.

Terry hoped that by moving his family to Webster he could keep it from disintegrating the way his parents' had. Instead of being separated by their careers and having different circles of friends, different burdensome social obligations that weren't social at all, Terry and Abigail could have their work in common, share proprietorship rather than laboring in some media conglomerate or law-firm pyramid scheme, and make a difference in the life of a single community. Nine-year-old Phoebe was the only one who dragged her feet.

Children are the great conservatives of family life, and to be uprooted from all that was comforting to her for no tangible reason made the move seem gratuitous as well as terrifying, even if it was to the familiar town that Phoebe herself had visited dozens of times before. But it was another loss, and her calluses were largely make-believe. She was sure she would never see her friends again—"It's true, basically, isn't it?" Terry said to her mother in private. "We won't see most of our friends either. Friends evidently are disposable in life"—and that the ones she might make in Webster could never compare to the ones she had made in New York, where she had attended just one school and lived in just one apartment her entire life. "Will the cat go with us?" she asked fearfully. "Can I come back and visit?" As the time for moving drew near, she dissolved in silent dread, excusing herself when the subject came up and after a while not even acknowledging that the move was forthcoming. She would look ahead to events in New York that would occur in their absence. Terry and Abigail contemplated sending her for a few sessions to a psychologist. "All her friends go," said Abigail. "They go right from the cradle to the couch around here."

Besides, Webster was not a cow town. It wasn't even the sleepy college town it had been when Terry had grown up there. The world had changed since then, including Webster, and it was his kind of place now, full of beards and progressive politics, with an old-fashioned downtown and a real sense of itself as someplace special. Webster was an old town, the earliest Puritan settlements dating back to the seventeenth century, but it took its name much later in honor of Daniel Webster, who had lived there for some years in his youth. As a community, the great compromiser's namesake was much less willing to deal. Some months before the hundredth anniversary of Webster's naming, Abigail served on a local commission appointed to plan an appropriate commemoration for this event, but the more the panel delved into history, the less it liked the man. Webster had been too willing to accommodate slavery, displayed xenophobia by supporting the notorious Tariff of Abominations, accepted bribes to support his lavish lifestyle, and as secretary of state paid off debts by dispensing federal jobs. How could the taxpayers' money be spent in good conscience for his further glorification? "The truth is," the commission reported, "that we need to pull this man off his pedestal." The commission's urgings were taken quite literally. For 100 years, a larger-than-life statue of the great man stood stern watch over the town park, gesturing in mid-oration, but after the commission's report and a good deal of public debate, the statue was unceremoniously removed.

The town engineer reported that tearing out the base would be much more expensive, though, and the suggestion arose that this pedestal be maintained as a caution against blind idolatry. Daniel Webster Remembrance Day came to be known simply as Residents' Day, and on the very first such occasion, the pedestal was solemnly rededicated. "And so there it remains," the *Chronicle* reported, "a fitting monument to all the people of Webster—the little people who toil anonymously, the ones who keep the roads repaired and the phones working and the children healthy and safe. People of all colors, races, and creeds. The real heroes, in other words. The ones who don't get the credit." The Empty Pedestal, as it was soon universally known, became something of a tourist attraction, and Webster itself, however unfairly, was inscribed in the guidebooks as "the town without a hero."

It was not lost on Terry that he was moving back to the town from which, during the endless abeyance of youth, he had pined for the same father he was now moving away from. Webster was the community in which he had passed his boyhood, spending weekends and vacations with his father when he could, but mostly observing the flash and sparkle of that comet moving across the nighttime firmament from his sleepy outpost in what had for a while been the family's summer home. Much of his time there, stranded in a small town with his mother and her fragile watercolors, was spent trying to catch the older man's eye; he lived for the holidays during which his father would "take him," as his mother put it to her friends, and kept one of Maury's publicity photos over his bed. As a small boy he would copy out elaborate maps of places he knew his father had visited, "for the next time you go," he would say, and early on started a scrapbook. As he got older, he bombarded his father with letters, articles, and school writings, which Maury marked up and sent back, always full of corrections but always too with a hint of encouragement and the vague promise of yet another reunion in the not-so-distant future. As a teenager in Webster, he read his father's newspaper columns (and later watched his television dispatches) religiously, whether the older man was reporting from Vietnam or Washington or his desk in New York, and despite the usual adolescent rebelliousness, frankly idolized him. As an adult, Terry sometimes felt that he was still forever trying to catch the older man's eye, and he seemed able to succeed only in the worst possible ways. It had always been thus; Maury would magically appear when Terry had done something particularly bad, or if the father couldn't come to the son, the son would be dispatched to the father, the two of them granting Maria a lonely respite from such exuberant alienation. Terry would go on the train and then the subway, ringing his father's doorbell, sometimes without warning, and would be greeted with a weary air of stern sympathy, as if they both knew, but could not say, that you could not be blamed for breaking windows and shoplifting if you were stuck in a fine place like Webster with a fine woman like his mother. Maury would phone with lugubrious word: "I don't know what happened, Maria, but he's here with me. We'll get it sorted out."

Until the onset of college, he lived all year for the annual week spent with his father at the seashore. They would swim and sun themselves, of course, the two of them brown as dates by the time they came home, but mostly they would talk. Terry would tell his father about his friends, his school, and what new efforts were being undertaken to cure him of his cursed stammer. His father was always patient when Terry spoke, but it was more fun for both of them when the son found a way to ask about the father's work. He could relax then, not concentrate on his speech, and listen in a kind of reverie as the older man described his adventures. Those summers were a chance for Terry to show his father how grown up he had become, and each year he saved up new tics and mannerisms to show off during their time together. As his schooling progressed, he could delight Maury with evidence of his learning. He was a brilliant if erratic student, the kind that drove teachers crazy by goldbricking all semester and then summarizing the textbook, committing the results to memory, and acing the finals. Languages came easily to him, as did math, literature, and whatever else he turned his attention toward, so that during summer vacations with his father his precocity was always on display. He did algebra in the sand, spoke French for an entire day followed by Spanish the next and Hebrew on the third. "Y-y-you need to learn Latin, Dad," he said seriously, wishing to fill his mouth with its delicious cadences. "There's a Pooh book that's pretty good, if you want to try it." Strangely, he spoke foreign languages without a trace of stutter, and later, when he had finished college and fantasized about playing basketball in Greece or Italy or even Cyprus, somewhere third-rate Americans were still wanted for this purpose, he imagined himself speaking casually to women in cafés, his accent improved by grappa and sunshine and his words flowing freely. In the summer after the Christmas for which his father had given him a telescope, he expounded glibly on the constellations and pretended he might pursue astronomy or write about science for *The New Yorker*. He strove to show as well how determined he was to overcome his speech impediment. One year, as a boy, he filled his mouth with stones and declaimed against the waves like some pint-sized Demosthenes. The year after that, frustrated beyond expression with his incurable stutter, he borrowed one of his father's razor blades and bravely tried to slice through his own frenum (the muscle under his tongue), resulting only in bloodshed and embarrassment. "I wanted to free my tongue," he explained later, the stitches and excitement somehow having done just that for a single bleary evening. His mouth tasted unpleasantly of iron for a while, but the injury wasn't serious, and the next day they were back on the beach, walking along the shore at sunset, Terry pausing to look for interesting shells and then running along to catch up, trying not to step in any fresh sand and so chasing his father by hopping from footstep to footstep, landing each time in and around the deep impressions left by his forward-striding dad.

chapter FOUR

L ooking at Jeffrey, Lucille Lyttle again began to worry. As he took off after the cat, she saw that half his bagel was stuck by its cream cheese topping to the textured surface of the refrigerator like some arch and oversized magnet, and now, from the other room, there was a sudden desperate *meow!* followed by a loud *bang.* Two-year-old Amy, at the breakfast table, thrust her lower lip forward in unhappy preamble. Her father's exasperated footsteps, his wing tips heavy on the wooden stairs, set her inexorably to wailing, and little Jeffrey, hearing them as well, darted back into the kitchen and sheepishly tried to resume his forsaken place at table. It was only 7:30, and already the house was a noisy shambles. In the background, on television, one of those white-haired TV sages droned on sententiously about the decline of the American family. It was Maury Mathers, Lucille saw at a glance, and she ignored him.

It was Jeffrey who preoccupied his mother now. He was large for a four-year-old, but slow, she had to admit, and difficult. He never sat still, didn't pay much attention to adults, and seemed unable to focus on anybody else. The word *autism* sometimes ran through her mind, even though he certainly wasn't autistic. But neither would he look you in the eye. His attention wandered all over even if you addressed him directly, and when he spoke he did so badly, unable to pronounce so that anyone but Lucille could understand, and even to her his speech was disjointed, fantastic, until sometimes she almost allowed herself to wonder if he were possessed. She knew that some people thought her son stupid.

"Jeffrey, no hitting!" his father said when he caught up with him. Wayne was a bulky man, largely bald and a little flabby around the gills. His green eyes were weary. "How many times am I supposed to tell you, *no hitting?!* Don't hit the cat, don't hit your friends, don't hit your sister or your mother or me!"

The boy, unmoved, smiled and muttered to himself as he began piling apricot preserves onto the other half of his bagel. There were crumbs in his fine blond hair. Wayne gave Lucille a what-are-you-sitting-there-for look, and she rolled her eyes.

"Jeffrey, sit down and eat your breakfast," she told her son, enunciating with care. She felt for debris in her own hair, which was cut to a fashionably uniform length but permed so that it stood out from her head like a tent. Her huge eyes and long, pale limbs added to the air of excitability she gave off, and her son's maddening behavior only exaggerated this electrified aura.

Things weren't supposed to be this way. Unlike so many of the mothers in Webster, Lucille was home most of the time, except for the many hours she spent at church. She had been taking Jeffrey to the Alphabet Soup Preschool five mornings a week, but mainly because she thought it would do him good to play with other kids his own age, learn to read early, get used to groups. And it was only for half a day. Lucille did not believe that mothers with small children should work, although she knew that many didn't have husbands like hers, who earned enough that, in a town like Webster where things didn't cost too terribly much, she didn't have to hold a job. At least you could say that for Wayne—he was a good provider. She had wondered sometimes if Alphabet Soup had been a huge mistake, and she felt guilty for it. It was time away from her children, time sometimes well spent on church activities or shopping more efficiently without them in tow, but time also spent luxuriously, with a drink and a cigarette and a couple of her favorite soap operas. She felt so guilty that sometimes she would make herself turn off the TV and have her drink and smoke instead with her Bible, which she always kept at hand and in whose terrible beauty she took solace when she was unhappy with Wayne, or when Jeffrey frankly drove her round the bend.

Enrolling Jeffrey in Alphabet Soup had itself been an act of altruism, she liked to recall. When her friends Emily and Frank took over the place, they had needed all the help they could get. They sat right here in this kitchen just bursting with their plans and not coming right out but wanting, it was obvious, Lucille and Wayne to send their kids, knowing that when they came aboard it would give the place a kind of Good Housekeeping seal of approval among many of the conservative, churchgoing parents who followed Lucille's lead, and many of the more secular executive types that knew Wayne from Rotary, golf, and so forth, all of which flowed from his job as Krieger's chief financial officer. Plus Lucille took pity because she knew what Emily and Frank had gone through in losing their little girl. But you couldn't skate on sympathy forever.

She looked over at the oatmeal-stained *Wall Street Journal,* held by her husband like a shield as he tried to eat.

Given what a boost she had provided the school, it was all the more outrageous that Frank would raise a hand to her little boy, and the more galling that he would offer no real apology. He had spanked her son, once evidently, but hard, without so much as a fare-thee-well, and although he acted contrite, it was obvious he wasn't really sorry; Emily even defended him. Lucille had become hooked on Alphabet Soup, she could admit that. She counted on the little window of peace and privacy she had each day when Jeffrey was in preschool and Amy in day care. They liked it too, liked the other children, the games, the birthday parties. And now, of course, she was stuck with them all day. Her son squirmed off his chair and seemed headed under the table.

"Jeffrey, sit down properly and eat some breakfast, will you please? No more bagels on the refrigerator."

Jeffrey submerged unhindered by these exhortations and Lucille, who resisted the impulse to grab him by his straw-colored hair and allowed the thought into her mind again that there might be something wrong with him. Her son was behind most of his peers, who shunned him as thuggish and dim, and Wayne was little help when she worried over it. "He's a guy," Wayne would say. "This is what boys are like. It's what I was like. He'll grow out of it." But it was obvious from her mother-in-law's dismay around her grandson that this was not what Wayne had been like. Jeffrey was different, and Lucille gnawed at herself trying to figure out why.

Sometimes, in her darkest moments, she thought she might be to blame. She had had a drinking problem once or twice in her life, but it was under control now and had been for years. She did not believe an occasional drink during pregnancy was really so bad; millions of people did it. She had done it carrying Amy, with no ill effects. She hadn't fallen down drunk while carrying Jeffrey; she had kept herself in check, and she refused to beat herself up for doing something that helped her relax. Wasn't it important to the fetus that the mother stay calm? She had drunk more in those days, sure, but part of the problem was she'd had to sneak the drinks when Wayne wasn't looking, which was stressful. She still did this; he only rarely saw her drink, and she clung to the fantasy that her breath mints and careful demeanor kept him from knowing how much she took in. She admitted to herself that on some days this was more than others, but not so much that she was out of control. She bought it with the money she saved on coupons, or combined her alcohol purchases with other items and put the whole mess on the Visa. Nobody would ever know.

No, her drinking wasn't the cause of Jeffrey's problems; if anything, it was the other way around. Her son's preschool was a much more plausible candidate.

Frank claimed he struck the boy because he just couldn't get Jeffrey's attention. Her son was disrupting the whole school, was taking up far too much of the teacher's time, didn't seem to know the first thing about how to behave. Blah blah blah. It was an affront. Later, on the phone, they only made things worse, acting put-upon and ignoring the whole incident. Denial, that's what they were in.

"Emily, you just don't get it, do you? Your husband struck my child."

"Lucille, for Pete's sake, he whacked Jeffrey once on the bottom after your son nearly killed the Peterson girl and wouldn't stop trying to bop half a dozen other kids with a bowling pin. It was an unfortunate incident, but your little boy has some problems that seem to go beyond what we can help him with here."

Lucille had been barely able to control her voice. "Are you saying he's no longer welcome at your facility?"

"He's welcome if he can calm down a little and not be such a disruption all the time."

"Well, doesn't that take the cake," Lucille had marveled. Emily had always condescended to her. "I made that place for you. If it wasn't for me you'd still have six kids to take care of. You'd have lost your shirt by now, and this is the way you repay your best friend."

Jeffrey batted the pepper shaker off the table with the butter knife, splattering some of the apricot preserves onto the wall. As he wound up to take a swing at the salt shaker, she grabbed his hand and wrenched the knife free. He wailed and swept the salt shaker off the table with a petulant fist, daring her with his unrepentant gaze to do something about it.

"Jeffrey, that is not OK! That is not OK! *That is not OK!*" she practically shrieked. "Do you understand me?"

Wayne, putting down the paper, looked stupefied. She felt herself on the verge of smacking him and smacking Jeffrey too, and she looked away momentarily. Lucille did not think an occasional whack was a bad thing for a child. She just felt that she ought to be the one to administer such correction. For them to do it at Alphabet Soup was a slap at her, and not on the bottom. Come to think, she had never heard of a school, no less a preschool, engaging in corporal punishment in this day and age. She felt sure it was prohibited in public school, and she knew it wasn't permitted in the church school either, because she'd taught Sunday Bible classes there herself. What on earth was it about Alphabet Soup?

"Wayne, I want you to go over there today."

"Where?"

"Alphabet Soup, that's where. I want you to go over there and let them know, *make them understand,* how serious this is. I don't think they take a woman seriously."

"Luce," Wayne sighed. "Maybe we're making a mountain out of a molehill on this thing. They didn't hurt him, and he really can get out of hand sometimes. Are you telling me you never wanted to smack this kid?"

"Wanting and doing are completely separate, can't you see that?" Lucille hissed. "I've *wanted* to sleep with the UPS man."

"I'm really busy at the office right now. Let me see if I can get over there one of these days."

"Just pathetic," she said, shaking her head.

He sighed and left without saying good-bye. With much effort Lucille got the children ready and then drove them to a new preschool she had found for them in a nearby town, the bagel still caulked neatly to the refrigerator when she returned. Wayne was gone, there was nothing at the church that day, and so Lucille, tired already from the morning's ordeal, poured herself a drink and sat down to take another look at the local newspaper. She got fidgety sometimes during this part of the morning when she wasn't at church. It was a slow part of the day, without much to do aside from the drudgery of housekeeping, and projects seemed to come to mind. She made lists, wrote down ideas.

Today, she began to see, her project was Jeffrey. As she often did when she had a couple of drinks, she found herself worrying about her son, only lately, settling over this bumpy road like a snowfall that colored and silenced everything else, there was the overwhelming issue of the spanking. Maybe Alphabet Soup really was to blame for her son's problems. Had he really been so bad before they'd brought him there? The more she thought about it, the angrier she became.

Lucille took down the Alphabet Soup phone list from the side of the refrigerator and browsed through it. Webster was a small place and, by name or face or brief personal encounter, she knew almost all of the families listed, but many of them still ranked as near-strangers. So she began by calling the handful of mothers with whom she was friendly, the ones she knew from church or as residents of her immediate outlying neighborhood, the ones whose kids she had driven, and who had driven her kids.

"Believe me," Lucille said earnestly. "I'm not trying to draw you into this, and I'm not trying to make a big deal out of something that's really between me and them. It's just that—well, the truth is my son has been acting strange ever since we started taking him there. . . . As a matter of fact, yes, thanks, he is a little better now. A little calmer. I really do think there's a difference! So anyway, I'm just calling a few of the mothers, very quietly, to find out what their experience has been, maybe see if they've noticed anything unusual in their kids, or if their kids have said anything about what goes on at Alphabet Soup on a daily basis."

They knew about the spanking, of course, and from their tone she could tell that many didn't want to get involved. They liked and even needed Alphabet Soup, and so didn't want to be troubled about the place, Lucille felt. Perhaps they thought of her as a little hysterical. Perhaps they had their own experience of her son's behavior on which to draw. When she called Belinda Jackson, on the other hand, she found someone less anxious to suppress any bad feelings she might have about the school, the way the other mothers obviously were doing.

She didn't get Belinda right away. She'd left a message, and later that afternoon her call was returned. Both women spoke into cordless phones tucked into their shoulders while they chased after their children.

"See, Tiffany's never been away from me," Belinda said. "But I just got in at Mart-World, so naturally I needed a place for her."

"Mart-World? My husband works in retailing," Lucille said. "He's at Krieger's."

"Oh, wow, our arch-enemy. I hope he don't hate me."

"Oh no, no. So tell me, has your daughter been acting strange at all since you've been taking her to Alphabet Soup?"

"Well as a matter of fact she has, now you mention it. Although they've been real nice, you know, giving me practically a free ride on the expenses and all. But they say she has behavior problems, and you know she's never had those before. I mean, just the usual kid stuff, that's all. Things they all do. But they say she's a problem. I don't know whether it's 'cause she's away from me or what. Also, they don't let her watch TV when she wants to—"

"This is so interesting," Lucille said, freshening her drink. "They said my boy had behavioral problems too."

"Really?"

"And you know, he's been much better since I took him out of that place."

"You took him out?"

"Sure did. He was the one they spanked! You probably read about that in the *Chronicle.*"

"I don't take the paper. They spanked him?"

"Can you believe it?" Lucille tried to keep the ice from tinkling into the phone.

"Did he deserve it?"

"Of course not! They're not supposed to hit other people's kids."

"Oh, right."

"The arrogance of it!"

"You know, they do seem awful snotty over there," Belinda said. "The old lady especially. She don't even like kids, far as I can tell."

"Makes you wonder, doesn't it?"

"It does. It really does."

Why, all of a sudden, was Frank so in favor of selling the school? That was what Pearl Gibson wanted to know. She drummed her fingers impatiently on the table.

"Emily, you decide," she said, looking away. "I really don't care anymore."

It wasn't strictly a lie. She was done; she had had her time. She knew this and was resigned to it, even though she couldn't quite get used to this business of being old, the creaky and flaccid vehicle her body had somehow become when she wasn't paying attention, the feel of the flesh at the back of her upper arms slapping gently against her sides when she moved a certain way, or the thought that before too very long she would follow her husband into the grave and that would be the end of her.

"I'm not especially eager to sell," Frank said. Pearl noticed his frayed shirt cuff as he gestured. *It was his own fault,* she thought. *They'd been doing fine.* "I just begin to wonder if our hearts are in this anymore, and the offer on the table—"

"Charlie Krieger's got a lot of money," she couldn't help interjecting. "Nobody's disputing that."

"—is almost absurdly generous. I mean, think about it. This property is so valuable we could sell it and earn as much on the principal as we do working so hard at running Alphabet Soup—without taking any flack for whacking some bully on the bottom."

Pearl noted with satisfaction that her daughter's eyes rolled nearly out of her head.

"We could even reopen Alphabet Soup somewhere else," Frank continued. This was so typically disingenuous that it just set her off. She slapped the table crisply.

"Do whatever you want when I'm dead and buried, but I won't let the Kriegers get it while I'm living. No, sir."

"Pearl. Just for spite? Is that really what this is about?"

"It has nothing to do with spite, and it has everything to do with standing up to that son of a bitch."

"Mother!"

"They're all asleep. The door's closed. Nobody can hear anything." She turned back to Frank. "The only reason we got the offer we did is that he's desperate, and I personally would rather take care of kids for the hardworking families around here than sit on my porch all day drinking tea with his dirty money. He's in trouble now, and I'm sure not going to be the one to bail him out."

She felt bad for her daughter; the pain of this discussion was written on Emily's face. She wanted to sell, Pearl could see that. She was tired; she and her husband had talked of moving to the city, starting fresh, perhaps with another bookstore like the one they'd used to have in Webster. Had anyone really contemplated that they would stay on forever? Pearl wondered at her own motives. Wasn't this really just about hanging onto her little girl?

"Daddy built something here," Emily said patiently to Frank, as if reading her mother's mind. "It will never be easy to let go of it."

Pearl could see him, a young man again, not unlike her son-in-law now except not a gambler who lost everything the family had on the ponies, cards, whatever. She could see her beloved Ernest, such a gentleman he had bored her at first with his dignity and reserve until she grew to love him so strongly over time, love the old-fashioned strength he had. She could see him among the wooden tables after the place had grown quite prosperous, a little department store in its own right at its peak, the beakers and jars of the old drugstore long since swept away to make room for the girdles and lace and other things people bought downtown in those days. A dime store they called it at first, when a dime was something. People still met at the soda fountain. He was from the old school, with a sparkling white shirt and lapel flower to match. Shoppers were Mrs. Somebody in those days, with gloves and little hats like a saddle across the top of their marcelled hair. We sold a lot of gloves in those days.

"Mom can tell you how he supervised the details personally," Emily continued, with a smile Pearl did not regard as wholly genuine. "How he got all this art deco stuff from catalogs, magazines. How children would come from miles around at Christmas. He poured himself into this place."

Pearl waited in vain for her to add the part about how her mother had astutely and intrepidly started the preschool in it when the old man died and the business flagged (or was strangled by the ruthless Krieger family). And how Frank and Emily came to it when they lost the bookstore.

"Just what are you going to do with all that money?" she demanded of Frank. "You've had a problem with large sums of money before."

Frank blushed, smiled, and looked at his wife. *You get old, you can say anything,* Pearl thought. *They just have to take it.*

"Mother, I think you'll agree that we had a hand in building up the school—"

"Which wouldn't even be here if it wasn't for me."

"—and so I'm not sure it's fair to berate Frank over something that happened long ago when we're trying to decide now what to do."

"Well it sounds like you've already decided," Pearl said, looking from one to the other. "It really doesn't matter what I say, does it?"

"Pearl, we would never sell this school without your agreement," Frank said resignedly, brushing imaginary lint from his trousers. "But at some level it just doesn't make sense. You don't enjoy it anymore. We can see that."

"You sound like a man trying to get away from something," Pearl said. He was a suspicious character, her son-in-law. She had never liked him, she told herself now, even though this was far from true. (She had doted on him at first, cherished his manners and taken his seriousness as flattery.) Now she heard noises from outside the teachers room and consulted the tiny gold watch face embedded in the fat of her arm. Nap time was coming to an end; she rose stiffly and shuffled out into the main area of the school. Alphabet Soup had four classrooms, but these were to some extent illusory, since they were created by deploying mobile dividers in a single huge space. It had been a temporary expedient when the school began, a way of converting the building quickly and cheaply, but the system had proved itself over time. It gave Emily the ability to combine rooms at will, wheel off all the dividers to create a single large space, or change classroom sizes to adapt to changing enrollments. At nap time, for instance, two of the four dividers were wheeled aside, making more room for bedrolls while making it easier for a single person (wakeful Emily, usually, although the teachers often slept among the children too) to keep an eye on everybody. Of course, the dividers on wheels served a subtle marketing function as well, helping give the school an open, flexible, down-to-earth air that pleased Webster parents.

As the children awakened, the preschool came groggily back to life. Today, as on most days, the same ones rose first, most of them four-year-olds: Jennifer, with the Prince Valiant haircut; quizzical Jared, whose hair was short all around except for a sort of tail in back; plump little Alyssa, whose blonde tresses, her mother admitted, had never been cut; and gentle Lennon, smaller than most, his skin tawny and his curly hair the same color. There was nervous Maxwell, always afraid no one would come and get him at the end of the day, and the biracial twins Jomo and Patrice, who were so attached to each other. And of course there was Tiffany, who was always so cranky and somehow frowsy-looking when she got up, with her hair in her dirty face and her brows knit into a frown. They had found her at their front door one drizzly fall day, standing there quietly waiting to be discovered like Moses among the bulrushes. Hours later a woman turned up in a red vest with a little gold nameplate that said "Belinda"; Pearl would never forget her damp shag haircut and the cigarette dangling from her lips. She tried to claim Tiffany had run off but finally confessed she had left her in desperation so she could start a new job. Pearl had wanted to call the police all along, but Emily, the softest touch in the world, was always ready to fall for a sob story and granted the little one a full scholarship. Maybe it was because Tiffany was a girl, and Emily felt her own lost little one was out there somewhere. Pearl had noticed her daughter was a lot more interested in reincarnation and other such occult nonsense after that horrible, horrible thing.

She had to admit that all the children slept easier now in the absence of Jeffrey, whose daily post-nap search-and-destroy missions often tore the others so rudely from the clammy arms of Morpheus. Teachers were beginning to turn the lights back on, and more students were rising as Pearl became aware that a man had entered the school, a man whose dark topcoat was open to reveal a dark suit and tie.

"Time for some cat stretches!" said one of the young teachers, but Pearl wasn't looking. "Ready to stretch all those sleepies out? Tiffany. Margaretta. You too now."

It was Wayne Lyttle; she could see that when she got him lined up in her trifocals. He had often picked up Jeffrey after school, and he nodded curtly, even sheepishly, as he headed for the office. Pearl decided to let Emily and Frank handle this. They were friendly with the Lyttles, God only knew why, and Pearl hoped they would iron everything out. She didn't trust herself to hold her own tongue.

Later, when the meeting with Wayne Lyttle was over, Emily was relieved. She was skeptical that place mattered all that much, but Webster was the place she knew, and it just felt too late to leave it now, which is what selling the school would entail. She didn't want to be the one to disappoint her husband, and so she was glad her mother had done the job for her. All she had had to do was disappoint Wayne instead, something at which she was experienced. It was funny to sit alone with him now after all these years, both of them with their disappointments, the weight of time tucked under their flesh like tacky souvenirs from the foolish, exciting trip of youth.

"Did he mention the spanking?" Frank asked afterward. This had been a sore subject between them.

"He did mention it," Emily said now, smiling wryly as she unwrapped a plateful of cookies and muffins and similar concoctions. They were in the school's kitchen. "He said he admired you for doing something he should have done years ago. Said he and Lu had read too many child-care books. Too many experts."

"So is Jeffrey coming back?"

"I don't think so. You know how Lucille is. She wants some kind of apology, some kind of pleading on our hands and knees that she give us back her darling son."

"I would apologize. The lawyer's the one who told us not to."

One of the two kettles she'd set to boil whistled, and Emily used a threadbare potholder to move it off the flame.

"It was stupid," Frank continued. "I admit it. But in a fairer world, his father wouldn't have to applaud us for it in secret."

"Lemme know when you move there."

But in truth, this was another reason Emily was relieved, for the spanking had made her furious at her husband and fearful about what the incident would do to the school's reputation. Alphabet Soup was a certain kind of place, largely because Webster was a certain kind of place. The snacks they served the children were always made of unrefined brown sugar and other fibrous or little-processed ingredients, all prepared as if for the pan-allergic offspring of ideologically committed vegans, since the children at the preschool (or more accurately, their parents) had so many special dietary requirements that aiming for the most austere was the only way to feed the same thing to everybody. The teachers conferred with the parents regularly about the emotional state of these same children, dissecting their play and characteristics with the fervor of ancient seers reading entrails. The parents were mostly well-to-do, and many were bent on getting their kids into the town's most selective private school. The reports that Alphabet Soup would provide when the kids graduated were considered crucial in this admissions process for five-year-olds and gave Emily unwanted power over the happiness of many families. She had tried to stop, but the parents had raised an outcry. Merely having their kids in Alphabet Soup was considered a huge advantage, but every possible edge was demanded, and so she found herself, year after year, writing cheerfully empty references for kids vying for kindergarten.

She did not have to wonder what this did to the children; with their hectic schedules and busy parents, they seemed already beset by the discontents of adulthood. The emotional state of the children at Alphabet Soup was a perennial subject for the teachers. Theirs was a caring profession, and they lived in a therapeutic age. The students wanted for nothing materially, were well-fed and clothed (as any teacher would learn if any child went home in some other child's sneakers). But some of them ached with want nonetheless, and the tiny band of Alphabet Soup teachers, all of whom adored children, did what they could to provide as much love and attention as humanly possible. Some of the teachers wanted to console the children with God, or at least with Bible stories and angels and miracles, but God had as little place in the preschool as in the rest of public life in Webster, where nobody could agree on whether there was one or what shape he, she, or it might take. On the other hand, all of the teachers could supply affection, and so except for Pearl they hugged and kissed the children, touched them freely, and on their birthdays each child got to sit on a teacher's lap and have a story read while the rest of the children had free play.

Treating the children this way filled a need for the teachers as well. Sue Steinhauer and her husband, Bob, shared their marriage with the son of God, whom they had accepted as their savior before they met one another. They came together through their church, which was the same as Lucille Lyttle's. Both found it difficult to talk to people and so had few friends. But their silences, once so comfortable, had grown vast and bleak. Julie Kennedy, Sue's young colleague, missed her boyfriend, who had moved to California. Despite his tortured letters, which arrived in bulging envelopes filled with pages of needy scribblings, he seemed so far away she had a hard time holding onto what he looked and felt like. They were trying to save money by not talking much on the telephone. Chris

Cutler, the new girl in plaid flannel and loose jeans, was lonely too. She missed her little brother and even, sometimes, her parents. She didn't know many people yet in Webster, which for a country girl could be an exciting place. Annette Martini's husband had a violent temper, and she doted preternaturally on their son. Mary Maloney, the eldest of a large family, mothered everyone.

It sometimes seemed to Emily, in fact, that all the maternal instincts of the entire town had come together in this one building, and that anyone who was of such a mind or heart was working here at Alphabet Soup, where the staff had formed such bonds of closeness that those who were still menstruating discovered long ago that they were doing so around the same time each month.

In such a time and place, the spanking of a child was a sin, so when the *Chronicle* story had appeared, with its gleeful tempest-in-a-teapot tone, Emily felt humiliated yet again by the man she had married. For what could be worse than for the world to see that her preschool, her own husband, for God's sake, must resort to physical force to control a little boy? Julie never would have done it, but she had been out sick—there was a bug going around—and Frank had covered the class and swatted the child.

"What exactly is the nature of this taboo against spanking a kid when he gets too far out of line?" he had asked when Emily assailed him for it, in the infuriating way he had of responding to her wrath with intellectualizing. "You've tried giving him time-outs, which is like calling time-out on a hurricane, and even when he sits still for one, why doesn't anybody complain that we're ostracizing kids in order to discipline them? Why is a quick smack on the ass worse than shunning?"

"Because it teaches kids that violence is the answer, that when you don't like what somebody's doing, you can hit them."

"Well what does a time-out teach? That you should withhold affection whenever you don't get your way? That emotional manipulation is a better way to go than physical force? Isn't compulsion the basis of it in any case?"

"Frank, parents in this town don't believe in spanking, especially our parents, the ones who send their kids here and write the checks. Is that a language that you understand? Because I'm assuming it would be a waste of breath for me to tell you how embarrassed I am to have the staff and everyone else see that we have to use violence, God save us, *violence,* to control a four-year-old."

Almost as soon as it happened, she called Bob Varity. He was their lawyer, one of the best known in Webster, and happened to have a four-year-old at Alphabet Soup. He had kept them out of trouble before— when someone had sued over their admissions procedures, for instance. "Frank probably was crazy to hit the kid, Em, even though I'd have belted that little monster long ago," Varity said. Emily sighed. She liked Bob, he wasn't haughty or bloodless like the other lawyers she knew. He had a sense of humor, of humility. She had always felt there was some special sympathy between them, and in her hardest times with Frank, when Varity was all that stood between them and bankruptcy or disgrace, she had wondered what life might have been like if she and Bob had married one another instead of their own disappointing spouses. "I kept hoping my son would belt him," Varity said of little Jeffrey. "The kids all hate him, you know. He's just a miserable little bully. But what's done is done, and now you have to be careful. Being in business these days means never having to say you're sorry."

"Well, that's convenient."

"But there's a reason for it. If you say you're sorry, you admit you were wrong, and believe me, you can't afford to be wrong. A wrong in my business is called a tort, which means that apologies, like written policies and so forth, just give people a better shot at you. Corporal punishment's not illegal in this state, and nobody was really hurt, correct? At least he hit the right kid. Have a talk with the parents, maybe. Hear them out, be sympathetic, and let it be understood that it won't happen again. But don't use any words too close to 'I'm sorry.'"

Emily and Frank had acted on this advice during their confrontation with Lucille Lyttle, and it also colored their approach to the unscheduled staff meeting that Emily had insisted upon to give everyone a chance to air their feelings. Arrayed in the little lunchroom they used for such gatherings, the group struck her now as frankly skeptical, the verdict of the inquisition guilty with dissenting votes only from Sue and perhaps

Annette. They all knew that any of them probably would have been fired for doing what Frank had done, and Frank's laconic style, rich in irony though it might be, had won him few admirers among the teachers except for Annette, of course.

Emily did her best at this meeting to explain the spanking and, without making light of it, keep it in proportion. Frank said little, as she made it clear that this had been an extraordinary event, that it wasn't expected to be repeated, and that although no laws had been broken it was, of course, the school's belief that good order could be maintained without corporal punishment.

"Obviously, if anybody has anything to share on this matter, the floor's open, as it always is," she said, surveying the faces, the haircuts, the outfits, and the body language of her listeners. Pearl sat heavily off to one side, her plump face inexpressive. Annette, in tight jeans, scowled slightly; she always looked embarrassed, or rather as if she were trying not to look embarrassed. Sue wore her usual flowered dress, prim white collar, and flat, low-cut shoes, and her usual expression of worry when unexpected things happened. Chris looked to be working as hard as ever to suppress a smirk. Julie, so very thoughtful, listening intently, pushed her dark blonde hair behind her ear. Mary, the good girl, was the picture of innocence and attentiveness. And Jesus (they pronounced this in Spanish: hay-*soos*) Mendoza, the maintenance man, sat solemnly in his khaki twill uniform, twisting a clean rag in his thick fingers. The familiar faces were mostly blank, but behind their eyes Emily could see a cruel judgment, and she knew it was likely thus outside the school as well.

"Frank looked like the cat that ate the bird," Chris said after the meeting. "He's proud of himself for hitting Jeffrey. He thinks he's a big man in the eyes of the women."

"I don't blame him one bit," said Sue, who taught Sunday school at her evangelical church. "Julie's been wanting to strangle that kid, or throw him out, or something."

"Jeffrey just made it hard for the others," said Julie, pushing the hair out of her face as if deflecting the homicidal tendencies attributed to her. "He takes so much energy that they all get less, and we end up just reinforcing his acting out by giving him attention. I've tried to ignore him, but his behavior just escalates to where it's not safe."

Emily did not like to have Frank in class, truth be told. He was a good man, she told herself, and he loved children, single-handedly taking their own son and his friends on trips of all kinds until finally they all grew up. But he was stern, old-fashioned, and a little rigid. He had wanted to have all the children at Alphabet Soup call the teachers ma'am and sir, as he had required of their own son, now safely off to college in Oregon, until Emily and Pearl persuaded him that it would kill the school, that the parents of modern-day Webster, who paid the bills, after all, would never go for it. Frank was out of step in other ways. He never slept, it sometimes seemed, and looked on the other teachers' nap-time habits with amusement. His sense of humor, at least, was unfailing. She loved his wicked impersonations of the people they knew, how he mocked their neighbors' pieties in thought and deed. He made fun of himself most of all, with his fragrant pipe tobacco and old-fashioned books. Imagine me here in Webster, he would say over drinks, and she understood: in a town so committed to the notion of the world's sinfulness, he was one of the few with any real experience of sin.

He was a fastidious man, another reason Emily had married him, and struggled heroically against his native hairiness. His hirsute body had taken getting used to; not just his chest but his shoulders, back, and arms were covered with black curls, and his beard was so exuberant that he shaved twice a day, retiring every afternoon into the staff bathroom to beat back the jungle at least to below his collar (although of course his head was mostly bald). "My hairy ape," Emily had called him during their courtship. He wore a coat and tie every day, an old-fashioned briarwood among the scraps of tobacco in his left-hand pocket, and she believed him when he said he was most comfortable this way. He was not well known in Webster, except for his deadpan wit and otherworldly air. Abigail Thorndike, who had served with him on the commission that had investigated Daniel Webster, said he was the true heir to the town's Puritan tradition, a man strangely in this world but not of it. Of his lifelong vice—gambling—he would say with smooth irony that all who suffered from it were the last truly religious people in a godless land. They were simply hoping for a sign of grace, which winning must be, and the tragedy was how consistently their hopes were dashed.

For all his hardheadedness, Frank for years had acquiesced in Emily's and her mother's refusal to sell the school's Clove Street building to make way for the Krieger's garage, even though the school had never been terribly profitable. They had been the last holdouts among several landowners whose properties were needed to make way for the project. The others had badly wanted to sell. But Alphabet Soup parents, not a few of them Krieger's employees, loved the preschool's central location, which enabled them to drop off their kids on the way to work downtown and sometimes even visit them at lunch, and had mobilized to save the place. The anti-parking forces, including the preschool's owners, had used the slogan "Choose children over cars," enraging opponents who insisted with pathetic futility that they loved children as much as anyone else. It was a classic Websterian conflict, a practical question turned into an emotional litmus test. Neighboring landholders still resented Alphabet Soup for standing in their way, and there was a faction in town that had wanted to condemn the school and the land to make it available for the parking structure. In this view, Emily's stubbornness was really just arrogance, and some people hadn't talked to her since.

Her secret, which she never mentioned to Frank, was that some part of her wanted to sell too. And even though she felt embedded in her hometown, it tickled her to think her husband still wished to abscond with her and commit adventures that would be theirs alone. Besides, running the school was ever more a burden. They tried to create an island of calm and joy for the children, but the place was buffeted by the same winds as the rest of Webster. Divorce, live-ins, step-siblings—all the accoutrements of family restructuring added unpleasant complication to her life. She had at least three restraining orders on file barring one parent or another from picking up a child, and end-of-day arrangements, once so casual, were now infused with caution lest a child be handed off to the wrong person. Of course, the real problem at Alphabet Soup wasn't kidnapping. On the contrary, the problem was that, once or twice a month, no one would come to claim a child at all.

Y ou have such a nice house!" Belinda said, giggling shyly, as Lucille freshened her drink.

Despite their differences, they had become fast friends since their first phone conversation. Lucille was part of a giant Christian congregation on the outskirts of town, its vast building surrounded by acres of parking and bristling with video screens. Belinda attended a little Baptist church on the seedy side of downtown, a world away. But both places took scripture literally, and in both places, it was hard to find people to drink with.

"Decorating's always been an interest of mine," Lucille said, succumbing easily to flattery. "I get all the magazines, go to the open houses. I used to dream of moving to New York. If I hadn't married Wayne and had these kids, I probably would have. Taxis, night life, the works."

"Sounds like you wish you had."

"Oh, well, the road not taken."

"Tell me about it! I didn't plan to get knocked up so fast, and not by Evan, believe me. I was just about to start cosmetology school. Asshole hasn't seen his own daughter twice since she was born and don't send nothing to keep us alive. He'd just as soon we drowned or something."

"It must be tough, making it on your own."

"It really is. I worked a while, used to leave Tiffany with Evan's sister, who's got three of her own, but her husband's such a dirtbag I had to stop. That guy gave me the creeps. I swear I was worried he was gonna molest my kid."

"You can't be too careful," Lucille nodded sympathetically. Both women took appreciative gulps from their drinks.

"We had an incident once," Belinda said, lowering her voice and looking at Lucille sideways. "I had a boyfriend who liked to walk around naked. I used to tell him, 'cover yourself, don't go in front of my daughter that way!' Then one night I thought he got up to pee and I found him in her room."

"No!"

"Yup. Said he wanted to check on her. I almost believed him, 'cause he

was always real nice to her—real fatherly type. But he was buck naked
and his prong was out to here!"

Belinda extended her arm to show how far. Lucille covered her mouth.
She could imagine it quivering there, erect like some snake poised to
strike.

"What did you do?" she asked.

"I told him never to go in there that way again, and from that day forward I watched him. 'Cause you never know. Know what I mean? He
dumped me not long after that, which made me even more suspicious. I
asked Tiffany if he ever did anything funny, but she says no. She misses
him! Kids."

"You really can't be too careful," Lucille repeated.

"That's right. I worry about that, that some pervert is somehow gonna
hurt my little girl. I had something like that. A minister once, when I was
real small. It was disgusting. I worry about it all the time, and I ask her too.
I want her to tell me if anybody does anything, not end up like me, living
hand-to-mouth with a daughter she can barely support and no husband. I
think it did something to my self-esteem, you know? That's partly why I
didn't work for so long. I didn't like the welfare; I never been on welfare
before in my life until then. But I just couldn't stand leaving my little lamb
with someone for all those hours and who knows what they're up to."

"Now you're making me worried," Lucille said.

"I know it," Belinda said with a guilty laugh. "Here we are with both
our kids in day care; we're having a good time and God knows what's
happening with them. But what choice do I have? I work most days. And
Alphabet Soup is supposed to be the best."

"Well that's what I thought," Lucille said, shaking her head. "But
that's not how it turned out for Jeffrey."

"What's the story over at that place, anyway? Why's it so popular?"

"Beats me. Fashion, I suppose. Emily and Frank are the darlings of the
well-to-do families here in town, and everybody thinks they just have to
have their kid in there. It's a real status thing."

"The old lady's so funny," said Belinda. "Really a sourpuss. I had
teachers like that one. Real Miss Grundy types. And that guy. Frank

Joseph. I can't decide about him. Sometimes he strikes me as really sexy; other times he almost gives me the creeps. So laid-back. With those lounge-lizard eyes. What does he do over there?"

"He's Emily's Svengali, I think. Not a happy man. Used to gamble, lost most of their savings that way. He seems real proper and quiet and all, but he's the one that hit my boy. Emily won't say boo to him." She took a big sip, and when she swallowed, added: "I'd have left a bum like that long ago."

"Well, I don't have much choice right now. I couldn't afford any place else, what with the scholarship they're giving me and all. But you're right about one thing—it's always the ones who don't look it! I better keep an eye on her over there."

"Charlie Krieger gets so mad—he calls the whole bunch a nest of pedophiles," Lucille said with a snort. She liked dropping his name.

"Pedophiles?!" Belinda looked worried. "Are they the ones hang around in the shoe department or something?"

Lucille looked at her. "What do shoes have to do with it?"

"Pedophiles. Ain't that people who get their jollies from looking at other people's feet? They like sandals and stuff?" She gave a little shiver. "Ugh!"

"Not feet—kids!" Lucille blurted through her laughter. "I'm sorry. I'm getting silly, I'm having such a good time. It means liking kids just a little too much."

"Oh! Oh, you mean like I suspected my boyfriend of being?"

"You got it."

"They're at Alphabet Soup?!"

"You gotta know Charlie. He gets carried away sometimes."

"Uh-huh," Belinda said, looking not entirely mollified. "Huh. Speaking of which, I better be going before somebody has to carry me away. They don't like me to leave Tiff too late. I'm not one of the paying customers, and the old lady never lets me forget it."

"They never do take a snow day, do they?"

"Not so far," Belinda said. "That's OK with me, though."

"Well it was great having you," Lucille said, getting up too. "You should come back again."

"Only maybe I'll have one less next time," Belinda said, grabbing her friend by the arm. She laughed heartily, conspiratorially, and lowered her voice. "Jeez, I'm gonna have to take it real slow this afternoon."

Belinda got into her car, which she knew needed a muffler and probably a rebuilt transmission at least, with a mixture of emotions roiling inside her. She had a grand feeling of well-being from the drinks and the knowledge that she was friends with one of those rich ladies in Barrington Vistas, the best part of Webster, but she was also nervous and resentful. The roads were treacherous, the light of day was waning, and her windshield was chronically fogged. She was in a hurry to get her daughter—she was already late, Pearl would certainly remind her—but there was traffic on the major artery going across town, with idiots turning left and snowbanks and rich little college kids walking every which way. "Look where you're going," she shouted when one walked practically into her car. She hated that, when they started toward her before she was entirely past. "Jesus H. Christ!" Why should she have to rush like this? Why was it her lot to go home to a trailer outside town and have Chef Boy-ar-dee for dinner, when kids like this could eat out every night and not have a care in the world? Luck. That's all any of this was. Plain dumb luck.

By the time she pulled up at the preschool she was in a lather, but she told herself to calm down, there was no real rush, everything was fine. When she got inside, though, Pearl asked to speak to her in the office.

"What? Is anything wrong? Is Tiffany okay?"

Pearl led her inside, closing the door behind them.

"Your daughter had a nosebleed today—"

"A nosebleed?" Belinda was relieved. "Oh, that's nothing. She has those."

"—and it took quite a while to stop it," Pearl continued.

"Ice on the forehead usually does it for me," Belinda said helpfully. She pretended to be looking for something in her bag.

"So we called you at Mart-World, and they said you were off on Wednesdays."

"Right. Oh, well not every Wednesday."

"Well, what exactly is your work schedule? They said you never work Wednesdays. They were quite specific."

"Look, what's this about? What's the difference whether I work Wednesdays?"

Emily slipped in and closed the door behind her. She noticed that Belinda was missing two of her lower teeth on the left.

"The difference," Pearl said, "is that we're granting your daughter very close to a full scholarship so you can hold a job, but on the days you aren't working we'd like you to make other arrangements. We've got a very full house, and it's all we can do to give everyone the attention they deserve."

"Well fine, she won't be back on Wednesdays," Belinda said. She felt like she was back in school, in the principal's office. "Is there anything else, or can we go now?"

"It's nothing personal," Emily said. "We're just overcrowded as it is, and if it's not essential for you to leave her here Wednesdays, it'd really be a help if you did something else."

"Fine, I already said we won't be back Wednesdays! Jesus!"

Belinda made for the door but yowled when she struck her hip against the large table in the middle of the room. Mouthing curses, her face contorted by pain, she rubbed the spot that hurt.

"Sit down," Emily urged. "Just sit down a minute."

"I'm OK! Let me just get my daughter."

"Would you like some coffee or something?" Emily asked. "I mean, are you going to be all right driving?"

"I'm fine," Belinda said, sidling around the other two women and hurrying out into the room full of children.

"Shouldn't we stop her?" Emily asked, looking at her mother. "She smells like a distillery."

But Pearl only shook her head and sent her eyes heavenward.

Belinda needed brakes too, and her tires were very nearly bald, as she was told after the accident. The funny thing was, she was being careful. She had had a DUI before and now felt light-headed as she made her way to her car, a little woozy, even, but also angry at Pearl and the preschool for the high-handed way it wanted to tell her how to run her life. Even Emily, with that Lady Bountiful routine of hers.

"He who pays the piper calls the tune," she said bitterly to her daughter, who sat on the bench seat beside her. "Always remember that, sweetie."

"Who's the piper, Mommy?" Tiffany asked. When she got no answer, she asked again, "Who's the piper?"

But her mother wasn't listening. They had the classic rock-and-roll station on the radio, and every now and then she would wipe down the inside of the windshield with her sleeve to clear a little spot she could see through.

"Is Mr. Frank the piper? He showed us his pipe today. In his pants he keeps it."

Traffic was slow getting out of central Webster, as it turned out because someone had rear-ended someone else right on Main Street, and there wasn't much room for them to get off to the side and sort out their insurance and so forth.

"What are you talkin' about, sweetie?" Belinda asked. They inched past the main gate of Bradfield College, where Belinda's mother had worked in the cafeteria. "I can't listen right now. I can barely see."

"His pipe—that he keeps in his pants! He even lets us hold it, but we're not supposed to tell."

When finally traffic broke free and Main Street opened up onto Route 32, Belinda was glad to give it some gas, feeling a serious need to get away from something. But what? She was uneasy somehow. She felt low about the way she had been treated at the school, and her need to get away was partly a flight from the town's righteous judgment of her wayward life. But there was something else. Something about her daughter's words bothered her. Something about that pipe. She made it fine out almost to the Old Mill Road, about a mile before the gravel track she'd use to reach the cluster of cottages and trailers where she lived. There's a poorly banked curve there, one that Terry Mathers had written about repeatedly for its risks, and you need to take it slower than she did, especially when you need tires and brakes and the wet from the melt earlier in the day is streaky ice now because this particular stretch has been in shade for so long. If your car does let go, there's not much you can do. You can't steer into the skid because you'll hit the oak tree, and you can't brake because you'll spin around and hit it sideways, which is exactly what Belinda's rusting blue Gran Torino ended up doing.

chapter FIVE

The next morning Emily was jolted out of her paperwork by a looming presence walking among the children who arrived at 7:30 A.M. She was frightened as soon as she set eyes on the man, and she would always remember what seemed in retrospect the precious innocence of the moments before this hulking figure came looming among her few little charges at that hour. Pearl and Annette, the only others present, tried not to stare. He appeared to be a bodybuilder; he was blonde, ruddy, and his massive torso seemed to precede him, so when he asked for Frank, Emily assumed it was about gambling, that he was some sort of enforcer sent to collect an overdue debt.

"I warn you, I'll call the police," she said. Her voice was shaking. "Whatever the problem is, you can't bring it here. There are children present, and I simply will not have it."

Hands and eyebrows upraised, Detective Jepson had answered, of course, that he was the police, and then Emily worried in a different way even though she knew there would be no violence. So she summoned Frank, who seemed genuinely surprised and strangely calm, like someone who truly had no idea what could be the matter, and she relaxed a little. The detective asked if he could speak to Frank in private, and then they went into the office and closed the door. When the detective left, her husband was ashen.

"Em, Tiffany Jackson is dead," he told her when she went in to him. "She was killed yesterday out on 32, driving home from here with her mother."

"Oh my God. Oh, Frank! Was Belinda—"

"Just cuts and bruises. She had been drinking, apparently."

"Jesus, Mom was right. Oh, Frank, that woman should be shot! That poor little girl—" Emily began to weep, and he held her. Neither would mention their own lost daughter, who filled their thoughts. "What's going to happen? Is Belinda going to be prosecuted, did the detective say?"

"He says she accuses me of abusing her daughter." Frank gave a little laugh, tried to sound astonished.

"What?! What are you talking about, what abuse?"

"Sexually, Em. She says I abused her little girl sexually." He sounded embarrassed not for himself but his accuser.

"What?" she repeated. "That stupid, lying drunk! You told that guy about her, right? How she left the kid here in the first place, how we practically have to bathe her, how she doesn't seem to get anything to eat at home?"

"I think he knows she's grasping at straws," Frank said, rubbing his left palm with his right thumb. "She's facing some pretty serious charges here, so what can you expect? She's probably hysterical, not even in her right mind. So now it's child abuse. She claims that's why we took Tiffany without charging. Says she was so distraught it drove her to drink, and she was so anxious to get her daughter away from here that she went off the road."

"I can't believe the police would even dignify this—would have the temerity to ask about it. She killed her child, Frank! She was careless and stupid and self-involved, and now that poor girl is dead, and she's blaming it on you. I can't believe it."

"Well, neither do the police, apparently. She was drunk, her tires were bald, the girl wasn't belted in properly. On and on and on. It's sad really. I can't get too mad at her, Em. I don't think I could live with myself now if I were her. I told Jepson they ought to keep an eye on her. I'm worried she'll kill herself."

"I can't believe the police are pursuing this. Do they know what they're doing to us? This will be all over town any minute, and no matter how much we deny it, we're screwed."

"Em, he swore up and down they never make an investigation public unless and until there are charges. And it's hard to see how there ever could be any. In fact, he asked me to keep this confidential. He seemed embarrassed, almost. It'll all blow over."

But Detective Jepson's visit weighed on Emily. That night, after dinner, she sat brushing out her chestnut hair, her best feature, she always felt, and gazed at her slender face in the mirror, marveling that it showed no sign of what she had been through. She would be considered attractive, she knew, if she could somehow rest and banish the weary circles under eyes. Her flesh sagged even though she was thin, and her sharp nose was red most of the time, even though she was rarely sick. People thought she was much more serious than she felt herself to be, yet even Frank complained that she didn't know how to have fun. *Anhedonic* was the word he used. The thought of this almost made her cry, but a photo of her son, tucked in the corner of her mirror, cheered her. She missed him banging the screen door in warm weather, raiding the refrigerator at all hours, letting her hug him even as a teenager, as long as the other kids didn't see. She missed him as a baby even after all these years, a fuzzy-headed baby laden with fat from the milk of her youth. And now here was this wild, revolting allegation. Child abuse! She caught herself brushing so hard it hurt, her hair crackling with static electricity, and realized she was thinking of her uncle Herman and his heavy flesh like hairy cheddar, the way he taught her to rub him, the importance of keeping their secret, and how well she had learned her lessons. What a good girl. She had never spoken of these things, never told a living soul except her therapist, and barely admitted them now to herself. When she had met Frank, it was almost instinct for her to wet her thumb and forefinger and do the same. He loved it, but it was what made her freeze inside, and eventually this realization made her understand that what had happened to her as a child at the hands of blithe Pearl's older brother was not normal and might have to do with the way she wept sometimes with Frank, and the joylessness she felt about sex to this day.

It was why she worried about the children so much as well; she had told Dr. Brauner that one of her deepest (and, she knew, most desperately irrational) fears was that somehow the intense pleasure she took in children would become sexual—already, the feelings she had for them were so intense—and that she would become her uncle. For a long time, she wouldn't handle the children at Alphabet Soup the way the younger women did, but Dr. Brauner had helped her a good deal, and finally she had come to realize that her fears were just that, only fears, and that her love for children was natural and good and could be expressed safely. "You're not your uncle," the doctor had said. "You don't belong to him, just because of what he did to you, and you won't become him. Your fears have more to do with the lost child in your life, with your own lost childhood, than with cursed Uncle Herman, may he rot in hell. Don't be afraid."

In the mirror, Emily saw her husband moving around behind her, undoing the cufflinks that were a badge of ironic vanity for him, emptying his pockets of wallet, keys, and money, undoing his wristwatch, and finally, quickly, removing his wedding band. She began to worry that he had a secret once again. She liked to think she could tell, but desperately wanted not to credit her judgment just now. There had been enough secrets. Without turning around, and in a quiet voice, she called to him, but amid the opening and closing of drawers and the running of the bathroom tap, he must not have heard, because he only brushed his teeth and didn't respond, and she didn't call him again.

When the phone rang, Lucille was in the middle of changing her daughter's diaper. Amy was a mess, and her mother grabbed for a wipe from the package before picking up the phone. "Hello," Lucille said, barking above the start and stop noises of the Nintendo game in the background. There was no response at first.

"Hello!" she said again. "Is anybody there?"

"H-H-H-H—Lu. Hi," she finally heard from the struggling male voice. "It's T-T-Terry Mathers at the *C-Chronicle.* I'm s-s-sorry to be calling at a time like this, but I was told you were friendly with Belinda Jackson. I thought you might be able to h-h-help us with the story we're working on."

"Story? What are you talking about? What's happened?"

"You haven't heard." Terry paused.

Adrenaline rushed into Lucille's system. "Is Belinda OK?"

"She's OK, but it's her daughter. I'm s-sorry to be the one to have to tell you, but there was an accident. Tiffany's been k-k-k-"

"Oh my Jesus," Lucille said, the unpronounceable word dawning on her. "She's been killed. Is that what you mean to say? O my dear Jesus Lord. How? What happened?"

"It was out on 32, she m-m-missed the curve and went off the road. There was ice. She's also ch-ch-charged with driving while intoxicated." His breath sounded caught, almost strangled. "Apparently, she'd been at your house before she picked her daughter up."

"But she only had one drink. One or two at most!"

"Do you remember what you were drinking?"

"I don't think I should discuss this. Oh God, this is terrible. Look, where is she now? Was she hurt?"

"B-B-Banged up a little," Terry said. "She's in Webster Memorial."

When Lucille called her, she was amazed for an instant to hear Belinda's voice on the phone, babyish and wary sounding. How could you simply dial and get someone who had just lost her child—whose child had been lying dead right next to her? It took Lucille a second to find her voice. She had an inkling, for just that moment, of what it must be like to stutter, to be Terry. But she didn't have to say much. She listened in guilty shock as Belinda told her what had happened. When she came to the part about the girl being thrown from the car, she could barely say the words.

"They say it was 'cause of the alcohol—"

"But you only had one drink over here, maybe with just a little freshening. Had you had anything before you came here?"

"—but it wasn't 'cause of the alcohol, it was 'cause I was so upset, which is also why I had been drinking. It was 'cause of what they were doing to her over there. That man, that Mr. Joseph guy, was molesting my daughter."

Lucille's stomach was churning. Her white skin, flushed now, was tingling.

"Don't you see what I'm saying to you?" Belinda continued. "Tiffany told me. It was hard for her, but on the way home she told me what I had known all along. I mean, I didn't drink that much, did I? But she told me. It's what she'd been trying to tell me all along, only I never wanted to hear it, I guess. She said he showed her his pipe, the one he kept in his pants. He let her touch it, Lu. It didn't register at first, but suddenly I realized what she was saying and I ran off the road. I got so upset I just lost control of the car. Tiffany was so upset and I was so upset and I just completely lost it. Didn't know where I was or anything. Like I blacked out. And now my little baby's gone, and it's all their fault. I don't even have the money to pay for a funeral, and they're talking about charging me with murder!" She dissolved into tears. "I can't believe this is happening to me. I keep waking during the night wanting to go check on my baby. I haven't slept more than a few minutes. Lu, I don't think I'll ever sleep again. Can a person live that way? If I don't get some sleep soon I think I'll go out of my mind."

"Tell the doctors, Belinda. Tell them that, and they'll give you something."

"The police don't believe me. They think I killed her. My own baby! But when she told me what that animal did to her, I just lost it. I just screamed out, and the next thing I know I'm in the hospital and they won't tell me where my baby is. They won't tell me at first, and so I know, which is even worse, until finally this doctor says he's really sorry but she's gone."

"Do you need anything, Belinda?" Lucille asked, but gazing at her own children across the room, the two of them frozen by the mysterious power of the television screen, her mind was elsewhere already. What she was hearing on the phone was too painful, too pathetic, too far away. She worried a little that there would be a scandal, talk of Belinda tanking up

at Lucille's, and this tightened her stomach further. How had she ever
become entangled with this trailer trash? She felt the bile rising thickly
at the back of her throat. If she wasn't careful, she knew, she would lose
her lunch. On the phone, she was all sympathy, however. She promised to
visit her friend soon and to ask her husband about lawyers, and then hung
up, never dreaming of doing the things she had promised to do. Looking
at her son, the pity of Belinda's situation was the last thing on her mind.

A cross town, in the gathering gloom of a wintry Webster afternoon,
Diana Shirley sat in her office with Al Jepson, going over his
account of his interview with Frank Joseph and wondering when he
would finally go away so she could leave. She had felt small and withdrawn at first next to Jepson's intimidating bulk and was now further
oppressed by his reluctance to go.

"He does kind of fit the profile," Jepson said. "Loner, addictive personality."

"And as we know from the spanking incident," Diana added, "violent."

Jepson shrugged, and Diana realized that to a police officer the spanking of a child hardly qualified as violence.

"And he talked to you freely, without asking for an attorney or anything."

"Quite freely. Denied everything. Acted like it was the most amazing
thing he'd ever heard in his entire life, which it probably was. In all hon-
esty, I felt awful asking him about it."

Diana was not surprised to hear these things. The allegation had been
made by a mother likely to be held responsible for her daughter's death, a
woman who was driving drunk and had a record of petty disorderliness
and misdeameanors, including shoplifting, that Mart-World had somehow overlooked. But Diana had done many such interviews, and she was
convinced after talking with Belinda Jackson that Tiffany had been
abused no matter what the circumstances of the allegation, which certainly didn't excuse drunken driving. Belinda hadn't really tried to
excuse herself, had acknowledged what she had done and how she would

always have to live with it, but seemed determined to spare the other children, and that was what impressed Diana, who had requested an examination of the corpse to see if there was any physical evidence of what the poor child might have suffered. She was not hopeful on this score; the physician who would perform this examination had attended a day-long seminar on recognizing sexual abuse in small children but had no other experience in the field. Consciousness of these issues was so new, and Webster so far from a major city, that it was difficult to bring to bear the kind of trained personnel that Diana considered necessary for investigating the sexual abuse of children. But it was true that abusers tended to prey on more than one child, and if Tiffany had had to live through this, chances are other children were as well.

Like the physician, Jepson was also new to the field and tended to follow Diana's lead, although he too had attended a seminar on investigating molestation. He seemed deeply affected by it; he had a powerful affection for kids, she could see. He was aware, too, of the sensitivity of these issues. He had thrown himself into his new beat with righteous ardor, phoning her frequently and vowing to leave no stone unturned in carrying their investigations to a successful conclusion. She suspected—correctly, it would turn out—that he was half in love with her, and so she made a point of asking often after his wife and children. To her relief, he was always ready to take out photos, and when a new batch arrived couldn't wait to show them off.

Today, as usual, he seemed reluctant to go, and they discussed how to proceed. While he lingered, the phone rang, and when Diana put it down, she gave him the news: Dr. Verdi had indeed found signs of abuse. Jepson looked stunned.

"It's horrible, I know," Diana said. She felt for him; he wasn't used to this, and she wondered if she herself was becoming hardened. Perhaps it was inevitable. "But it's good news, really. At least now we have some physical evidence. She's faxing me her report as soon as she gets it done."

"Get me a copy of that, will you?" Jepson said through gritted teeth.

Diana looked over Jepson's report, wondering when he would leave. If it wasn't in the next five minutes, she would be late. Then she chided herself for being so selfish. She had seen abuse aplenty from uncles, boyfriends, and other men who passed through the life of children at home, but this was the first time she had ever worked on a case involving a school, where the abuser had access to so many children and so much privacy. Where the opportunity, in other words, was so vast. She had read about pedophiles running Boy Scout troops and the like, and knew, of course, that they were drawn to such positions, readily volunteering to shepherd young people around in order to satisfy their twisted desires. Now here she was with a pedophile whose actual business was day care. Of course. It made perfect sense.

That evening, changing hurriedly into her good suit, she wondered sorrowfully how much pedophilia there was in the world, and how anyone could ever hope to eradicate such a thing. It was depressing, and so she tried to think instead about the other children and how, in some terrible sense, Tiffany had died to save them.

Diana was cold all the time lately, and so she took care to dress warmly. Perhaps it was just being alone, sleeping alone, knowing at the end of every day that there was no one special to go home to and embrace. Webster felt like the coldest place she had ever been. Why was it that hell was always described as so hot? Burns were painful, but as a Californian, it had always seemed to her that the world would end not in heat but in some bleak Ice Age of remorseless darkness and cold, a fearsome, frigid solitude that (in her current imaginings) would spread outward from Webster to engulf the planet with its phony rectitude. It was all so bleak—the climate, the landscape, the terrible things people did to children. She felt guilty too about the way her last relationship had ended, even if she had given Alix the house they had bought together. For a brief time there was peace, but this was just the quiet before the storm, and soon the raging letters began to arrive in envelopes thick with grieving pages, and packages of Diana's few remaining things including a box containing nothing but broken glass—crystal from which they had toasted their mutual devotion.

She felt bad about everything. If it makes you feel any better, she wanted to write back, I'm not happy either, although she was trying to console herself with positive thinking. She was lonely, but Webster had at least welcomed her, and the flattering profile that had appeared in the

Chronicle was already helping. People had begun to recognize her around town. Calls were already beginning to come in. Perhaps here she could make a real difference.

Driving downtown, Diana picked her way gingerly along streets narrowed by frozen snowbanks and, when she'd parked, shivered as she walked carefully through the icy municipal parking lot, which made the row of businesses in front of it, their faces turned hopefully toward the street, seem almost like false fronts. Despite her woolen tights, her lower body was cold in the skirt she had decided to wear for her first date with a man in nearly three years.

chapter SIX

Dimly, from somewhere outside his trancelike state, Terry heard the old man speaking.

"I've had a full battery of tests," the voice said, "and now it's only a matter of time. I have a fairly clear idea what the results will be."

Even under the circumstances, his father spoke in the same oracular vein he did on television. Even when the subject was his own body. Terry felt no pressure to respond because of the Guatemalan woman walking up and down on his back. She held onto a couple of railings mounted along the ceiling. His joints cracked and popped colorfully.

"Like a piano," she said shyly from somewhere up above, a smile in her voice. Maury's Guatemalan giggled.

"Dad, you've been to the finest doctors," Terry said at last. "Mayo. *Uhh.* Mass. *Uh.* General. You name it. *Uhhh.* You're healthy as a horse. Grandma and Grampa lived into their *uhhh* nineties. Never took a pill. It's all in your head."

"Son, if it makes you feel better to believe that, it's a load off my"—a sudden exhalation here, as Maury's back-walker passed over his abdomen—"mind. The only reason I'm so dogged about this is you and Abby and the grandchildren. That's why I came up here. While I still have the illusion of immortality, I thought I could indulge my loved ones."

They were in the massage room at the Splendid Valley Spa, one of the most expensive (and discreet) such places in the country, which happened to be situated in the hills twenty minutes from Webster. Maury was a regular at their Arizona campus, but Terry knew he didn't want to get too tan during the winter lest he come across on TV as some kind of aristocrat instead of the man of the people he pretended to be.

"How's Marcia?" Terry asked. Marcia was Maury's young wife.

"Marcia," the old man snorted, whether in disdain or from the weight on his back Terry couldn't tell, "felt the need to visit St. Bart."

Terry tried not to smile, which was easy given what he was enduring. He was envious, both of his father's conquests and of these young women who were forever replacing him as the focus of Maury's affections, and he saw himself someday, if his father ever really did kick the bucket, owing the *Chronicle* to the old man's thirty-year-old former research assistant. Marcia was sweet but jealous of her husband's past, and this sudden separation made it more likely Maury would be willing to extend further support to his son's beleaguered newspaper. As his masseuse balanced between his shoulder blades, rocking back and forth, the phrase *good money after bad* flashed through Terry's mind, and he resolved to come clean about how unlikely it was the loan would be repaid. He had been meaning to do this for weeks now, but in spite of what he'd told Abigail, no such conversation had occurred.

"Dad," Terry began.

"I know what you're thinking," Maury interrupted, "but I didn't come up here just to end my marriage. Believe me, I'm quite capable of doing that from home." Both men spoke face down into the hole in the middle of the pad at the top of their massage tables. "I came to see you. Also to dispose of some property."

"Property?"

"Out on 32, near Rockton. Some land I bought. Long ago *uhhh,* some scrubland. A couple of us got into it after the war. I was holding it for you, but somebody with a lot of money wants to put up some kind of strip development."

So at least he's flush, Terry thought, ready to plunge ahead.

"Besides," his father added. "It's expensive being Maury Mathers. I need the money. Guy like me can't start going to McDonald's."

"Well," Terry said finally, losing his nerve. "We're really glad you came."

"Wow," Maury said afterward, grinning vividly as they walked to the locker room. "It's nice to have somebody walk all over me now and then."

Glowing red, Maury puffed his chest out. Terry had his mother's lankier build, but his father was thickset and muscular, his large teeth giving him a carnivorous air when exposed too broadly. What looked like a bit of a totter in street clothes was springy and athletic naked in the locker room, although his movements were still slower and less precise than in a younger man. He picked up his towel with a swipe, like some old bear, and he seemed a little more delicately balanced every time Terry saw him.

The heat was shocking when they entered the sauna, and settling themselves, they talked about the news. Terry was touched at the way his father was always careful to question him about this and act as if the doings he covered in Webster were the most important in the world.

"We had something a few days ago," Terry reported. "A tragic death. Little girl killed 'cause of her mother's carelessness."

"Awful," Maury said, shaking his head. Neither said what he was thinking, which was: great story! *Bad news is good news,* Terry thought. Our motto.

He told his father what happened. "There's an especially ugly twist that I picked up from somebody in an absolute position to know, which is that the mother claims it was all because her child was abused at a local preschool."

"Geez, can you imagine that? Everybody's ready to point the finger at somebody else."

"Yup. She was on her way home from there and says when her daughter told her in the car, you know, told her about the abuse, she just r-r-ran off the road."

"Wow." Maury said. "What a story. What did you do?"

"Just report the accident. I could never print some garbage like that."

"But don't you have an obligation to report what she says *caused* the accident? I mean, you'd include the guy's denial, but otherwise you're convicting her in the paper."

"Dad, I c-can't smear some highly respected people—you remember Pearl Gibson? It's her son-in-law, OK?—based on the self-serving allegation of some negligent drunk. The kid wasn't even b-buckled in. Something like this could destroy them and their school, and it's obviously not true."

"Well, but we don't know that. We just think it."

"D-Dad, gimme a break, it's irresponsible. What are you gonna do, dignify every far-fetched allegation?"

Dinner that night was at the Saddle & Crop, where Terry went only under duress. It was Maury and Abby's shared joke. "They have vegetables, for God's sake," his father said, and Abby added, "You'll love the mashed potatoes." The two of them got this way together. Maury flirted shamelessly with her, which was nothing new. Both Terry's parents had always acted as if they preferred his wife to their own son, as if glad at last to shift the focus of their attention to some hopeful new face, some other couple's handiwork free of all the guilt and regret that went with one's own children. Abby had been a special favorite of Terry's mother; they were drawn together by their husbands, whom they saw as birds of a feather. Now here she was basking in the attention of the older of the two, simpering infuriatingly and acting like nothing in the world could be more interesting than the Machiavellian politics of network television.

But otherwise Maury was on his best behavior, having been carefully briefed by his son not to ruin their outing with any talk about failing marriages or the troubles of the newspaper business. "It's been a stressful time," Terry said. "Abby's earned a little break."

They dropped Maury off, and Terry rode back to town with Abigail, who made small talk about the children. "Come and say good night to them at least," she said when they reached the house they had used to share. "I think they're still up."

They were glad to see him, he could tell, even though it confused them, but when Terry began to leave, Marty began to cry and couldn't or wouldn't stop, until finally he snuggled down with his father on the sofa, where the two of them ended up spending the night. Terry told himself the boy wasn't doing all that badly, really. At least he hadn't begun to stutter.

The next day, the editor of the *Webster Chronicle* lifted his woolen Yankee cap and seated it farther down on his itchy forehead, peering into his amber computer screen at the list of stories for the coming week's edition. An avalanche of advertising for and against a takeover of Krieger's gave him so much extra space that he would run almost anything he could get his hands on—including a weather story, some extra photos, and more people items. There would be a follow-up to the death of Tiffany Jackson, but no mention of the bizarre allegation her mother had made. The whole thing was a shame, really, and he made a mental note, when things died down, to produce some kind of probing psychological portrait of Tiffany's mother, her life shattered, making some wild accusation that she herself might even believe, if only because facing her own guilt would otherwise be so excruciating.

He thumbed through the stack of phone messages on his desk. On the outside of his glass door was a sign in 72-point Bodoni saying, "Be Brief," and inside he sat at a battered steel desk surrounded by a putty-colored IBM XT with an astonishing 10-megabyte hard drive, various ad layouts, and a bulletin board full of stuff he never looked at. Next to his desk was a tiny refrigerator, and on a table in the corner he kept some copies of the *Chronicle* from the ancien régime, with their bizarre typefaces and news judgment. A local plant closing that had cost ninety-five jobs ended up as an inside brief. The annual blood drive made page one. Nothing but good things ever seemed to happen to supermarkets, car dealers, and real estate brokers, that holy trinity of newspapers everywhere, and the paper had loved publishing lists: of entries on the local police blotter, building permits pulled, homes bought and sold, court cases, bankruptcies, and even divorces. The former owner, a laconic old man who had seen Terry and his ideals coming a mile off, explained that all those lists kept costs down by filling space cheaply, and besides, people pored over them. "We don't print gossip, but those lists give people plenty to jaw about, believe you me," the man had said.

But they were all shit lists, Terry felt, lists you might read in smug superiority, or maybe just relief that you weren't on them. They were like the town stocks, whose purpose was humiliation. He had swept them all from the paper, although he hadn't abandoned the *idea* of lists; newspapers had long ago served a useful gazetteer function, listing the arrival of salesmen, ships, war wounded, and so forth. But who really needed a list of divorces? Instead he instituted a list of good deeds. Someone at the post office had supplied a missing stamp on a Christmas package. A man too poor to own a car was able to keep his job thanks to the good Samaritan next door, who drove him to work. An anonymous donor dropped groceries off, mysteriously, at the Tabernacle of the Resurrection Church in the middle of the night. The good deeds were a hit; the more the *Chronicle* ran, it seemed, the more good deeds there were. Examples of samaritanship began to pour in. Readers submitted them, reporters observed them, and Terry himself saw them all around. "It's incredible, but in some subtle way we've already made things better around here, not that we'll get any thanks for it," he said to Abigail. "M-M-Maybe it's just knowing that someone is watching. See, it's h-h-hard to be good without God."

In the old days, Herb the postman, who came to work each night after supper still in uniform, wrote a friendly local column of comings and goings: who was taking a Hawaiian vacation, whose daughter had made what sorority at Webster State. "Cookin' with Herb," it was called, and it was getting stale even before Terry and Abigail took over. A couple whose joyful cruise made Herb's column came back to find their house cleaned out. Webster was changing. The kind of people Herb wrote about, the old-timers, were being replaced by a very different group. You could see it in the wedding notices. Nowadays the young newlyweds were out-numbered by people who had been married before and already had children. Terry had made the decision to carry gay "weddings," even though these did not carry the force of law, and in place of Herb, he got a local professor of physics to write a science column called "The Wonder of the Invisible." He gave himself a column too, under the modest pseudonym of Tartaglia, the pathetic stammerer of the commedia dell'arte. He redesigned the paper as well, imposing a clean, modern look on what was once a relic, and hired hungry young reporters eager to break into the business. Instead of rewriting handouts and covering boring town meetings, the *Chronicle* was suddenly digging for dirt, pointing at problems, highlighting conflicts. New features accumulated; Terry himself began reviewing church services. Why not? John O'Hara had covered sermons in his youth, and knowing a community's clergymen was a good way to keep your finger on the pulse of a place.

Besides, even in the absence of a knowable God, he found himself strongly drawn to the spiritual. He talked to no one about this, knowing that if he did, he would only discover others who felt the same, which would be unfortunate. He felt people's religious impulses needed to be channeled somehow lest they dissolve into the mush-brained pantheism so much in evidence around Webster, and in fact, Terry found it relaxing to visit places of worship, the grander the better: when he lay on the floor of his office, giving his troublesome back a rest, he loved looking up at the distant ceiling of the former church that soared high above the glass partitions of his work space. His faintly Jewish father and Unitarian mother had left him with no particular religion to speak of, but he often had strong feelings of déjà vu and powerfully vivid dreams that sometimes left him struggling to awaken from them. He dreamed he was in hiding from some nameless pursuers who were always drawing closer, and he dreamed again and again of his wife's death until he realized it was his mother's instead. After writing a long article about truck safety in town, he dreamed that Webster was burning, the result of a colossal tanker-truck accident at the main intersection—the flames were everywhere, like an animated orange snowfall, and people walked among them squinting and sweating from the heat. Later he dreamed that Webster was beset by a plague, and it was his job to go house to house and interview the dying. Terry had strong intimations of another world too, another life. It was as if he could feel in his bones the various Hasids and Puritans from whom he was descended. He felt that in an earlier go-round he might have been a minister himself and sometimes even dreamed that he was speaking eloquently, passionately and without stumbling, before an entire grateful congregation, all the dull and the weak, the gullible and the garrulous, the needy and the self-satisfied—all the same sort of people, in other words, that he encountered in churches and synagogues today.

Catholic churches, perhaps owing to their natural exoticism against the stringent backdrop of Protestant Webster, he found most alluring of all. It was his fantasy someday to enter the confessional booth and in its humid intimacy utter unto God the profundity of his failings—their banality being foremost among them. It was so appealing, this idea of a single secret place to let go of all your betrayals and vacillations and childish sorrow about not measuring up, a place to drop the mask of sanity and acknowledge the mess within. Maybe this accounted for the popularity of therapists in Webster, who outnumbered even dentists, as if the quantity of sin exceeded even that of teeth.

And he crusaded. Terry editorialized tirelessly against cigarettes, suburban sprawl and handguns, TV and cheap gasoline, and every year, lest parents forget, he wrote in favor of inoculations for schoolchildren. He was a longstanding opponent of parking and in fact of driving, but his most enduring—and hopeless—crusade was on behalf of fluoride in the local water. He had waged this battle almost from his first day in Webster, belittling naysayers and arranging to sell fluoride treatments from the *Chronicle* building. Science was on his side, as were the county dental association and the local teachers' union. But an odd coalition of opponents, including right-wing nuts, Christian fundamentalists, cheerful Luddites and New Agers who, like Terry, had fled the failures and complications of city life for some pastoral ideal of Webster, furiously opposed what they regarded as the mass poisoning of the community. Their leader, of course, was Willie Niedleman.

Niedleman was Terry's self-appointed nemesis, a man with time on his hands whose reason for waking up in the morning was to make the

editor of the *Webster Chronicle* miserable. Mainly, for Terry, it was embarrassing. His father had used to say that you could judge a man by his enemies; Maury had made Richard Nixon's famous enemies list back in the
golden age of Watergate. Terry had an irascible little small-town retiree
who still used Brylcreem in his hair. Niedleman's determined enmity was
the unkindest proclamation of Terry's failure, a thought that flashed
through his mind anew on seeing a message from Niedleman among the
stack of pink phone slips on his desk.

His in-basket was full, he hadn't returned any phone calls, and the
mail had already come, but he pushed these things out of his mind,
struggling to concentrate on a new editorial. He was looking for the right
beginning. Staring out through the glass of his office, where he knew he
would not find it, he surveyed the troops, his gaze stopping first at Ariadne, who stood next to her desk practicing ballet poses while she talked
on the phone, her blonde hair tumbling over the earpiece. Next to her sat
Margaret O'Hanlon, the graying office secretary who did a little of just
about everything, including a knitting column, and at a drafting table in
the corner, temperamental Alfred Blake, well turned out in a cotton knit
sweater of dusty olive with a pomegranate-colored kerchief tied like an
ascot. One of Terry and Abigail's first acts, on taking over the *Chronicle,*
had been to eliminate the composing room in favor of Alfred and his
newfangled computers, which magically produced what was known as
cold type. Terry had been a Newspaper Guild activist back in his former
life, but as an owner he saw things differently. This way was much
cheaper and infinitely more flexible. "You're becoming a Republican in
your old age," Abigail would tease, and he worried sometimes that she
might be right.

Such worries were in his mind as he turned back toward his monitor.
The *Chronicle* wasn't just against this takeover, he would make clear in his
editorial, it was against all of them, and he soon warmed to the task of
flaying asset-shuffling corporate raiders with no loyalty to workers, communities, or customers. Like all journalists, he was happy with this image
of himself as a crusader, and when the phone rang he ignored it, waving
Margaret away when, from the corner of his eye, he saw her approaching
the glass. A company, Terry contended (thinking only briefly of the

paper's half-dozen former composing room workers) is nothing more than the people who work for it, not some set of embossed securities or electronic blips or capitalistic clay that can be molded into any shape or hurled across the border if things are cheaper there. *People's lives and their livelihoods cannot be reduced to commodities, nor can the hearts and souls of communities like Webster all over America, held hostage to the whims of Wall Street tycoons already so rich that money is just how they keep score.* He must be careful here; it would be easy to start talking about Webster being crucified on a cross of gold. Stick to the facts. He cited coverage in the news pages of the *Chronicle* on what proportion of the local taxes were paid by Krieger's, what effect a closing might have on local unemployment, and how residents, lacking a Krieger's for competition, would be forced to pay more at the Rothwax stores in surrounding communities. Shoppers would have to drive farther too, which meant more pollution and also more accidents. The paper even quoted Delia Kornfeld, the famously provocative professor of gender studies at Web State, as saying that the closing of Krieger's would result in a certain number of deaths over the next decade as a result of the additional driving and the decline in air quality it would bring about. The conclusion was clear, although Terry didn't say it in so many words. Rothwax didn't just pillage. He was a murderer.

At the glass he saw Alfred, his long, slender head at a rueful angle, waving for attention. He held a full-size mock-up of a newspaper page against the window. "I need the rest of those layouts by this PM & I'm not kidding," it said in 60-point Times Roman. In smaller type below: "I can't do any more late nights this week!!" Terry took off his hat and buried his face in his hands. Through his fingers, he saw that Alfred was taping the page to the glass. "Get that fucking thing off there," he yelled, as the phone went off. He looked over at Margaret's desk, saw that she was gone, and answered with his "don't bother me" voice. It was the Reverend Floyd Albertson, pastor of the evangelical Tabernacle of the Resurrection Church, a ramshackle former supermarket filled with born-agains and holy rollers. Almost all of them, it seemed, had been down on their luck, much as their minister had been; the editor remembered him as the town drunk way back when, before Albertson found sobriety and religion during the late seventies. Terry had once written a funny but ultimately favorable review of one of Albertson's sermons, and since then they had struck up a kind of friendship.

"*Mister* Mathers," the reverend said, his voice throaty from years of cigarettes and alcohol followed by years more of preaching. What was that accent of his? Southern? Western, somehow. Texas, Wyoming, someplace like that. "Maybe you can help me. I sent you a press release some time ago, I wrote it myself, describing a wonderful program of service that we have here for the seventh-graders at the Tabernacle of the Resurrection religious school. Some of these youngsters are writing letters to the inmates at the state penitentiary. Others are reading to the elderly at the Eiderdown Home. Others still are tutoring the first-graders in reading, if they need a little extra help." The cadences! It was like talking to a TV announcer. "The *point* is, they *all* have to do *some* kind of *community service* in order to advance to the *eighth grade.*"

"Well, that's wonderful, Reverend—"

"Well I certainly think so. But when I talked to your young reporter about this, she told me that according to you, it's quote 'not news.' Those were the very words: 'It's not news'! And so I decided I'd call up myself and make sure you were quoted correctly, since I can't believe you'd reject a story of hope in this day and age, in favor of the usual stuff about young people carrying guns and robbing old folks and so forth. I said to her, 'That can't be Terry Mathers who said that.'"

Terry sighed, a sigh that said, yes, as you well know, Terry Mathers did say that. "I guess my thinking was that we still hadn't reached the point where the failure of a group of twelve-year-olds to commit mayhem is a big story, especially here in Webster. You've been doing this service thing for years, no?"

"Failure to commit mayhem?! Why, that's right, we've been doing it for years, we're very proud of it . . ."

"And the *Chronicle* has reported on this before, hasn't it?" This was a wild bluff.

"Well not in several years," Albertson said defensively. "Not since you've been here, anyway. Didn't you once tell me a story is something the press hasn't carried in a couple of years? We're overdue for one of those lunches we used to have, aren't we?"

About once a month, Terry and the reverend went for Indian food on Main Street, where there was a little place with a really cheap vegetarian buffet. Albertson was the only person Terry knew who had less money than he did, although of course in a minister this was a virtue. But the last one had not gone well. The good reverend had questioned him about his faith, only to discover that Terry had none.

"Atheism is an error your people seem especially prone to," Albertson had said with what appeared to be sympathy. His huge face, behind aviator glasses, was like much-used leather, and his gray hair, rising delicately from his scalp and swept back with hair oil, suggested the memory of a pompadour in its wastrel youth.

"Error? P-P-People?"

"The congregational nature of your fathers' faith." There was a grain of yellow basmati rice at the corner of Albertson's enormous mouth. "The emphasis on individual understanding, on personal inquiry, and a God caught up in the struggle between good and evil—inevitably some people's inquiries lead them astray. They become faithless." Albertson chewed. "Turn their energies to tax law. Modern architecture. Heatwave thermodynamics. Instead of Talmud."

"My f-f-father's f-f-faith is in his makeup man," Terry said.

"I was speaking of *all* your fathers," Albertson replied with a smile. "All the men who came before and made you and your world. You cannot shake their faith from this vantage, nor can they redeem you now by remote control from their deserved place in the heavens."

Now, on the phone, the reverend changed the subject.

"So about Bob. Can I count on you?"

"Bob." Terry was at a loss.

"Bob Varity."

"Wait a minute, is he gonna run for DA? Last time I talked to him, he was going to wait till Cal Hawthorne's ambition led him elsewhere."

"Nosiree. Bob Varity is going to be our next district attorney. From there, the sky's the limit."

Terry smiled. During Albertson's substance-abuse period, Varity had defended him for free, kept after him to get treatment—basically, saved his life. Albertson, who looked a little like a Saint Bernard, never forgot. Now he was laboring on behalf of Varity's embryonic political aspirations.

"We'll endorse him," Terry said. "Sure. Unless he does something drastic between now and the election. Like give up marijuana."

"Oh ye of little faith," Albertson said. "If only you boys would listen to your pastor."

"If I listened to you, I'd have to accept Jesus as my savior."

"And think how much better off you would be!" Albertson said plaintively. "How much happier! My advice: *pretend* to embrace him. *Make believe.* You might just surprise yourself."

That was how the day went by. It was how they all went by, until finally Terry looked up and discovered that it was night. The place was quiet but not deserted, and after the twelve-hour day he had already put in, he felt himself start to sag. He couldn't face his apartment though, and his in-basket towered with junk, so he withdrew a fistful from the pile, turned his back to the door, and propped his feet on the little table behind him. The condition of his shoes was dismal. With a yawn he started going through the stuff, pitching most of it into the wastebasket, saving the odd press release, setting aside letters to the editor and the like until a page of small black-and-white photos stopped him. With a guilty glance toward Abigail's office, he let his gaze linger over the contact sheet for the shots that had run with his profile of Diana Shirley.

"She's pretty," a familiar voice said neutrally. His stepdaughter stood over him, lanky and precocious. Not yet sixteen, she already had the neurotic's ability to divine weakness.

"Y-Y-You think so?" Terry could barely get the words out. He felt caught, flustered.

"Mom's still sexier. This one looks a little crazed to me."

"Ph-Ph-Phoebe, I really wish you wouldn't c-c-creep up on me that way."

"I'm like the fog," she said. Her cheeks glowed—was that rouge?—and a small gold ring pierced her flesh above the right eyebrow. "I come in on little cat's feet."

"We need a horn then."

She bellowed like a foghorn, trailing off dramatically. One of Terry's weaknesses was that, educated in the love of children by the arrival of Marty, he had come to love Phoebe retroactively as well, love her almost as if she were his own. In subtle ways, she had reciprocated this, and so her cold shoulder nowadays hurt.

"Sorry," she said with a shrug. Terry couldn't help looking at the silver stud at the side of her nose. "I came to see Mom anyway. We're having dinner with Charlie Krieger tonight. He's a really nice guy."

"Great," he said, recognizing this as calculated. They all knew he hated Krieger. "Glad to hear it."

"Later."

He wanted to ask her what this was all about, this business of dinner with Krieger, but she slipped away as easily as she had appeared. She had her mother's hair, Terry noticed as she left, and was beginning to fill out her overalls in the same womanly way, leaning forward like her mother as she walked. She had her mother's air of gravity as well, a seriousness edging toward melancholy, and Terry felt he'd been granted a visit from some younger Abigail who was in the dark about everything that was to come, and whose innocence of her fate stirred him.

chapter **SEVEN**

Yet another cold front moved across Vanatee County, casting its frigid shadow all across Webster and giving a hostile air to what was normally a friendly place. People made jokes about it, ran through more firewood than they thought they would, and occasionally died from it. But despite the unspeakable weather, the Webster City Council mustered an impressive turnout for its regular monthly meeting, and it was a testament to the citizenry's powers of concentration that no one sitting in the overheated council chambers fell into a coma during the droning report of the town's Peace and Justice Commission, which was in charge of making sure Webster did business with firms that had clean hands.

This was not always an easy task, and the commission had a staff of three to investigate, say, whether a maker of personal computers did business with the Defense Department or a vendor of toilet paper was making or selling products in countries where human rights were abridged. The problem lately was gasoline; the oil companies did business everywhere, with all kinds of horrible regimes, and it was increasingly difficult to obtain morally acceptable fuel for city police cars and other vehicles. Lately, due to a civil-rights crackdown in the African oil-producing nation of Khanderia, another big oil firm had been struck from the acceptable list. As a result, the town would buy no-name gasoline from a supplier in Rockford who gave assurances that it came from Alaskan crude. "Is that really any kind of improvement?" asked Councilwoman Dana Fontanelle, a stout woman with short gray hair and blue eyes. "We don't even know if they're telling the truth, and if they are, we're basically saying it's OK to despoil the wilderness to fuel our cars."

Willie Niedleman, brandishing a clipboard, caught the commission up short. Dressed in his usual thin black tie and Ivy League suit, his wardrobe frozen in his own heyday, he was the picture of the local crank. His own research, he said, indicated that Webster's police uniforms, the phones in Town Hall and various computer components used by the city were made in China. "They do a great job killing people over there. Why are you all so worried about Khanderia? They're not nearly as organized as the Red Chinese."

Terry thought this was clever but wouldn't give Niedleman the satisfaction of any more ink. He was an older man, bald but with a fringe of yellow-gray hair hanging down over his collar, and he pretended to go about in a permanent state of astonishment at the gross stupidity of the people who ran the world. He was like the man who spun plates on a series of sticks on the old *Ted Mack Amateur Hour*. How on earth did he keep them all going at once? Niedleman had used to sell suits downtown, but in his retirement he had made opposition to Terry and his newspaper into the focus of his days. He submitted not just letters for publication, but also personal notes chiding the *Chronicle*'s editor for even the tiniest mistakes. "Never underestimate a haberdasher," he liked to say. "Harry Truman sold suits once upon a time."

Terry bent down, pretending to search for a dropped pen and hoping Niedleman wouldn't spot him, but when he sat up the older man smiled, held up a finger, and gathered up his things. Good grief, he was planning to come and sit! Public meetings were the bane of life in Webster, and this one would be no different. Terry no longer had the patience. He pointed at himself, the door, and mouthed the word *Sorry,* smiling broadly. Then he got up and walked out.

One of the advantages of not driving much, Terry felt, is that you could drink whatever you wanted and then just go out into the night and deal with yourself. After the meeting he had stopped at Costello's, his favorite tavern, to kill a little time and recover from the idea that he was still the editor of the *Webster Chronicle,* and as he stumbled down the front steps and out into the street, he checked his watch to make sure the woman he was going to see would be home.

The trek from Webster proper—the old Webster that predated the automobile and remained accessible to pedestrians—to the sprawl of condominiums, tract homes, and shopping strips that had accreted around it since then was a spooky one on foot, no matter how sober or inebriated Terry found himself. After a period of years in which the village had fallen into a general state of decrepitude, the close-in homes had been restored by antique-loving young couples who had money to spend in the new shops that resuscitated the old commercial buildings on Main Street even out to the edge of town. Thus as Terry walked, he passed In the Soup, all whitewash and Douglas fir and stainless steel pots and ladles, followed by a fancy florist and a high-end bicycle shop, a hip women's store called Vocabulary, and his favorite bookstore, Webster's Fictionary. As Main Street turned into Vanatee County Route 32 though, the sidewalks dropped away and a more generic flavor of commercial enterprises began to appear, ones catering to the more plebeian tastes and incomes of regular people. Many of the businesses seemed geared to caring for the very automobiles that made their own existence possible. You could get your brakes and muffler fixed here, pay less for gas, or have a car wash. Pumping his legs harder to ascend the road's sharp grade as it climbed out of town, he was disgusted by the smell of frying that announced the approach of Webster's Hamburger Alley, with its forest of giant fast-food signs and lethal offerings made from dead animals. Determinedly vegetarian, he bristled at a world full of ads for lethal food. These outlets were like death ships bobbing in a sea of consumption, Terry thought in disgust, their masts sporting not sails but signs of the contagions they

carried. The carrion trade, catering to the working classes and the igno-
rant young enslaved by those darkest of ancestral longings: for fat, salt,
and flesh.

The billboards and strip malls came next, the giant supermarket paired
with the Mart-World store that had replaced the old five-and-dime and
now threatened even mighty Krieger's with its cut-rate prices and public
address system and acres of paved parking it seemed to take forever to tra-
verse. Terry wrapped his scarf more tightly around his neck. He was the
only pedestrian in sight, the only one for miles around probably, and with
the cars zooming by and the signs towering overhead, automotive fumes
mixing nauseously with the odor of frying fat, he felt as if plunged into his
own hellish vision of modern commerce. He imagined that Dante would
have drawn us in such an orgy, eternally poisoning one another.

He turned off Route 32 onto the lane that led to the apartment complex. Even here there was some traffic—there was traffic everywhere, it
seemed—and as he trudged along the narrow strip of crushed shale running beside the country road to his destination, he wondered idly if it
would hurt much to be hit by one of the oncoming vehicles that roared
past at infrequent intervals. It was so cold that even a stubbed toe was
unusually painful, and despite his unhappiness and confusion, Terry
clung to the brush that ran along the shale, as far from the roadway as he
could walk.

But when Diana opened the door looking radiant in her nightgown,
her hair held off her face with a ribbon of yarn, his foul mood floated
away. She kissed him warmly and took him inside like a highwayman she
must spirit from the authorities. Her embrace was taut and her limbs
lean and smooth, almost boyish in his arms. He loved her soapy fragrance, her minimalist penmanship, the three earrings marching up her
left ear, the laughing porpoise tattooed on her firm right buttock like the
label on a melon. Her interests and worldview were so very different from
his that it was exciting just to consider what she thought and read and
knew, but better yet, her interests were very different from Abigail's as
well. She wasn't obsessed with money and did not reflect back at him his
own innermost disdain for the small-town life they had chosen together
and regretted separately. In short, he was smitten.

New lovers are the only people who really live for love, but despite their headlong plunge, Terry and Diana each had had the impulse—an instinct, really—that as their affair flourished it should be kept quiet, a sign that love always has context. Perhaps they told themselves that it needed privacy from the prying eyes of small-town life, or maybe a dollop of clandestineness simply added to the excitement. And of course, one of them was married. This conspiratorial element in their mutual obsession made it all the stranger that Diana told him nothing of her investigation into child abuse at Alphabet Soup. She had professional reasons for keeping her secret, of course, especially from the editor of the town's newspaper. Yet she was startled to discover how much she liked holding back this important information. Knowing something that Terry—her pedantic, omniscient sweetheart who could hold forth, it sometimes seemed, on any subject—didn't know gave her an immense feeling of power and importance that she needed to maintain herself in the face of a lover whose personality might otherwise be overwhelming.

Besides, she hardly knew him. She hadn't imagined that they would fall into bed so easily; she had expected something more gradual, their fraught relations evolving almost imperceptibly from journalist and official to friends to intimates to, finally, something more. Instead they came together as if they had been kept apart by force, as if they had surmounted distance and other enemies to unite again after many years apart.

Tonight she served him tea and oatmeal cookies in front of the television. His father was on, interviewing Ronald Reagan.

"I still can't believe that fool was re-elected," Diana said.

"I interviewed him once," Terry said.

"Really?"

"Sure. Of course, he wasn't p-p-president yet. He was still the retired actor in those days, running for governor of California. We had a little lunchroom, sort of, in the basement of the *Weekly*, with folding tables and chairs. It was really pathetic. College paper stuff. He drank a Coke and ate Twinkies."

"You probably did better with him than this guy."

"You don't like the guy asking questions?"

"He's kind of bogus, don't you think? All that white hair combed across his head."

"Careful now, pussycat. You're talking about family here."

On her worried look, Terry told her.

"Maury Mathers is your father?!" Her eyes widened, and she leaned around into his field of vision. "Terry, that's incredible." She looked at the screen and then at her lover. "You never told me that."

"You thought I was the Beaver, remember? Jerry Mathers. Son of Ward Cleaver."

"Well, it must have been subconscious," she said, looking from Terry to the screen and back again. "At least it's the same medium."

"Can you see the resemblance?"

"Oh my God, it's uncanny!"

"Yeah, we—"

"Shh!"

They listened as Maury finished a question about immigration and Reagan launched into some dubious recollections. Terry hit the mute button on the remote control.

"If anybody ever asks," he said, "tell them you watch. He's having a little ratings trouble."

"I gather you have some issues here," she said. "You don't want to hear any more?"

"If you'd heard as much of him as I had, you wouldn't want to hear him either. I come from a long line of people from whom everyone always heard a great deal."

"Really? Are they all great talkers and writers?"

"Every one of them a speechifier, a thumb-sucker—a pundit. Each fish swimming in a bigger pond, until me."

"Terry. Why are you so hard on yourself? You worked at the best newspaper in the country, and now you publish the best small-town weekly anyone has ever seen."

"I m-might have been on TV, but I s-s-stutter." He did a little Porky Pig riff. "Be-he-be-he-be-he, uh, that's all folks!"

"Is it really that bad?" She rubbed his thigh. "I never even notice it."

"I don't s-stutter around people I really like. I just don't like that many people. So one thing led to another, and the n-next thing you know I'm running a one-man newsroom, practically, and my staff is terrible."

"Sweetheart. Do you see much of your father?"

"Every day," he said, pointing at the TV. He blushed then. "H-H-He's with me all the time though. Seriously. I imagine him watching almost everything I do. I speak for his ears. I carry myself the way he would. It's pathetic. When we were looking for a house here in Webster, I kept looking at them with the image in my mind of him driving up one day and being suitably impressed. Having kids made me see what I was doing."

"Do you have pictures of them?"

He rose and retrieved his wallet from the pants he had flung onto the little chair in the corner.

"Oh, you're so lucky!" Diana said when she saw them. "So very, very lucky." She gave a sigh and then asked if they'd gone to Alphabet Soup.

"Phoebe was too old when we got here," Terry said. "Marty was at Ducks in a Row, out near Web State. Ducks, webbed feet. Get it? The campus mascot is a mallard."

"Well that's good."

"Why? It wasn't convenient, but they had some kind of experimental program Abigail liked, so we schlepped them there and back every day. Also, he didn't get into Alphabet Soup. Didn't measure up somehow."

"I was just wondering."

"Is something going on at Alphabet Soup?"

"You can't write about this," she said.

"About what?"

"Promise first. Promise you won't write about it."

"Better not tell me."

"Aren't you a man of your word?"

"I am. That's why I can't give it."

"Terry, this is terrible. So I'm never going to be able to tell you when we have something big in the works?"

"What if I find out about it elsewhere?" He was already thinking of the Krieger's story again, and the confidences he had had to juggle. "I'd want to be able to use it without your thinking I broke my promise. I run a newspaper. I'm the last person in Webster anyone ought to tell any secrets."

"OK, then I guess I can't say anything more."

"So does it have to do with Alphabet Soup??"

Diana flushed.

"It does and it doesn't," she said, and then shook her head. "Sweetheart, I can't. I took an oath or something, I can't remember, but I just can't. I'm not the only person in the world who can answer a question. Come to bed—I have other virtues."

B ut the editor of the *Webster Chronicle* had bigger fish to fry than some evanescent tip about a preschool he hated even to think about for the simple reason that it had rejected his own son, and so he instead threw himself into the Krieger's story with his customary manic energy. He mastered Krieger's finances with the help of an accountant friend and called on a former college roommate for help in cultivating investment banking sources so he could keep up with the rumors on Wall Street. Along the way he educated himself about tender offers, white knights, "highly confident" letters, and all the other strange verdure that flourished in the financial landscape of the period. In addition to the usual stream of articles, headlines, and so forth, the *Chronicle*'s editor churned out stories about the stores, their role in the community, the personality of the combatants, and the quirks of their right-hand men. He had the most fun doing a profile of Ed Krcyszyki, the union leader. Terry conducted this interview at Costello's, where the two of them drank and gossiped until they were both so bleary and sodden that, unable to drive, they shared a cab home.

"Jus' remember," Krcyszyki had slurred as he tumbled out into the night, his heavy eyeglasses halfway down his nose. "Rothwax has to deal with us. Whatever he thinks he's buying from Charlie Krieger, he's got nothin' if we decide to walk."

And with these words he tottered uncertainly in the direction of his front porch.

If every story was an obsession, it was easy for Terry to lose himself in this one. Krieger and Rothwax, in their war for control of what was basically a tired and piddling department store chain, conducted their campaign from Wall Street all the way back to Webster. They fought for the hearts and minds of investors, legislators, judges, regulators, and anyone who could influence such people, carrying the fight onto the roadways with bumper stickers and billboards, into the homes of Webster and the pages of the *Chronicle,* and even into outer space on errant airwaves, stalking the souls of the influential wherever public opinion might lurk. Terry was inundated with warring press releases in which each side accused the other of acting against the best interests of investors and "communities." He learned that Krieger's was considered to be "in play," meaning that even if Rothwax didn't succeed, somebody else probably would, and he also began to get an inkling that matters weren't as simple as he had assumed them to be. Rothwax himself helped him see this.

"Yours is a very conservative position," he said quietly. They sat in his office, where the famous raider got to play the role of philosopher, and Terry, in his great ignorance, was cast in the role of student.

"Very conservative," Rothwax continued. "You're against change. You believe the same people should maintain control over some other people's lives and assets just because they've always done so. You don't stop to ask if change would be better, or compare how much benefit would stack up against how much hurt."

Terry was still surprised Rothwax had agreed to grant an interview. He had dressed up only to find his host in an open-necked dress shirt and nondescript pants, like some old Israeli parliamentarian. He was mostly bald, with some gray hair combed over a sun-spotted pate, and he had the lively eyes and modest pot belly Terry associated with professors at alternative colleges. His office overlooking a good chunk of the Delaware Valley was filled with primitive art, and he sat among three desks arrayed with blinking phones and three glowing computer screens. At the front, on the desk facing visitors, a small Hindu sculpture rested.

"Lakshmi," Rothwax explained. "The goddess of wealth and fortune."

Terry felt his own deities—the tattered gods of journalism—smiling at him, and said: "Mammon, in other words."

"Mammon was a false god, if you remember your Bible. This one is real. Worship her and everything improves."

"The goddess of wealth?"

"Of fortune too, remember. Which I interpret to mean chance, the sense of mystery that lies behind things. I find it always pays to pretend that there's a god, even if you don't really believe in one. Keeps you from thinking the world revolves around you, which it doesn't."

Who was this greedy little man pretending to be a philosopher? He was clever, you had to give him that. Yet Terry hated Rothwax nonetheless. He was embarrassed by him, for one thing. They were all Jews, these raiders. Why? How could a people so obsessed with the cause of justice, so over-represented in the academy, as lawyers and judges and so forth, produce so many soulless capitalists? "I'm no more soulless than you are, my friend," Rothwax had insisted. "The existence of the human soul is an entirely different discussion, but I think it's safe to say that the outcome doesn't depend on business or politics." Yet he could also contend that his heedless pursuit of profit was itself a form of justice. "Doing well is the only way to really do any good," he asserted with a twinkle. He shifted almost sideways in his chair, so that the arm was against his back. "Look out that way. You see that campus? University of Pennsylvania. The Marxists and deconstructionists and video artists and all the rest eat from my table, drink from my vineyard. They're there because people like me do what we do. And it's not just them. All the gains in longevity, civil rights, pollution control, and so forth, almost all that stuff is the result of rising affluence, not advances in science or legislation. Prosperity. *Moola.*" Rothwax rubbed his fingers together; the gesture was self-consciously coarse. "Try some one of these days. It'll set you free."

Was he offering a bribe? Terry had to give him the benefit of the doubt. But it was as if his own threadbare clothes were transparent and Rothwax could see through him. Without admitting wrongdoing, Rothwax had once paid a fine to settle some civil charges brought by the Securities and Exchange Commission, but when Terry asked about it on the phone, the financier had scoffed. "Sloppy bookkeeping," he said. With his sharp beak and high forehead, this high-finance buccaneer could almost be the devil, saying the worst things with the most bemused expression, confident in human frailty. The devil always knew people would sell to the highest bidder.

"But why not just *make* widgets?" Terry asked. "Why restrict yourself to asset-shuffling and financial manipulations? You could do well in other ways and make jobs rather than eliminating them."

"Because I can do far more well, and therefore far more good, in *this* way. I can change the whole widget business, bring it up to date, force it to get efficient. I'm like the unions. Just knowing about me changes behavior in executive suites. They do the things they should be doing, just to keep me at bay. Unfortunately, they also do some things they shouldn't be doing, and your Mr. Krieger happens to fall into that particular category himself."

"But you make this sound like nothing more than a struggle between capital. What about all the other people who have something at stake? What about the workers? What about the communities?"

"I'm the best friend they ever had, because I'm the only one who will give them the medicine they're too squeamish to take on their own. You think Krieger is the workers' friend? He doesn't give a shit about anybody, and when his business goes down the tubes, as it inevitably will if I don't get the chance to save it, they'll all be unemployed. I *grow* businesses. I create jobs the only way you can, which is by creating *wealth*. Besides, what about all those other workers condemned to high prices and poor choices when they shop at Krieger's? This is not about feeling good, my friend, it's about *doing* good. People who do well inevitably do good." He chuckled. "Hardly anybody does as well as Ira Rothwax."

On the plane home, with his tiny vodka bottles and his shiny blue blazer, Terry found himself surrounded by exemplars of the life he might have chosen but hadn't. They spoke heartily to one another as they settled themselves, baring their silky button-downs and folding their suit coats inside out before laying them atop their briefcases in the rack above their seats. Their clothes fit, their teeth were even and white. They were at ease in the world, not worried or confused or plagued by doubts. It must be the end of their day, yet they still looked well-shaved and alert. The air of proprietorship they carried with them! Terry was revolted. He couldn't even take solace in his special status anymore. They all read the *Tribune,* after all, but who had ever heard of the *Webster Chronicle*? It was pathetic, infuriating! Terry had a window seat, and the darkness outside served mainly to reflect his brooding expression back at him from the glass of the plane's windows. He was surrounded by his contemporaries, even some younger men, and all of them out-earned him probably by a factor of five. He remembered that when Abigail had Marty, she took three months off and adopted an ironic stance toward her new role. She took to wearing frilly aprons, left a carpet-sweeper standing around the apartment, made a casserole once. "The breadwinner is here," she told their newborn son when Terry came home from work. "Crumbwinner," he'd correct, exhausted from a day at the paper. "Occasionally I win a c-c-crouton." And despite five years of ceaseless toil in Webster, it was even more true today. *I could make more teaching school or driving a cab,* Terry thought, *or doing any of the other things people do when they aren't even conscious of their own obscurity.* Without Maury's infusions over the years, they would have been living in a homeless shelter long ago. He loathed these subsidies, knowing they were a way for his father to keep his son a little boy, maintain power, feel better about his absence during Terry's childhood, stave off his own mortality. Whatever. He regarded his own participation—his willingness to sell the old man indulgences in this way—as pathological and embarrassing. He had never cared about money, but he had come to agree with Dostoyevsky: *money is coined liberty.* It's a marker, a telltale by-product of success, just like certain antibodies were a telltale sign of disease or like worldly success was a sign of Calvinistic grace.

When he got back to Webster, Terry went straight to the office and hit the keyboard as Tartaglia, the nom de plume he had adopted for his iconoclastic weekly column. Tartaglia, he knew, lurked deep within himself, banging away on his ribs and shouting "This is bullshit!" whenever the smiles and patience and compromises of life in Webster became unendurable. Tartaglia had met a kindred spirit in Rothwax and, under the latter's influence, saw the struggle over Krieger's in a new light. "When Charlie Krieger's father crushed competing stores with union-busting and lower prices, there was no pious wailing from Krieger's about the need to protect anybody from the ravages of the competitive marketplace," he wrote, typing furiously. "The rise of Ira Rothwax is just more of the same, so why get excited? He who lives by the sword dies the same way. Besides, Krieger's has grown complacent under the current generation. Maybe some new management blood will freshen up its stores."

That night, sleepless and unable to withstand the loneliness of his apartment, Terry slipped out of the house and made his way to the dingy men's locker room in the basement of the YMCA. A handful of local big shots who were also good athletes had keys, and Terry was one of them, enabling him to use the place off-hours. He rarely encountered any of the others late at night, since the big shots of Webster, like big shots everywhere, rose early, but sometimes he managed to pick up a game even at midnight. He had a permanent locker too and subscribed to the laundry service, so he could come and go anytime he wanted.

Changing into his workout clothes, which were wrinkled and damp from being washed in a mesh bag with all the other stuff the Y washed every day, Terry felt better already. He loved the old building at this hour. It was silent now except for the far-off noises of water, heat, and sewage rumbling powerfully in its bowels, and wending his way through its stony labyrinth of bumpy corridors and scuffed weight rooms, his sense of proprietorship was undisturbed by intruding yuppies or children foolishly brought during the school day instead of being taught to read and write. (He promised himself yet again to write an editorial about this.)

He worried about the Y's monthly fee; the bills he knew were piled high on his wife's desk, and his father's loan worst of all, but he left these worries at the door of the gym, as he always had done, and by the time he had wrestled a rack of basketballs out of the janitor's closet he was thinking about nothing but shooting. Auspiciously, the first couple he threw up went *swish,* and chasing rebounds, he quickly felt himself beginning to get loose. The marijuana helped, even if it usually did hurt his accuracy. He'd had a joint in the car on the way over, driving slowly along the back streets where he knew he wouldn't be stopped, listening to Miles Davis on tape. He shot some more and found he had a hot hand in spite of all this, wondering if exhaustion and cannabis might have relaxed him for this purpose, just as they were helpful with his speech. He drilled a lean jumpshot from the top of the key and then ran some layups the full length of the court. The gym was chilly; the heat was turned down for the night, and he could tell it was getting cold just from the feeling in his fingers. But he wore a sweatshirt and kept moving. Soon enough he was warm.

He missed a couple of long shots, made another from the top of the key and then, before he got too sweaty, lay down in the tip-off circle and sighed, listening for the sounds of his bones settling themselves against wood as he knew they must someday one last time. *"Sic transit ignominia mundi,"* he mumbled, pleased to be alone. Too many years alternately hunched over a keyboard and running up and down the court had left him frequently achy and stiff, but the floor, he had come to believe, was the poor man's chiropractor, and lying on it helped enough that he did it three or four times a day. Staff members at the paper were accustomed to conversing with their editor while he was flat on his back, spewing pronouncements like an oracle embedded in the carpet. It was especially pleasurable to lie down at the bottom of a great room such as this one. Gazing at the network of ceiling trusses and bright lights that formed a man-made firmament above the hardwood, Terry inflated his rib cage with all the air he could hold and heard more cracking. He groaned lightly as he exhaled. Sitting up, he twisted his upper back against his lower body until he heard a satisfying pop in his spine, and then did the same in the other direction, knowing that for some reason he would not be similarly rewarded on that side. He lay back down and imagined himself floating at sea, a mote in the eye of the universe. What was he doing here, in the gymnasium of the YMCA in Webster in the middle of the night, well into his fortieth unprofitable year? In the grown-up newspapers he read compulsively every day, his contemporaries were becoming chief executives, governors, cabinet secretaries. His own father had won his first Pulitzer Prize at thirty-five. All an illusion, Terry told himself, striving to take a Buddhist's pleasure in the wood against his skull and the astonishing symmetry of the construction overhead. It reminded him of those European train stations, but in miniature. He spread his arms and legs in the circle, thinking of Leonardo, wishing for a life of simple proportions and beauty. He stretched again, this time grabbing his toes and pulling himself down, holding on as long as he could. Finally, slowly, he lay back down, closed his eyes and gave himself to the vast quiet. He loved the feel of the wood, with its hard assurance under his hands and feet that he was not at the office, where the countless duties and details of putting out the paper plagued him like a thousand mosquitoes. The wood assured him too, at this hour, that he was not at home, where he was reminded by the tiny space and rented furniture and sculpted pile carpets of the ugly wreckage of his marriage. As he tried to muster the energy to rise off the floor, it came to him for the first time that he might find a more permanent home, that just as he would rise there in that chilly gymnasium, so too would he leave his house and marriage behind and find himself upright anew.

"Hallo?" The voice came from above, back by the door, and Terry looked around. "Buenas noches, Señor Terry. It's OK?"

It was Jesus Mendoza, the night custodian. He was one of perhaps two dozen hardworking Mexicans who had appeared in Webster during the 1980s, gradually replacing some of the black families who had lived for so long in Johnson's Hollow, a ramshackle section of town on the wrong side of the river. Jesus was mildly retarded and spoke almost no English, but he held down two jobs.

"Buenas noches, Señor Jesus," he replied. "I'm fine. No problem."

Jesus, laughing, waved in apologetic relief. Terry could see that the other man was just as embarrassed as he was, and with nothing more to say, Jesus wheeled his heavy bucket and mop off down the corridor, his many keys jangling on his belt.

Sheepishly, Terry hopped up onto his feet, holding the crouch for just a minute to let the dizziness pass. He wished he had eaten more during the day. The ball he dribbled, its leather pebbles so sexy against his fingertips, seemed much too loud after his little idyll, striking the maple floor with a resounding smack that rang like a shot through the empty gym, but it helped bring him back to the present, and with sudden speed he moved into the left-hand corner, his favorite, where he stopped, gave the little pump fake that had worked so well just days earlier against his friend Errol Jones from the District Attorney's Office, and then launched a long, high shot that bounded off the back of the iron out toward center court. "Shit!" Terry said, glad nobody was watching.

Thankfully, it had been different that day against Errol.

Terry was tough one-on-one; he was tall, he hustled, and beating him required both an outside shot *and* a good move to the basket. Errol was young and fast, and although Terry usually prevailed, in the second of their customary three-game set he had climbed to within a point, until Terry took him to the corner, faked him into the air and then fired the softest shot he knew how, which dropped straight through the net long after his opponent had returned unhappily to earth. Jones looked up at the ceiling in frustration and finally turned toward Terry with a smile. "You wiseass son of a gun," he said. "Again." Sure enough, he got some of his own back in the third game. Terry was winded, spent, and his shots went awry. Errol out-hustled him and won the game easily.

"I had Mary Jane on my side, didn't I?" he panted, laughing.

"I'm through with Mary," Terry said bent over, gasping for breath. He never stammered when winded. It was the same when he sang; in the shower, bellowing rock lyrics, he was fluent. "I'm old. That's my problem. I could be your father."

"You were with a black girl when you were ten?" Errol scoffed. "Don't kid me, man, you're still seeing Mary; it's in your eyes. Every time we play you got less wind. Demon weed! I oughta prosecute your ass."

Terry played a lot of pickup basketball, but for weeks afterward he would think of the fake that won him the second game, and of the soft, double-pump shot he lobbed with such flawless delicacy it seemed to rise and fall in slow motion. It was not just the beauty of the thing that he remembered, but the chance to feel superior, because both men knew that Terry would never take such a fake. He would never take *any* fake. It was a matter of pride, one of those fundamentals Coach Hardesty had drummed into the boys all through high school. Take a fake and you had to hop around the gym three times like a rabbit. The other guys would laugh at you, and you'd deserve it, Terry always thought. You'd deserve it.

chapter EIGHT

While Terry struggled to cover the battle over Krieger's, Abigail and Charles plotted how best to preserve the status quo that both of them (for different reasons) depended upon. Time was short, and so there was a sense of urgency about their late-night strategy sessions. They convened in Krieger's leathery office in a large turret jutting from the upper corner of the building containing his store, the club chairs and carpets expensive and masculine, old-looking without seeming shabby. In the distance, the dim lights of outlying Webster twinkled faintly until they petered out in the countryside, where a black gulf separated the edge of town from the comparative supernova of Webster State University, its arrogant towers blinking a red warning to low flying aircraft and its low-slung library emitting dashes of light from bunker-slit windows.

Abigail quickly came to look forward to these encounters with Charles, at which they would sit around his handsome red mahogany desk and talk about how to stave off the takeover. They plotted strategies and tactics financial and political, means of persuasion and aversion, scenarios of every kind. They dissected the personality of Ira Rothwax and tried to put themselves in his no doubt ostentatious shoes, the better to predict his movements. And sooner or later, in the cocoon of warm light that left the rest of the room—the rest of the world—in darkness, they talked of other things: of their beliefs, their children, and their vulnerabilities. Krieger was an odd capitalist, one whose faith in the system depended on its fetters.

"Nobody wants *truly* free markets," he maintained. "Can you imagine? We'd be like chipmunks on a treadmill, forever running as fast as we could, always looking over our shoulder. And for what? Imperfect markets are like imperfect people. They're what make life interesting."

"There are competing interests, naturally," Abigail said. "Employees, communities, traditions. But surely you can see that shareholders want a good return on their investment."

"Obviously we all need to *pretend* we believe in free markets. Think what a god-awful mess we'd have otherwise. But it's important for everyone to remember that we're *just* pretending. Otherwise we might end up buying and selling everything and even one another by auction. It's efficient, but it's not the world I'd want to live in."

"Charlie, in business that's precisely the world we live in," Abigail said with some impatience. "If I can't improve the *Chronicle's* performance, it's dead meat. It doesn't matter how many hundred years it's been publishing."

"Listen, don't get me wrong; this whole episode has given me a strong dose of free-market religion. If we ever get out of this, I'm going to address all our operational issues, bring in some strong new managers, the works. And most of all get some goddamned parking for our flagship store"—here Charles pointed downward, to the selling floors below—"which is ideally situated to serve shoppers who arrive by streetcar. Otherwise we can't compete with the malls."

For Abigail, it was all very stimulating. It reminded her of the old days in New York when she had been in the thick of such struggles, when resources were so ample that no one thought about the costs of messengers or first-class travel or ad campaigns in giant regional dailies and the national business press. Her newfound role as Krieger's chief adviser and confidante was a relief from the pettiness of the *Chronicle,* where she slaved over spreadsheets and expenses, and from the *Chronicle*'s piety as well. She would make a poor missionary, she now knew. It had been hard enough being any kind of decent missionary wife.

Besides all this, there was the money. She had been stringing along suppliers, sweet-talking bankers, holding back payroll taxes owed the government, and taking every other step she could think of to hang onto cash and accelerate collections. For the past year she had been keeping the patient alive with transfusions from her share of her family's small trust, which was rapidly being exhausted. Even Terry didn't know how bad things really were at the *Chronicle.* By her own optimistic projections, the paper had no more than six months to live if nothing changed, and if it died, she was convinced, it would drag what was left of her marriage down with it, to say nothing of impoverishing her and her children. Abigail had never been poor but knew it was a fate to be avoided at all costs. The stock options she was to receive for her work with Charles could pull the *Chronicle* out of the hole and then some, giving her and Terry a chance to pay attention to other problems without the hot breath of their creditors forever on their necks.

Yet the money paled next to the guilty pleasure of it all. Abigail noticed that she dressed more carefully for these meetings, making a point of washing her hair and putting on a fragrance. She had spent more than an hour at the perfume counter at Krieger's, confused by a cloud of competing scents until she finally settled on the first one she'd tried, and she had a new, more stylish haircut, which she obtained, she had to admit, in part because she liked flirting with Charles. They met in secret, lest they seem to compromise the *Chronicle*'s coverage or give Terry cause for alarm, and when they grew hungry they ordered in from Food for Thought, a kosher delicatessen founded by an anthropology professor at Webster State who could no longer bear life without the delicacies of his longed-for New York. He now made far more running a polite and witty small-town eatery than he ever would as a college teacher. Abigail and Charles would fax a list of knishes, sandwiches, a kind of bogus stuffed derma that was a Food for Thought specialty, and toast their efforts to defeat Rothwax with Dr. Brown's Cel-Ray. It was strange *traif.* The forbidden fruit they relished, delivered by a quiet young woman with dark blond hair and a ring through her nose, came in fragrant white bags emblazoned with the deli's motto, "Pastrami without the fat, tongue without the lip!"

Throughout, Krieger's obsession with parking never flagged. It was the single dimension of the whole struggle, aside from the stock price, that came up again and again during their regular strategy sessions with what had become Krieger's anti-takeover working group. Wayne Lyttle was there, as were Ed Krcyszyki and Mayor Loquendi, among others. Abigail had been introduced to everyone at one point or another but still couldn't name everyone in the room.

"Look, not to seem obtuse, but is parking really such a big deal?" she asked at last. "It's not going to make Ira Rothwax go away."

"You don't understand," Krieger said. "It's the key to everything nowadays. You can't sell a pair of shoelaces in this country without first giving the buyer someplace to leave her car. See, Americans aren't like your husband. They see him walking all over the place, just bopping along, and they think he's really weird. Homeless people walk, Abigail. Black people, when they don't have the bus fare. Meh-hee-ca-no Americans! But my customer, she doesn't walk. She drives. In the long run, that's the business we're in: parking. Because if she can't find a safe, free, convenient place to park, preferably protected from rain and snow, she's not coming into my store."

"Why not take another run at the preschool?" Ed offered. "You've got plenty of money this time around, thanks to you folks down at Flemington"—he nodded toward one of the younger men present—"and I can't even see that it matters much what price we pay. They might even be willing to take stock, if we give them enough of it."

"That's actually quite a creative idea," Abigail agreed. She sat with one leg crossed over the other, a cordovan pump dangling from her toes. She was conscious of being the only woman in the room.

"Those bastards wouldn't give us ice in a blizzard," Krieger said. "They've got it in for me and my whole family, as if it's my fault that my father was a better merchant than their guy. And they don't seem to care about money."

"It's not about money, and it's not even about what happened all those years ago," Wayne said patiently. "We know these folks. Lucy and I know Emily real well. She's the problem. Frank would sell in a minute, and Pearl couldn't hold out against the two of them. What we need to do is explain to Emily somehow. Do something to get her with the program."

"For the love of Christ, Dom, can't we do something about this?" Krieger demanded. "Are we gonna let a collection of sprout-eaters hold the entire town hostage?"

"Charlie, I wish I could do something," the mayor said.

"Dom, c'mon, we're dying over here. I know we've been through this, but it matters now. It really, really matters."

"There's nothing I can do that I could do in time. Nothing that would work as well as going over there, knocking on the door, and offering them some money."

"I think we've been around this bush once or twice before," Wayne said wearily, "and it doesn't get any smaller. Let's talk cash for a minute, everybody. I've got a plane to catch."

Cash was for once plentiful at Krieger's, thanks to the debt the company had issued with the expensive assistance of its new investment banker friends, and Abigail made sure the *Chronicle* got its hands on some of it by persuading Charles to step up advertising in the region's newspapers—including, of course, the *Chronicle*—explaining why it was so important for Krieger's to remain unacquired. These ads stressed the virtues of local ownership, the anchoring role of the six Krieger's stores in central business districts of the small communities they occupied, their historic importance in sponsoring cultural and sporting events, the taxes they pay, the employees who are friends and neighbors.

"We can do even better," she suggested. "Let's run a series with local residents; a woman remembers getting her wedding dress, an employee who put in forty-five years, the group of elderly ladies who eat cucumber sandwiches in the café every Wednesday."

"Are you trying to save Krieger's or the *Chronicle,* with all this advertising?"

"Charles, count your blessings, ads in the *Chronicle* are dirt cheap compared to what even a small daily would charge. And believe me, Rothwax will be doing it too, mark my words."

"I'm putty in your hands, Abby. Draw up a budget and we'll move on it."

"Me? But I'm selling the ads, I can't—"

"Of *course* you can. And raise your rates! As you say, it's chicken feed, and besides, from this point on I'm spending Rothwax's money, since the experts say Krieger's is all but his. I'll fight him with his own dough, and that of the arbs who were generous enough to buy up our stock. Develop some ads, come up with a budget, and we're in business."

And so they were. One bleary night, in the shadowy light of Krieger's antique desk lamp, fed by the briny aroma of corned beef and kosher pickles, he took her hand and kissed the inside of her wrist. Then he reached over and put his mouth on her neck just below the ear. "Sit down, Charles," she said, trying to control her breathing. *We're tired and hungry,* she thought, chewing carefully, and although the warmth of his mouth had made her shiver it seemed more in keeping with those other needs, of rest and nourishment and an end to isolation. Later she would acknowledge all those things in wondering what confluence of planets, events, and bodily humors had driven her into his arms.

Like many couples, Emily Joseph and her husband had discovered over time that they had little in common aside from their troubles, and with the death of their youngest child receding far enough into the past that they thought of it no more than briefly every day, and with their son drifting off into adulthood, there was less and less to hold Frank and Emily together, other than Alphabet Soup. Now, with the death of Tiffany and the wild allegation that followed, even that seemed to be driving them apart.

Thus it was that on the bittersweet occasion of Emily's fortieth birthday, she would skip dinner with her husband, who had proposed the Saddle & Crop despite her distaste for red meat and her ambivalence toward an entire evening with Frank in a restaurant. The prospect was embarrassing. She saw the two of them sometimes as she imagined that others must, sitting forlornly together, without animation, tired without possibility of rest or renewal, coping bravely with the disappointments life had dealt them. She thought it must depress other diners and half-expected them to complain to the waiters, as they would about smokers. So she begged off on dinner, asking sweetly if Frank would mind if she had an evening with the girls. He was welcome, she said, in a way that made it clear he wasn't, and he cheerfully declined. Frank was always happiest by himself, and she was pleased to spend the evening of her birthday in the company of the people she felt closest to: some of the teachers from Alphabet Soup. And so on this cold New England night she sat snugly with her young friends in the candlelit parlor room of an old house, the windows sealed with plastic against the draft.

"*Emily!*"

She blushed crimson as her name rang out on all sides, not slowly the way it would be said by a group of children in unison, but eerily nonetheless.

"*EMILY!*"

The women sat in a circle, the room lit only by candles, and they sang her name, chanted it, shouted it, and simply spoke it, sometimes in unison but other times not, the disembodied cry of "Emily" suddenly ringing loudly and out of synch with the hypnotic repetition of the rest. It was embarrassing, maddening almost, until finally it lost its meaning and she could just, well, *soak up the energy,* as the girls liked to put it. Her well-meaning features remained frozen in a smile.

In honor of Emily's birthday, Julie and Mary had invited her with great seriousness to their "group," as they called it, with a special emphasis to indicate that it was really something else. And she had to admit that if she could just get over feeling so foolish, this was kind of fun. Dressed in robes and other baroque thrift-store finery, they were holding a kind of worship service. She'd thought they were talking about baskets at first. Wicker baskets.

"No no, *Wicca.* It's all about energy," Julie said when she begged Emily to attend one of the sessions. Her fresh-faced looks made her seem even more earnest than she was. "The Native Americans had the idea that rocks and plants and even people are just temporary energy swirls, which was really an amazing intuitive recognition that matter is just energy."

"It is, isn't it?" Emily said helpfully.

"Of course, when Einstein came up with it, everybody made a fuss."

They began by standing in a circle. It was Julie's living room, and all the furniture had been pushed to the sides or carried into the dining room. The candlelight was cozy and the warm air was filled with complex odors, patchouli at first but then incense, which was burning on a small, linen-covered table that functioned as a kind of altar at the center of the room. There was silence for a little while, a pregnant silence, until Julie, looking with a tiara in her hair more princess than priestess, rose from her place in the circle, walked to the table, and took up an old, wood-handled bread knife, pointing it solemnly first at the ceiling and then at the floor. Heavens and earth thus saluted, she walked to one end of the circle followed by two other women, both of them bearing cups of some kind. "Hail to the guardians of the East," Julie cried.

Powers of Air!
We invoke thy grace
And call upon thy whirlwind presence.
Bestow on us the Goddess breath that is her essence!

As she spoke these words, she made an elaborate shape in the air with her knife, and then one of her acolytes flicked water three times from the cup, intoning, "With salt and water I purify the East!"

"With fire and air I charge the East!" recited the other in rapid succession, making the same elaborate shape in the air as Julie had with the knife. The three women did the same, more or less, to the south, west, and north. Julie, in her role as high priestess, saluted the earth and sky again with her big knife ("it's called an *athame,*" she corrected Emily later), and then dipped it into a large, colorful salad bowl on the altar. Emily recognized this bowl from some of their lunches at school, and this connection reinforced the air of children playing dress-up. In a flash of melancholy, she wished again for the daughter who might have grown up just like Julie, now stumbling momentarily and coolly adjusting her crown. Looking around the circle, Emily could see a little of the same indulgent parent smile that she herself was wearing reflected in the face of Chris, one of the newer teachers, whose boyish presence she hadn't before noted. Then she heard Julie recite in a loud, clear voice:

Out of time, exempt from night and day,
The circle is cast, the wider world at bay.
Earth and sky, fire and water,
Each is to the Goddess daughter.
Seein' with your starlight vision,
Our humble coven's really bitchin'.
And so we nestle, safe and sound,
Our gentle circle strong as round.

One of the assistant priestesses lit some candles on the altar and then all three took their places in the circle again, Julie's being just to the right of Emily, to whom she turned and said, "In perfect love and perfect trust, to send a kiss is only just." Smiling sweetly, Julie kissed her on the cheek. "Now you do the same on your left." Emily was so touched she had to swallow a catch in her throat. "In perfect love and perfect trust," she warbled, and then had to be helped with the rest. Gently, with surprising pleasure, she kissed the downy cheek on her left, and so the kiss went around the circle.

The ritual, Emily guessed it was called, went on to include a ceremonial purification not unlike the use of holy water she remembered from her long-ago Catholic youth, a kind of group word association game, and a lesson for the newcomers in "grounding" and "centering" themselves so that they could channel the earth's energy up their spines. She tried to concentrate and take everything seriously, but it was hard sometimes not to think about how very glad she was that her husband wasn't around. Frank wouldn't even say anything, she knew that; the look on his face would do all the talking.

Yet it was striking how you could get lost in the thing. She felt herself slip into a delicious light trance during the relaxation exercise. They started by progressively clenching their entire bodies, from their toes all the way up to their scalps, and then, when the tension just seemed unendurable, they exhaled and relaxed, Emily feeling the carpet fibers under her hands and through the fabric of her blouse as Julie, like some Hollywood hypnotist, chanted, "You're utterly, completely relaxed. You're just completely, totally relaxed, there's not an ounce of tension in your body . . ."

Emily drifted back to the Japanese spa she had visited so long ago with her old friend Lucille Lyttle, who had had no children in those days, and whose life had not yet been blighted by religion or drink. It was somehow comforting to think of Lucille in those times, to remind herself that Lu wasn't always the wreck she had become. Emily had only recently resumed wanting to live enough to do something nice for herself, and Frank had been left with their son so she could have a little pampering with a girlfriend. She and Lucille spent the day having facials, mudbaths, herbal rubs. It had seemed almost evilly indulgent. They had lounged for hours in the sulfurous hot tub until it was time for their massage.

"Do you ever wonder what your life would be like if things had worked out different?" Lucille had asked. "If you had made different choices?"

"Sometimes. Sure."

"Me too. I wonder sometimes if you had married Wayne instead of me. If you hadn't dumped him back in high school. What things would be like now."

"Talk about water under the bridge! Wayne loves you, Luce. He and I—it wasn't meant to be."

"I don't know whether anything's meant to be, or whether we just grope our way through and live with all our mistakes. Sometimes I wish you'd stayed with him, know what I mean? I'd lead a different life, that's for sure. Not married to any accountant."

Emily was startled to hear this.

"Are you unhappy with Wayne?"

"Not unhappy. I mean, you know. It's never like it was at first, being married. Isn't that the way it is with Frank?"

"Yes." She wondered sometimes what her life might have been with Wayne, yet here was his wife, testifying that the road not taken looked just like the one she was on. "But you get surprises too. Frank has surprised me in some good ways as well as in some bad. He was a tower of strength during Roberta's illness, and now for all his failings, it's hard to imagine anything tearing us apart after that."

"We should go out and find us some guys some night. Guys with tattoos or something, just once, just for the hell of it. Something different. Before we're so worn out we don't even want to anymore."

"Luce, I think I'm there already." She was only a couple of years older than Lucille but had always seemed a big sister to her friend.

"No you're not," Lucille said, frowning.

It was summer. Single people from all over the region came to the resort's bar on weekend nights, and Lucille wanted to have some fun. They had a couple of drinks with dinner, more than Emily had had in recent memory, and perhaps as a result, and in keeping with the climate of indulgence, she agreed to go along. Lucille first hid all their stockings, insisting they go bare-legged and wear only their sexiest dresses. They giggled as they made themselves up, drinking and taking turns with lipstick and eyeliner until the sadness in Emily's face had retreated to the corners of her eyes and mouth, where it peeked out from behind the mask of her levity only occasionally during the night. When they hit the bar, their wedding rings were buried at the bottoms of their purses.

"Remember, the thing to do is not to let one of them pick you," Lucille had warned. "You go after the one you want."

That's just what she had done. Emily was too good even to flirt much, but Lucille had zeroed in on somebody and left with him. Emily hadn't liked her selection from the first; there was something impatient and condescending in his banter, something hurried about the way he ordered more drinks, as if he couldn't even be bothered to maintain any pretense about what he was doing. Later, assuming Lucille had gone elsewhere with the guy, Emily had returned to their room in the nick of time. She could hear the noise of their struggle from down the hall, and when she finally got the key to work and got inside, he was hopping to get his pants on while Lucille tried to cover herself with what was left of her torn dress. The room was a shambles, lit scarily by a lamp lying sideways on the floor.

"Fucking cock tease!" he sputtered, dressing hastily and storming for the door. "I thought the other one might be a lesbian, but I guess it's the both o' you."

"I'm calling the police," Emily said, shaking with rage. She mainly wanted to scare him away. When they got home, Lucille had claimed the black eye was from Emily's elbow in the swimming pool.

Emily had reminded Lucille of all this in a telephone call after the spanking. It was for Jeffrey's sake, really, because she thought he was better off at Alphabet Soup than home with his troubled mother. And for Wayne's, because she still had a soft spot for him.

"Do you remember how much I read to you, Luce? All your favorites from when you were a kid? Just because you needed that when you were up in the hospital? You said you couldn't have survived Summerville otherwise. Couldn't have lived without a drink."

"All I wanted was an apology, Em. But you and your husband were too important, and now I thank God because otherwise I never would have known. For years you used to tell me what an odd duck Frank was, and now I see. You've known all along, haven't you?"

"Known what?"

"What Tiffany told us, finally. Before she died."

"Lu, that's ridiculous, Frank would never—I mean, he's just not the type."

"You're not really sure though, are you?" Lucille persisted. "You don't really have any idea."

She scoffed, but a little voice inside said: *Well, who really knew?* It seemed inconceivable that she hadn't noticed, but there was a lot about her husband she tended not to notice, until someone held it up in her face. This was the worst thing about these crazy charges—that somewhere inside she found it a little too easy to believe.

The ceremony in Julie's living room ended with a farewell to all their visions and the powers of the four directions, and after a brief, silent meditation, the women came back to themselves. The lights were turned on, and they hugged and kissed and talked about how refreshed and renewed they felt. It was dark out by now, and Emily realized that she had lost all track of time. Afterward there was food, an insipid non-alcoholic wine and the din of animated chatter.

"So what were those shapes you were making?" Emily asked. "Were those anything?"

"Pentagrams," said Julie. "They have all kinds of special significance for witches."

"But do you all really believe you're witches?"

"We *are* witches," Mary insisted. "It's just that witches aren't born, they're made, and the craft is more a way of life than anything else. We don't ride brooms or stick pins through dolls to give someone appendicitis."

It was surprising hearing this from freckled, working-class Mary, who had attended St. Brigid's and seemed always about to get fat, but Emily knew she looked up to Julie as an avatar of the worldly, sophisticated Webster she had admired from afar, and this sort of thing was not surprising in Julie, who during nap time at the school would meditate sometimes, chanting her mantra inwardly, or when she slept, imagine a circle of protective energy around the building.

"But you do magic." Emily meant it as a question.

"Sure," said Julie. "What's magic except concentrated consciousness? How's it different from prayer? There are studies showing that patients who were prayed for by strangers across the country, and who didn't even know it, did better than those who weren't prayed for."

"It's a very old religion," Mary added quickly, "and a lot of women have turned to it lately because it's an alternative to the rigid, patriarchal spiritualities most of us grew up with. It's creative, and everyone gets to take part."

Emily learned more, more perhaps than she wanted to know. Their coven, which she was invited to join, was called Ariel and limited to thirteen members. Initiation required quite an apprenticeship including readings, exercises, and a certain amount of ritual attending. These rituals seemed made up, although there was a handbook called the *Witches Rede*, and a lot of what they did they wrote down in a sort of worship diary. Julie said they sometimes danced and even undressed at their ceremonies. "We reenact myths too, with costumes and everything. Just like in the theater, suspending disbelief is part of the exercise." The girls seemed to Emily so tender, so earnest and innocent—such girls. Emily could see that for them to be in a traditional church, with the long and bloody histories these faiths carried, was like accepting a sullied world. She was touched that they had included her in a ceremony. She was not particularly happy about turning forty, but the coven's magic evidently worked because later, on the way home, she had a good cry and then felt better.

Frank Joseph, meanwhile, stood out on Main Street, mesmerized. He was piloting his large and aging Oldsmobile through the icy streets of Webster when, just blocks short of his furtive destination, he found himself stranded in traffic. Main Street was a parking lot, thronged with cars and people, everything made worse by the snow. The police were out in force, but there seemed little they could or would do. Curious, he got out and walked toward the commotion. Cars on the street crept along at perhaps five miles per hour, and pickets walked with signs reading, "Fight the Carpetbagger!" and "Don't Let Krieger's Go!" The noise was deafening; the pickets shouted "Save Our Store! Save Our Jobs!"—led by what he imagined were shop stewards with bullhorns, who occasionally changed the chant. "Parking Now!" the leaders suddenly began, and there was a moment of confusion as the new chant made its way up and down the street, flowing like the tide across footprints in the sand. Frank was transfixed. He had never seen the main street of Webster so packed with cars and pedestrians. It was festive, exciting. There were TV cameras and reporters running around with notebooks and microphones. Suddenly, a lean, energetic man mounted the back of a pickup truck, and the protesters erupted in cheers.

"First I want to apologize," he said, and shouts of "No!" and "No way, José!" bobbed up here and there. He held up a hand, dipped his head. "I want to apologize to the working people of Webster for tying things up in the evening rush. I know you're tired, and you've got families to get home to."

It was Ed Krcyszyki, Frank realized. He knew Ed from the Daniel Webster Historical Commission, on which they both had served. They had taken very different views of Webster's behavior and how the town should react all these years later.

"But I also hope you'll understand that those of us who work at Krieger's are here for you just as much as for ourselves." At this a huge cheer went up, dwarfing the tiny shops and buildings along the old high street. "We're here to say that this town won't let some greedy carpetbagger from Philadelphia come in and take away any of our livelihoods, or kill our local institutions, or walk all over our way of life, just because he's got a few bucks!"

An even larger cheer arose from the crowd, and Frank turned away. He was sympathetic to the workers, despite Pearl's loathing for Charlie Krieger, and sympathetic also to the idea that Webster should be saved from having to do all its shopping in a soulless concrete tilt-up out in some former cornfield beyond the edge of town. But he needed to go, shouldn't even have left his car. When he got back to it, he managed a U-turn and took a detour past the old electronics factory, now shuttered and awaiting some chimerical arts organization to breathe life back into it, and the long, grimy row of narrow company houses standing primly in line across from it, their tiny porches bearing old sofas, plastic jack-o'-lanterns and other such weary paraphernalia. He turned left, drove a few more minutes, and the neighborhood improved gradually until he made a right and slowed to look for the right driveway. When he reached Annette Martini's place, he pulled around to the back, sliding this way and that on her ice-glazed lawn until he came to a stop well short of her Celica.

Frank understood by now that to have a lover while you are married means that every encounter is unpredictably charged. Often he could tell the state of the emotional weather inside the house even before he reached Annette's back porch, with its aluminum storm door and wind chimes and images of screeching cats and pumpkins and the like left over from Halloween. The level of the blinds, the state of the porch, the presence or absence of smoke rising from the chimney—these were all clues as to whether he would be welcomed or assailed or some combination of the two.

Leaving the car, he was struck once again by how achingly cold it was. Tonight, he knew, Annette would read him the same way he usually read her, simply from the way he greeted her. She would smell the mournful air of termination he brought in with him, feel it in his arms and hands when they hugged, and perhaps begin to respond even before he could open his mouth. Surely she must have seen this coming. Surely she must have understood all along that this thing she, above all others, had wanted could not continue. But when he got inside, he couldn't tell if Annette had read his message in his face or felt it through his hands or missed it altogether, because in response to his warm greeting, she only hugged him distractedly.

"Frank, this custody thing is just killing me," she said. "I don't know what that judge is thinking with all this delay. How can they separate a little boy from his mother? Just because the father has a better job and a new wife? How is that fair?"

Annette was bony and a little raw, the skin of her nose and lips always a little red and chapped, the weather seeming to take a more severe toll on her than on others. She always looked as if she had been crying—or perhaps was cried out. Worry, Frank saw, was her native expression. In that moment he recognized anew the extent to which he was drawn to women who needed to be cared for, and the frequency with which he fell down on the job.

"Annie, they're not going to take your boy away," he said impatiently, thinking: *Not like my little girl, whom the fates chose to take from us.* "It's just a visit. Look, maybe joint custody isn't so bad. Maybe it's good for the boy. Isn't that ultimately what you want?"

"Are you kidding?" Her dark eyes widened. "Don't you remember how he used to beat me up? He takes psychotropic drugs by the handful every morning just to get through the day. I don't mind Andy seeing his father, I just want sole and uncontested custody of my boy."

Frank noticed the complex smells of Annette's cooking and saw the table set with her good dishes, the candlelight reflected off the shoulder of an open bottle of red wine. He was not large but grew up in the Irish macho tradition and had had enough scrapes not to fear a fight. He had warned Annette's husband, Ray was his name, not to lay another hand on his wife unless he was prepared to lay hands on Frank as well. That was the beginning of his and Annette's special friendship.

"I don't know what I'm going to do, Frank. I'm frantic. Sometimes I think I should just take Andy and run away with him."

He looked at her hands and saw that the cuticles had been chewed bloody. He felt himself fill with feeling for her and for anyone who worried over a child.

"He's never harmed the boy, has he?"

"He's never harmed him, no, but I don't trust him. That's why I left him. I can't trust him."

Frank was embarrassed. The words, he felt, might as well be aimed at himself, and he could practically hear Emily saying them. God knew she would be entitled.

"Ray wouldn't try anything now, Annie. C'mon, it smells great in here. Let's enjoy ourselves."

They kissed gently, and he hugged her. Frank knew he should try to empathize with Ray. Like Frank, he had been beaten by his father as a child. And Frank certainly understood compulsion. Some part of him even understood the impulse to strike out at others for their failure to comply, for their insistence on getting in the way. He caught himself sometimes handling a child too peremptorily, gripping too sternly, and saw that for someone unbalanced it would be too easy to inflict violence on a frustrating wife or child.

"I was afraid you were coming over to leave me tonight," Annette said, searching his face. "You said you wanted to talk."

"I always need to talk." He hugged her. "Let's talk while we eat. Everything's fine, Annie. As fine as it can be."

Later that night, when he got home, Emily was reading in the big chair next to the bed, her feet curled up beside her. The light was soft and blended into the darkness only a little ways from her head. His wife looked ever so slightly abashed to him, and he loved her for it, loved her shyness about herself, which mirrored his own deep reticence. Taking off his jacket and shoes, he walked toward her, secure in her indulgent gaze, and kissed her hair, her oily forehead, and her chapped lips, sticky with balm. Her flannel nightie was fragrant and soft, and Frank wished that he had saved himself for her, for the comfort and closeness he craved just now, even if their lovemaking was always such a trial. What was he doing? Why hadn't he done what he'd meant to do about Annette?

"Mm, you taste good," Emily said. "Where've you been?"

"I had a quiet dinner at La Madeleine and then stopped at Costello's," he said, hoping neither had burned down to make a liar of him.

"Did they have the game on?"

"I didn't even notice."

"Pensive guy." Emily leaned her head against the chair back.

"Did you have fun with the girls?"

"Yeah," she said. "Yeah, we did."

"Where?"

"Julie's house. We just made a nice meal, had some nice wine. It was very sweet. They were so kind to me. We talked about life and feelings and all that stuff you can't get enough of talking about." She bit her tongue to show that she was teasing. "Julie and Mary are so young, I feel like their mother." She shook her head and sighed. "Forty!"

"Come to bed, old timer," he said, going off to brush his teeth.

When he returned he switched off the light on his side and joined her under the covers, where he kissed her again. She turned around so he could fold her in his arms, and she took one and thrust it under her night-gown, between her breasts.

chapter NINE

Towering, upright Cal Hawthorne spoke with characteristic vigor, pronouncing the words slowly and biting them off as if his dim-witted audience had driven him to the quivering limits of his patience. He had just finished enumerating his accomplishments, which were indisputable. Since his appointment to fill out the term of his predecessor, who had died of a heart attack at the wheel of his car after just a month in office, the new DA had tightened up the office, brought some consistency to the prosecution of drug offenses, and expanded the pursuit of white-collar crime. He smiled as he went on, surveying a room full of paying supporters. "And so I ask you today for something I have never before asked for in my life, which is your vote. I ask you next fall to re-elect me to a full four-year term as Vanatee County district attorney so that I can complete the job I've started and clean up our communities."

The dining room erupted in applause. A few people even leaped to their feet, and others felt compelled to follow. The speaker basked in the mounting ovation, offering a toothy grimace in lieu of a smile.

Errol Jones smiled too, although weakly. He was abashed by the cynicism of this display. What did these people care? As long as the district attorney didn't let the homeless get too far out of hand, these prosperous burghers paid little attention to the DA's office. But they were not fools. Hawthorne was an attractive and dynamic candidate, and reporters from well beyond Webster had turned out for his anticipated announcement. His name had already been bruited for governor someday. Local lawyers, real estate agents, insurance brokers, and other ambitious types liked the idea of getting in on the ground floor. All of them were glad to pony up $100 for a bad lunch and burned-tasting coffee with Hawthorne at the Web State Inn. It was a bargain.

The turnout was excellent. Looking around, Errol could see everyone who was anyone locally. Here was his friend Terry Mathers at one of the press tables up front, among the political writers sent by newspapers and radio stations from all over the state. He looked around farther and spotted Charles Krieger, resplendent with his wintertime tan, surrounded by a tableful of lieutenants (odd to see Terry's wife among them). Krieger was Hawthorne's biggest backer, single-handedly donating or raising huge sums of "soft" money for a separate campaign committee not covered by the state's low limits on individual campaign contributions. God knew it would be awkward if Charlie ever did anything indictable, although probably, knowing Cal, the DA would be thrilled.

Errol could see that his boss, always revved up, was truly wired today. A model of self-control, Hawthorne had eaten a little salad, picked at his entrée, and devoured the fruit he'd ordered for dessert. He had washed it all down with four cups of coffee and a glass of orange juice. The pH in his stomach was unthinkable.

Errol's distaste for the gathering was not so strong that he couldn't take comfort in his boss's announcement. He was Hawthorne's chief deputy, although for a while, when he lost the biggest case the District Attorney's Office had prosecuted in years, he thought he might be Hawthorne's biggest liability. The case had made headlines all over the state, and the trial had been an ordeal. A little girl was dead, murdered, and the suspects were her parents. Jones knew in his innermost soul that one of them was guilty, but even he wasn't sure which. The jury acquitted both of them. Afterward you'd see them around, just like normal people. He'd run into the father once at the dry cleaners. Eventually, to everyone's relief, they had moved away.

"What can we learn from this?" Hawthorne had asked after the verdict. They spent a long time talking about what happened, looking for patterns and conclusions. Hawthorne always seemed to reach them first, but there had been no rancor, nothing but understanding. Errol had given it his best shot, and Hawthorne said flatly he did not believe he himself might have done any better. "That's why I picked you," he said with a sly smile and a shrug. "Better you than me."

That was Hawthorne. In victory, his office would get the credit, but in defeat the loss was Errol's, and as long as Hawthorne did not hold it against him, he was willing to take the blame. Now here was Hawthorne announcing his candidacy for a term of his own and, if the papers were to be believed, he was not only the front-runner but likely to go much farther as well.

So he was wired. Knowing this, Jones was prepared, when they charged out into the cold for the short walk back to the District Attorney's Office, to deliver the rapid-fire briefing on the day that Hawthorne was certain to want.

"We've gone through the candidates to replace Millstein," Errol began. "We've narrowed the list down to four, and he's agreed to stay on an extra month until we pick one of them. I think we finally got the arraignments under control with the new schedule, even if people are still bellyaching about it. The attorney in the Rollefson murder wants to do a deal, if you have any interest. And then there's this business of the kid from Alphabet Soup who died in the crash. We have a meeting about it"—Errol looked at his watch—"five minutes ago."

"A meeting? What's the issue? The mother was drunk; she killed her kid. What else do we need to know? Who's her lawyer?"

"It's not that. The woman claims her kid accused the principal or somebody at her preschool of sexual abuse, and that's why she went off the road. She was so shocked when the daughter told her."

"What? Give me a fucking break. She'll plead or we go for murder. I can't listen to this crap."

"I hear you, man. The thing is, we have a second allegation now. From another kid."

Hawthorne stopped for a minute, the wind blowing his hair as if electrical current were passing through him. "Don't tell me this, Errol."

"Cal, I can't make this go away."

"OK, let's have it." Hawthorne didn't move, which annoyed Errol. It took an effort to keep his teeth from chattering.

"The case was developed by Diana Shirley," he said, "the county's new specialist in this whole area. Alphabet Soup is a popular place, no record of violations or other troubles, and they have a big waiting list."

"Yeah, yeah."

"But in fact there's all kinds of data about how prevalent this is, even in affluent white counties like this one. And of course the *Chronicle* made a big deal about Shirley coming to town to save all the children."

"Who's the newest allegator? I mean who's the family?"

Errol consulted a slip of paper in his breast pocket. His cotton shirt felt icy against his nipple. "Lucille Lyttle. The mother is all I have. Maybe no father in the picture, I don't know."

"Oh, shit," Hawthorne said.

"What?" Errol asked. "You know her?"

"Tell me about Shirley," Hawthorne said.

"About thirty-five, good background, worked with prosecutors before. They say she knows how to make a case."

"I need everything, Errol."

"No family. Lesbian, as far as anyone knows. I think she's OK."

"Kind of a babe, from what I saw the other night," Hawthorne said.

"No barrier, apparently. Bottom line is, a tough case with a big payoff. You protect the children of Webster from these monsters over at the preschool, you're a hero. But it's gonna depend on the testimony of some very small kids, and the people who run the preschool are liable to have some very strong support in the community."

"Not for long," Hawthorne said. "Shit."

"That's why you need to take the lead on this. It's going to be very high profile, far beyond Webster."

"C'mon Errol. There's no life beyond Webster."

Errol had to laugh. After three years as his chief deputy, he neither liked nor fully trusted Cal Hawthorne, even as he managed to admire him. He appreciated his boss's level of calculation; you could almost see him weighing possible advantages behind that expressionless facade, kind of like a computer with no video display. As a black man in a white world, Errol could empathize. Hawthorne could emulate emotional states, for instance, with perfect verisimilitude: anger, passion, grief, whatever the microphones and cameras might demand, yet Errol had to wonder whether his boss had ever genuinely felt any of these. There was an impatience about the man, a sense of sufferance for the slow and untidy world around him. Hawthorne was a man who seemed to wish that others would exercise the same degree of self-control that he did. No empty calories passed the bar of his teeth, nor were empty minutes permitted to elapse in the day. His distaste for a fat person, or a sloppy one, was palpable.

In their gray suits, Errol and his boss took a short cut through the parking lot of the Staple Gun convenience store, past a smoking employee in company-issue red-striped shirt scratching at lottery tickets atop a trash can. Hawthorne had made a big deal of enforcing the county's progressive new no-smoking law, and now you saw these poor devils all over Webster, miserably puffing and shivering outside every building in town. The prosecutors walked quickly. Errol was solidly built, bespectacled, prematurely bald and so closely cropped on the rest of his head that he was almost hairless. Hawthorne was balding too, forcing him to envelope himself in a cloud of hair spray every morning to keep what was left of his wiry gray hair over his scalp. He was taller and leaner than his deputy, his posture so straight he was almost a caricature of the overweening attorney, and on weekdays he rose at dawn for a punishing martial arts workout at the Y (like Terry, he too had his own key); after three years as a brown belt in tae kwan do, he was saving up vacation time to make the big push for black. Hawthorne had a tough beard which he kept closely shaved, and he made sure his face was powdered before doing TV.

The nice thing about Hawthorne was that he kept you on your toes. Errol himself had an ambition for excellence; it nauseated him to think that people might assume he was not quite up to snuff or that allowances must be made because of his color. He would never have admitted it to himself, but he also wanted badly to fit in, to avoid the humiliation of being mistaken for someone else, and so he never went about publicly in sweatpants or tattered jeans, instead sending his entire "casual" wardrobe to the cleaners, so that he was always crisply pressed, even when it made him look stuffy and pretentious, as in Webster it so often did. His effacing style clashed slightly with this tendency to be over-dressed, however painfully good his taste, and despite his gentle voice and mild manners, people wondered if he was patronizing them. He knew this, but knew also in his heart that he did condescend, finding people who pumped gas and flipped burgers despite the great advantages of whiteness just a little pathetic. Hawthorne at least was ambitious. He captured something in Webster, managing to embody the contradiction between the community's remarkable tolerance and its persecuting spirit, both of which seemed to coexist in people's hearts without any difficulty. And of course, he was ruthless. Errol considered his future to be bright.

They arrived at the office to find a small woman and a huge man seated uncomfortably around the small table in a little conference room they used mainly for plea negotiations. Jepson seemed to fill the place with his bulk and even his breath, but it was Diana who took over the meeting.

Hawthorne listened in what seemed physical pain as she and Jepson explained that since the initial complaint, which had been against Frank Joseph, co-owner of the preschool, Lucille Lyttle's son had also implicated his wife, Emily, and her elderly mother, Pearl. So not only did they have medical evidence, they even had a second victim.

"How old is this kid?" Hawthorne asked.

"His name's Jeffrey, and he's just four," Diana said. "I've questioned a lot of children in this situation, and I'm quite familiar with the literature as well. One thing that's clear is, kids don't make this stuff up. I mean, why would they? If you saw how difficult it is for them to disclose, you'd realize that they're speaking the truth. The whole premise of any abuse case is that you've got to believe the children. Otherwise, what do you have? You'd never make a case of child abuse, ever."

"No eyewitnesses?" Jones asked, knowing the answer but wanting to save Hawthorne from seeming doubtful.

"None that we know of yet," Jepson said. "I mean, when you're gonna screw a kid, you don't do it in Throgmorton Park at high noon."

"There might be some witnesses," said Diana, "which is why we're here. We want to contact the other parents and find out what the other children saw and, of course, whether any of them were abused."

"We've got an obligation," said Jepson. "And I personally find it hard to believe that these three abusers focused on just two kids, to the exclusion of all the others. Or that these two kids were the very first ones. There are probably older kids in this town, maybe even grown-ups, who've been abused by this family."

"Any allegation like this is awfully serious, but I'm troubled by the idea that Emily and that old lady might be involved," Hawthorne said. "I've got to believe a jury would be troubled too. I mean, Pearl Gibson? She's got to be, what, seventy?"

"Sixty-seven," Jepson corrected.

"Geez, I see her every year when I go to vote. You're telling me this nice old lady is—well, exactly what I don't know—to some little kid? Just what is she supposed to have been doing to him?"

"Cal, you'd be very surprised," Diana said. "There's a tendency to assume that elderly women in our society are asexual, but it's not true, just as there's a tendency to assume that men are the only ones who abuse children, which is also not true. One of the things we've been trying to do in this field is make people aware of the way their stereotypes are limiting their ability to perceive the abuse going on around them. I think you'll see from the report of my interviews with Jeffrey that Mrs. Gibson was quite sexual indeed."

"And the school shouldn't be surprising," Errol said to Hawthorne, as Jepson nodded his agreement. "You often see abusers as scoutmasters and so forth—in places where they have responsibility for kids and access to them."

"Sounds like a hell of a report, Diana." Hawthorne invoked people's names like a salesman. He was wide-eyed now with apparent enthusiasm. Sometimes he made Errol's skin crawl. "The thing is, I don't believe any of this happened. Nor do I think for one minute that it could stand up in a court of law."

He waited a beat, relishing the sense that he had kicked three people in the stomach simultaneously, then continued.

"Forget Belinda Jackson; that's a joke. This is all about Lucille Lyttle's kid, right?" Hawthorne continued. "Do you people know anything about her? When we were young, she'd get older guys to buy her booze in exchange for blow jobs, and she's been up in Summerville for at least one extended stay. For a while her husband had to send the kids to the grand-parents' because she couldn't be trusted around them. She's your star wit-ness?"

"Pardon me, but I cannot believe the things I'm hearing here." Diana's voice was shaking. "This woman's past is *not* the *issue* at this meet-ing. The abuse was disclosed by her *son,* to me *personally,* so please don't visit the supposed sins of the mothers on the children."

"He made some 'disclosure'"—here Hawthorne made mocking quo-tation marks with his fingers—"to his mother first, though, isn't that correct? And his mother is a drunk and maybe psychotic as well. Isn't that also correct?"

"And so your idea is to do nothing? To forget the whole thing?"

"My plan is for you to go and find some more evidence before we go off half-cocked on the word of a lunatic. If you find it, great. I'll nail 'em to the wall personally, so help me God. But we don't have enough right now to make a case like this against three respected members of the com-munity." Hawthorne turned to the others. "So what's next? What's the plan?"

"We're sending a letter to all the Alphabet Soup parents," Jepson said, "asking them about any suspicious activities at the school."

"Isn't that a little prejudicial?" Hawthorne looked around the room. "If you don't have enough to charge anybody, how can you write to all these parents asking about abuse? Don't you think you need to hold off and see what else you can turn up before you paper the town with this thing?"

"Mr. District Attorney, I'm sorry, but I have to disagree with you," Jepson said. Jones could see him bristling even as the big detective restrained himself verbally. "We feel there's a serious public safety issue, which overrides certain evidentiary niceties that won't matter in the end anyway, because I know in my gut that there's something very serious going on in that school. I'm a parent, and the parents of those kids have a right to know about it."

"Let's wait on that," Hawthorne said, his eyes glittering with contempt. "Let's just wait a bit and see what we can turn up first. You've already questioned Frank Joseph. I imagine if there's a ring of child-abusers over there, you've already put the fear of God into them. The kids are probably safe for a couple more weeks."

After the meeting, Hawthorne motioned Jones to stay.

"So what do you think?" he asked.

"What do I think? Seems like you've already made up your mind on this one."

"I'm asking you."

"I think you're making a mistake. I think there could be something very serious here, and you can't just dismiss it because this woman was the town slut when you were in high school."

"Really? So what would you do? If you were me."

"I'd get personally involved, prosecute the case myself, deal with the press, the whole nine yards. It's too big for you to do otherwise, and the exposure would be tremendous. Where's the down side? Nobody likes child abusers; you could string 'em up and not have anybody outside holding a candlelight vigil, the way they do for some murderer on death row."

"You're not giving me options, Errol."

"You don't have any options. Unless you think there's nothing there."

"In which case I'm the one who didn't believe the children." Errol said nothing. "Who let the abusers get away. 'DA Lets Child Molesters Walk.' "

"Not just in the *Chronicle,* either. And heaven help you if you lose a case like this."

"Very astute. You got most of it. Now let me tell you what I think," Hawthorne said. "First, I know very well we may have to prosecute this case, but it'll be miserable for all concerned, with children under cross-examination, public opinion divided, years of appeals, fundraisers for the defendants, and God knows what else. There is very little upside here for us, Errol. Second, I know we'll never make a case on what these bozos have so far. And third, I know at least some of the allegations will be false. They already are."

"But what about the kids? If they're being abused, we have to stop it. Right? Let's assume for a minute that they might be. How do we proceed?"

"Who the hell knows about the kids? We haven't heard a peep out of them until now. You can't even get into that school; parents sign up two years in advance, now all of a sudden it's a den of pederasty. We may never know about the kids. Look," Hawthorne said, rubbing his face and shifting into a different tone, "I'm going to need you to spend some time on this. Make sure that if there is a case, we don't lose it. And make sure we win in a court of law *and* in the court of public opinion."

Hawthorne pronounced those last words with distaste—for the cliché he consciously invoked or for the judge and jury of this demotic venue? Errol wasn't sure which, but he called Diana and told her he would be working the Alphabet Soup investigation from the District Attorney's Office, and that it would be better if, before anything else drastic was done, he might be informed.

"I think I might be able to help," he said, thinking: *I mean this. This is serious. I'll put up with a lot, but this Machiavelli routine of Hawthorne's is just too much when the lives of kids are at stake. I'm not paid enough to be that cynical.* "To be perfectly honest, the district attorney is less than positive that we have a case, but I'm convinced that kids—little kids, who aren't otherwise sexually aware—don't make this stuff up."

"Thank you, Errol." Diana's gratitude touched him. "Thank you so much for this."

Jones arrived at Costello's to find the editor of the *Webster Chronicle* already seated and watching Michigan against Indiana, shown on television from one of those far-off camera angles that made even big-time college basketball seem quaint and old-fashioned compared to the pros. They both liked the college game, had both played it in a small way, and Jones knew Terry would want to get out of the house, although lately his friend was less frequently available on such short notice. He was a cagey character, Terry, and elusive. There was a ghostly ubiquity about him in Webster, a sense that he took up more space than most people. Hawthorne had noticed it too, seeing him around the Y. Errol thought he was up to something, a new girlfriend perhaps. Tonight, as usual at Costello's, Terry ate french fries and a bowl of vegetarian chili, while Errol scarfed down Costello's famous bacon avocado cheeseburger smothered in onions and peppers, promising himself once again to do something about his intake of fat and salt. It would be so wearisomely banal as a black man to get high blood pressure and heart disease. Almost like going to prison or getting shot. You so rarely met black vegetarians. The two men had a pitcher of beer between them, and then another, taking turns ferrying this golden liquid by bladder to the men's room and thence into the sea.

Finally, Errol followed Terry rather than waiting for him to return from the bathroom, and walked up to the urinal next to him. It was a small room, pervaded by the smell of ammonia. The two men stood facing a crumbling plaster wall covered with a thousand small graffiti.

"Hey," said Errol as he worked to free himself. "You remember that poor little kid who was killed out on 32? One whose mother ran into the oak tree on that curve?"

"Tiffany Jackson, right? Mother was drunk, as I recall."

Errol gave a long, low groan as he emptied himself into the camphor-filled drain.

"What about her?" Terry prompted. He shook the last drops from his own flaccid member.

"You ever look into that?" Errol asked, his voice a parody of innocent curiosity.

"Look into it how? She was drunk; her kid wasn't even buckled in; she wasn't much of a mother anyway. She killed her daughter through her own fucking negligence."

"That's one way to look at it," Errol said.

Terry looked at him.

"And the other is?"

"She claimed she ran off the road because her daughter told her that someone at the school was abusing her. Sexually abusing her."

"And you credit that?" Terry asked. "Of course the daughter is conveniently dead, so we can't ask her. Now all of a sudden the mother is suffering—what? Post-disclosure stress syndrome? The main symptom being impaired driving skills, correct?"

"Sounds fishy, huh?"

Terry looked at him again.

"I'm getting a vibe here, Errol. But generally it's more effective to communicate through words, don't you think? There's n-n-nobody else in here, and you know I'm n-not gonna tell."

"Tell what?"

"Where I heard it."

"You didn't hear anything."

"OK," Terry sighed. "OK."

The next day at work, Terry Mathers felt the rush that came of knowing he was onto something. The thing now was to pin it down. Diana was an obvious place to start, but he wanted to find out everything he could beforehand, by any means he could. Pondering whether to try some of his sources on the Webster Police, something made him call Bob Varity first.

"Bob, I understand the District Attorney's Office is investigating some allegations of child abuse against Alphabet Soup. You used to represent the Josephs in one thing and another. Wanna get their side in here?" It was a classic bluff, but Terry was betting that Varity would go for it.

"What? That's just incredible. Terry, I don't know where you're getting your information, but I'd be very careful before I ran a story that damaging. I've had no communications with the district attorney about this, nor have my clients."

"So you're telling me it's not true?"

"I'm not privy to what goes on in Cal Hawthorne's mind or office, I'm just telling you that you're playing with fire here. You and I both know there's no child abuse at Alphabet Soup, but a story like this, just one story, could destroy everything they've worked for over there. And believe me, the kids of Webster will be worse off elsewhere, worse off even at home. My own son is with Emily and Frank right now. You think I'd have my kid over there if they were running some kind of kiddy porn ring?"

If anything, the scent was now even stronger. With the Krieger's story percolating at a low level, he dumped that whole mess on Ariadne Tidwell, which had the added advantage of keeping him away from Abigail's machinations, and turned his full attention to the school. Terry always considered himself lucky, and so he decided to take a guess. His guess was that Frank Joseph was the problem here. It was not a difficult assumption to make. It was even a little creepy to think of Frank, whom Terry knew only slightly, lurking around a preschool. Frank was an anachronism, the kind of man one expected to find wearing hair oil and a well-creased homburg. He liked to gamble. He was not a nurturer.

As it turned out, Frank had had his troubles. The Josephs had narrowly avoided bankruptcy when their bookstore failed, and Frank's fondness for the horses was easy to discover, as was his tendency to spend time at the nearest Indian casino, a mere fifty miles away. The shocking thing came practically out of nowhere, in a routine check with the police in Rockton: that Frank had actually been charged with sexual abuse of a minor. The Josephs, it seemed, had used to take in foster children, troubled teens, and preadolescents who needed a home.

The precise disposition of the case never became clear, but there had been an allegation in the days when the Josephs had lived in Rockton, an allegation and an arrest. There was no conviction; it all seemed to vanish like the young girl who had made the charge in the first place. Terry was never able to learn her identity, never able to ask her what happened. All he knew was that she wasn't quite sixteen—Phoebe's age. That didn't mean the authorities were now after him in Webster, of course. But Terry knew from experience that someone who does something sleazy in one arena often does unsavory things in others as well. There are people who don't seem to live under the same constraints as the rest of us. Evidently Frank was one of them.

Yet no one seemed willing to give him the missing piece: what was it that the police in Webster were investigating? Did they really think Frank Joseph was a child molester?

Ultimately it was Diana who told him. She described Tiffany's allegations, but what clinched it for him was that a second child had come forward—a little boy who had leveled similar accusations against Frank, Emily, and even Pearl. Terry and Diana were in bed, in the dark, and she spoke in a whisper as if the walls themselves might have ears. "I've wanted to talk to you about this for so long," she said. "They aren't letting us move fast enough, and so these kids are all condemned to attending a preschool with at least one abuser and probably more. The more we find out, the worse it looks. It's horrible, Terry. I don't know how else to stop it. Maybe if you write something in the newspaper, it will shake things up."

Terry was astonished. His mother had known Pearl when both women were young, and he had slightly known Emily growing up. He remembered their old house, with its odd, moldy smell and the loose banister no one ever seemed to get around to fixing. It was all inconceivable. Yet wasn't it always inconceivable? Wasn't that Diana's point? Fortunately, at some level it wasn't up to Terry. If the District Attorney's Office had gone this far and there were two separate allegations, how could he ignore it? It wasn't as if his sourcing was poor. Diana had done the questioning herself, although of course she couldn't be named.

With what he learned from her, Terry went back to Errol, who stalled for an afternoon. Finally he called back and, "on deepest background," made plain that the District Attorney's Office—not merely the Webster PD—was conducting a supersensitive investigation into child molestation at the Alphabet Soup preschool.

Soon after Terry left a message at the school, he looked up to see Bob Varity hurrying through the newsroom. When he reached the editor's office, he closed the door, lowered the blinds, and pulled up a chair to make his pitch. "Terry," he said. "Is this what we're really about? Destroying the kind of people who turn away big bucks from a developer so they can continue to spend their lives taking care of little children? This isn't you, Terry. This isn't why we go back all these years."

But Terry bristled at this maudlin abuse of their long friendship, and anyway by now he was committed. How could he *not* run it? "Bob, it'll come out sooner or later anyway. Do you think these parents don't talk to one another?" He promised to give prominent play to the school's side of things, which was that the whole affair was a fiction arising from the addled imagination of a single, guilt-stricken parent and then taken up by another with an ax to grind.

Abigail asked whether they should play it like the initial spanking, which was Varity's fall-back position, but Terry refused. And she too wondered what was the rush.

"Lucille Lyttle is crazy, Terry. You know that."

"But it's her son. He doesn't have a drinking problem, does he? And I'm not running this investigation, the DA's Office is. I'm just reporting the facts. Errol himself is involved, which means the DA thinks it's big. Imagine if Marty were in that school and the paper had the information but didn't publish it."

On the day the *Chronicle* story appeared, under a banner headline on page one, the sun rose over the Vanatee River as it always did and life in Webster seemed to go on in much the usual way, for the people of this enlightened community were not mere cattle prone to stampeding at the surprise of a loud noise. Men and women ate breakfast, dressed, bid the postman hello, drank coffee at work and wondered, as the meat-locker chill of a brutal winter persisted, whether spring would ever come. Yet later, looking backward with the clarity of hindsight, the story had the impact of a giant asteroid whose thud was nothing compared to the climatological upheaval that was to follow.

When it first came off the press though, there was no way to know where it would lead, even if Terry was proud of the scoop. At last, he thought, casually stuffing a paper into a manila envelope and addressing it to his father. Something to push this business about Krieger's below the fold. "You were right," he scribbled on the back of the envelope. "As usual."

chapter TEN

Emily hadn't known about the girl in Rockton. Hadn't known and hadn't suspected. Anja was her name. Bleached blond, sprayed-on jeans, halters. Her navel never covered the whole time. Not Frank's type, that much Emily knew, although she also knew that for most men, in some primal way, *type* simply meant *female.* The whole thing happened during the week she was visiting an old college friend in Florida. They had been in one of their protracted rough spots, and he hadn't wanted to make it any worse by telling her about the accusation. It all went away when the girl confessed in tears; she was only trying to get sent back to the city so she could be with her boyfriend there. She had even agreed not to mention it to Emily, thought she was doing him a favor. But that was the thing with Frank. You never knew the magnitude of what you didn't know.

By the end of the day the *Chronicle* article appeared, she was a wreck. Most parents chose to leave their children at the school, either because they disbelieved the allegations, because they had no other choice on such short notice, or because they hadn't yet seen or heard about the newspaper article. Many were full of sympathy; one spoke of her outrage. Between meetings with anxious parents, Emily got on the phone and tried to call those who hadn't come in. She wanted to warn them of the story and thus remove its sting, explain that there was no basis to it, that the Josephs and their school, the school all the children so loved, had been the innocent target of a wanton smear campaign.

But it was hard. There was so little time, so many phone machines, so much doubt. Parents don't take chances with their children, she knew. When the first call had come in that morning, from Elana Auerbach, whose little girl had clung to Emily for weeks after starting preschool, Emily's stomach leaped into her throat. Heart pounding, she had made Elana read her the article. Elana was a second soprano in the Rockton Community College choir, in which Emily also sang. They were friends, or at least friendly. She read in a clear voice words that were like nails in Emily's flesh. The only part she heard clearly was the beginning:

> The Vanatee County District Attorney's Office is investigating a pair of child-abuse allegations against staff members at the Alphabet Soup preschool, according to sources with personal knowledge of the inquiry.

Elana, thank God, understood when Emily explained and distrusted the police anyway, a feeling that for a fleeting instant Emily thought might be so widespread in Webster that other parents would behave similarly. Indeed, many of the mothers, and the fathers dispatched by the mothers, picked up their children sheepishly, even apologetically. Many of them had known Emily and her husband for years, saw them socially, had entrusted one or two prior children to their care. The children didn't want to leave. Jomo and Patrice tried to hide and threw toys at their mother, who seemed on the verge of tears. Emily and Julie had to round them up, hold them for a minute, assure them they would be back.

"I love you, Julie," said Patrice. "Will you save me some graham crackers?"

"Here," said Julie, dashing for the tin. On the wall above it was a giant cutout of Humpty Dumpty. "Here's one for each of you. For later, OK?"

Emily knew at that moment that, despite all her best efforts, the school would have to close. She did not admit this to herself except for the barest instant, when the shadow of this grim thought flashed across her consciousness like the silhouette of a vulture. She knew she must ignore this shadow and, despite everything, went through the motions of determination that she expected of herself. She had always assumed the worst in life, and she did so now, hoping that, as usual, the sheer mundaneness of reality would prove her most pessimistic assumptions outlandish.

She had some reason to hope. What Emily did not guess at first was the extent to which the parents were motivated to rationalize the newspaper story. The truth was that they needed Alphabet Soup, indeed depended upon it, and wanted desperately to believe that it was a good place for their children. In most cases, it was the *only* place, unless someone was going to stay home from work, and hardly anyone considered that an option.

Meanwhile, Emily was grateful that the day was hectic, because this distracted her from considering, in all its fullness, that her husband and partner in the school had been accused in print before the entire town of being a child molester. Toward evening, as parents came to pick up their children, she could see them searching her face—for signs of what, it was hard to say. Perversity? Gratitude? Strength? Despair?

Somehow the day went by, and at the end, after crying silently in her office, she slipped out the back door and drove slowly home. She found Frank in the living room, sitting in the dark listening to something dire.

"What is that?" she asked.

"The music? Schubert."

"Is it the Polish guy you love so much?"

"Horszowski. Yup. If only he'd played cards like he played piano. It's the C Minor Sonata."

She sniffed his glass.

"Bourbon?"

"The good one I save for special occasions. How often do I get accused of child abuse?"

"Let me get a glass."

"Was it really that bad today?"

Emily shook her head unconvincingly. "Can't I just have a little of your special bourbon if I want to?"

"Was I bogarting the bourbon?" He poured. "That's what the guys would say in the navy. 'Don't bogart that joint, man.'"

"We only lost a few kids, but I spent the whole day explaining." She took a sip, enjoying the ice against her lips. "That's what life is going to be like around here for a while, isn't it? We'll spend all our time explaining. Even after this is all blown over. Even then, the stain won't be washed away."

"I'm so sorry, Em. I've disgraced you again. I'm so ashamed of that."

"Oh, hush. You made a little mistake. This isn't your fault."

"It's never my fault, and it's always my fault. As you said, even when this thing blows over, there'll be a cloud. Maybe we should think about leaving Webster. Selling the damned school and leaving."

"And go where?"

"Wherever. What difference does it make? Where we'll be unknown and free."

"Maybe," Emily said, trying to seem intrigued. She was so exhausted she felt faint.

"Em, if you don't want me around, I'll understand that."

"I'll always want you around." She took his arm, and her spirits rose on the strength of her own devotion. "Always. Isn't it obvious that if I haven't dumped you by now I'm not going to? After the bookies and the loan sharks. And Anja. I'm a barnacle. What can I say?"

They considered going out to dinner, not just because neither had the energy to cook, but as a show of transcendence that would let everybody know the charges were preposterous. But Emily had been telling people he was out of town, and neither of them really wanted to go anyway. They weren't much hungry, so they just ate some cheese and crackers. Afterward her husband said he was going for a walk and might be a while.

. . .

Without particularly setting out for it, Frank headed in the direction of Annette's house. In the cold he walked quickly, his footfalls marked by the rhythmic crunch of snow and his breath hovering before him like steam from the anger he felt boiling inside. There were a few snow-encrusted cars gliding up and down the streets, some of them looking torn as if by archaeologists from a glacier, but he could see from the blue flicker of the televisions in most of the living rooms that otherwise Webster was hunkered down in the nightly postprandial coma that preceded bed.

He turned onto a little street of decrepit older homes, dowagers that in some earlier day were where the upper crust lived but that now served to house gangs of college students. He took this lane, the herringbone pattern of the brick sidewalks undulant with roots under the snow, to Main Street, which in this outlying part of Webster was the setting for even grander old homes, and then turned to walk in the opposite direction from downtown.

He walked with care on the icy, narrow sidewalk until he reached the little street that led to Annette's house, unaware of the large, dark car that cruised past twice during his approach. Walking toward the porch, he was stopped by the sound of somebody crying. He went around quietly to the back door, looking in the windows but seeing nothing amiss. Finally he reached the back door and knocked. Out of nowhere, Annette flung the door open. Later he would remember the shiny copper bottoms of the pots hanging on the rack behind her, the homely array of oils and herbs next to the stove, the plastic-looking ivy in a pot near the window. Such order. Such bliss.

"Ray's told the police you molested Andy." She looked frantic. "He says Andy told him all the things you did, how you threatened him if he ever told anybody. He's gone to the police, Frank."

"How remarkable," Frank said in genuine wonder. "Where is this abuse supposed to have occurred?"

"Here. Ray says it was right here!"

"But I've never been here when you've had Andy."

"That's not what Ray told the cops."

"And what does Andy say? Have you spoken to him?"

"They won't let me! Frank, they won't let me speak to my son! They're saying I'm a bad mother, I let a married man come into the house and molest him. I can't believe this is happening."

Frank wasn't sure what to say, except to marvel at the awfulness of what had arisen, the amazing, insane wrongheadedness of it, and so, at a loss, he sat down and asked if he might have a drink.

"You can't stay here," Annette said. "You can't come here anymore. I can't take any more chances. Do you understand? These lies are more dangerous than Ray ever was."

He took her red hands in his own and tried to kiss them.

"Don't," she said. "I'm afraid I'm gonna lose my boy, Frank."

As she dissolved into tears, he took her into his arms. "I'm sorry, Annie," he said. "I'll do whatever will help."

On the way home, the walk seemed more difficult, more dangerous, the traffic faster, and his mind raced with the possibilities arising from the information he had just received. Some part of him felt as if he'd got away with something; with no effort at all, he was extricated at last from an inconvenient affair. Yet he now found himself accused of the same ludicrous crime from a wholly new quarter, by a child who didn't even attend Alphabet Soup, and for reasons that could destroy his marriage. He wasn't sure how to proceed on the news he'd just been given. He couldn't very well tell Emily. Could he even tell their lawyer? Should he? What proof could there be of these preposterous allegations? There were no witnesses, no tapes, no photos, no evidence of any kind, *since nothing at all had happened.* His main fears had to do with the scandal and the effect it would have on Emily. Groping for the reassuring bottom presented by the worst possible case, he fleetingly considered that the destruction of his marriage could prove fatal to his defense, but he still couldn't imagine needing to provide one. Once everyone saw things clearly, the whole ugly business would become just a bad memory.

Days passed during which he kept to himself the news that Annette's ex-husband was sponsoring allegations against him. He slept little during this time, although not much less than usual, and found that the growing intimacy he had enjoyed with his wife of late was undermined by the poisonous information he withheld from her. He tried to tell her, again and again, but finally let himself off the hook by deciding that perhaps there would be no need. Perhaps the allegations, so preposterous on their face, would collapse of their own accord.

Emily had asked him to take some time off, and he avoided going out, spending his days instead around the house, reading Milton, Anne Bradstreet, *The Pilgrim's Progress,* and other old favorites nobody looked at anymore. Under normal circumstances he took pleasure in holding himself apart from the quotidian whirl of life in Webster, ignoring the latest songs and dances and television shows like bad weather that would surely pass. He tried now to draw on the satisfaction of his customary pose. What would it be like, he wondered, to live this way all this time? It's what must happen to old men, why they come to seem crotchety and even cynical. They've seen it all come and go, know it won't amount to anything, and haven't any way to manifest themselves or their experience on the young, who must make the same mistakes all over again. The Josephs' house was from roughly 1920, with high ceilings and generous proportions, and Frank wandered these gracious rooms in his stocking feet, pretending to be a housecat and not minding the role after all, napping and reading and snacking in the luxurious quiet and privacy of a clean, empty home.

When the postal carrier came, Frank laid aside his practice of not opening mail, for it seemed only fair that he should take on some of the burdens he normally left to his wife—just as he had done with the laundry. But the mail was a sensitive subject. There had been a time when he did everything in his power to intercept it, like an unruly schoolboy hoping to snag a teacher's communication, and so leaving it for Emily was part of the reforms that had made it possible for them to stay together.

But nowadays he opened the mail, paying the bills by check with the fountain pen he loved to use at Emily's sunny writing table and keeping the envelopes with the Christmas cards in case she might want the return address. Would they send cards under the circumstances? Could they afford not to? Every step, it seemed, must be weighed in light of whether it implied innocence or guilt, as if, in an adaptation of medieval practice, he should be subject to trial by social obligation.

He even read some of the closely printed Christmas letters that poured in. He was startled at the volume of these. A letter from an old school friend of Emily's reported that she had at last broken up with her boyfriend of three years, that she should have done this long ago, she now realized, and that that her mother had finally married the man with whom she had been living. Another, from Emily's cousin in Pittsburgh, reported that her oldest had taken a marvelous trip to Washington with the school chess club and that they had had to put the dog to sleep after a tumor was discovered in his abdomen. Should he and Emily send a holiday letter on green paper describing how they were being investigated for pederasty? A letter from Julie, Frank's favorite among the teachers (despite his dalliance with Annette), reported that she was still at Alphabet Soup and still loving it, and that she had taken up the guitar again with a vengeance, hoping at last to make her playing passable. Women are life's grand self-improvers, Frank noted, as well as its communicators. The letter went on: "Ariel, meanwhile, continues to thrive, its members enriching one another's spiritual lives and looking forward to another year of ever-deeper connection with the Earth and the Goddess. Blessed be." Ariel? What could she be talking about? A club of some kind? It was comforting to receive these epistles from normality, comforting to think there was a humdrum everyday world from which to dissent in his quiet way, and so he cherished these letters with their decorative paper and smiling snapshots, cherished the arched-eyebrow tone taken toward the young and the enthusiasm for reporting the pointless exertions of one and all in pursuit of happiness.

Yet he worried about what Annette's former husband might be brewing. Frank should have punched him when he'd had the chance; at least then the record would show a clear-cut motive for vengeance aside from the affair. He was nervous about appearing in public, but he needed to see his attorney, needed to air somehow the terrible lies that had sprung like offspring from his own glum deceptions, and so he drove to Bob Varity's office on the edge of town, where he found a parking space behind the nondescript brick building that Varity shared with a CPA, a child psychologist, and a couple of other professional hand-holders.

"Bob, I need to tell you about something," Frank began and noticed at once that Varity looked different than usual. Normally so easy to read, the lawyer wore now a poker face, and with a shiver Frank realized that this might be more serious than he had assumed.

"I think there's going to be another allegation against me," he continued.

"More than one, actually," said Varity.

"You—you know about this?"

"I know that three other kids have come forward claiming they were sexually abused at Alphabet Soup."

"Three?! At the school?"

"From the school, I mean. The abuse supposedly occurred there and elsewhere. You're a major recurring theme in these tales, but Pearl is featured as a sort of ringleader, in keeping with the well-known stereotype of grandmothers as child-abusing monsters." Varity rubbed his face unhappily. "I've been a lawyer for a long time, Frank, and I want to tell you, this is really strange."

"Jesus Christ. I came here to tell you that I did something extremely stupid, but now I don't even know if it matters. Do you know Annette Martini, one of our teachers?"

"To say hello. Josh has mentioned her, says she's real nice."

Annette's identity established in this way through Varity's son, Frank took a deep breath and told the whole story.

"Does Emily know?" Varity asked, without missing a beat.

"Does Emily know," Frank repeated thoughtfully, as if the question posed an interesting semantic problem.

"Have you told her?" Varity asked helpfully.

"No. I wanted to tell her, but I haven't been able. I thought maybe I mightn't have to. Shit, I wasn't sure what to do. Mainly I've just stayed around the house and worried. I've thought of getting away for a while, maybe going to the Caribbean or something. Get away from this god-awful cold."

"I wouldn't go far right now, Frank. Stick around. Wait'll we clear all this up."

Frank wanted to ask: *Are you kidding? Am I about to be arrested?* But he felt that this would be a breach of some unspoken compact that had arisen between them, some crucial etiquette that permitted discussion and kept violence and hysteria at bay.

"Would it help if I told the police about this business with Annette? You know, volunteered? I do want to cooperate. I mean, for Chrissake, what's a little philandering in Webster? I've got nothing to hide except for what's legal."

"It's the District Attorney's Office, not the police." Varity said. "And from the sound of it, they already know. But I'll talk to them, let them know there's another side to all this."

"And what about these new allegations? I mean aside from Annette's ex-husband."

"I don't know a lot yet. I just know they're weird. All the stuff you've heard before, only more so. Lots of urine, feces, bodily orifices, nakedness, threats, spooky dances. They make it sound almost ritualized. Photo sessions too. Supposedly you all photographed naked kids over there every day."

Outside you could hear the traffic passing. The road sounded wet. There were golf trophies and unreadable plaques at the top of Varity's bookshelves.

"Bob, where is this going? Can't everybody see how crazy this is? The other day Em took a call from a real estate agent. He wanted to know if we had considered 'disposing of' the school property—as if we were about to pack up our tents and sneak off into the night. Over what? Where are all those children going to end up, if not at Alphabet Soup?"

"The silver lining, if you could call it that, is that the allegations get stranger and stranger, and I'm beginning to get a sense of 'give a man enough rope' in this whole thing. It's a virus that people catch from one another. I'm hoping they get sick for a while and then get better."

"So you're thinking it will pass."

"I'm hoping it will pass. But I don't know what's going to happen. My crystal ball is cloudy, Frank. I really don't know."

When Frank was gone, Bob Varity went out into the waiting room he shared with the accountant and was relieved to find there was still some coffee in the pot. He had piles of work on his desk, but instead of plunging in when he returned, he stared out the window, relishing the heat of his drink, which warmed him inside even as he felt it tighten his stomach with every gulp. The last thing he wanted to do was go over the depositions of the poor devils some of his clients were suing. Oh, they weren't all poor devils. Plenty were assholes, of course. Just like Varity's clients. He represented people injured by doctors, victims of contractor rip-offs, now and then even the wrongly accused. But mostly he fattened himself by swimming through the same vast tide of divorce, criminal recidivism, and trumped-up personal injury on which he and his fellow attorneys fed like whales sifting the ocean for plankton. There were hoods bent on avoiding jail, philandering fathers trying to weasel out of child support, anxious bankrupts happy to repudiate their debts. The thickest file on his desk was the result of a suit by an alcoholic, drug-addicted homeless man who fell asleep in a miasma of intoxicants on the tracks of the old Vanatee & Kesiwick Railroad, which were still used to haul freight. A locomotive neatly amputated his right hand just above the wrist, and Varity had won him $4.3 million. The case was on appeal, of course, but the victory made a settlement likely, and it would be a rich one. There were other such cases. There was the man who, clearing out his gutters, left a ladder standing next to his house while he went inside for supper. Unaware what an attractive nuisance a ladder can be in the eyes of children and lawyers, the man found himself legally responsible for the broken leg suffered by a neighborhood teenager who, Varity felt sure, had climbed the ladder to rob the place.

These were the cases he took. The ones he turned away were even more depressing. The people of Webster, it now seemed, expected compensation for all of life's misfortunes. They wanted the courts to solve all their differences. Divorce cases could be like annuities for him, with warring couples fighting over money, houses, children, far-off job opportunities and just sheer vengeance. What a way to embark on middle age, he thought, sipping coffee sourly—chasing ambulances, calculating the value of fuel oil in the heating tank at house closings, helping people allocate and reallocate their meager belongings among their ungrateful descendants. Like all the other fathers he knew, he was divorced and only dimly aware of what his son did and thought aside from wishing that mom and dad could be reunited. But his son loved school, that much he knew.

Now, out of the blue, the people who ran the place were accused of sexually abusing three- and four-year-olds. Varity had been shocked when the police first questioned Frank and horrified that Terry Mathers would think to dignify the whole nasty business with a story based entirely on allegations the paper itself had no chance to assess. But Varity was a political animal and accustomed to the ways of newspapers. He imagined taking Cal Hawthorne's job some day and worried now that too many people were motivated to make a mountain out of this particular molehill. Nor did he overlook the chance that it might pile up right on top of him. Certainly he was unlikely to endear himself to voters by defending people seen as child molesters, although he decided on the spot that he wouldn't let this influence him. He wouldn't have been able to stand thinking of himself that way. Hawthorne, on the other hand, was concerned enough about re-election that he might very well pursue the Alphabet Soup case, even if the allegations weren't credible—especially, perhaps, because his chief opponent might well be Varity, whom he might try to tar as a defender of child abusers and vanquish at trial. And there might be pressure to press the case. People saw child molesters behind every bush these days. You couldn't give a kid an apple at Halloween without arousing fears of hidden razors or cyanide poisoning. Varity also understood Terry. He knew that, like most journalists, his friend was always eager for a big story, an eagerness compounded in this case by Terry's disdain for the mundane facts of life in a place like Webster—and his great need to prove something to himself. As for Lucille, he knew that vengeance was just the spark to ignite the flammable mix of alcohol, envy, and mental instability that were her hallmarks. Under normal circumstances, it was hard to believe she was a danger to anybody but herself. That had changed now.

The question was, what would happen next? Varity didn't believe Hawthorne had any real basis for anything like a criminal case, but the quiet was scary, and he feared it masked the descent of a giant snowball that would soon become an avalanche. Who knew, maybe Frank was guilty. Why had Emily married this man? Why did they stay married?

No, he could begin to see now. He was no longer eaten up with jealousy and infatuation. The flame in the torch he carried had been turned down long ago, and he could see more clearly by its dimmer light. There was something about Frank, some wrecked grandeur he could see only now that he was no longer hopeful about Emily. He too would stand by Frank; he knew that. Acting on an impulse, he called Terry. It was time to fight back, to do something while there was still time to counteract the craziness. He figured they could play some ball, drink some beer, and hash this out. He'd make him see how preposterous all this was on its face.

"I'm g-glad you called, Bob. I need to run something else by you." Terry sounded suspiciously cool. "Evidently there are some more allegations."

When he got as much out of Terry as he could about the nature of the accusations and where they came from, Varity dismissed them all as ridiculous, the product of "just the kind of publicity and leaks that made it so tough to defend an innocent person's reputation around here." But behind the bluster, he felt nauseated. Always afflicted with a sensitive stomach, he spent the next few days feeling as if he had imbibed a gallon of battery acid, his innards roiling as he waited for the next edition of the *Chronicle* to come out. He sensed that the rest of the town was similarly on edge, and although people still talked about Krieger's (for who wanted to discuss child abuse allegations in public?), it was clear there was something more on their minds. It all seemed incredible, a bad dream, until the next issue of the *Chronicle* carried a banner headline reporting that at least five children had now "come forward with disclosures" of abuse at Alphabet Soup. *Disclosures?* According to the story, authorities were "assisting" the children by permitting them to describe what happened with dolls and stories, which might account for the metaphorical nature of some of the allegations. Indeed, Alphabet Soup staff members were now accused of making children watch while the teachers impaled babies on barbecue sticks and ate them, burying the bones in the backyard. The allegations had spread beyond Frank, Emily, and Pearl as well. Varity read all this in disbelief. Even more upsetting was the editorial Terry had written to go with the stories. He accused the district attorney of dragging his feet, of holding back the investigation. "Does the county's top cop think innocent children make up stories about being abused by the powerful and intimidating people in whose care they are entrusted daily? Believe the children, Mr. Hawthorne. Believe the children."

It got worse. Three days later, his own little boy still among the dwindling band of children brought daily to Alphabet Soup, Varity got a call from another lawyer with whom he sometimes played racquetball. This man and, evidently, all the other Alphabet Soup parents had received letters from the police about possible sex abuse at the preschool. One of the letters had arrived at the lawyer's home, and his wife had faxed it to him. He in turn faxed it to Varity, who could only assume that his own letter was sitting in the mailbox out in front of his house. He felt his head pounding as he held the greasy fax paper in his hands.

> The Webster Police Dept. has received allegations of child abuse against an employee or employees of the Alphabet Soup Preschool. To fully investigate these charges, we need the cooperation of parents whose children attend the school. We are requesting that all parents examine their children, question them about their activities at the school, and report any concerns to the Department or to the county's new Child Intervention Services Agency. Your cooperation is appreciated.

Errol Jones could feel his dislike for his boss growing as the Alphabet Soup disclosures mounted. Hawthorne's skepticism was almost perverse—disbelieving credible witnesses, discounting any incriminating factors in the suspects' backgrounds, and generally flaunting his doubts before the assembled believers as if faith in the word of children was the sign of a weak mind. There was a sense of relish in this that Errol resented, and so the more dubious his superior seemed, the harder Errol worked to make the case.

"There's a guy I want you to meet," Errol said. "I think you need to hear this with your own ears. He's right outside, it'll just take a minute."

Errol buzzed, and Detective Jepson appeared with a skinny older man in a baggy tan corduroy jacket, blue shirt, and black trousers. His hair, plastered down in a valiant application of Vitalis, stuck out on the sides as if in protest. The back of his neck and hands looked like dried leather, and his walk was shambling. Errol noticed Hawthorne looking at the man's shoes, which screamed *new* and *cheap* to anyone who would listen.

"Cal, this is Gabriel Demming. Mr. Demming, District Attorney Hawthorne."

chapter ELEVEN

The *Webster Chronicle*'s Christmas party—traditionally attended by everyone who was anyone in Webster—this year was fun for all but the couple who threw it. Abigail stood with Melissa Faircloth and Ariadne Tidwell, listening unhappily as Alfred Blake complained about his boyfriend troubles. The other two women wore looks of absorption.

"I'm not sure what he's up to," Alfred said, in a throwing-up-of-hands voice. "Philip's always been very private, OK? He stays within himself. But now I'm really getting suspicious. He's finding too many reasons to go to Boston."

"Doesn't he ever invite you along?" Ariadne asked, squinting. She was his favorite foil, clueless in all things but love. "Or maybe you need to invite yourself."

"He doesn't, and I don't push it. I know he needs a certain amount of space."

The women looked at each other.

"I don't know, Alfred," Ariadne said. Abigail, embarrassed at the turn things were taking, emptied her drink. Melissa finally asked, "Have you tried talking to him about it?"

"Look, I know where this is going," Alfred said. "He's talked about moving out, which is fine with me. Just fine. What the heck, he's just so good-looking I figure I'll hang in while I can. After that, I don't know. It's so hard to meet people around here."

"It can't really be hard for you, can it?" Melissa asked, meaning to offer a compliment. "There are bright men at the colleges and so forth."

"Hairy legs only help if you're a dyke," he lamented. "Webster is a lesbian town; everybody knows that. It's not just Bradfield College, either; they go to Web State because of it. A gay guy can't get laid around here for love or money. Philip was such a catch, even if he is kind of a bore when he gets going on Lewis Mumford."

Charles Krieger arrived at that moment as if on cue, entering magisterially, his face alight with expectation, and Terry, cornered by the director of the YMCA, had to stand still while the merchant prince approached wearing his carnivorous smile.

"Well, hello!" Krieger said, gripping Terry's bicep and interrupting the YMCA director mid-sentence. "Great party! Great paper!"

"Whaddya say, Charlie. You know"—Terry blanked for just an instant, then recovered—"Gwendolyn Hanker, don't you? Who's doing such a grand job over at the Y?"

"As a matter of fact, I don't believe I've had the pleasure," he said grandly, beaming at her as if she were Catherine Deneuve. "I'll have to get over there one of these days. We're practically neighbors after all."

"You should become a regular," Hanker urged. "Fitness is so important, and you just can't beat the range of our offerings."

"Well you know I do get to the Club fairly often, play a lot of tennis and so forth—do you have tennis?"

"No, I'm afraid—"

"But a lot of my employees swear by the Y, so I know the kind of job you must be doing."

"Why not give them some of Rothwax's money?" Terry asked. "Help 'em spruce up the place."

"Exactly what I was thinking," Krieger said. He glanced at the glass in Terry's hand. The fluent speech and undisguised needling were signs he'd had a few. "Now isn't that amazing? Tell you what, Ms. Wanker—"

"It's *Hanker.*"

"—Ms. Hanker, I'm sorry. Listen, call my secretary, will you, and we'll set something up. I'd really like to look around the place, see what I can do to help."

Terry rolled his eyes.

"Oh, that would be just wonderful," Gwendolyn said.

"Don't thank me; it's good for business. The kind of people you're getting nowadays are just the kind we want in our store. Excuse me now," he said, looking pointedly at Abigail. "There's really somebody I have to talk to."

Terry took a large gulp from his drink and looked away. Gwendolyn began talking about how excited she was at last to be meeting Krieger, whose support she had attempted to enlist almost from the day she had arrived in town, but Terry wasn't listening. Behind her he could see Delia Kornfeld. Terry liked Delia; she had boyish short hair and always wore a pantsuit, with an open-necked shirt and colorful scarf, but even in this getup she was ineffably feminine. Now she was giving Margaret O'Hanlon her side of her latest dispute with the university, which Margaret had read about in the *Chronicle.* It was over the granting of college credit for life experience. Web State was big on this, but there was growing dissent from the practice, and one case in particular, a student advocated by Delia, had crystallized the opposition.

"It's typical of the kind of thinking you get in any administration," she said. "How can you come up with a more significant aspect of life experience for credit than 'Maternal Thinking and Practice'? I mean, c'mon. It's only the single most important topic in human history. But these guys just don't get it."

"Maternal Thinking and—you mean motherhood?" Margaret asked, eyebrows aloft.

"Exactly. With all that that entails."

"But how can you give credit for—for having a baby? I had four. I should put in for a Ph.D."

"But it's not just for having a baby, or even for raising one. It's for the learning that's involved. The applicant in this case wrote a twenty-page essay outlining the hard-won insights she's gained in all her years of motherhood and felt she knew something about the subject because her son grew up and got a job, didn't go to jail and so forth, even though his father was a dirtball who walked out while she was pregnant."

"—and what I'm really hoping is that Mr. Krieger can be persuaded to rebuild our pool for us. Terry? So that's why I'm asking whether he likes to swim."

With a start, he realized that Gwendolyn was asking him a question.

"Like a shark," Terry said. "In high school, swimming was his thing. I played ball; he swam. It was a great way to avoid one another."

Gwendolyn prattled on, and the editor of the *Webster Chronicle,* wishing someone would rescue him now that his wife wouldn't, scanned the room while nodding. They were all here, he noted sourly: the tweedy graybeards from the various faculties, their smug-looking young nemeses in black and gray, ready to pounce on improper speech, Mayor Loquendi, whispering into the ear of the library director. That was supposed to be over, yet they looked awfully chummy. Others no doubt had noticed the great distance between the editor and the publisher during the party. Terry and Abigail, as if by unspoken agreement, always seemed to be working opposite ends of the room.

Soon enough Terry retreated to his glass-walled cloister, where he closed the door against the noise. The frantic materialism of the season made him cynical, but despite his annual disdain for all the shopping and stress, this year more than ever he felt left out of all the fuss. Diana was off with relatives, and Phoebe was with her father in California. He was glad the *Chronicle* was so huge, as it typically was this time of year; filling its many extra pages helped fill his time and kept him from feeling sorry for himself.

At home that night in his rented digs, with their orange plaid sofas and pumpernickel-colored carpets, Terry popped open a beer and carefully rolled a joint, prolonging the delicious anticipation with his fastidiousness. The spicy weed smelled somehow like sex and made him think of Diana. For dinner, he made himself a couple of peanut butter sandwiches using a copy of *Gourmet* magazine as a plate. With his food he drank a quart of cold milk straight from the carton, which featured a missing child on one side. He remembered making buses out of these cartons in first grade, when milk containers had flat tops instead of gabled roofs (and were usually bottles anyway). The marijuana took the edge off his terrible apartment, but still he felt lonely, and so, glancing at the clock to see if it was too late, he dialed his father. Maury was having a hard time of it; he had slept with one of his producers and his third wife had filed for divorce. It was becoming messy, had made a couple of the tabloids. He'd had to intercede with a friend to kill an item in *People* magazine. Calling his father now afforded Terry a chance to season the pain of impoverishment and exile with harmless schadenfreude purchased cheaply for mere sympathy.

"I'm glad you called," Maury said, his late-night voice throaty and intimate. "Listen, if anybody asks you about that $200,000 I loaned you, tell 'em they're mistaken."

"M-Mistaken?"

"There was no loan. It was a gift! I want to keep it out of her hands, understand? She's gonna take me to the cleaners if she can, shrink my balls down to the size of marbles, and I want to keep as much of that stuff away from her as I can. What she doesn't know she can't get a chunk of."

"G-G-Gift?! Dad, really, I c-can't accept—"

"It's not *really* a gift." Maury sounded impatient. "That's only for public consumption, only so there'll be a little something left when she and her lawyers get done fighting over the carcass. I wish it *could* be a gift, but I'm afraid I'm gonna need it back. Badly, in fact."

"Oh." Terry did not like the sound of this. "Sure, of course."

"It's no big deal. We told the bank it was a gift anyway, remember? So it would seem you and Abigail had more equity."

Terry thought of his father's youth, before the war, when he was an eager little Communist like all the other bright and earnest young Jews of the period, who smoked a lot and slept around and conducted their fervent doctrinal disputes in publications long since shouldered into obscurity by the elephantine culture whose downfall they'd so smugly foretold. Maury had somehow survived the fifties, although he'd had to become an editor for a while and keep his name out of the paper. He'd never named names, God bless him. "Not because they didn't deserve naming," he said later. "But because I didn't like anybody pushing me around. That's what Uncle Sam was doing in those days. Who the fuck were they to ask about people's beliefs?" The faith they had had! Terry had aspired to such faith in the sixties, inspired by the civil rights movement and the war. Yet even then his faith had never seemed as powerful or pure as the Communism of the fathers. Theirs was a religion. "We were like the Orthodox," Maury had said once. "Like the Hasidim, almost. We wanted to sanctify the world, to ennoble everyday acts. Making spark plugs would be consecrated by the collective nature of ownership. Working with your hands, which none of us did except to type, was going to be a sacrament." Now the idea was to shelter assets from his estranged wife's lawyers.

"A gift, that's right," Terry said now. "We can stick to that story."

"Take my advice, stick with Abigail too. I never should have left your mother, I admit that now. What a jerk I was. I followed my dick and look where it got me. I'm grappling with a vengeful woman who can't be happy and doesn't want anybody else to be either. She wants every penny."

"C'mon, Dad, you've still got plenty. What about that property you've got up here in Webster?"

"There are some very serious environmental problems, as it turns out. That land may be unbuildable. I made a lot of ill-advised real estate investments over the years, as well as some ill-advised marriages. Between the two of them, your old man's living paycheck to paycheck. Aside from my apartment, my biggest asset is my clothes."

"I h-h-had no idea it was that bad."

"You can't imagine the legal bills," Maury fretted into the phone. "We had a limited partnership in Arizona—I'll tell you about it one of these days. My manager got me into it as the general; he was gonna take care of everything and I was gonna make a bundle, avoid taxes, the whole nine yards. What a joke. So believe me, it's a good thing you borrowed that two hundred grand, 'cause I'd have lost it by now. And it's a good thing you're gonna pay it back soon, once I get all this crap settled."

"I intend to pay it back, absolutely, but—"

"I know what you're gonna say. How can you pay me and not have it show up in my account, right? Smart boy. I'll give you the name of an off-shore bank."

"D-D-Dad, you're kidding."

"You can wire the money when the time comes. I know it's hard to believe, but this is what I'm reduced to. Careful where that dick of yours leads you, son. Believe me."

Terry recalled flirting with his father's latest soon-to-be ex-wife the last time they had been together, at a hugely expensive house Maury had bought for her on Nantucket (a house she was in the process of acquiring for herself by means of divorce). Maury made a lot of money, and no doubt this was one of his attractions to such a woman. Why not? Poverty was bad enough; Lord knew there was no need to marry it.

"She did seem awfully concerned about money," Terry said. "Always r-r-redecorating, always the f-fanciest restaurants and clothes."

"That woman's charge bills would make your eyes pop," Maury said, glad to have an opening. "Twenty, thirty thousand a month just in department stores, restaurants, first-class travel. My God, amounts that I never saw in a year when I was a young kid."

It crossed Terry's mind that his father's misadventures were depleting his estate. And if he claimed the money were a gift, wouldn't he owe taxes on it? Surely it wouldn't come to this.

"M-maybe you're r-right about Abigail," he said.

"Of course I'm right."

"She's just—I don't know, just s-s-such a dutiful little girl sometimes. So insipid."

"Please don't say that. I used to think the same thing about your mother, and it was ridiculous. We mistake virtue for dullness. You think heaven is bad; try hell. Really, it was just a matter of my wanting other women."

"But she is a bit of a pill, no?"

"So what are you, flawless? Am I Superman or something? Don't make the same mistake I did." Maury sighed heavily, as if even he knew what an old and scratchy recording this was. He sang the praises of Terry's mother after every romantic fiasco, and changed his tune whenever the next young woman put the song back into him. "So what's happening at the paper, Terry? And how's business? Or is that Abigail's department?"

It is Abigail's department, Terry thought when his father was off the phone. Abigail, of whom he heard little and saw less. And Phoebe! He missed her too. Sighing, he rolled another joint. What a failure he was. An aging, impoverished pothead condemned to chronicle the life of a fly-speck town blessed with good coffee and a surfeit of ethnic restaurants. A certain anesthetized clarity came over him thanks to the marijuana. It was useful. You could face the Gorgon this way and not turn to stone. It was practically the only way to get a good look.

It helped at such times to do some palpable good, and he spent Saturday with Floyd Albertson, working on a decrepit old house that Albertson's church was renovating for a needy family.

"Six kids. Can you believe it?" Albertson said, smiling.

"In this town? No."

Then the whine of the saw blade. They were laying a subfloor, whole sheets of plywood because neither of them liked the emissions from particle board or the way it acted when it got wet. It was nice to build something again. Terry had learned this kind of work from his maternal grandfather, one of those men for whom it was a sin not to do these jobs for yourself. He had made up projects, on his farm outside of town, just to keep his grandson occupied. "Idle hands," he used to say, handing Terry a hammer. Now the tools were Albertson's.

"So what do you think you're doing?" the reverend asked, and Terry looked at the nail gun in his hand.

"What? Am I forgetting something?"

"Your wife. Your marriage. Your family. That's all you're forgetting."

There was no beer when you worked with Albertson, although it was just as well around these power tools.

"Floyd. Are we doing a subfloor?"

Terry turned and quickly nailed down a sheet. Blam! Blam! Blam! Wanting to forestall conversation, he used more nails than he needed to.

"What we're doing is damage to the foundation."

"Floyd, if I wanted metaphor, I'd be home on the sofa reading poetry. You're confusing me now. You'll tell me I'm missing the floor joists, and I won't know whether you mean here or at home."

Albertson had a sort of unsmiling laugh, just a tight-lipped grimace, really, so you couldn't always tell when he was making fun of you.

"You haven't answered my question."

"Which was?" Terry was wrestling a whole sheet from the pile, the reverend pointedly failing to assist.

"What do you think you're doing? With Abigail, I mean? Why are you playing games with a good woman?"

"Are you going to help me here?" Terry asked, hiding behind a sheet of wood.

"I'm trying to help you."

"I'm an atheist, Reverend," Terry said. "You g-got no standing with me. Grab hold of this plywood."

On Sundays Marty was his, and they spent the days at the playground, the pizza parlor, watching action pictures at the Bijou Quadraplex, and in other manly pursuits. The two of them cherished this time, although it was hard work keeping the sadness at bay. On this rainy morning, they found themselves, with Marty's nervous friend Kent, at Imagination Place, a kind of indoor playground at the mall where, for $3 each, children could tumble around in a sea of rubber balls, climb various obstacles, slide, hide out, and generally carry on without regard to the elements, all in an environment as thickly padded as a Victorian armchair. The place made money selling junk food. Terry disapproved of IP, as it was known, but had to acknowledge that it was a godsend on a day like this. The place was crowded with energetic children and sluggish-looking parents, the latter hovering along the walls drinking coffee and interceding when necessary. Terry joined this motley crowd, their pudgy physiques stuffed into sweatshirts and acid-washed jeans, and sat back to watch Marty solemnly dash around with the others, brow furrowed as he concentrated on looking like a big boy for his father. He and Kent were playing a game on the bridge between two slides, something about fleeing the aliens, reaching Plasma Four. Kent was quiet but animated. He was a cute kid, half-Korean, and Marty seemed to appreciate the gravity he brought to play.

It was then Terry noticed the girl. She was nine, maybe ten, and he caught himself looking longer than seemed right. What was it about her? He looked away and then found her again as she pranced from place to place, running on her toes, her calves lined with slender muscle, athletically pulling herself up and around the jungle gym. Her taut midriff peeked out from between a skimpy stretch top and tiny denim shorts—IP regulars knew the place would be stuffy—and her great intensity made her stand out from the pack of girls she'd come with, girls she easily eclipsed and ordered about. She frowned gorgeously at them now, wisps of brown hair working loose from her ponytail, which swept from side to side behind her as she dashed about, lips parted slightly. Terry smiled, but sheepishly, for it had begun to dawn that what held his gaze was desire. His interest was not fatherly but sexual—and deaf to all the taboos it violated. He turned away but couldn't make himself not want to look.

We're all just fine," Abigail said into the telephone days later. Phoebe, hearing this, sighed disgustedly and left the kitchen, where the one-sided conversation followed her more faintly. "Terry's fine too. We're all great."

There was a pause and then, "I think he's at the office. He's been putting in some awfully long hours lately. Really, we're fine."

Phoebe heard her mother saying good-bye and waited for her to come out, but it was soon clear enough that she wouldn't, and so the discussion would have to happen in the kitchen. With her coat on, about to leave, she went in.

"Mom, this is sick. When you are gonna tell Mom-Mom that Terry's moved out?"

"In my own good time," Abigail said, pretending to look for something in the refrigerator. Phoebe started to say something else when her mother turned to face her.

"In my own good time! I've got my hands full right now and I really don't need any family therapy from you at this particular moment."

"Well, get it somewhere!" Phoebe said and stalked out. She had half a mind to call her grandmother back and tell her everything. It was such an insufferable charade, insulting even, to let the poor woman sit up there in Toronto believing they were a happy family. She was shopping for presents for a son-in-law who'd deserted them all.

She turned around to see her mother right behind her.

"The reason is that this is not finished," her mother said. "Do you understand? This isn't like your father and me, a big mistake long ago in the misty past. This is still alive, still working itself out, and I don't want her interference. I don't want her or anyone else to make things any worse than they are."

"It's embarrassing, Mom." Phoebe started to roll her eyes.

"It's not your job to be embarrassed for me," Abigail said. "Do you really have so much free time? You're failing math and chemistry, your room is a wreck, and you don't lift a finger around here to help, so maybe you can redirect some of that energy you're putting into embarrassment toward something you can control."

Phoebe rolled her eyes in earnest this time and looked at her watch.

"Do you know what it's like to have to defend your parents and your husband to one another year after year?" Abigail went on. "And now to give them this, this disgusting satisfaction, and then to live with their pity and superiority forever after—no, I won't do it. It's none of their business. They withdrew from this long ago."

"He's got someone else," Phoebe said. Wasn't it time for her mother to face facts? "You've got someone else too. Life goes on."

Abigail sighed.

"Phoebe, look. I've got something in the oven," she said, turning to leave. "Don't stay out too late, OK? Do I need to pick you up somewhere? Do you need some money?"

"No. I'll get a ride."

Suddenly Phoebe felt terrible for her mother, whose life was a series of mistakes she knew she would never make. But she didn't know what to do, how to behave. She wanted to go to her, but didn't want to embarrass her further and was already overdue to meet Tim, whom Abigail didn't even know about. *I can keep secrets too,* Phoebe thought, *and why shouldn't I? You do it.* She had a vision of mothers and daughters in the family keeping their secrets all the way back to the Middle Ages, husbanding their mysteries in castles and huts by the spooky light of cooking fires.

The darkness of Webster was freezing, and her leather coat and short skirt were almost useless against the cold. When oh when would she be old enough to drive? Her mother was so sweet; she didn't even say "you're not going out that way!" anymore, even though someone really ought to. But Phoebe knew that without suffering there is no art, and so she bore the cold as well as she could, knowing she looked really cool. It reminded her of Wallace Stevens, who they were doing in school with the supremely cool Mr. Chollet, who pronounced his name the French way and was entitled, if you asked Phoebe or any of the other girls. "Death is the mother of beauty" was his big thing. "Let's just hope nobody decides to kill themselves 'cause they couldn't get a prom date," she had told her boyfriend, "or Mr. Chollet is in big trouble with the school board." Phoebe had been the student representative one year. What a bunch of hypocrites the trustees had turned out to be. As if this was some surprise.

Tim didn't like Mr. Chollet, but she told him he shouldn't be jealous. Anyway, he would be a happy camper this evening when she told him about her surprise. She knew how he hated wearing those awful rubbers, and so she had started tracking her periods, which were nicely regular, using the system the Catholics used to use before they stopped pretending not to believe in birth control. It was pretty reliable, if you did it right, and she was even leaving a margin of safety. So tonight, no rubber.

She was shivering now, and she still had another mile to go. So fucking damp here on top of everything else. If it weren't for Tim, she would move to LA and get away from all these crazy people and spoiled college kids. That would give Dad one helluva scare.

Through the curtains, you could see televisions on in almost all the houses, and Phoebe promised herself again that she wouldn't live in one of these tidy places, wasting her life soaking up radiation from the tube. Just up Sycamore she recognized Julie Kennedy's little gray Toyota with the Witches Sweep! bumper sticker, the same car she had used to drive when she was a lifeguard at the municipal pool. Phoebe kept meaning to stop in one day and say hi. It was awful she had to work at that disgusting pre-school with that child molester, Joseph what's-his-name. Thank God Mom and Terry had had sense enough to keep Marty out of that place. One of the rare smart moves they had ever made. Maybe her stepfather's reporting would finally close the thing down one of these days. She wished she and her friends had the guts to torch the place in the middle of the night. It was a moral imperative, practically, yet nobody was doing anything. Just sit-ting around, waiting for this jerk to molest someone else's kid. Ugh!

I should get going," Chris said quietly the next morning, draining her mug of tea and wanting to be contradicted. But silence yawned and so, nonchalantly, she asked: "What are you doing today?"

"Oh, a lot of boring stuff I've got piled up," Julie answered with a nervous smile. Outside her kitchen window, looking toward Sycamore, she could see water dripping from icicles on the bushes as the sun struggled weakly through the clouds. "Return some library books. Laun-dromat. Grocery shopping."

"Well, I'll get out of your hair for a while," Chris said. She had that knowing look that was at once so maddening and so appealing, as if she could tell that Julie couldn't wait for her to go but didn't entirely want her to.

But already Julie's mind was on all the things she needed to do on this particular Saturday, the first in a while that snow had not made too diffi-cult. Besides, errands were innocent. *I'm just going to the hardware store,* she would think. *Now I'm filling the car with gas, just like everybody else.* She was someone who liked feeling a certain ordinariness about her life. It made departures from the usual course both easier and less threatening.

Yet as they walked outside, she was sorry to see Chris go. She wished they could do the errands together, in the relaxing way she remembered from when she was with Andrew, before he had gone to California and found someone else.

"I should clear off the rest of this walk, now that it's warmed up a little," she said, making conversation to prolong the moment. She gave a nervous laugh. Chris had already teased her about suffering a serious case of the *I shoulds*. Whenever she walked outside, came into the house, entered a room, she was overwhelmed by all the things she should be doing. *I should make curtains. I should make a pie out of these old apples. I should really paint the bathroom.* But she liked this about herself.

"Got a shovel?" Chris asked, boyish with her hands jammed into the pockets of her jeans. "I could do that for you."

"I need the exercise," Julie said. "Besides, I've really got to get going."

"OK." Chris smiled. "You got plans tonight?"

In the light of day, Julie felt on edge with her new lover, nervous about what still seemed, even in the Webster of this day and age, something furtive, illicit. There was not the go-everywhere, show-him-off impulse she might have had about a new boyfriend, and Chris's wicked expression seemed to capture the forbidden fruit aspect of Julie's amazing decision to sleep with her.

She had never been with a woman before, never imagined being with one, but she was curious, and lonely without Andrew. Chris had been after her ever since coming to Alphabet Soup. And Julie felt that being with a woman somehow didn't count as any kind of betrayal. The door was still open for Andrew; if he asked, she could honestly say there was no new boyfriend. This was just something different, some passing thing that she wanted to try. In her innocence, she still felt it was almost in the same category as masturbating. There wasn't even that same feeling of giving yourself as when somebody was inside you. It wasn't remotely the same as with Andrew.

But it was delicious in its own way, interesting and surprising and completely different than she'd imagined. It was taking her a little while to figure out where she stood in this thing, who she was, how to be.

"I know this is stupid," Julie had said. "But it makes me wonder who's the man. Not that we're not both women. I love it that you're a woman. But it just makes me wonder."

"About who's in charge? Who's hard and who's soft? Who leads and who follows?"

"Yeah. Exactly."

"That's the fun of it. We both do. We make it up as we go. We take turns."

Lovemaking was that way too. It reminded her of English class, when they had studied dramatic form. But rather than climbing a hill and sliding down the other side, it was more like exploring a series of rooms— like visiting a spa, almost, and having one blissful experience after another, all of them warm and soft. The image of them was airbrushed in her mind. It was so different than with eager, angular Andrew, all elbows and knees, who was so immediately spent when he was, well, spent.

"Such a pussycat," Chris whispered, hugging her and then sliding her hands down to her hips. Now it was Julie's turn to blush. "So are you OK?"

Julie nodded and smiled. She felt her lover's hand rubbing the lowest part of her back. It glowed so warm her forehead tingled.

"Sure?"

She nodded and smiled again and, sighing, squeezed the other woman to herself. In doing so, she spied a man watching them from a large, dark automobile parked across the street. *He thinks we're cousins or maybe even sisters,* she thought. *He can't really imagine.*

"Call me later," she told Chris, not wanting to let go but unwilling to be hugged that way with somebody watching.

"Well, all right," Chris said happily. There was a little country girl that came and went in her manner. Julie thought it was adorable.

Inside, she wandered around a little, unsure what to do next and unused to the silence after spending the night and morning with somebody. These were the only times she was lonely, but they reminded her of why people mated, and she wished again that Andrew hadn't gone. She still hoped to visit him in spring. As she was about to sit down and finish reading the newspaper, the doorbell rang, and when she opened it, she realized it was the man from the automobile.

"I'm Detective Al Jepson of the Webster Police," he said. "Mind if I have a word with you?"

She had been waiting for this moment ever since the investigation of Alphabet Soup had become public. She had rehearsed in her mind the impassioned speech she would give in defense of Emily and Frank, only to have it falter in the face of a single nagging uncertainty—which was that she didn't exactly *know* about Frank. That is, she was sure he wasn't guilty, sure no children had ever been abused at the school, sure enough to stake her life on Emily's innocence. But Frank was such a mystery. Without some sense of inner certainty, as she had about Emily and the other women at the school, who could ever be positive of a negative? She hardly knew Frank. Nobody did. And yet it seemed ludicrous, insane, inconceivable that—

"Ma'am, are you a witch?"

Jepson's question made her blush; it was so ridiculous, and she had never been a ma'am before. But this passed quickly; Julie had worried for some time that eventually she might find herself accused. She and the others had talked about it, but it seemed so far-fetched. It was precisely the inconceivable that she heard in Jepson's question, precisely the way the rest of the world, in the gathering climate of suspicion that was engulfing Webster, might react to the Wicca she and her friends practiced so innocently. An image of the coven flashed through her mind, she and the others just children, really, feeling that they were playing with fire but having no idea what conflagration might result. Suddenly she felt twenty years older.

"What kind of a question is that?" she asked.

"It's a simple question. Are you a witch?"

"Do you believe in witchcraft?"

"What I believe doesn't matter."

"That's exactly what I think. My religion is nobody's business but my own, and you'll need to talk to my lawyer about anything having to do with Alphabet Soup."

"You're not gonna put a spell on me, now." He would bait her. "Make a little doll and stick pins in it?"

"Will you please leave now?" She felt no particular fear, she would remember later, just a kind of dismissive loathing. "Right now. This instant."

"One last thing," Jepson said on the way out. "Will you tell your roommate I'll want to speak to her as well?"

"What roommate?"

"The woman who left here this morning."

"She's not my roommate. I don't have a roommate."

"Oh, I'm sorry. I thought since she spent the night. I must be mistaken."

Jepson did not have anything against women who love other women. He was a man of the world, in his own mind. But he felt licensed—even obligated—to use every lever at his disposal to pry the lid off the hideous Pandora's box that was, in his view, Alphabet Soup, and the prosecutor was almost no help at all.

Heaving his bulk behind the steering wheel of his car and driving back to his office, he thought of the way Hawthorne had treated his witness. It says something about a man when he can't even take the trouble to show a little courtesy to an old guy like Gabriel Demming. From the moment Demming had entered, Jepson could see that Hawthorne was filled with scorn. When they shook hands, for instance, Hawthorne squeezed wickedly, you could see it from the way Demming winced even as he radiated a desire to please. Jepson thought of an elderly Labrador. A golden retriever.

"Where do you live, Mr. Demming?" Hawthorne had asked.

"Well, right now I'm staying at the Tabernacle Resurrection Shelter until I can get another job, get back on my feet. Just temporary."

"What was the last job you held?"

"Short-order cook. I worked in Rockton." Demming looked uneasily at Jepson. He nodded slightly. *Don't worry about this part,* they seemed to say. Jones in particular had seen this before. Hawthorne spotted the man as homeless the minute he walked in, which cast doubt in advance on whatever Demming would have to say. This was fine with Jones, who knew his boss would accept testimony more readily if he felt he knew everything about the testifier. They could all get down to business now.

"I joined with them, see," Demming said, looking from time to time to Jones and Jepson for reassurance. Hawthorne's unwavering gaze had him spooked. "I came walking by, on my way back to the shelter after, you know, visiting with some friends."

Hawthorne interjected: "You were drinking."

"Not a lot. Just with some friends, no big deal. You can't come in the shelter if you too drunk."

He looked again from Jepson to Jones.

"Go ahead," Hawthorne said quietly.

"So I joined with them, see. In the circle."

Hawthorne looked at his deputy unhappily.

"Start at the beginning," Jones said to Demming. "The way you told it to the cop."

Demming took a deep breath and began, explaining how he had been walking past the Alphabet Soup Preschool when he saw a group of young women sitting cross-legged in the cold outside the building. He asked one of them what they were doing, and they tried to get rid of him at first, but he persisted. They were good-looking, and so finally they got him to join them in their ritual. The idea was to form a protective circle shielding the building from harm. He did it because they were good-looking, he emphasized, and because they gave him a sandwich and some hot tea from a Thermos. "It was cold that night, man, I'm telling you," Demming said.

Jones noticed that Hawthorne wasn't asking any more questions. He expected his deputy to ask the questions; that way he could test both questioner and questioned.

"What do you remember about this ritual you took part in?" Errol asked. "You described it to the police officer, as I recall."

"*North and east, of ill be released. South and west, evil spirits we arrest.* Something like that. We said it over and over, along with some other things. Chanted, kinda. And the cutest one, Julie her name was, went around the whole building with a broom and a box of salt—"

"What did you think you were doing there, Mr. Demming?" Hawthorne asked. Demming looked from Jepson to Jones and seemed about to protest his innocence when Hawthorne, eyes half-closed, brushed this aside. "I mean, what did you think this was all about?"

"Well, that's the thing. They said they were witches, see, and I was in with their coven for a night. Their coven! Name of Ariel. I told 'em I don't believe in witchcraft. And you all much too young and pretty to be no kinda witches. But that's why I did it. Because I knew they ain't witches."

"And because they were young and pretty."

"You got me there," Demming said, affecting a good-natured laugh. "They *were* young and pretty. Educated too. I could tell."

"How could you tell?"

"From the way they talked and dressed. Carried themselves. You can tell."

"And who were these educated young witches you met there on the street that night?" Jones asked. "Do you have any idea?"

"I don't know any names, except Julie, and maybe Mary. I think there was a Mary. But they worked at Alphabet Soup, they told me as much. That much I know." Demming looked about with an air of triumph. His fingernails were lined with ribbons of black that made Jones rub his hands together in distaste.

"They worked at Alphabet Soup, that's what they said," Demming continued. "But they were only playing, you could tell. With the knife and the five-sided star and all that. Like a Star of David."

"That's a six-pointed star," said Jepson, for Hawthorne's benefit. "A five-pointed star is called a pentagram. It's a traditional symbol used by Satanists the world over."

"They were playing their little game." Demming shook his head. "Young girls. What do they know about anything? They were only playing with me too. I knew that. I'm not stupid, you know? I worked in an office; I been around. I was playing with them. See? They thought they were playing with me, but I was playing with them."

"Very astute, Mr. Demming," said Hawthorne. "Very astute indeed."

To Jepson, the problem with Cal Hawthorne was an excess of rationalism. Because the district attorney did not believe in Satan, he could not imagine that anyone else might—that others might go so far as to worship Satan in conjunction with their twisted sexual longings. Like most of the Webster Police Department, Jepson was a local kid—not local in the way that Terry Mathers was local, always shuttling down to New York to see his big-shot father, but really local, rooted in Webster in ways the newcomers wouldn't be for a couple of generations. Jepson's family went way back. They had had 600 acres on Scism Road outside of town going back a century at least, until his grandfather had pissed it away, and there were still Jepsons all over town. *Do not underestimate me,* he liked to think of as the family motto. Unlike most of his local relatives, Detective Jepson had traveled widely when he was in the service and had taken a Japanese wife. He spoke Spanish, knew how to cook. He imagined himself not provincial but rooted. And he prided himself on keeping up with developments in law enforcement, in particular involving the sexual abuse of children. He read everything he could find on this subject, subscribed to newsletters, attended conferences. And one of the things he knew from his readings was that there were Satanists in America, some of whom preyed on little children. Suspiciously consistent signs of Satanic ritual had been found in abuse cases in far-flung parts of the country, enough to suggest to some leading thinkers in the field a conspiracy of child abusers who considered themselves in league with the devil.

Thus, the handful of parents whose children claimed they were abused at Alphabet Soup were asked by the police whether they or their kids had noticed any signs of Satanism—five-sided stars, the ritualized use of animal bones, any kind of potions or incantations, or other hocus pocus they could recall. To avoid giving suggestible witnesses any ideas, Jepson was careful to ask this only of those already reporting abuse. But he hadn't reckoned on the phone tree.

At this point, it remained informal. Started by Lucille Lyttle, it was simply a network of mothers who reported to one another the latest questions, answers, and rumors arising from the investigation of Alphabet Soup. The earliest participants were mostly true believers, although there were a couple of skeptics as well. And so when three or four mothers were asked about signs of Satanism at the school, word spread to other mothers, until before long a large number were worriedly interrogating their children about this. It was inevitable that, with everyone searching for the devil, hoofprints would soon be reported.

Some children now said they had been forced to worship Satan at a scary black altar constructed in a secret room. Others said the teachers rode around on brooms, and that Frank Joseph sprouted horns. "Probably a costume," Diana explained. Teachers and children alike drank the blood of sacrificial animals and danced naked, singing songs in praise of "their prince."

The kids were warned that if they revealed what went on, their parents would be skewered and cooked over an open flame and then eaten at the school. The pattern of disclosures was always the same: reluctant at first, volunteering nothing, but gradually, under Diana's patient questioning, the children opened up. It helped when parents followed Diana's advice to reward their kids with affection and toys. Once the children felt safe and saw that the adults wanted them to tell, they became founts of accusation. Satan—or Satanism—figured in more and more of their stories.

Belinda struggled to hold onto her attorney's words as he spoke them, but they seemed to slip through her fingers like sand. She was woozy from being in bed for so long. Her neck hurt.

"You're still in a state of shock," he said calmly. His fleshy features were hard somehow. "You need round-the-clock monitoring. Frankly, I've been worried you might harm yourself."

"Puh," she said, with a weary wave of her hand.

"You're suffering post-traumatic stress syndrome," he said insistently, as if she had interrupted him. He was a heavyset man in a blue-gray suit who had volunteered many kindnesses upon hearing of her situation. "We have to be careful. You need help. You need rest. Just stay put for a while."

"I don't know if my insurance will cover this," she fretted. There was a note of whining in her voice, of pleading. "I just started at Mart-World and now—"

"Never mind all that. I've made it clear to the administration that you've been through some serious trauma, and they have a responsibility, regardless of your ability to pay. This hospital will do right by you."

"Mr. Kalkstein, I'm scared." She began to cry quietly. "I killed my daughter—"

"Belinda, listen to me—"

"—and I don't even know if I can live with myself—"

"Listen to me. That was a tragedy. That was a tragedy that befell you that you'll always have to live with. All of us will. But you bear a very small part of the responsibility. What those people did at that school—who can begin to describe the awfulness of it?"

"I'm not even sure what happened," Belinda said fearfully. "I mean, I thought I knew, but I'm not sure."

"I know it's hard—"

"I don't want anybody to get in any trouble," she said.

"I know it's hard," the lawyer said with quiet persistence. "But the only one who'll be in trouble if you won't speak out is you. I've got to be honest with you."

They sat in silence while Belinda pondered this. Mr. Kalkstein began going through his large leather briefcase, and she was afraid suddenly that he was getting ready to go, that he would leave her to her fate in wordless disgust. But just as she was about to announce her readiness to help in any way she could, he spoke.

"Belinda, I want your permission to move ahead civilly," he said, handing over some papers. "I've prepared this complaint. That's what a lawsuit is, an official complaint that we submit to the court against the people we think have harmed us. Take a look at this."

The language was foreign to her, incomprehensibly old-fashioned and formal, with all the lines numbered on the side. "Comes now plaintiff Belinda Jackson," it began and grew only more involute. She noticed she was named at the top in capital letters, versus a whole list of people and things including the people who ran Alphabet Soup, the teachers, and the school itself.

"You sue everybody," Mr. Kalkstein said simply when she looked up at him in puzzlement. "You let the courts sort that out. A child is dead, and countless others are scarred for life. Somebody's got to take responsibility. I would anticipate that we won't be alone in this. I'm expecting other suits, and there's a good chance they'll be consolidated."

"Mr. Kalkstein, I really appreciate all the work you've been doing, but I gotta tell you, I got nothing. I don't know how I can even begin to pay you the first dime on this."

"Confidentially, I should tell you that you have a local philanthropist named Charles Krieger to thank. Besides which, our firm may be able to recoup its future investment in this case after we file this action. I want to get started on this because first, your criminal defense is going to take money, and you're not out of the woods there, by any means, although in that matter too Mr. Krieger has been very generous. And second, this should help us show our determination to pursue the real criminals in this matter."

"What's the point?" she asked. "Aren't these people charged with child abuse anyway?"

"Yes, and we want to remind the world, and any potential jurors in it, that we hold these people responsible for the tragedy that happened out on that road the day you hit the tree. If nothing else, this suit sends a message." He sighed. "Remember also that the school has insurance, and the individuals have some assets. The land, the building. These things have some value. You can't just abuse little children in this society and keep your worldly possessions while families suffer and pay for counseling and medical care and attorneys. We can't allow it."

Belinda, nodding and avoiding his gaze, tried to suppress the sobs that were forever surprising her at inopportune moments since the death of her daughter. Mr. Kalkstein tactfully looked away.

When Terry got home that night, he turned on the stereo, which he kept tuned to the Web State jazz station, and rolled himself a joint before going for the phone machine. When he hit the button, he heard an oddly brisk message from his father about where to wire the money to repay the *Chronicle*'s loan, and he realized that it would be impossible any longer to put off a reckoning on this score. The tone of the message itself was a kind of dare, a demand to show his cards. He sighed and listened to the other three messages, all of them from Lucille, each more urgent than the last. She would call again, he knew, and so he settled down to smoke and think and enjoy the peace and quiet that were the only consolations of the tacky little dump he was lately calling home.

These late-night phone calls had become a tiresome habit with Lucille. He was happy to have her as a source, happy to go along with whatever subconscious fantasies helped a source deliver useful information, but as time wore on he chafed at being enlisted in someone else's fantastic crusade, at the you-and-me, secret-society aspect the whole thing had begun to take on. She called in the small hours, when the rest of Webster was in bed, and she liked to stay on the phone, speculating, gossiping, trading tidbits with him, and using him (as all sources did) as much as he used her. The question was, what was she using him for? A creepy sexual undertone had slipped into their telephone liaisons, and Terry knew he had done little to dampen this. He was usually stoned, and he could hear the ice clinking in her drinks. She spoke in a whisper, ostensibly not to wake anyone in her family, and he used a strange, late night voice mellowed by marijuana. It was like she was some secret lover. When he picked up the phone at two A.M. it was like an assignation.

"Terry," she said, starting right in. "Has anyone talked to you about the photographs?"

"Photographs?"

"They took pictures of the kids. Thousands of pictures. The place was a porno mill, evidently, and there are photos of our kids doing these horrible things. Just a whole gigantic cache. I've got to assume that a lot of these pictures have already been copied and passed around and made their way all over the world by now among this whole goddamn network of pedophiles."

"Have you seen any of these?"

"Of course I haven't seen them," Lucille said. "They're evidence. But the police have seen them, from what I understand. It's just so awful. You wouldn't publish pictures like that, would you?"

"Of course not."

"That's what I told the others. Some of the mothers were worried that these things would get into the newspapers."

"I'm astonished to hear about these pictures. Where did they keep them, at the school? And how did they get them developed?"

"By now I wouldn't think anything would astonish you. I mean, who'd have thought that Alphabet Soup was run by child molesters? And believe me, it doesn't stop there. My son has been disclosing like mad, God bless him, and if you knew all the people in this town involved in sexually abusing children, you wouldn't let your own kids leave the house."

"You're telling me it goes beyond Alphabet Soup?"

"Don't be naive, Terry. The kids have been reporting abuse in places all over town, in the car wash, barber shop, some little insurance office out on 32, you name it. Not just one of them either, but several confirming each of these things. Some of it is so awful, I can't begin to describe it." She lowered her voice. "My son was taken to a kennel in Rockton. A kennel, Terry!"

Could this really be happening? Surely this could not all be a tissue of lies, yet how could they abuse kids in a barber shop without anyone noticing? Why haul them all the way up to Rockton, for Pete's sake? The more he talked to Lucille, the more unbalanced she seemed, which was in a way a relief, because it would account for a lot of the wilder allegations. It could stand next to the core of truth in all this—that something at Alphabet Soup had gone horribly, horribly wrong. He took another drag, and the dope hit him like a tidal wave.

"Terry? Terry, are you there?"

"Yeah, I'm here." He began to feel frightened, paranoid. "Lucille. Let me ask you something, Lucille. Now I want you to think carefully about this one. Have any of the children, to your knowledge, said anything about a dancing bear?"

"A dancing bear."

"Yeah. You know, like the Russians have in circuses. A dancing bear."

"I don't think so, but I don't know. I can check into it."

"Would you do that? It's just something I picked up."

"Can you elaborate a little?"

"I don't know much more than I've already told you. Just that there was a dancing bear. I'm wondering what it means myself."

"That's a new one on me, but nothing would be surprise me by now," she said bitterly. He could hear her voice start to crack. "Not a damned thing."

"Lucille, listen. I need to get going. I've got to be in New York early tomorrow."

"Business or pleasure?" she asked. *My great friend,* Terry thought with distaste. How had this started? How could he end it?

"Neither," he said.

"I'll find out about that dancing bear business. When are you coming back?"

"Next day, I guess. Maybe even the same night. It's just a long way from here, you know."

Dancing bear. Now where the fuck had that come from? And what had made him toss it out the way he had? The desire to be liked for giving something back, for participating in some crackpot minuet with this woman? It was just the first thing that had popped into his head. He racked his brain but could find no explanation. No one had told him about it, he felt sure of that, and it had nothing to do with Alphabet Soup. No, it was more likely just his old habit of making private fun of people, mocking those who can't know they're being mocked. He did this often in Webster and was ashamed of it. When it worked, it gave him no pleasure, and yet he persisted, finding it a habit, like marijuana, that was tough to break. Perhaps one last joint before bed, he thought, looking down at the package of rolling papers on the coffee table. Suddenly he yelped with laughter. Dancing Bear was his brand, of course. There he was, on the cover, an Indian chief in full Hollywood regalia, a single eyebrow raised quizzically. Dancing Bear Rolling Papers. *For the love of God,* he wondered, *what is happening to me?* He realized that he held the minuscule remains of a sizable reefer, and he carefully set it to rest in the ashtray.

chapter TWELVE

Maury Mathers was waving an edition of the *Chronicle* that Terry had brought all the way from Webster. "This business with the Satanism is unbelievable," he said.

"I d-didn't believe it either, Dad. But it's what the investigators are hearing. It's what's coming out of the kids. And it's s-such a complete outrage. We just had to cover the hell out of it."

They sat in Maury's clubby office, the father at home in ascot and woolens behind his grand mahogany desk, the son slouched down in a cordovan leather wing chair. Terry felt dazed, removed from himself and the scene at hand. He had been on a bus since 6 A.M., sleepless as it raced along the highway to reach New York in time for the morbid procession of rush-hour traffic creeping into the city. He was nervous about broaching the true subject of his pilgrimage, which was the money owed to his father, and silently he thanked the gods for giving him the amazing Alphabet Soup story to show for his efforts and investment. At least Maury would feel that he was funding something worthwhile.

"It's all just incredible," Maury said. As he spoke, Terry stole glances at a photograph of his father's new girlfriend, a woman in her mid-thirties with short blond hair, perfect teeth, and huge green eyes. It hurt to look at her. "What do people think up there?"

"About the allegations?" Terry groggily considered this. His speech was better when he was sleepy. "The town's divided. There are old f-friends in Webster, even relatives, who aren't talking to one another over this. Some think the folks at Alphabet Soup are the d-d-devil incar-nate; others believe ardently in their innocence. It's been interesting; since the whole thing started, they've lost a lot of kids, but others have actually come in. They had a waiting list, remember. And the mothers really need day care; they just can't live without it. So Alphabet Soup struggles on."

"And what do you think?"

"I think it's a hell of a story."

"Did they do it or didn't they?"

"Dad, I still can't believe it at some level, but I know the people look-ing into this and they're very, very good. I also know that the disbelief of parents and other grown-ups is precisely how this kind of thing goes on. It's why there are probably millions of people walking around out there who were abused as kids. So yeah. I believe something is going on at that school. I believe s-somebody there is as g-guilty as s-sin."

"You've been way ahead on this thing, from what I can see. Nothing even in the New York papers yet." Terry was overwhelmed by how com-pletely his father's manner had been subsumed by his television persona. It was as if space aliens had taken over the body of the man he'd used to know. "Shoo-in for the Pulitzer if it turns out to be true."

"I don't w-worry much about prizes," Terry said. "They r-reinforce all our worst instincts, don't you think?"

They drank tea together from expensive-looking white china that made Terry feel silly, with its tiny, baroque handles and scalloped saucers. It was so delicate he felt he could snap off a piece with his teeth.

"Satan in Webster," Maury said. "Hard to believe."

"I've thought about that, Dad, and it is odd, but I'm not going to get too carried away with that angle. The real issue is not whether there's a religious aspect to child abuse; it's just whether there is child abuse. And the evidence appears overwhelming."

"But there's a sense in which they're right," Maury said, musing theatrically. He sank deep into his chair, shrugged his shoulders a couple of times, and looked flirtatiously up at the ceiling. Terry noticed for the first time that it was painted with clouds. "The people who talk about Satan, I mean. What could be more evil, more purely Satanic, than conspiring with other people to sexually molest children? We don't talk about this stuff anymore, but in the old days, when people said someone was possessed by the devil, they kind of had a point. They meant the person was in the grip of some truly incomprehensible evil. Isn't that what we're talking about here?"

"It's like when people attributed natural disasters to the gods," said Terry, "instead of the m-m-movement of geothermal forces, or bad luck, or whatever."

"We cloak our ignorance in science," Maury agreed. "The other day my doctor said I might have some sort of a low-grade infection, and when I thought about it afterward I realized he was no different than some medieval conjurer who says he thinks I'm possessed. I *am* possessed—by some kind of bacteria, no? I mean, they've got into me; they're coursing all through my bloodstream. You don't know whether you're talking to me or to the microbes. What difference does it make whether you call them devils or bacteria or the Prince of Wales? Whether there are really Satanic rituals going on up there in Webster is almost beside the point, because what's going on is evil. It doesn't matter what name you give it."

"You're r-r-right, Dad. But there is some kind of religious aspect to this whole thing. The authorities have s-seen it elsewhere, apparently. There really are S-S-Satanists in this country, just like there are Methodists and Presbyterians."

"You're doing great work up there, son. It's only a matter of time before the story breaks out and the entire country sits up and notices."

"I think when indictments come down, we can expect a lot of attention up in Webster."

"Maybe I should come and do something," Maury said, as if testing the idea aloud. It dawned on Terry that his father had been working up to this all along and that was why he was free on such short notice this morning. "I could make it personal, talk about how the town I've known all these years has discovered a darker side of itself. It'd be a chance to address the entire issue of child abuse, day care, all that stuff."

"G-Great," said Terry without enthusiasm. The biggest story of his career and just when it's about to amount to something, his father needs to come and steal his thunder. "Of course, there's no telling how all this will play out. I mean, it could just blow over—"

"Our Children at Risk," said Maury, indicating the titles with a sweep of his hand. He sat up suddenly. "You know, I've been looking for a way to get out of this fucking mausoleum and talk to some real people. Maybe there really is something there. Are you willing to appear on air?"

"M-M-Me?" Terry's voice turned shrill. "I'm n-n-not a player in any of this."

"Of course you are. If I'm going to do this, don't you think I'm going to give my own son credit?"

"I'll p-p-p-probably choke!" Terry's face burned as the words burst forth.

"It's only videotape, my boy. It doesn't cost anything, and I'll make sure the crew has all the time in the world. Might do you good. That whole problem seems to be getting better as you get older."

"It's b-better, yes. When I'm n-n-not self-conscious about it. W-W-When I'm n-n-not talking to more than one or—one or—person at a time."

"You might even work with the producer, get yourself a nice little fee out of this thing. Assuming the *Chronicle* remains as lucrative as it's always been."

"N-n-no change there." Terry sighed artificially. His heart began to pound. "W-W-W-e really need to talk about that."

"Let's do talk about it," Maury said, and his look made it clear he knew everything.

Terry took a deep breath. "D-D-Dad, we j-j-just d-d-don't have y-your money. I think you can see that j-j-j-journalistically the *Chronicle* is doing an incredible job with the s-s-scant resources at our d-d-disposal, but the paper barely breaks even, and then o-o-only when Abigail and I d-d-don't pay ourselves."

"Let me be honest with you, Terry. I'm sure you've read that our ratings have been stuck at the bottom for six months now, and my contract is up for renewal this summer. There's a new anchorman—anchorwoman, I should say—and a lot of talk about bringing in fresh blood." He spoke with studied weariness here, as if in disdain of such unseemly exigencies. "The new owners, being from another business altogether, also have a different way of looking at expenditures." He snorted. "They pay so much for football these days, there doesn't seem to be any money left for anything else. Some of the new managers no doubt hold the view that talk is cheap, and really, talk is all I'm selling."

Terry was embarrassed by this speech. He had known that his father's viewer approval ratings were down and of course couldn't blame the old man for emphasizing circumstances rather than his own slipping popularity. But what would become of Maury Mathers without an audience? The American people no longer knew the meaning of loyalty, of gratitude; it was no different than in Webster. How could the vast and mercurial assembly out there in TV land, with its gnatlike attention span and hunger for fresh celebrity, fail to fail its most trusted preacher?

"I'm skating on thin ice," Maury continued. "That's the bottom line. Thin ice. Can you believe this, at my age? My colleagues make a fortune giving speeches, run around the country addressing grocers' associations and dental organizations, but Maury Mathers can't. He cannot do it. It would devalue his most precious commodity, which is trust—the illusion of which entitles him to a platform in the first place."

"Not an illusion, Dad. You won't do speaking engagements for m-m-money because you think it's dishonest, c-c-corrupting. You deserve the people's trust."

Maury shrugged.

"These days, it doesn't count for much," he said, smiling indulgently. He saw through their petty transparencies, he meant to say. He was a man of irony, impervious to such manifest folly. "To these guys I'm just a brand, a pretty good one, but tired, on a product no one really seems to want. They want younger people, lighter stories. Nobody cares about foreign policy, arms control, the latest shenanigans at the White House or State. And nobody wants to be hectored about consumerism or pollution or the end of family life. Without God, we got no grip on anybody."

"That's not fair. Your audience is in the millions. Try c-c-c-covering the Webster City C-Council."

"The *Webster Chronicle* can run long, probing stories about public affairs. In television land, we fall all over ourselves to divine what people want and then give it to them. We've got AIDS spreading so fast people are afraid to get laid, the Japanese are buying everything in sight, the president's a superannuated actor who's flummoxed by facts, and we serve up a kind of 'lite' journalism that makes people feel better about things even when they're only getting worse."

"Not just lite stories. Stories that resonate. Stories with emotional content. Old-fashioned stories, really. Stories like Alphabet Soup."

"The point is, when I loaned you the money, I was flush. It was a couple of divorces ago. I was a lot younger. Old men are like dogs, you know. Each year counts for eight. Woof woof."

"We'll r-r-repay you, Dad, I promise you that. It's just a m-m-matter of time. Meanwhile, why not c-c-come up and do one of those stories? You'll have it exclusively. Indictments are c-c-coming, I know it for a fact, and the charges will be shocking. The prosecution will allege that the folks at Alphabet Soup have systematically molested hundreds of children over the years and then terrorized them into silence. It will be a major national story." An idea struck him. "Why not come up early, get all kinds of stuff on tape, and the day I break it, go on the air?"

"You've got some kind of pipeline. But can you be sure they'll feed you the indictment in advance?"

"I'll b-break it, I guarantee you. And if I b-b-break it, you b-break it. 'One Town's Trauma.' Brought to you exclusively by Maury Mathers."

"And Terry Mathers. 'Cause I'm not gonna do it unless you go on air."

"D-Dad, there's something else I should m-m-mention. Um. It turns out that I've been seeing this woman who is the county's chief sex-abuse investigator."

"You've been seeing her."

"Yeah."

"All of her."

"Yes, D-Dad, all of her."

"And you're also covering this story."

"It didn't start out that way. We got involved before. Before I knew anything about any of this."

"And this is why you're not with your wife? Because you're *shtupping* this source?"

"Leave A-Abby out of this, will you? It has nothing to do with her."

"So then what? Look, if it's the ethics you're worried about, I don't think it's such a problem. You got involved with a public official, and then a big story comes up and she's involved. But it's not *about* her. Correct? It's about somebody else; if you were involved with *them*, well, that could be a problem."

"I guess there is a distinction there."

"See, Webster in that sense is not so different from Washington. Basically very incestuous. Like any beat you cover. You fight like dogs and cats, you get fleas. Besides, in your case what's the alternative? How many reporters you have up there on the *Chronicle*?"

"Real reporters? Not counting me or the woman who does the knitting column?"

"And you're their editor anyway, right? Is there anybody else who could direct the coverage? And you own the goddamn newspaper. So there's no way to somehow recuse yourself from this thing, let other people pick up on it now that it seems a little sticky in your mind. So I don't know what you can do, other than run a big story about your relationship."

Terry snorted.

"Or dump this babe," his father continued. "Which I hope will happen sooner or later, because I love your wife. But not until I get on air with this thing, if you don't mind. See if you can hold out a little longer. Force yourself. And of course, introduce me. Is she good-looking?"

Back in Webster, Terry felt a great weight lifted from his shoulders. There was no longer any pretense that his father could be repaid any time soon, and that news had been delivered. What was the big deal, really? Maury was always proclaiming himself impoverished, but Terry suspected him of financial hypochondria—weren't they served tea by a uniformed housekeeper? He hated the idea of Maury taking over his big story, just as Maury had dominated every other aspect of his life, but what the hell, it made it easier for his father to swallow the news about the money. He knew that when the time came, he would dread going on camera, and in the meantime he enjoyed anticipating some of the exposure he felt he had deserved all along.

Freed of his own biggest worry, he was able to turn his attention fully to the increasingly consuming story of Alphabet Soup. It was natural that he would do so, even aside from its obvious merits. Webster was seething over child abuse at the preschool, and Terry received so much information, rumor, gossip, and speculation that it was all he could do to find time for the other big ongoing story that competed for his attention: the fate of Krieger's. The Krieger's story, in fact, was a nightmare; there was the fact that Krieger's was the paper's biggest advertiser, the longstanding mutual dislike between Terry and Charles Krieger, and the maddeningly well-sourced national business press, which broke stories about the takeover battle long before Terry, with his cloutless weekly, could learn about them or get them into print. And of course, there was his strong suspicion that Krieger was sleeping with his wife. Bad enough that Abigail was his chief strategist. Everything he did in connection with Krieger's was painful, reminding him of his pathetic financial circumstances, his shattered marriage, and his lowly position in the vast and ruthless media food chain.

Alphabet Soup, on the other hand, was about people, not money, and competition was scant. Not surprisingly, given their friendship and Cal Hawthorne's ambitions, Errol was always ready to help as long as he wasn't quoted by name. He provided leads Terry was free to hunt down elsewhere and could confirm or refute things Terry had picked up on his own. Terry was not naive about this. It was how the District Attorney's Office obtained a pipeline into the *Chronicle,* but he handled what he got from Errol with care and considered the bargain well worth the price. He talked to Diana too, of course, and she laid to rest any nascent doubts he might have. The child abuse probe was part of their mutual discovery. They discussed the case incessantly, Diana dropping all pretense of confidentiality and Terry no longer giving speeches about what she should and should not tell him. Each of them simply made judgments based on trust, pleasure, and mutual advantage. They gossiped about Errol, Hawthorne, Jepson and the others, Terry providing context and background from his lifelong involvement with Webster and Diana revealing things about the investigation.

The chilling accounts of the children, as elicited by Diana's expert questioning, made Lucille Lyttle's ravings seem marginal, and all the more unfortunate in light of what actually occurred at the preschool. The excitement of this drew Diana and Terry closer. They shared the thrill of the hunt as well as the indignation of the righteous. They found themselves mourning together not only what had happened to the children of Webster, but to the illusion of innocence in which its residents had wrapped themselves.

Terry discovered that the Alphabet Soup scandal—for that is what it had become, a scandal the likes of which hadn't been seen in Webster probably in all its history—had a similar effect on the couples whose children claimed to have been abused at the formerly admired preschool. Many of the mothers quit their jobs to spend more time with their offspring, promote "healing," and perhaps assuage their own guilt for entrusting their kids to fiends. Husbands, doubtful and bewildered at first, came home from work earlier and showed more love and understanding to their wives, their children, even their pets. Couples began communicating more, even as sex began to die out in the homes of children who had disclosed. For some mothers, tormented for years by hamhanded husbands and possibly, in the past, an abusive boyfriend or two, it was a good excuse at last for calling a halt. Indeed, a by-product of the burgeoning sex-abuse charges was the growing power and self-possession of the women whose children leveled the allegations.

Terry met these women and knew some of them from life in Webster before all this had happened. Aside from Lucille Lyttle, they were well-organized and articulate, eager to talk to one another and ready now to tackle the terrible new problem their children's preschool had thrust upon them. They carried those fold-out organizers full of phone numbers and appointments, and several had taken to wearing beepers so they could be reached at any time. One or two of these mothers edged toward officious, but he made allowances. Look what they were going through, after all. And in his advancing years, he had come to see this particular brand of officiousness as a way of keeping sex at bay, of saying to the world that there was no place for it here, and this was fine too, since in fact he dimly lusted for several of these women and caught himself commiserating too freely, gathering too many phone numbers, turning on his charm the way he might unscrew the cap on a bottle of cheap sparkling wine.

These women had been talking to one another long before they began talking to Terry, and their informal network grew into a system, with each woman assigned to call three others so that news, accusations, and rumors spread instantly. Dutifully, with all the love and delicacy at their disposal, these good mothers questioned their children about whether *they* had ever been made to play the "naked movie star" game or whether *they* had ever been molested on a trip to the Fire Engine Museum in Rockton. Many of the children, who already stood in wonder before a parent never previously available at this hour of the day, reported when asked that indeed they *had* played such games or been touched in such and such a place, in such and such a way. As they had come to expect by now, the right answers led to hugs, kisses, ice cream, new tricycles, trips to Grandma's, and many other consummations much more concrete than the modest fantasies they had traded for them.

With all this fertilizer and so much pollen in the air, the telephone tree bore an embarrassment of fruit. When one child disclosed that she had been photographed hanging nude upside down in the Josephs' private office, Diana asked other children about this. The allegation was spread all along the mighty telephone tree that connected the mothers in their agony, and these mothers promptly asked their own children if any such thing had happened to them. Soon other kids came forward with similar allegations, even kids who had previously denied any abuse at all. Parents who at first supported the Alphabet Soup teachers were shocked to find their own children admitting to abuse.

There were so many charges that it was a challenge keeping track of them. Already several other preschools and day-care centers in the region had closed their doors, some amid allegations of abuse and others because fearful parents had withdrawn their kids or because fearful schoolmasters no longer felt it was worth the risk. Parents who wanted or needed day care for their small children were in a quandary. Some found themselves driving great distances to find a place in another preschool, while others hired housekeepers to watch the kids at home. For many mothers, the scandal was license to indulge their innermost desire, which was to stop working and stay home with their kids. Terry used the togetherness of these families, the newfound value they placed on time at home rather than money, to infuse his profiles of suffering families with hope. The children would get better and the families would emerge stronger. The truth, they had come to learn, would set them free.

Yet the children in Webster did not thrive during those dark days. The Alphabet Soup children had screaming fits, night terrors, eating disorders, skin problems, pill habits, self-destructive tics. One compulsively tugged at his eyelashes until they were all gone. Their personalities seemed to change. The grown-ups suffered too—even the ones who had never been to Webster. For the madness of that time changed the country's ideas about childhood. People came to think that perverts lurked behind every bush waiting to snatch their children, and those who worked with children learned not to hug them or even touch them for more than an instant. Teachers' unions around the country began providing training videos on how to stay out of trouble for "inappropriate touching." Five-year-olds were arrested for kissing other five-year-olds on the cheek. Well-to-do parents who left their children with nannies began to install hidden video cameras to keep an eye on things in their absence.

In Webster, meanwhile, the disclosures were abetted by community support. Terry wrote in the *Chronicle* about the families who had decided to go public with their pain, and he was inundated with calls of support and offers of help. A local cab company offered free rides to the county social services building. A wealthy retiree offered to fly the brave families to Disney World. Terry got a lump in his throat as he described in print the way public Webster responded—the way evil begat goodness many times over.

The only sour note came from Krieger's, which delivered to the county's Child Intervention Services Agency a shipment of numbered tokens once used by the coat-check department in the days when Krieger's checked its patrons' outerwear. The agency would give a token to each child who disclosed. And each token was redeemable at Krieger's for $100 worth of toys. *Charlie doesn't miss a trick,* Terry thought, having no choice but to report such generosity. He tried to imagine the cynicism behind this move on the part of Charles Krieger and wondered how he could possibly be married to somebody who might even dream of sleeping with such a person.

A hundred dollars, Charles?" Abigail had asked him. "But I saw piles and piles of them today. There must be a thousand tokens there."

"Easily," he said. "I had them brought down from the attics and storage bins of all our stores. They're sort of collectors' items."

"But this could run into an awful lot of money."

"Yes, my darling, but whose? Everyone tells me we can't beat Rothwax, so it comes out of his pocket, ultimately. What better cause than the children of Webster? He's a charitable guy. He's probably glad to be of service."

"I'm sure he'll be very grateful," she said, reaching down under the covers for the hardness she had felt there.

Krieger moaned and said that he could not imagine Rothwax being any more grateful than he, Krieger, felt at this particular instant, although, hard as it was to believe, his gratitude was increasing now at every moment.

"It's very hard, Charles," she whispered. "Very hard indeed."

Men are funny, Abigail thought. All so different, and yet all so much alike. She had been with no one but Terry in years, and although she had decided to give Charlie Krieger a try without any particularly strong feelings beyond her superficial attraction to him, she was delighted now that she had done so. He *was* different: less hairy than Terry, shorter, thicker, and most surprising of all, uncircumcised, so that his penis arose from a kind of silo, and in repose lay hooded like some sleeping cobra she was pleased to know that she could charm. Of course Charles made love differently too—maybe not so much because he was a different person as because he was a *new* person, and new people make love differently from people who've been together for a long, long time.

Yet they were alike too, Terry and Charles, much as they would hate the idea. Her new lover liked her to wear heels, liked it when she kept her jewelry on when she was naked, liked to do it in some of the same ways as Terry did. She really was quite a good lover, she decided, maybe precisely because she held Krieger in just the right level of regard. She felt affection for him, friendship, a certain cool admiration, even a strange kinship, but no love and, at this point in her life, found this to be a wonderful basis for sexual adventure. She did something under the covers that seemed to work well, and so she held on, drawing herself down to where she could bring her mouth into play. She loved this part. It crossed her mind that he might well ask her to marry him, when the takeover was complete. (And despite her best efforts, she expected it to succeed.) He would be richer than ever, what with the price Rothwax was offering, and free of Webster too. Although she did not now love her lover, she liked him well enough and did not rule out that she might accept such an offer, were he to make it. She was old enough to know that love, in the traditional sense, need not be the basis for a successful marriage, even if it made a fine premise for a failed one.

She imagined spending every night in this lovely bedroom, with its modern four-poster bed of some obscure black wood and its walls that resembled old parchment in the light of carefully dimmed sconces. She would never marry for money, but money happened to be one of Charles' attributes, like wit and worldliness, or a flat stomach. Why should she not take account of them all? Where was it written that she must always be condemned to poverty and struggle with a quixotic spouse who didn't even appreciate her heroic efforts to keep them afloat financially? Who disdained those efforts, in fact? As she slid her lover in and out of her mouth, she reached down and felt her own wetness, drawing it up and rubbing it with a delicate finger up and down, which made her wetter still. She thought perhaps she would stop and ride him, but couldn't quite resist what she was doing to herself, and so kept at it, slowing the movements of her mouth while she made herself come in her own right hand. Then she pulled Charles on top of her, hoping she might come again. It touched her that they all seemed to retain the eagerness of young men as they mounted to their climax—that no matter how grizzled and weary they might be otherwise, at this moment they were in the bloom of youth and boys again. She smiled at him and nodded that it was OK, surprising herself with the pleasure she took in leaving behind all the heavy baggage that normally cluttered the bed when she and Terry were in it—all the battered luggage of their journey together, poking them in the ribs and smelling of musty depths. It was like being on vacation or getting to the bathroom when you really had to pee. There was a luscious quality of letting go that made it so easy. She had cried and cried when Terry left, but she was cried out now and had come to her senses. What, after all, was there to lose?

Now that she had begun to explore the idea that there might be life after her husband, dealing with him was strangely tolerable. Ever the workaholic, he was consumed now by the Alphabet Soup scandal, which somewhat to her consternation had pushed Krieger's down below the fold and, in one regrettable edition, off page one altogether. He had a lover, she knew, but his dismayed look whenever Charlie's name arose confirmed her idea that there remained unfinished business, if not an unfinished life, between them. She liked to watch her husband through the glass of her office, peering at him by lifting a corner of the drawn blinds just for the sheer pleasure of spying. One day she watched him retrieve a file from the cabinet and become absorbed, his head held sideways, tongue protruding slightly, like a boy hunched over his homework. She imagined herself Thetis watching over Achilles, a hidden protector and secret cheering squad, groaning as she watched his face contort when his words wouldn't come during a phone call or recalling him in his jeans as a younger man, and she a younger woman.

She worked to save the *Chronicle* as if it were their marriage. It was like voodoo. The newspaper was a doll to which she fed chicken soup and exhortation, inserting pins only as a kind of acupuncture, the goal being to cure rather than to harm. And saving the *Chronicle,* Abigail knew, meant saving Krieger's, which is why she worked so furiously on this as well, taking over not only the chain's public relations strategy but sponsoring a lobbying effort in the state capital, overseeing employee relations and tackling the financial strategy. She was indebted to Terry in this department. Why, he demanded, were the employees always left out of these discussions? Why was the debate only about capital and never about the people with the most riding on the outcome?

"Can't you see, it's not just about ownership? Remember in *The Grapes of Wrath*? What makes the land yours? Working it, living on it, dying on it, the whole enchilada. The workers at Krieger's have all the disadvantages of ownership, like toil and responsibility and risk, and none of the advantages. You want to mobilize them to save the company's independence. Why not give them something in return?"

She had no ready answer for his argument, beyond the easy one that owners of capital have options employees don't, and the theoretical one that serving the owners' interest serves everyone's too. That was how she got the idea that the workers should be given stock or at least induced to invest in the company. This would give them a stake and, not coincidentally, place more shares in friendly hands. Let them buy stock at a discount, Abigail suggested the next time she found herself eating pastrami with the merchant prince, in return for agreeing not to sell for some extended period.

"The union's been clamoring for a better retirement package," Krieger said. "Why not give it to them? A retirement plan made of Krieger's stock! As an incentive, we'll match the shares they buy. And we'll start a campaign to get them on board. We'll show them what a great deal this is, the tax advantages, how beautiful and really *good* it can be to own Krieger's shares. We'll even put Ed Krcyszyki on the board."

"My only concern here," Abigail said, signaling for a moment's grace while she swallowed, "is that, in the event of some sort of meltdown, things could get ugly. These people aren't rich, Charles."

"But what sort of meltdown might that be? If we get taken over, they'll make money on their stock. And if we stay independent, we'll continue with the improvements we've been making, the stock in the long run will do about as well as any stock, and our employees will have safeguarded their jobs and the independence of a pillar of their community. What are we, elitists? Most of these people don't have two nickels put away for their retirement. They're depending on Social Security, for Chrissake."

That sounded reasonable to Abigail. If the employees were to have a greater stake, they must accept a greater risk. No one will put a gun to people's heads and force them to buy Krieger shares. *These are grown-ups,* she thought. *They might as well start acting like ones.*

Despite all the time she spent at Krieger's, Abigail did her own shopping at the mall just like everyone else. Even on a Thursday afternoon, there were a good many cars in the parking lot, all huddled closely around the building as if for warmth, the rest of the acreage given over to streaks of ice and, at the edges, snowdrifts. Inside it was a little too warm, and Abigail opened her coat, which seemed a lead weight on her shoulders. Maybe take it off, but as she considered this, she spotted her daughter tucked away in a corner behind a big potted plant. Could it be? Phoebe's back was to her, and Abigail had time to duck. Almost without thinking, she did so, hiding in the entryway of a sporting goods store and peeking back through the window, between sneakers. It was a joke at first; she assumed Phoebe's friend had spotted her, and she would show enough of herself to get a wry smile out of them, make them blush a little, and then go say hello.

But she didn't recognize the boy her daughter was with, and he obviously didn't know her. Phoebe was absorbed in flirtatious conversation, her head barely poking out of the mound of cloth formed by the hood of her sweatshirt. She held a cigarette down between her knees, puffing furtively now and then. Abigail noticed now that her hand was on his thigh.

It was at once touching and unsettling to see her daughter here—to see that Phoebe had a whole unheralded life, to realize with a start the extent to which she was already gone. Abigail's face flushed. What with the paper, Charles, the need to avoid all kinds of unpleasant topics and ambiguities, some part of her had been too eager to remain busily out of reach to her own offspring. Once or twice, Phoebe had even made noises about an unscheduled trip to Los Angeles. Abigail had broached this with her ex-husband, who had hemmed and hawed before offering a weak facsimile of welcome. She was not vindictive and could not bring herself to tell Phoebe she wasn't wanted there. She would not compete for her daughter's affections on that basis.

When Phoebe and her boyfriend—is that what he was?—kissed, Abigail hurriedly turned away, blushing for all of them. Looking at the fancy sneakers and overpriced basketball jerseys floating in the air of the shop's windows, she thought of Terry and her own lost youth and began to feel the tears come. She choked them back as well as she could, intent on not being noticed, but her face crumpled silently and she rested her forehead against the glass, helpless against this wave of despair. *Let it pass,* she thought. *I don't want to stand crying in a shopping mall.* But it didn't pass, and she felt her big shoulders heave and knew she was a sight, with her back hunched and her cheeks covered with running makeup. These thoughts were enough to settle her just enough, and covering her eyes with Kleenex, she breathed determinedly in and out, in and out, until the worst of it was over and she could escape to her car. She wanted to lower the seat and take a nap, but it was too cold without the engine running, and she was afraid of the fumes. This worry cheered her; she wanted to live, didn't even want to flirt with suicide, and when her face was dry she went back inside, determined to happen cheerily across her daughter and meet the object of her affection. But by that time they were gone.

Back at the *Chronicle* that afternoon, she closed the blinds to her private office and hung out the Do Not Disturb sign. Then she buzzed for Terry. "There's something very important I need to show you," she said. She glanced around, making sure once again that the blinds were closed tight. "Something you've just got to see for yourself." When he got there, she said, "Close the door." She stood behind it wearing only a blouse and stockings.

"Abby."

"I felt you just had to see this," she said, removing her shirt.

She felt his warm mouth on her neck and his cold fingers at the clasp of her lacy bra and knew that he was still hers. Though the blinds were drawn, the incomplete walls and the staff just outside added urgency to their quick, explosive sex.

"There," she whispered contentedly when he was inside her. "That's where you belong." His face, so like Marty's, attested reluctant agreement. She liked seeing Terry confused, liked knowing she could still do this to him. It somehow cleared the air between them even as it seemed, on the surface, to cloud their relationship. Afterward they clasped one another tightly, almost desperately, and for a while at least found themselves spared the discomfort of having to act like strangers despite their years of entanglement. For the rest of the day, when she looked at him, it was with an air of proprietary triumph, and it wasn't until evening, along with the children, Marty parked in front of the television and Phoebe immersed in a book, neither of them paying her the slightest bit of attention, that doubts set in. Fixing their dinner, she asked herself whether she wasn't being irrational about her husband, whether she was failing to let go of something already gone, but she felt too powerfully that it wasn't gone, that maybe it would never go, and now that she was over the initial sorrow and had taken an interesting lover of her own, she saw no reason to suppress her feelings about her foolish, wayward spouse, whom she loved in spite of everything.

She found excuses to go back to the mall, charging through the place in hopes her daughter would spot her. But she never spied Phoebe again. Had she and her beau gone elsewhere? Abigail worried about this; was it better just to let them fuck in their own rooms, where at least they're safe? Why can't they make out in parked cars the way young people are supposed to? She didn't learn anything more about her daughter's social life, but she did come to see the mall in a different light. It was like Krieger's, in a way, but a latter-day Krieger's in which the various departments had been sold off to specialists who lived and died by their own performance. So each of them was vastly more up-to-the-minute fashion conscious than the scuffed tables full of brassieres and girdles available at Krieger's. Nobody at Rockton Plaza would dream of wearing a girdle.

When she reported all this to Charles, it was obvious he already knew all about it. Sometimes, he said, he heard the mothers in the wood-paneled elevators, marveling with their kids at the high-toned trappings of the store. They reminisced about lunches with *their* mothers in the old Garden Court, where the ladies wore hats, and they remembered putting together a trousseau at Krieger's. "What is that, like lace or something?" a daughter would say, slightly annoyed by this boring topic.

"As if anyone would ever again amass a chestful of fancy linens before getting married," he said. "They all see the place as a kind of museum, except sanctified by their own memories. A place to buy ugly furniture that will last you a lifetime, in an age when nobody in his right mind would ever want such a thing. The mothers take the daughters and maybe buy them something they'll never wear, but none of the younger people would dream of shopping for themselves here."

"But maybe we can work with that," Abigail replied. "Not with the ugly furniture, but with the memories, with the idea of shopping as something special—of Krieger's as something special, something that sets you apart from the mall rats. Isn't that the basis of all marketing these days? That the product makes you somebody special?"

She wondered if Charles was only pretending to greet her idea with enthusiasm. He acted determined to save Krieger's and preserve its independence, to bring the stores up to date and embrace the changes that had swept through retailing just as they had swept through the rest of society. Yet there was an element of performance in his mien, something to which she was exquisitely attuned after years of marriage to Terry. She wondered what was really going on in Charles' head and in darker moments got the sense that he considered himself to be presiding over a hopeless dinosaur, with its hulking building and many departments, each less stylish than the last. He was the tiny head of this great moribund beast, and only he was smart enough to know for sure that it was lumbering off into the sunset, carrying him along at its very pinnacle.

chapter THIRTEEN

The raid didn't so much kill Alphabet Soup as put it out of its misery. The police came in force one unseasonably warm night with a search warrant, and so Frank and Emily met Bob Varity there and watched as Jepson and the other grim-faced officers took everything: every scrap of paper, every student's file, every coffee mug. Everything.

Emily witnessed this event in numbed silence, standing by as the uniformed officers roughly emptied out the cabinets and dumped the contents of her desk drawers into plastic bags. They went through the staff members' cubbyholes, the bathroom cabinets, the supply room, the kitchen, and the storage areas. "How could this be happening?" Frank wondered aloud. But Emily said nothing.

Left without even a list of home phones, she had no way to notify parents, and so numbly she posted a handwritten sign that would tell everyone the next day to go home. The school was closed, she wrote in crayon, "until further notice." She lettered these words carefully, as if in a dream. Then she and Frank went home and finished what was left of his special bourbon. While they drank, they speculated about what their lives might be like elsewhere and whether these lives would be conducted as one.

"What I always wondered was, why Annette? Because I knew, of course. Somewhere I knew. I pretended to myself not to, I guess because choosing someone like that just meant you were unhappy with me. I couldn't imagine there were any qualities of hers that you wanted so badly."

"I just fell into it, Em." He was embarrassed, worried that she would suggest it was because of her difficulties with sex and that he would then have to lie some more. "It's just the way men are. Maybe I needed somebody to take care of."

"How could I have married such a stupid man? I've cleaned up your messes all these years, and now when you get around to feeling you should take care of somebody else, you settle on the least interesting woman we know." Emily puffed on a cigarette. She was cultivating this habit after years of abstention. "Who else?"

"Maybe it was because she wasn't interesting. Because she needed me, needed help the way anyone might need help. It was a little chance to be whole again, to walk without a limp."

"Who else, Frank?" she said, her voice hard as the blade of a shovel. "And what else? Tell me everything."

"Emily." He rubbed his face. "She needed me in a way you never would."

"I'm not going to prison because of your lies, do you hear me?" she practically shrieked. "Did you do what they say you did? Did you fondle any of those kids? I need to know, Frank. Tell me what you did!"

"Don't you see this is the only way they can win? To sow doubt?"

Suddenly she was swept by a wave of unreality. Surely she wasn't having a discussion with her philandering husband about whether they were both likely to be imprisoned forever for child abuse. Surely their school wasn't closed, their lives weren't shattered. Surely this was all some computer error, some nightmare from which at any moment she would awake.

"Emily? Do you see that?"

Already, they were out of touch with the other teachers. Their lawyers had advised them not to have any further communication.

"You're the man with nine lives, Frank. What do you think? Will we survive this one?"

"Absolutely."

"I don't mean will we go to prison. I know it won't get that far. I mean you and me, and each of us. How will we go on with life after this? I'll never look at the world the same way again. And I know that some people will always believe the charges, no matter what the grand jury decides. Either way, of course, the thing we've built together is gone, smashed to bits." She took a sip of her drink. "It's a relief, really. I would never have said this before, or to anyone else, but it's a relief. The end of our marriage is a relief too."

"Emily, please—"

"Don't be stupid, Frank. I could never leave you now. Not until this is all over."

"Em, I can't give you a good reason to stay except that I love you."

"They say we're in league with the devil, Frank. Sometimes I think it must be true. Look at you, with your devil's peak and swarthy skin. Your hairy body. Your cloven hooves." She let herself be drunk for a minute and began to slur, to wag her finger. "The others don't know about the cloven hooves, but I do."

She began to cry then. Her own joke set her off, throwing her plight into relief too sharp for her to bear, and she broke down, doubling over and covering her face. Frank went to her, knelt down and gingerly placed his hand on her back until finally, sensing that she would allow it, he could enfold her.

They began waiting now. At Varity's suggestion, they each kept a small bag packed in case they were to be arrested, and in the interim they waited for what they were told would be their indictment. Waiting became their hobby, their sport, their calling. It was like waiting to die, the little time left polluted by the knowledge of what was coming next. They prepared in different ways: Emily made lists and set about accomplishing everything on them so that, eventually, she would sit in a chair with her hands folded, as if at an airport, all the frantic planning and preparation behind her. She liquidated their investments, cashed in their insurance policy and tapped their home equity to the fullest, all in preparation for what she was warned would be gigantic legal bills if and when she came to trial. Frank, on the other hand, seemed to focus on preparing himself mentally and even spiritually. He read some of his favorites, consuming not just *Inferno* but also *Purgatorio,* not just the Old Testament but the New. He packed two bags, one with his clothes and shaving paraphernalia and the other with books. It helped him to think of himself as a martyr, perhaps because he had grown up with the Catholic martyrs, so often were they invoked at school, and also because martyrdom ultimately meant vindication at the cost of mere suffering in the here and now. He and Emily went forth into the streets of Webster when they had to, although they tried to arrange their errands when things were quietest, and they cooked one another elaborate meals that they would remember if they found themselves subsisting for several days on prison fare. They stopped worrying about cholesterol, played cards, became connoisseurs of the TV listings, wrote letters to their bewildered son urging him not to come. They didn't talk much at first about what was coming, and to Frank his wife seemed permanently stiffened by anger and disappointment, even as she yielded to his hugs and allowed him to hold her through the night. It was hurtful but necessary, he knew, and he held her in spite of it, even made it in his mind an aspect of his martyrdom. He had earned this mortification and would relish it. He saw too, as he always did at times of trouble, how much she meant to him. His consistently expressed love for her gilded this blighted period of their lives for a while, but Bob Varity one day brought them back to earth.

"Emily, I can't represent you anymore," he said on the phone.

"You can't represent me?"

"You or Frank." Always he sought to reassure, but today she heard a metallic hardness in his voice. "Evidently your husband abused my son. I can't say much about it because frankly I'm in a state of shock. I don't blame you, Em. I really don't think any of this has been your doing. But you'll need to find another lawyer."

"Bob, you can't believe—"

"I don't know what to believe. You just need another lawyer. There's any number of good ones out there. Better than me, in fact. I just can't be involved in your defense any further. Get somebody soon. The charges are very serious, and this morning I learned that Belinda Jackson's attorneys are seeking to place a lien on the school property. I can't help you with that either. Everything you've told me up till now is protected by attorney-client privilege, but that's it."

Emily hung up the phone in a panic verging on euphoria, as if she had been struggling with all her might to hold onto a window ledge and could finally savor the release of letting go.

It was late, and the Food for Thought sandwich on Errol Jones' desk seemed to grow more inert the longer it took him to eat it. He drank stale coffee poured from the bottom of the office pot and worked feverishly with a legal pad to make sense of the multiplying list of victims and charges arising before him.

The creeping growth of allegations metastasizing outward from Alphabet Soup was the source of much anguish to the chief deputy district attorney, who recognized that hysteria was settling over Vanatee County. He worried that all the static surrounding the case would obscure the genuine abuse he was certain had occurred. That would make it harder to convict the real criminals. Cal Hawthorne would know all this, and so the entire enterprise was threatened from that quarter as well. Or was it? Could Hawthorne really pull the plug on this thing now? Was not the growing hysteria an asset inasmuch as it would force the prosecutor to act, even if he didn't want to?

The signs of mass hysteria were laid out on Errol's desk. Allegations of child abuse were popping up all over Vanatee County and the surrounding area. Alphabet Soup children alleged that they had been abused in the local McDonald's, a working class bar in the east end of town, three different drug stores, the basement of an unoccupied private home, the parking lot of the public library, and behind some bushes in Throgmorton Park. Some of these children contended that the network of abusers went far beyond staff members at the school, and it was possible that there was some truth to these allegations. Why should the conspiracy be limited only to members of the teaching profession? So when children pointed at postal workers, plumbers, bank tellers, waiters, and the like, investigators overcame the natural tendency to dismiss these assertions as childish confusion arising from the ordeal. Instead, they investigated. When children implicated a mysterious naval officer in a series of appalling sex acts, investigators were stymied until Jepson realized that the only people in Webster who wore nautical-looking attire were the pilots who flew commuter planes in and out of Webster Airport. Only half a dozen of these were regulars in Webster, and all were now under suspicion.

There was no hiding from it. Obviously, a climate had been created in which it was too easy to "disclose" abuse. Children who did so were lavishly rewarded with toys, treats, and attention, and the local culture had clasped families of disclosing children in the full embrace of media affection. Hawthorne had been right, Errol began to see, about what a bad deal the whole thing would be for Webster. As the allegations spread to more schools, more teachers, more and more people from all walks of life, the posture of adults toward children changed markedly. Errol saw this himself on the streets, in the stores, even in his own behavior. He had always liked children, but now they made him nervous, and he knew he was not alone in this. Adults in Webster were no longer particularly friendly toward little children. They no longer smiled indulgently, no longer picked them up or tickled them or chatted teasingly.

Finally, there was the problem of Lucille, whose son had made so many accusations, against so many people, that they had lost all credibility. Jones often found himself awakened in the middle of the night by Lucille, whom he had rashly given his home telephone number, calling to report that her son had been abused by a local minister, the Chevy dealer in Rockton, the manager of the Food-O-Rama when the family went grocery shopping, and even the manager's German shepherd, somehow, when the manager was off duty. Her late-night ravings were frightening, indiscriminate, venomous. There was an undercurrent of threat in her boozy diatribes, as if she knew that her listeners' faith was eroding even as she ranted. She hinted that the mayor might be involved. Lucille was the fly in the ointment, someone it would be hard for a jury not to see as crazy and vicious, especially in comparison to the nice, decent folks who ran Alphabet Soup. When she suggested that the district attorney was dragging his feet because he himself had a taste for young boys, Errol stopped taking her calls. But he couldn't stop his own doubts about where all this was leading.

The next morning, bright and early, he laid things out for Hawthorne. They sat in the district attorney's office with a third man, introduced as Elliott Gordon. "My new media consultant," Hawthorne pronounced, eyebrows raised in his best what's-the-world-coming-to style. "He's here to get a feel for what we do, how we work. The election is always sooner than you think."

Gordon was from New York. His clothes were slouchy and European looking, in fashionable shades of gray and blue only barely discernible from one another. His gray hair was cropped short and covered only the sides of his head, and his eyeglasses were the arty, fragile kind that in certain Webster bars were enough by themselves to get you punched in the face. He said little as Errol launched into his pitch. It was thorough, concise, and politically savvy, but Errol was sure Hawthorne would see that his heart wasn't in it. He was conflicted, he wanted to say. The case was a mess. They might never sort out what truly happened.

"Correct me if I'm wrong," Hawthorne finally said. "We have many more allegations and supposed perps than this."

"That's correct."

"But we can't charge everybody, right? Because then we'd be indicting half the people in town."

Errol shrugged, giving Hawthorne a way out. "We could indict based on the most credible accusations and acknowledge that the general atmosphere has led to a certain inevitable hysteria and some unfounded reports of child abuse far beyond Alphabet Soup. It's a problem, no doubt about it."

"So basically we're in the position of deciding that some are guilty and not others. On what basis are we drawing this distinction?" Errol noticed that Hawthorne hardly ever moved his head as he talked. "Is it strictly temporal? Allegations made before a certain date are credible, while those made later are not?"

"It's not just that—"

"Free child abuse after January 1? Kind of like off-season fares to the Caribbean. And it's not based on the credibility of the accuser, right? Because little Jeffrey Lyttle has been abused by Doberman pinschers, Martians, Volvos—"

"No one can blame the kid for being screwed up, after what he's been through. We just need to sort out the wheat from the chaff in this case, and that means focusing on the school, at least right now."

"Options?" Hawthorne was playing professor again, and it was annoying.

"If you don't bring some charges in this case, you're toast," Errol replied. "And a bunch of babyfuckers walk. I don't think those are acceptable outcomes."

"My feelings exactly. We indict everybody from the school. Everybody else walks. This is not going to be pretty, but it's got to be done. These people are monsters, I'm convinced of that now. Let's time the announcement for maximum impact. Get it on the television news. National. And let's understand: once we do this, there will be no looking back. The people we indict are guilty. They're child molesters, and we'll pursue them to the ends of the earth."

Terry busied himself in the kitchen while Diana reproached him for canceling the dinner they were supposed to have with his father.

"I just couldn't, somehow," he said. "It's always such an ordeal. I wanted to be with you." *Or more truthfully,* he thought with a pang, *I wasn't sure I wanted you entangled any further in my life. Just in case.*

"But just to leave a message that way. What if he didn't get it? He might be waiting for you at the restaurant, and there's no way he can get hold of you. He doesn't have this number, right?"

"L-L-Let's not worry so much about Dad, OK?"

"He needs your help, Terry. He calls me now and then, but of course I can't tell him anything. Nobody in the press knows the story the way you do."

"And I intend to keep it that way."

"He's probably lonely, too. Nobody to eat with."

"He's got his crew with him. Whole fucking entourage."

Diana sighed, but Terry was unrepentant. He wouldn't be scolded about his father by someone who had no idea of what had come before, and he didn't want to feel guilty about blowing off their dinner date. He and Diana were opening cartons of takeout.

"Here, we can visit with him the way the rest of America does," he said, flipping on the television. "He's at his best that way anyhow."

They watched a few minutes of the news until Maury was introduced—with a special report, entitled "Children at Risk."

"What the hell is this?" Terry wondered aloud. "He didn't tell me he was going with anything yet."

"Downtown Webster." The voice was Maury's, over shots of the quaintest stretch of Main Street. "In many ways, it's a throwback. Fred still runs the local hardware store with an old-fashioned postal window in back. People still sit on their front porches, weather permitting. And they still take the time to say hello." Maury, walking along a porch-lined side street, nods warmly at an old man walking a poodle. "With roots going back to the seventeenth century and many residents who seem to have lived here just as long, it's a place where everybody really does know your name." There were shots of kids making snowmen, of Phil Marcantonio, the cop at the main intersection at rush hour, holding up traffic for a little old lady to cross, of a homeowner shoveling his walk. "For years, in my wastrel youth, I spent summers in this town. My son still lives here. It's a great place to escape the rat race of the big city, and thanks to the universities, there are good restaurants, a jazz club, a couple of theaters. Webster would seem the ideal place to raise a family"—a mother shepherding some young charges into a van, some kids playing soccer behind the junior high—"away from the crime, dirt, and indifference of city life."

Suddenly, in front of City Hall, Maury was back. He was wearing a trench coat.

"But as it turns out, the children of Webster weren't as safe as residents thought they were. For weeks now, the venerable Alphabet Soup Preschool"—sinister long shot of the deserted building—"has been under investigation for possible child molestation by one or more of its staff members. The allegations have rocked this close-knit community. Alphabet Soup was popular—so popular that my own grandson couldn't get in. Well, thank God for that. Earlier today, in the nearby county seat of Rockton, the investigation reached its culmination. A grand jury indicted nine members of what it described as a ring of Satan worshipers on charges they sexually abused dozens and dozens of children in their care. The 673-count indictment, due to be unsealed tomorrow, catalogs a series of horrors that would be difficult to believe if the children themselves had not attested to their accuracy."

"What the fuck is this?!" Terry said in astonishment.

"Oh my God, indictments!" Diana's face flushed with excitement. "Terry, Hawthorne didn't even tell *me.*"

Now a woman was speaking on screen, but she didn't look or sound normal, and Maury came on after a sentence or two to explain that her voice had been altered and she was wearing a disguise. The wig was grotesque, her voice processed like that of some turncoat hitman testifying before Congress. Her face was a blurry collage of computer-generated colors. Yet it was obvious from her body that it was Elana Auerbach, one of the mothers Terry had told his father about. *How could this be happening?*

"You can't imagine the sense of betrayal," she croaked electronically. It was Darth Vader as soccer mom. "The sense of violation, when someone does this to your kids. I was one of the ones who thought the charges were false. I believed the teachers, not the children."

"What made you change your mind?" Maury asked helpfully.

"My own child," she said, her voice wavering, her head quivering with rage around the pastiche of colors that replaced her face. "My own daughter was abused at that school. She finally disclosed—disclosed what they did to her in that awful, awful place."

"How did it feel"—Maury shook his head, as if in disbelief—"when you first got the news?"

"Like I'd been shot. I can't even describe it. You entrust your children, the most precious things in the world." Her voice broke for an instant, but she gathered herself. "It's beyond your worst nightmare. Beyond anything you can imagine." In a cutaway shot, Maury's face was arranged to reflect the unfathomable horror. Elana continued: "Sometimes I wonder if we'll ever be able to put our lives back together. My husband wanted to kill them. And I don't blame him. I wanted to kill somebody too."

Maury was back, still in the trench coat. "Mrs. A, as we'll call her to protect what is left of her privacy, has channeled her pain and anger into an informal organization of Webster women whose children say they were abused at what was once the town's premier preschool. They share information, help one another cope, and provide comfort and support as they try to work through what is surely the second worst thing that could happen to a parent. Vanatee County District Attorney Cal Hawthorne declined to comment on an indictment that hasn't been released, but sources close to his office tell us the allegations include almost every conceivable sexual act, in many cases accompanied by Satanic religious rituals. Authorities believe the abuse went on for years, but went undiscovered in part because the accused threatened to hurt the children's parents if they ever told anyone about what was happening to them.

"Authorities credit a single courageous child for coming forward, and the innovative work of Vanatee County's new Child Intervention Services Agency for using advanced techniques to elicit the testimony that broke this extraordinary case."

Now a new face appeared. He looked familiar, but Terry's shock was such that he couldn't come up with the name, wasn't sure of the connection.

"We've never, and I mean never, had anything like this happen in Webster." MAYOR DOMINIC LOQUENDI, it said across the speaker's chest. He was the picture of sincerity—shocked, horrified, "clearly shaken," in newspaper parlance. "This is just the worst thing I can think has ever happened around here. Until these indictments you're telling me about—which I haven't seen, of course—the town was divided about all this. There were a lot of people who felt the charges were outrageous, that it couldn't be true."

"What do *you* think, Mayor?" Maury asked, his brow knit with concern.

"That's for a judge and jury to decide. But I find it hard to believe that little children would lie about something like this. I mean, how would they even know what to report, what to make up, if it hadn't happened to them? This stuff is just so far outside the experience of most children—as it should be. It's tragic, really." The camera moved in close here. "That it can happen in such a nice town."

"But if it happens here—" Maury prompted innocently.

"It can happen anywhere," the mayor obliged. "Absolutely."

"Are America's children safe *anyplace?*" Maury's face was covered with pathos.

"I've been asking myself the same thing for the past few weeks," the mayor said.

Maury, in his trench coat again, out in front of the preschool. It wasn't just closed; it was cordoned with yellow police tape, as if it were the site of a murder.

"It's important to remember," he intoned, "that what we have here are allegations. *Charges.* In our system, remember, people are innocent until proven guilty. Proving all this in court may be the biggest test yet for the authorities, the parents, and most of all, the children of this quintessentially American community.

"From the little town of Webster, itself no longer innocent, I'm—"

Terry didn't wait for him to finish, didn't get his coat, didn't say a word to Diana. He just pulled on his boots, dashed for his car, and drove. The best hotel in Webster was out near Webster State, and Terry raced for it. He wanted to get there fast, husband his anger before it dissolved into resignation, self-pity, God knew what else. The roads were clear and dry for once, and he made good time, pulling up to the hotel with a theatrical screech and leaving his car right out front, at the curb. He dashed for the elevator, remembering his father's room number.

"Terry! I've been looking all over for you. A guy in your position ought to have a beeper."

It was him, right there in the lobby. He would brazen it out with a smile on his face.

"You son of a bitch!" Terry let him have it at the top of his lungs. Let the entire place hear. Let him blush every time he faces the desk clerk. Visiting academics, flabby parents of undergraduates, all of them looked stunned. "You manipulative cocksucker!" Terry ran right up into his father's face. He wanted to hit him, grab him by the lapels, and lift him off the ground. "What the fuck was that on TV just now? What kind of pathological fucker would do something like that to his own son—"

"Terry, stop it!" The color had drained from Maury's face as he looked around, embarrassed to his blood cells. "Stop screaming. Are you crazy?"

"You pathetic old fraud! Are you really that desperate?"

"Outside!" Maury grabbed him and began dragging him toward the door, but Terry grappled free and wouldn't be led. He began shouting again, Maury went for his shirtfront, and Terry grabbed him back, each surprising the other with his strength.

"Outside?!" Terry exclaimed. "You shameless whore, if I take you outside, I'll beat the living crap out of you."

"Terry," Maury said, trying solemnity. His hair was disheveled, but he made calming gestures with his hands. A security guard appeared and the elder Mathers shook him off. "Terry. Terry, please. You've vented, now come into the bar and listen to me. Come—listen, listen to me! Son—I was going to tell you at dinner. I tried calling you at the paper, at your apartment. I spoke to Abigail, you can ask her yourself."

"You're unbelievable! Get away from me!"

Terry stalked outside, but his father followed, grabbing his son by the shirt, its tails already hanging out of his pants. They grappled there by the car, Maury vowing, "I'm not letting you go until you give me a chance to explain!"

"Don't make me hit you, Dad," he said finally and, when his father let down his guard, tossed him aside. Terry quickly got into the car, but Maury got in front of it.

"You'll have to run me over," he said. "You'll have to run me down before I let this go."

Terry covered his face in despair; was there no getting away from this man? *He's inside me,* he thought. *It's like running from myself.* As if reading his mind, Maury said, "I'll never stop being your father. Even if you do run me down."

"A f-f-fucking martyr on top of everything else," Terry said, pounding the wheel with his fist. "H-H-How the fuck could you do it?" He got out of the car again and went up to his father. The wind was brutal. "J-J-Just explain that, p-p-p—just please explain, and I'll be happy. I'll understand. That's all I want to do, understand."

"They weren't going to let you have it," Maury said. "They wanted exposure. Cal Hawthorne wants to get re-elected by a landslide so he can try for attorney general, governor, president, dictator for life. I didn't come here for this. I was going to do a curtain-raiser, just build on what you've done. But after I made contact, *they* approached me. Claimed they couldn't time the announcement for a weekly anyway."

"And you felt it was best to say nothing about any of this."

"I wanted to wait until, what? Thursday, so we could break the story together, me on TV, you in the paper, but they told me if I didn't go today they would give it to NBC. The series was slotted already, ready to go except now there was this peg. Besides, this will be good for you too. Believe me."

Terry looked at him.

"Trust me once in a while, will you, son? And think about shaving. They're not gonna want that beard on camera."

"What are you talking about?"

"They want you as a special consultant. It'll be lucrative, and you'll get a lot of face time."

"D-D-Dad, I don't want any f-f-face time. I just want to be able to do my job without this kind of interference."

"Terry, what did you think was going to happen?" his father said in exasperation. "That a story like this would sit around and wait for you to do something once a week? I guarantee you this will be everywhere tomorrow, the next day, the next year. It'll be *Time, Newsweek,* the works. It doesn't mean the people of Webster won't still look to the *Chronicle,* and nobody is sourced the way you are. But that's the way of the world."

"And you had no choice, right? You just made the best of a tough situation."

"I'm not going to lie to you, son. I needed a story like this. It helps put me back on the map, remind people that Maury Mathers is still around. Think of it as interest on the two hundred K. When you needed it, I was there. Correct? Always have been, always will be. But sometimes it's my turn."

Compared to the original story in the *Chronicle*, Maury's report was a hydrogen bomb that went off in the wake of a popgun. Terry felt the scales drop from his eyes, felt he could see in all its nakedness the self-delusion of people who flung words at one another on paper, the futility of print in the late twentieth century. He was astonished the first time he was on network television—by the magnitude of the operation, the casual power of the technology, the mass of resources brought effortlessly to bear, the attention to image, the distance between that image and the underlying reality. They were making little movies, really, telling stories cinematically, and they acted like petty moguls, reorganizing the raw material offered them by the world into the scenes required to grab at the emotions. The *Chronicle* by comparison was a joke. Even the mighty *Tribune* paled into insignificance, except to the extent it influenced these workaday producers, camera crews, and on-air personalities who set the tone of the nation's unconscious with their quotidian output. These people spoke directly to millions as easily and as intimately as any spouse—perhaps more so.

Alphabet Soup put Terry on television. As the case unfolded, he found himself more and more in demand on camera and somehow found the ability to speak without stuttering too badly. It turned out to be easy, since he was really only speaking to the small group of technicians and others who would relay his words to the masses. He had no sense of speaking before an audience at all. What stutter remained endeared him to many viewers, particularly women, who in the months ahead would read about TV's new "Halting Hunk" in *Redbook, Cosmo,* and *TV Guide.* There were the inevitable father-son stories. He got a new haircut, with some touch-up to cover the gray at his temples and beard, always closely cropped now. He got used to makeup and learned to milk a story emotionally. He grew to like TV, like being instantly recognized instead of laboring in mindless obscurity, like having his pronouncements reach millions instead of the few indifferent thousands who mostly bought the paper for the supermarket coupons anyway.

The network was pleased too; it always struggled to appeal to women and could boast now of employing the handicapped. Terry's stutter was "irrelevant when you consider the great wealth of knowledge and expertise he brings us," a network spokeswoman told the *Tribune* when the paper carried an item about the phenomenon. "The network has always been committed to diversity, and this is just an example of how viewers benefit when we engage the talents and resources of all quarters of our society in delivering the news."

chapter FOURTEEN

The arraignment was grim. It was like some awful theater—nine anguished figures awaiting their turn before bland little Evan Prine, a political hack in judicial robes whose long experience taking pleas did not include anything quite like this. He looked nervous, and his air today was that of a mortician.

The editor of the *Webster Chronicle* knew all of the defendants at least by sight but hadn't seen any of them for a while. They had declined his requests for interviews and wouldn't even talk on the phone, letting their lawyers field all inquiries. The result had been coverage that gave short shrift to their protestations of innocence and tended to subject their bizarre explanation for what was going on to banal summary. Now, however, he would get some idea of what it was like to stand accused of child abuse. The courtroom was packed, and when the defendants were brought in, the benches erupted in a sea of catcalls and hisses. Terry was stunned, not just at this but at the defendants' haggard, shipwrecked appearance. One or two seemed in a state of shock, unable to absorb what was going on around them. The scorn of the full house, which Prine eventually gaveled into submission, lent a whiff of the gallows to the place.

Frank Joseph was the first called before the judge. His plea was "not guilty," which was always the plea at arraignments, but when the words were spoken the audience erupted again, and the defendant looked bitterly amused. Judge Prine, a small man of about fifty with an immaculately cropped dark beard, plaid shirt and knit tie, twice threatened to clear the courtroom, but Terry was sure he never would, and the others too seemed to regard the threats as hollow.

"Counselor, state your position on bail."

"Your Honor, we believe the defendant should be held without bail," said Errol Jones, who was representing the District Attorney's Office. "In light of the allegations, Mr. Joseph is a serious flight risk, and at the time of arrest was found with his bags packed."

"That's ridiculous, Your Honor." This was the guy who had succeeded Varity, Terry knew. From out of town, supposedly very good. "He had a bag packed because I told him to anticipate being arrested, which is exactly what occurred. Like all these defendants, my client has the deepest possible roots in this community, and regardless of what people may think, he is innocent until proven otherwise. I move for $25,000."

This speech elicited further grumbling and a couple of thwacks with the gavel.

"So the choice is between letting him walk virtually on his own recognizance and holding him no matter what, huh? Not much choice. Set bail at $500,000."

"If it please the court," the defense lawyer said in injured tones. "The defendant can't possibly meet that figure, you're basically punishing him without trial in the absence of any priors—"

"Can't win 'em all, counselor. Next defendant."

All the women were given $250,000 bail, in keeping with their even deeper local roots. Pearl, looking unspeakably old and weak, seemed nearly to faint when the charges were read. Finally Jesus Mendoza was called. He looked terrified, and Reverend Albertson popped up next to Terry.

"Your Honor, may I assist the defendant?" he said in his booming church voice. "I'm his pastor, and I speak Spanish."

In a flash, Albertson charged forward to stand beside Jesus. He placed his hand on the defendant's shoulder and served as translator. When the subject of bail came up, Albertson said, "Your Honor, I can personally vouch for this young man. There is no more honest or law-abiding member of this community."

When this was unavailing and bail was set at $250,000, Albertson said: "Thank you, Your Honor. Who do I see about posting that bail so this young man can be released?"

As Terry described it in the next edition of the *Chronicle,* Albertson put up the Tabernacle church building—the former supermarket, the parking lot, the works. He persuaded the church trustees to go along in part by pledging his own house and car as well. Thus, Jesus was released while his co-defendants languished in jail. Albertson also launched a campaign to exonerate his quiet parishioner, organizing a vigil at the church and speaking out against the charges. "The district attorney has spoken of perversion," Terry quoted him as saying. "But the only perversion here is a perversion of justice."

"How can you say these things?" Terry demanded. "You don't know what happened at that school. You think these kids just got together and decided to accuse grown-ups of things they never even knew existed before? I have kids; they don't just come in and claim someone stuck something up their ass the way they'd ask for a pony."

"But see, I know Jesus is innocent. And I've talked to his lawyer, so I know how those kids came to make these allegations. They didn't just well up. This is something infectious, something brought in among our children and then spread by adults, until the kids understand what they're supposed to 'disclose' and say what we want to hear."

" 'S-Something brought in among our kids, s-something infectious.' But who brought it in? Satan maybe? The Easter bunny? D-Do you know how d-difficult it is for these kids to tell anyone that they were abused?"

"You keep telling me you're not a man of faith, Terry. But you seem to have faith in other people's goblins. I'm appealing to reason. I don't believe we've got a coterie of Satan worshipers caring for children here in

Webster, except to the extent the kids are left in front of the television. I think it's all hysteria, craziness. Nobody reads Chesterton anymore, but he would surprise you. He was the one who said: 'When a man ceases to believe in God, he does not believe in nothing. He believes in anything.' "

How could anyone be so blind? Religious faith must be an effective conditioner for preposterous beliefs of all kinds, Terry decided, and so it was easy for Albertson to believe his own narrative about Alphabet Soup. This in the face of new disclosures every day. Diana barely had time to see Terry, so busy was she eliciting testimony from shell-shocked children who had suffered at the hands of the school's staff, and Krieger's had already distributed buckets full of tokens, each good for $100 worth of toys, to kids who had revealed what was done to them.

Not everyone in Albertson's flock believed his version of events either. Terry had heard from some Tabernacle parishioners none too happy at hocking everything to free a Mexican immigrant who, of all the defendants, posed the greatest flight risk, and a good many of these parishioners doubted his innocence. How could they feel otherwise? Television, radio, and all the newspapers (including the *Chronicle*) hawked lurid accounts of ritualized abuse the defendants had inflicted on the innocent children of Webster. At a press conference outlining the charges in the indictment, Cal Hawthorne had condemned the school "as nothing more than a convenient pretext for bringing children together for the purpose of ritualized sexual abuse. Silence was enforced through naked terror. Children were intimidated by threats to themselves and their parents, ritualized killings of animals, and repeated invocations of the devil, witchcraft, and the black arts." He added, "We now know that the children of Alphabet Soup were submitted to the most horrifying possible regime of physical and sexual abuse. They were forced to consume urine and feces, forced to submit to every conceivable sex act, photographed and videotaped for the production of child pornography, and used as playthings by a group of twisted adults whose perversions are now, thank God, now longer possible. Based on the charges we've brought and the evidence we've compiled, we intend to put the perpetrators of these awful crimes away for the rest of their lives, which is unfortunately the severest punishment available to us under the law."

t's amazing that I casually moved to Webster, and now here we are with one of the most egregious cases of child abuse ever documented," Diana said one night over dinner. "And Terry, these people really are Satan worshipers. I mean, they *believe* this stuff. They had a coven over there called Ariel, and one of them, this really femme, all-American girl-next-door type, kept a witch's diary of their meetings and so forth, although of course she doesn't mention all the really serious stuff they did. They even called themselves witches. It's all in keeping with what we've heard from the kids. They tell us about all kinds of ritual sacrifices and other spooky stuff— they'd kill cats in front of a kid, rabbits, snakes, let the animals bleed to death slowly. Can you imagine the impact of this on a four-year-old? The police are checking around now with people whose pets are missing."

"K-K-kind of gives you the chills, no? That we have such good evidence in favor of Satan, and no evidence at all in favor of God."

"Terry, there's evidence of God all around us! That these children are free at last—I mean, think about what they've been *living* with. Or that you and I met, out of all the people in the world." She smiled and ran a fingernail up his thigh. "Lots of things."

Later they watched his father deliver a special report on the charges in Webster. It was gripping stuff. Maury detailed the allegations again, showing mug shots of every defendant in the classic juxtaposition of guilt: full face right next to left-facing profile.

"The suspects are behind bars now," Maury intoned, addressing America from in front of the Vanatee County Detention Center, its concrete brutalism standing for the crushing weight of justice. He wore the trench coat again. "They're locked up for what prosecutors and a lot of other people hope will be a long, long time, held here in this institution behind me under the tightest possible security—for their own protection as well as the safety of the children of Webster. The arrest of these nine individuals has stopped the abuse of children at one preschool, but it hasn't stopped the effects of this case from rippling out far and wide all across this country. Since the news of abuse in Webster broke, similar reports of sexual abuse have arisen at no fewer than thirty-nine preschools or day-care facilities from coast to coast, many of them echoing in chilling detail what authorities have found here. In Knoxville, Pittsburgh, Dallas, St. Paul, Boise, San Diego, and elsewhere, the very people entrusted with the care of our children are accused of sexually molesting them while their parents were away at work."

Cut to a bland-looking man of about thirty-eight in a white shirt and nondescript tie.

"We see a real pattern to these things," the man said, as the words REYNOLDS OLSON, FBI CHILD-ABUSE SPECIALIST appeared across his chest. "It starts with a single child getting the help and finding the courage to come forward. The key to this whole thing is breaking the silence, overcoming the shame. The abusers deny everything, but then others start to disclose. It's typical to hear from the kids about all kinds of sexual abuse, as well as a variety of quasi-religious practices surrounding the abuse and aimed also at terrorizing the youngsters into silence. There are often mutilations of animals, for example, and threats of harm against the kids' moms and dads."

"What on earth can we conclude from the amazing similarity of these cases from one place to another?" Maury asked in horrified bewilderment.

"We take this as a sign that there are people into this sort of thing everywhere. And that they communicate with each other. They're in touch."

"Are you saying you're investigating a national ring of Satanic child abusers? A massive conspiracy of some kind?"

"I can't comment on specific investigations, but certainly we're looking into the connections and similarities between these cases. Sure."

Now Maury was at one of those big, curved desks they rig up only in TV news studios. With him was a dark-haired former sportscaster. Terry suspected she was his father's latest.

"Suzie, nobody has as much insight into this whole situation as Terry Mathers, our man on the scene."

"There you are!" said Diana, who still couldn't get over the way he would pop up on television.

"Terry, how deeply scarred are these children? Will they ever get over the things they've been through?"

"Psychologically, perhaps never," Terry said from the same sweet spot in front of the jail. "One kid I heard about asked his mother, 'Mommy, when I die, will the bad memories go away then?' "

"My God," said Maury, shaking his big head. "Keep us posted on this tragic story, will you Terry? We don't want to miss a beat on this thing."

"Will do, Dad."

"Okay," Suzie said somberly, looking down for an instant and then brightening. "In a moment, we'll find out about a new medical procedure that can leave you looking—and maybe even feeling—happier. Sound far-fetched? Don't go away."

Terry hit the mute button on the remote in order to avoid the blast of sound from the commercial. He was a part of this now, he realized, a part of the great beast of televised culture that swept all before it.

"You were great," Diana said, giving him a hug. "How's it feel to be a TV star?"

"I've got to admit, it feels great," Terry said.

But he was still editor of the *Webster Chronicle,* which meant he didn't spend all his time jetting from one big story to another, legitimizing events with his mere presence. There was the battle for Krieger's, for instance, which had taken a backseat during the astonishing business of Alphabet Soup. Miraculously, Krieger's was now considered to have an even chance of shaking off Rothwax. The employee stock ownership plan that Abigail cooked up had been adopted, and with backing from the union, the store's workers shifted nearly three-quarters of their retirement money into Krieger's stock, prompted by a generous company matching plan that multiplied their shares—and thereby further diluted the raider's holdings.

"Don't you see?" Rothwax said on the phone. There was pity in his voice, and it was infuriating. "This plan is terribly ill-advised. These people are risking not just their jobs but their savings. When Krieger's tanks—and it inevitably will, believe me—they're totally screwed. They'll be out of work at the same time their retirement nest egg turns to ashes. These people are not kids, Terry. Have you looked at the average age up there? It's forty-seven, which in retailing is prehistoric. A quarter of the work force is over fifty-five."

"Of course, you're not entirely objective about this," Terry said, "given that the stock plan makes it harder for you to acquire the company."

"You're talking to me about objective?!" Rothwax was yelling now. "Excuse me, my friend, but your wife is Charlie Krieger's chief strategist—"

"We're separated, and I don't know that she's exactly—"

"She's in bed with Krieger and so is your newspaper, of which she remains the publisher all the while she's working against me. And your paper supports this whole thing editorially, no? Correct me if I'm wrong. Whatever happened to journalistic ethics, to all those ideals you brought in here along with the vow of poverty? To read the *Chronicle,* you'd think the ESOP was the long-awaited coming of the worker's paradise. Krieger's is your biggest advertiser and you have consistently danced to its tune—except for that Tartaglia guy, God bless him, who right now seems to be the only one in Webster who's got his head screwed on straight. If I wasn't trying to buy this company, I'd be shorting the crap out of it."

Tartaglia, in fact, had become the devil's advocate on this issue, speculating on what a nice place Webster would be without Krieger's and expressing thoughts otherwise forbidden in polite company. But by now Alphabet Soup had come to overshadow everything else in Webster, which had become famous for its hellish preschool. Late-night comedians made jokes about it, and using his lavish new television expense account to search through Nexis, the miraculous periodical database he could never before afford, Terry discovered stories about Alphabet Soup all over the world. The *Straits Times* of Singapore found reason to tut, tut, and an English-language newspaper in India wondered how Americans could give advice to others about the care of children when its own were placed in such jeopardy. Locally, Alphabet Soup was what people obsessed over. The courthouse vigil on the day of the arraignments was one of many public events arising out of the allegations, and as the editor of the *Webster Chronicle,* Terry assigned himself to cover almost all of them. All this public theater was convenient now that he was doing television, which demands a never-ending diet of political performance art.

Thus did he find himself directing a camera crew to cover perhaps three dozen Webster women protesting the Alphabet Soup prosecutions. They took to the streets on a cold Saturday morning, marching up and down Main chanting "Free the Eight! Free the Eight!" and handing out literature about the injustice being done, the history of Goddess worship, the religious rights of those who pursue Wicca, and so forth. "We are all witches," the flyers said, in an *ich bin ein Berliner* vein. The marchers, mostly women, had short hair and nondescript attire except for the yellow scarves that all of them wore. Many were swathed in overalls and denim, flannel and construction boots. A few marched in long black costumes, pointy hats, and Halloween masks, complete with nose warts and pointy chins. They walked with cardboard signs around their necks that said, "Don't burn us!"

"It's just a witch-hunt of the worst kind," Delia Kornfeld said for the cameras. She identified herself as "one of the coordinators" of the rally, and she urged Terry to see a Professor Meisner, a psychologist who was "doing some interesting work on the suggestibility of children." Terry barely heard this; people from the colleges were forever trying to get him to write about their pet projects (or their friends' pet projects). Besides, he was talking to Delia because she didn't hesitate to throw bombs in the form of sound bites. "Suppressing Wicca has long been a way that societies have silenced and oppressed powerful women. Now it's being used as an excuse to vilify these teachers. No one would dream of making their Catholicism or Judaism part of the charges against these people."

The protesters were met with some polite heckling at first, but soon crowds gathered along their route. People came out of stores, stopped in their tracks, and spontaneously began countering the hypnotic chant of "Free the Eight" with shouts of "Believe the Children! Believe the Children!" until finally Webster's Main Street was divided into warring choruses, each side shouting its faith at the other until the marchers moved past the heart of town, leaving flyers and astonishment in their wake.

"F-F-First and f-foremost," Terry explained to his father, outlining the taxonomy of opinion in Webster, "there's a hard core of people who believe the children wholeheartedly and expected others to do the same. This group includes the parents of the abused kids, of course, but also their friends and relatives, and most of the right-thinking people who set the public and political tone around here."

"They're the ones behind all these yellow buttons and bumper stickers, right?"

"That's right, and in Webster nowadays it's tough to say no when you're asked to wear one. Disbelieving the children is tantamount to joining their abusers. It's siding with the patriarchy that's been abusing women and children since the Greeks—"

"If not since Neanderthal times."

"I'm working up a piece about all this," Terry continued, sipping his coffee. They were in Aiello's, Maury glad to be back after so long. He wore radiantly new casual clothes, his white sneakers and white hair equally immaculate. "See, to disbelieve the children is to reject the whole idea of disclosure, which in turn would be a rejection of the talking cure that has itself acquired religious status around here."

"But how about regular folks? Joe and Jane Chardonnay?"

"M-Mainstream opinion seems to have coalesced around the true believers. People know that what happened at the school is still pretty murky, but they also know something bad did happen, and the mothers of the victims support this much larger c-cloud of b-belief that has settled onto the town."

"But there must be somebody who thinks this is all a pile of crap."

"Here too, there's a corps of activists who believe the Alphabet Soup Eight are innocent. In this view, they're victims of the displaced guilt felt by harried parents stuck on the capitalist treadmill of production and consumption. Floyd A-Albertson—"

"The minister, right? Former boozehound?"

"Right. A-Albertson is a de facto leader of this group not just because he believes in the cause and I quote him a lot, but also because his opponents want him in that role."

"Really? Why?"

"He's a religious figure, which enables them to dismiss his views as yet another reactionary outburst from p-p-people mired in the medievalism of church, God and so forth. And he's a man, which hurts his credibility too. His arguments on behalf of Jesus Mendoza's innocence—"

"Tell me who that is again?" Maury was scribbling in a tiny notepad.

"The school's janitor. Also the janitor at the Y, by the way. Very sad case. Anyway, in defending Jesus, Albertson is basically denying all the evidence. In this town, that just won't wash."

"What a business," Maury said, closing his pad. "Thanks for the briefing."

"B-B-But, Dad, there are complications. Look at the campus feminists. Most of them believe; the allegations have the ring of truth about them, and the school seemed patriarchal in nature, with F-F-F-Frank Joseph presiding over all these women like some bantam cock."

"Sheesh," Maury marveled, scribbling again.

"Yeah. But among some feminist intellectuals, the idea of all these women has actually added credence to the charges. They consider the surprise at the women's involvement proof of society's assumptions about the limits of female s-s-sexuality. And they want more regulation of day care. On the other side of the question, conservative Christians see the case as proof women belong at home with their kids."

"That's a pipe dream," Maury said flatly. "People aren't going back. We work for the nation's leading baby-sitter: television."

Just then a large group trooped in. Terry noticed their bus idling outside and gestured for his father to look. "Grief counselors," he said quietly. "The county's brought them in, volunteers from all over the state. I did a phoner with the ringleader; she said they respond to all kinds of emergencies this way. Just like the Red Cross."

Maury shook his head in disbelief.

"By the way, the lesbian g-g-grapevine here in town has c-carried news of this whole thing for a while, and now there's a bad split between the c-campus lesbians and the non-lesbian feminists."

"Are there any?"

"Dad, p-please. You know about Ariel, right?"

"Ariel?"

"The c-c-coven. Some of the women at Alphabet Soup would get together and shake bones at the sky, chant, whatever. Well, it turns out that a lot of young lesbians in Webster have dabbled in Wicca. Many live here precisely because it's such a good place for women who love women—

a place where they could walk hand-in-hand without fear of assault or even much staring. Anyway, the point is that the lesbians have mobilized around two of the accused women, who are lovers. And even though there is every reason to think the investigators are especially sensitive to this issue, the fear is that their lesbianism will be used to convict them."

"Burn them at the stake," Maury said sonorously. "Like in the good old days."

That night, in the supermarket, Terry walked along the checkout counters in search of a short line. Late-night mega-store faces, seen in the deathly fluorescent glare of consumerism, were always depressing, but this evening his fellow townspeople looked drugged, catatonic. Pilgrims bound for the River Styx. He had joined the long "ten items or less" line when he was jolted by a familiar voice.

"Get thee behind me, Satan!"

It was Niedleman, hands upraised, feigning holy terror. He wore a putty-colored raincoat with blisters where the fusing had separated at the pockets, and in his basket on the floor was a quart of nonfat milk, three cans of gourmet cat food, a bunch of carrots, a bag of frozen peas, and three packages of chicken drumsticks, which were on sale. Terry blushed. There were three packages in his own basket as well.

"I had just gone over to the rack to get a magazine, which is why I left my basket here," Niedleman said. "Do you mind?"

"H-How could the devil object to any request of yours?"

"You see this? We're in *Time* this week. 'The Devil and Denial in Webster.' So now sensible people who don't believe all this superstitious nonsense are in denial, as if we just can't accept reality. Can you believe it?"

"The *Chronicle* no longer publishes *Time* magazine," Terry said wearily. "I'm not my brother journalist's keeper."

"You people in the media are the only ones who believe in all this Satanic bullshit. Now you got all those schoolteachers locked up for nothing, including a fat old lady who never harmed a fly. Molesting a bunch of schoolchildren! My ass!"

"F-F-From the sage himself!" Terry was livid. "The man who's so eager to protect our kids from f-f-fluoridated water doesn't mind if dozens of them report being molested in their own preschool."

"What the hell does fluoride—"

"You only believe in threats nobody can see or document, isn't that it, Niedleman?" Terry said. "Or are you so jealous and obsessed that if I say the sky is blue, you contend it's red? Why don't you get a life and give the rest of us a break?"

"Because your stupidity is so dangerous it's got a bunch of innocent people behind bars, that's why. And because it's got all the teachers in Vanatee County afraid to touch their pupils and all the parents cowering lest their little ones go running to the authorities if they don't get exactly what they want when they want it."

"I'm sorry, but your ignorance is just unbelievable," said the heavyset woman in front of Niedleman. She swung around to face him like a battleship coming around to bring all its guns to bear. On her swollen bosom he spotted a yellow Believe the Children button. "My nephew was at that school, and the things he went through I wouldn't wish on any-body, even somebody as blind and pathetic as you are!"

"See what you've done?" Niedleman said to Terry. "Everything was fine until people got all swept up in this." He turned to the woman with the button. "I understand your concerns, madam. Sex is no doubt quite alien to you, but if you stopped to think for a minute, you'd realize it's extremely unlikely that dozens of kids could be molested for years right under everyone's nose—for years, mind you, but no ill effects until now."

"You little twerp, I ought to stomp the bejesus out of you right here in this store! If my husband was here, you wouldn't dare say such a thing to me, you filthy little coward!"

The manager came hustling over to calm things down, and Terry took the opportunity to skulk off. Niedleman was outrageous, an unbelievable boor, yet there was often a kernel of truth in his ravings. The children of Webster *had* seemed fine. Now, at least according to their parents, they were not so fine. They had night terrors, wouldn't eat, were suddenly afraid of the dark, suffered from stranger anxiety, didn't want to be left alone, regressed in unpredictable ways. Terry and Abigail had seen some of this in Marty, but who knew if it had to do with the atmosphere in Webster? He'd been having problems ever since his father moved out, and Terry had read that more than half of Webster's children would spend some time in a single-parent household by the age of eighteen. Yet parents suddenly were positive that sexual abuse was at the root of their kids' problems; some of them said their children had had these problems even before the scandal broke, and now at least they knew why.

A truck went by and the fixtures in the store shook slightly, reminding Terry of his days in California, where he'd lived through a couple of earthquakes. The situation of Webster's children seemed analogous; an earthquake gets everybody's adrenaline going. But that doesn't mean the ground didn't move.

chapter FIFTEEN

Melissa Faircloth had never been in a jail before, and though she was working hard to put on a reassuring face, it was all she could do not to shriek or flee as she walked coolly down the cinder-block corridors of the Vanatee County Detention Center. She held her head high and kept a steady gait as she followed the fat woman in the blue uniform with the jangling keys. Cool had always been Melissa's specialty—not cool in the way of hip clothes and body piercings, but cool in the face of woe. She didn't panic, never raised her voice. Some part of her secretly welcomed trouble, for the chance to remain calm in its face. She took pride in her dignity the way other people took pride in their looks or their cars. It was a useful vanity, hard-won for a pale, gawky child who tended to stand out just for her height. People sometimes dismissed the grown-up Melissa as a remote Southern princess, she knew; good posture and unflappability were not fashionable in Webster, but she had always found the pose useful.

"How're you doing, sweetheart?" she asked through the glass via the disgustingly sticky telephone. *My beautiful cousin,* Melissa thought. *You look like death itself.* "Are you eating? It's important to try and eat."

"I'm OK, Mel." Emily spoke in a raspy whisper. She was smoking again, Melissa knew, and said it helped her. "They have to keep me separate from the other inmates. I get death threats in the mail. But you'd be surprised. You gain something when you lose everything. I'll survive."

"I've talked to Dad about augmenting your legal team. His lawyer friends say these charges can't hold up, that it'll all collapse when it gets to court."

"They wanted me to plead, Mel. The prosecution. Admit everything and get off with a light sentence—as if five years is light. But with parole and so forth. Counseling. They're very big on counseling."

"What did you tell them?"

"That I'd rather die. They've already taken everything, so what do I have to lose?"

"Em, we'll get through this," Melissa said. "I promise you, we'll get through it. And Em—Em, if you did want to plead, it wouldn't change anything. We know you're innocent. Honey, just do what's best for you. We know it's all madness."

"Plead to what? What should I confess to? How about eating babies?"

"Em—"

"They tried to make it seem like the others were about to confess. Isn't that incredible? Like there was anything *to* confess. And still not a scrap of evidence. Just the ravings of a bunch of brainwashed three-year-olds."

"They've been excavating the school," Melissa said. "I don't know if your lawyer told you. Digging tunnels under the building. All over the property."

"Nothing would surprise me now."

"Looking for kiddie porn, apparently. They also want to find evidence of ritual sacrifices—bones, carcasses, whatever. Even a human body. Some kid said you all killed a little boy and buried him out back. They busted up the playground to get underneath. As if you could kill one of your charges and nobody would come around asking whatever happened to their kid."

"The world's gone crazy." Emily wiped at her eyes with a tissue. "Stark raving crazy."

"Emily, Annette's confessed."

Emily covered her mouth with her hand.

"They took her little boy," Melissa said. "She couldn't bear it, couldn't bear thinking she might never see her child again. That he might be left with that asshole husband of hers. He used to beat hell out of both of them, you probably know that. She's got no money to defend herself, so they got her a court-appointed lawyer, some geek from Rockton who doesn't seem to know anything. I don't know if she's in her right mind or not."

Emily leaned her forehead against the glass. Melissa reached forward to touch it and balled her hand into a fist against its bulletproof thickness.

"Em, listen to me, it's not the end of the world. The lawyers tell me they weren't surprised. Stalin got lots of people to confess. They use torture, brainwashing, whatever. People confess all the time when they're under duress. It's only natural."

"How could she do this!? First my husband and now this. That woman is insane!"

"Em, don't. It doesn't do any good. Let's focus on getting you out of here. Sooner or later, it's all going to come out. As God is my witness, I believe that."

"I can't say much about God right now." Emily swept her hair out of her face. It was chopped short and colorless. "I try to pray, but He's not here. I'm by myself right now. I try to understand. I think: this must be for some purpose—"

"I love you, Em. While I'm in the world, you're never by yourself." They both started to weep. "I promise you I will never rest until you're out of here. And Em, believe me, I'm not the only one. You have such extraordinary support in this town."

"My impression is that the whole world thinks we're all guilty."

"Well, we're certainly learning who our friends are," Melissa said. "You'd be surprised. There are people in this town who won't speak to me, won't even say hello anymore, but that's just a few. A good many can't believe it. They just can't. They've had their kids in the school, they've known you and your mom all these years. An elderly lady, doing those things to kids? It just doesn't make sense."

Melissa didn't mention that she had been snubbed in stores on Main Street, had come out of her house to find her car covered with animal blood, would lift the morning paper off her doorstep, and find "Move!" scrawled across page one in red crayon. Her neighbor for eight years since she had arrived from the South, Mrs. Ellicott, wasn't speaking to her anymore, and she wasn't welcome in the fish store because the owner's kid claimed he'd been abused at Alphabet Soup. Her own children were hounded and ostracized at school. She didn't mention, in other words, that for Emily's defenders Webster was becoming a living hell. Melissa didn't altogether mind having another pretext for her enormous aplomb. She did not exactly believe that the world was a reasonable or decent place but had found that pretending it was, subscribing to decency and charity and good sense, were more effective ways to get through life. She handled moral complexity well. She did not love her husband, for example, yet showed him the utmost kindness and loyalty, which he returned unstintingly to her and their two children. The two affairs she had had in their married life were conducted so discreetly, facilitated by the lockboxes that grant realtors access to the empty homes they are selling, that even in Webster almost no one knew about them. She didn't deserve to have an extramarital relationship if she was so clumsy about it that she let it hurt her family.

Back in Atlanta, when Melissa found herself sitting alone at open houses, she took to carrying a beautiful little gun that she cared for meticulously and learned to fire accurately. She was taller than her husband, and although she made a show of ladylike deference, it was her will to which his needs were subordinate. She was the one who had wanted to come to Webster, for example, to live near the cousin with whom she had spent summers as a child, and since Ted worked from home and was originally from the North, there was little objection. Her faith in her ability to control the situations she encountered partly explained why she calmly rang the doorbell on the imposing center-hall colonial just blocks from her own home in the twenty-five- or thirty-year-old Barrington Vistas development, where she had sold any number of houses to "executive" families just like the one that lived in this one.

There was no answer, and so she rang again and again until finally she spoke through the door. "Lucille," she said. "Please open up. I really need to talk to you."

Children's footprints moved antically across the snowy lawn, and the remains of a snowman slumped morbidly in the sunshine. Here and there were indentations Melissa knew were someone's attempts at a snow angel. She was about to give up when the door opened and Lucille appeared defiantly before her.

"I've got nothing to say to you, Melissa."

"You've got no quarrel with me, Lu. Please. Let's just talk for a minute. I know things are bad right now. Please."

Because Melissa was in the real estate business, she was used to seeing other people's messes, but the state of the house shocked her. It was out of whack somehow. The furniture looked out of place, clothes and toys were all over the floor, and the dining room table was covered with files and paperwork. Black plastic trashbags, stuffed and tied, lined the walls. It was like entering a disordered mind. When she walked past Lucille she smelled alcohol on her breath. It was ten A.M.

In the den, Lucille's children stared in wary silence at their visitor and responded to her warm smile only by shuffling their feet a little. It seemed for an instant that the little girl might say something, but she was cowed into holding her tongue by her brother's unflinching gaze, and as Melissa expected, Lucille did not offer her any coffee or even a chair.

"May I sit down?"

"Help yourself."

"I wonder if it would be better if we talked alone," Melissa ventured.

"I can't leave my kids right now, I'm sorry. You didn't give me much notice."

Melissa again smiled at the children, who returned to their play even as they remained alert to her, while she gathered her thoughts. She heard some dim scratching and decided there must be a cat somewhere in the house.

"Lu, I know you must be going through a terrible time with all this," Melissa said. "I am so sorry about everything that's happened."

Lucille shook her head but said nothing.

"I feel like we've all fallen into some kind of horrible, horrible dream and can't wake up. I try to see how we got here, and I can't. I can't believe this is what anybody intended."

"I don't know why you're here," Lucille said at last. "There's nothing I can do. I wish all those people hadn't abused my child, but they did. And now they'll have to pay for it."

"Lu, what's this really all about? Is it about the spanking? That was so unfortunate. We all know that."

"It's ironic. I guess I should be grateful."

"How do you mean?"

"If Frank hadn't done that, none of this ever would have come out. They'd have gone right on with their abuse and Satan-worship and so forth, and nobody would have been the wiser."

"Do you really believe that's what was going on at Alphabet Soup?"

"Do you think my son is a liar? Is that what you're saying?"

"Not at all, Lu. But sometimes people are mistaken, especially little children. And so that's why I asked if you really believed, all that time before, that your son was being savaged at school. And you didn't have the slightest clue. You, his mother, who knows him better than anybody on earth."

"I wish I could help you, Melissa. Honestly I do. I feel bad for Em sometimes, sitting in that jail cell. But then I remember what she did, what they all did, to my boy. I blame Frank, really. She got it from him, that's what I think. You know Jeffrey has nightmares now. He can't sleep, can't eat. He has diarrhea every other day. I don't know how much therapy it's going to take to get us all through this."

"But Lu, surely you know Em and her mom would never do anything like this. They would never harm a child in their care. Surely you know that."

"Em is an icy and condescending bitch," she said. Melissa glanced at the children, who did not flinch.

"Why do you say that? When you were in trouble, Lu, she helped you. She visited you when you were in the hospital those times. You hated the food, remember? So she brought you things you liked to eat. Eighty miles each way. Remember that? The times you begged her not to go, and she called home and Frank took care of their boy and she stayed. She was there. And Lu, she needs you now. This business at the school—these things didn't happen. You *know* that. You know Emily and her mom aren't capable. What happened with Frank—that he spanked your little boy—that was an aberration. Everyone is sorry about that."

"It's a little late for that, don't you think?"

It was hard to argue with this. Melissa wasn't even sure what she'd been after. Maybe she believed that if only some sensible person would point out what madness this all was, it would dissipate, like some evil spell that depended on people's beliefs for its power. But afterward she came to see her visit with Lucille as part of the hubris of reason, a desire to demonstrate that the world simply could not be so irrational. It was like hearing that someone has cancer; you want to know that the person smoked so you can feel safe because you abstain. Otherwise nobody was safe.

It was shortly after Terry's profile of Detective Jepson in the *Chronicle* as "a man on a mission to protect Webster's kids" that the Webster Police Department began a series of follow-up arrests. Taken into custody were a short-order cook, the woman who read to little children at the library Saturday mornings, a part-time employee of Webster's pet store, and a cabby accused of abusing little children with the meter off. They were taken from their homes and offices, dragged from cars, kitchens, and even their own beds to answer charges that they were part of the evil Satanists who, for a time, held the children of Webster in their power. It was risky, bringing charges against people with no outward ties to Alphabet Soup. But they were connected, as Detective Jepson was certain he could prove. They were people who had participated in abusing children at the school, people who had provided facilities for abuse away from the school, people who took pictures and made videos and took part in the rituals.

"It's an uphill fight," he told the *Chronicle*. "These people have more resources than we do, and they're expert at camouflaging their activities. I believe they're part of a network of child-abusing Satanists around the country, and perhaps even internationally. They trade pornography and even missing children. They are so brilliant at keeping their activities secret that until recently nobody had an inkling. Personally, I'm convinced that that's where at least a few of the children on the milk cartons have gone."

Jepson's technique was to ride around town with Lucille and Jeffrey in search of locations and suspects. Jepson had learned from Diana that sometimes children, when set at ease, will point out important things as a matter of course, and so these drives at first were simply an opportunity for Jeffrey to ride in a police cruiser. He got to talk on the police radio and, outside of town, work the siren and lights while Jepson floored the pedal and they raced along the country roads to the north of town. Jeffrey was soon asking to ride in the police cruiser again, just as Jepson had hoped he would, so that instead of having to be coaxed, the little boy was eager. From there it was a small step to asking Jeffrey whether, as the car crisscrossed Webster and his towhead bobbed up and down barely above the bottom of the window, he had ever been in a given shop or office or home. Really? And what had he done there? Who had taken him there? Had anyone touched him in a bad way? He knew by now what *bad touching* meant, as did all the other children of Webster. Even those who made no claim to having been abused had been taught in school by now the difference between good touching and bad touching and how to react to the bad touching that sometimes adults want to do. Diana Shirley had worked with the Webster school board to develop just such programs. At least once a month, teachers conducted a quick review to make sure the lessons were not lost.

Jepson drove other kids around Webster as well, playing a game called "Where Have You Been?" Kids got points for every place they could point to that they'd been inside. Sometimes it was just the supermarket or the dentist's office, but sometimes it was a place nobody among the grown-ups had ever known you'd been, and this was really fun, because you got to explain how you'd ended up there. Jepson made it easy to do that, so then you got your points and at the end usually you had enough for an ice cream cone. Sometimes kids pointed to places they hadn't been in order to score extra points, but Detective Jepson was a father and had a way with children. He was certain he could tell when they were just joshing and when they had actually been inside a place.

Diana, who had been on some of these cruises, knew that there was an effective method to his seeming madness. She noticed, for example, that sooner or later he took all the children past the Tabernacle of the Resurrection Church—Catholic children, Jewish children, upper-class Episcopalians, none of them with any reason to visit the church or its attendant school. To her surprise, several of these Alphabet Soup children claimed points for having been there. At first they gave no good explanation for their visits, but under questioning they conceded that they had been taken by "Mr. Frank."

Jepson boasted to Diana of the horror and grief shown by some of the people he had arrested—all because their secret was finally out. She hated child abusers—who didn't?—yet reacted viscerally to the pleasure Jepson seemed to derive from shattering their peaceful lives. She had a suspicion that all this was calculated at least partly to impress her.

"Believe me, we're not any happier than you are," Errol said glumly when she complained to him. "Cal has made him stop. We let these people out on minimal bail, and I'm sure we won't try any of these cases. It's potentially a huge liability."

"It can't help our case against the teachers, can it?" Diana asked.

"The more people he brings in, the more bizarre and unbelievable this whole thing becomes. I think we can agree that something horrible went on in that school, but he's arrested a bank teller, a guy who works in the bicycle shop on Main—he even pulled in the guy who works on Hawthorne's car."

"Oh, God."

"Cal went absolutely ballistic. Little Armenian guy, been working on imports for years. Jepson backed off of that one. But he said two different kids told him they'd been taken there and made to strip naked and jam tools up their heinies."

"So just because he works on Hawthorne's car, your boss made Jepson drop the charges?"

"Diana, the guy's not a child molester. He's got nothing to do with Alphabet Soup, he's got three kids of his own who are doing just fine, and the district attorney has known him personally for seven years."

"Maybe it's not him. Maybe the kids were brought to his shop at night or when he wasn't around. Maybe they were taken into the rest room. Have you questioned him?"

"Diana."

"Two different kids, Errol. Kids don't make this stuff up."

"Jepson made it a game! They want to win, so they point out places. This isn't *investigating*. Don't worry about Cal's mechanic. Worry about all the others we've got to do something with."

Diana didn't want to argue, but she hung up the phone uneasily. Errol Jones did likewise.

The thought kept ringing in Terry's head like one of those car alarms that used to keep him awake in the city: *What if Diana was wrong?* All these arrests—it was terrifying, incredible. People were spooked. It was beginning to feel like a reign of terror, but in the face of it, Webster seemed paralyzed by indecision: its almost religious belief in civil liberties was counterbalanced by the belief that many more people had been subject to sexual abuse than was acknowledged.

Terry's doubts about the course of the investigation were linked to his doubts about Diana, yet as time wore on her convictions only seemed to harden. A process of disillusionment had begun. As the drama of courtship faded and he spent more time with her, he was struck by how little she had to say, how her anecdotes rambled until they petered out with no clear purpose, how scant and banal were her interests aside from her work. He knew her story by now, and while they still had fun in bed, he got antsy sometimes. But he blamed himself. He readily attributed his doubts to his own pathological indecisiveness, which made them seem all the more worth suppressing. He wanted Diana, but he also wanted Abigail. Hamlet's disease, they could call it in the medical texts. His stutter seemed powerfully metaphorical at such times, aptly expressing his inability to choose. Even Tartaglia was just a convenient way to hold opposing views at the same time—to see in both directions, Janus-like. Had he ever really given himself fully to anything? Not his work, not really; like those thin women who perennially diet, he could never work hard enough—or try hard enough—to satisfy himself. Niedleman was wrong about most things, but he had Terry's number, all right. He called himself lazy, a dense, plodding egoist who couldn't seem to grow up. And all because of the way he held himself back, valued himself so highly he couldn't quite give himself, not to his work or to his wife either, for that matter. Now that they had parted, thoughts of her kept him from giving himself fully to someone else.

But they hadn't really parted. Terry and Abigail still ran the *Chronicle* together, still collaborated in raising the children. Sometimes, they even still made love. The conspiratorial nature of their couplings, the knowledge that each was involved with another, the sense of one's spouse having become one's paramour—all these things made sex especially seductive for two people who in various ways were unable to let go of one another. It was sexy too, they discovered, to have a life pared down to work and love, with most of the mundane matters—what to have for dinner? when to get the house painted?—eliminated from their discourse. Stripped down to shared passions, life can be very interesting, as Terry and Abigail began to see, and the durability of their relationship—its flowering, even, in the face of conflict and infidelity—was paradoxically helped by not knowing what choices each would ultimately make.

The two of them watched a late-night news program on the Alphabet Soup scandal, which was now a major story from coast to coast. The host was Maury, who reported on all the arrests in Webster and interviewed Cal Hawthorne and Al Jepson on camera. The former was careful in his comments to condemn only those his grand jury had indicted, while the latter contended that in Webster the authorities at last had the opening they had been looking for to crack a nationwide network of child abusers. At the end, from the desk of a studio in New York, Maury interviewed his son. The interview was taped with Terry in front of the Alphabet Soup building, its doors and windows covered with plywood after the glass had been broken by vandals. The masonry above the windows was blackened by a fire someone had set before the building was secured, and the walls were covered with angry graffiti. The place looked almost bombed. If you looked closely, you could make out the words ROAST IN HELL!

Terry clicked off the remote just before his recorded self could open his mouth.

"Terry!" Abigail complained. "I wanted to see that!"

"Do you love Charlie Krieger?" he asked, his long frame sprawled on the carpet and his stockinged feet propped on the sofa. They had fallen into the habit of talking late into the night, after the children were in bed.

She shook her head quickly and gave a tight smile. "But you love Diana. Or you're infatuated, at least."

"Why are you with him, then?" he persisted. He poured some more wine, emptying the bottle into the tumblers they used instead of wine glasses because these fit into the dishwasher. He liked this homely, parental sort of habit; Diana used oversized stemware. It was like drinking out of a fishbowl.

"Don't be silly," Abigail said. "It takes a long time to love somebody, which you may yet find out for yourself."

"Do you think all these people, all over Webster, are Satan-worshiping child molesters?"

"I've never thought that, Terry."

"Well, you're biased."

"Look who's talking! I'm not the one who's biased."

"Yes, you are."

"I'm not. I may be a little jealous from time to time, but I'm perfectly willing to believe that this kind of thing happens. I just don't think it's happened at Alphabet Soup or on the scale that's being talked about."

"Abby, come on. Somebody's confessed already, and from what I hear one or two more are likely to."

"At Salem, fifty-five people confessed. I looked it up. Do you believe in witches?"

"The teachers at Alphabet Soup think *they're* witches. They had a coven, with secret meetings and spells and all that stuff. Ariel, they called it."

"But we don't believe in witches, right?"

"So you think it's all a hoax."

"Not a hoax exactly——"

"You think something like forty children are making this stuff up."

"What do you think, Terry? That's the important question. From the tone of the coverage, you think most of these people are guilty."

She had taken off his right sock and began to massage his foot, which was nestled in her lap.

"I don't know what I think," he said with a sigh. "There's a lot of evidence, multiple allegations. Errol is completely sure about it."

"Well, that's something. He's a smart guy." Abigail went to work on his heel and then his ankle. Her hands were warm from the friction.

"I'm just concerned about where this is going."

"I'm concerned about where *you're* going," Abigail said.

"Tonight?"

"Tonight, nowhere," she said, squeezing his leg harder. "I know about tonight. It's the rest of the time I'm worried about."

"You shouldn't worry."

"Really? Let's see, my husband's moved out, he's involved with a younger woman——"

"Only a couple of years!"

"Oh well, in that case . . ."

"She's not you, Abby," Terry said.

"That's the point, isn't it?"

The next day, sitting in a small room with a beat-up steel table, Terry fell in love with Diana all over again. Watching her through the one-way mirror as she worked with a little boy, easily winning his trust, who wouldn't fall for her? The boy obviously had.

"Okay, now watch this, Matthew," Terry heard her say. Her voice, piped into the windowless room, sounded electronically altered. It was especially strange coming from the gamine figure he knew so well, clad now in a leotard with two different colored legs and a stretch top with bells on the points of a jagged little skirt and even a jester's hat, all with the aim of setting the children at ease. "I'm going to lock the door so no one can get in. OK? You can get out any time you want, although I hope you'll stay and keep me company here for a few minutes at least." She locked the door with a key on a string that she placed around the little boy's neck.

"See? You're completely safe here. Nobody in the whole wide world can get in but us, unless you want them to!"

Matthew, who had a huge mop of dark hair and looked to be about four, fingered the key with interest. Then Diana invited him to come and look at her toys.

"Let's see," she said. "What do we have here in this bin?"

Terry had been watching her for a while now and was alternately impressed and uneasy. The idea was to write a piece about how the authorities managed to get children to disclose, and observing the questioning first-hand was illuminating. Terry discovered that Diana often used anatomically correct dolls with the kids (or perhaps anatomically exaggerated would be a better description, given their giant breasts and penises), making one of these goofy animals stand in for Frank Joseph, another for Emily, a third for Pearl, etc., and the children were encouraged to show what the big dolls did with the little children dolls. The kids were always reluctant at first and confused about what it was possible to show. It was confusing for Terry just to keep track of which doll stood for which person or whether a given doll stood for anyone at all. Yet inevitably, things began to emerge, and there was enough consistency in what the children told her to make a lot of it hard to discount. Usually, for instance, when the children were given a pencil they used it show how Mr. Frank had stuck his sword, his pole, his whatever, into the heinie of the little children dolls. Most of the children took the clothes off of Mrs. Big Rabbit and implied that Emily had done the same on a regular basis. Several took the clothes off the children dolls, and two of them said Mr. Big Rabbit liked to take their picture this way. Some kids said "no" again and again when asked whether they had any secrets, but sooner or later they caved.

Matthew was shy, a sweet boy who reminded Terry a little of his own son, and he peered curiously into the box of toys without immediately reaching for any, so Diana helpfully began taking some of them out. They were trucks, mostly, and various other things that would engage a four-year-old. They played around with these for a while, and eventually Diana brought the discussion around to Alphabet Soup.

"Did you like it there at Alphabet Soup?" she asked.

"Yup." Matthew focused on the ambulance he was playing with, moving it in circles around a miniature earth mover.

"Did you always like it there?"

"Yup."

"You know, some children have said some really yucky things went on there. And the other day, all the moms and dads got together, and they all talked, and they said we want to make sure no more yucky things happen to our children. So let's see which ones are big enough boys and girls to tell us about the yucky things that happened, and that way we can make sure it doesn't ever happen again."

Matthew picked up the ambulance and spun the wheels with his fingers.

"I told them I didn't know if you were big enough to tell those things," Diana said. "Not all children can do it, although I think you can."

"I can," Matthew affirmed, but he remained absorbed by his toy and said nothing.

"Well, some of the children said they used to play certain yucky games with Mr. Frank. Did Mr. Frank ever touch you?"

"No."

"He never touched you at all?"

"No."

"Did he ever touch your wee-wee?"

"No."

"Did anyone else touch your wee-wee?"

"No."

"Matthew." Diana squinted at him good-naturedly. "Did anybody touch you there?"

"No," he said but after a moment's hesitation.

"I don't know if you have any secrets to tell after all," Diana said. "Here, why don't you start by showing me? Mr. Big Rabbit can be Mr.

Frank, and this little boy doll can be you. We'll call him Matthew, OK? Can you show me now how Mr. Frank touched you?"

Terry watched as the boy took up the dolls and jammed them together, Mr. Big Rabbit up against the back of the little boy doll. Matthew banged the dolls and then twisted them one against the other, screwing up his face at the same time into a mask of anger and disgust.

"Ooh, that's really yucky," Diana said. "Did Mr. Frank put his wee-wee in your heinie that way?"

Matthew said nothing. He just kept banging the two dolls together, back to front, harder and harder.

"What else did Mr. Frank do?"

Matthew looked around among the toys on the floor and picked up a pencil, which he jammed into Mrs. Big Rabbit. He poked it in her face, her back, her stomach and her private parts. Then he took two other dolls—who did they represent? Terry couldn't keep track—and jammed their heads together. He did this with a variety of dolls now, warming to the project, until he came back to Mr. Big Rabbit, whom he seized.

"Don't tinkle on the floor," he said, bouncing Mr. Big Rabbit lightly up and down. A little smile came over Matthew's face. "Tinkle in the street, tinkle in the car, tinkle on everybody."

"Does Mr. Big Rabbit do that?" Diana asked. "Does he tinkle on everybody?"

"Everybody," Matthew affirmed, shaking his head vigorously. He pointed with the doll to another on a shelf. "Even Mr. Dancing Bear."

"Mr. Dancing Bear?"

"Mr. Big Rabbit likes Mr. Dancing Bear," explained Matthew quietly, almost as if to himself. "They play together, dance together, go together."

Terry felt his feet go sweaty in the overheated observation room. As he watched, Diana brought down the teddy bear and gave it to Matthew, who immediately started banging it with the Mr. Big Rabbit doll. Mr. Big Rabbit had a large erect penis, as did all the other male dolls Diana used, and Matthew began poking the bear with it, particularly around the face and mouth.

"Mr. Big Rabbit likes bears, doesn't he?" Diana said, smiling.

"Yup," said Matthew, grinning widely. "Likes Dancing Bear best of all."

When Terry got to the office that afternoon, Margaret O'Hanlon looked sick. "They've arrested Reverend Albertson," she said.

The district attorney had authorized it because the connection to Alphabet Soup seemed so strong. They had come for him during services the previous morning, waiting at the back of the church, behind the rows and rows of folding chairs, and later they would point to their patience and restraint in not seizing their man right out of the pulpit.

Something changed in Terry then. It was like a fall from grace. For the shocking arrest of the Reverend Albertson he blamed himself, and his coverage of the story in the *Chronicle* was palpably outraged. Tartaglia, meanwhile, let the bear out of the bag, explaining that this "ursine bogey" was just something a well-known local journalist, deep in his cups, had thrown out in a late-night discussion with one of the Alphabet Soup mothers, and how this selfsame bear had magically resurfaced in the stream of consciousness poured forth by an unrelated Alphabet Soup pupil under official questioning. Now the police were looking for a large, hairy man, identity unknown, who might have been associated with suspects from the school—a man who, in the parlance of the gay sexual bestiary, happened to be a "bear." Tartaglia had to wonder if the investigation had now achieved perfect circularity, with concepts arising in any one subconscious telepathically bobbing up in someone else's. The district attorney's political ambitions, the arrests of seeming bystanders, the charges against Reverend Albertson—taken together, they cast doubt on the entire investigation. "This thing has gone off the rails," Tartaglia wrote. Always without willpower in the face of gossip, the Stammerer couldn't resist noting that this very same local journalist, whose coverage of the investigation was so thorough and unflinching, was known to keep frequent company with the Grand Inquisitor whose interviews resulted in so very many disclosures of abuse.

chapter SIXTEEN

Apostasy is never welcome in a religious community, so when Tartaglia lost faith, his enemies in Webster quickly multiplied. Outrage poured in by telephone, fax, and mail, and the punishments inflicted on ancient heretics weren't considered severe enough. People demanded to know how the *Chronicle* could print such filth while allowing its cowardly author to hide behind the cloak of anonymity. "How can you publish such irresponsible lies in the face of such suffering?" one fax demanded. "These people have RAPED OUR CHILDREN, and you sit there and pooh-pooh the whole thing."

But Terry did not feel beaten down by threats and insults because he was already in mourning, his profound loss of faith having turned him inward. It is a lonely thing to peer into the empty maw at the center of yourself where once there was the solid core of certitude. You couldn't will the gap full; its very existence embarrassed you. It was like being conned.

Such were his thoughts at the end of the bar at Costello's on the night the Tartaglia column was published. He had lost track of how many beers he had consumed, except they were cheap and he was already working his way through a second $20 bill, when Ed Krcyszyki appeared. The bartender—it was Wendy tonight, his favorite—jerked her head in his direction, and Ed came down. Terry nodded hello, knowing it was obvious he was shit-faced.

"Fancy meeting you here," his friend said with the disconcerting casualness of sobriety. "I just tried calling you."

"I'm on a retreat," Terry said. He spoke perfectly when drunk.

"Am I intruding?"

"No no, I need the break, my back's already a bloody pulp. Not that I don't deserve it."

"I got something that's gonna make you feel much better. A juicy story. Very big. Nobody knows about it. Are you ready?"

"I'm sitting down."

"Krieger's is gonna get that garage after all. We're buying Alphabet Soup."

"Jesus, don't tell me—"

"It's where they wanted to put it in the first place, remember? Best of all, we're gettin' it for a song." Ed hung onto that old-time Webster accent that some working people retained in spite of television and all the outsiders the colleges had brought to town. "It's out of business now. The people who run the place were scumbags, of course, and the real estate people say nobody else wanted it. The building's considered kinda tainted, like someone was murdered there or something. Which I suppose they were, if you think how they murdered all those childhoods."

"Ed, don't tell me this." Terry slammed his fist down onto the bar, and Wendy shot him a look. "Don't fucking tell me this!"

"Terry boy, I don't get it. You should be happy. It's looking like Krieger's is gonna make it. Your biggest advertiser, remember? The place where all my members make a living? A lot of Webster families are counting on this."

"It's all wrong! All this Satanic bullshit, it's some kind of hysteria, some kind of spontaneous combustion. Nobody molested any kids at

Alphabet Soup. There's no evidence at all. These kids get the message loud and clear that all the grown-ups want them to disclose. So they cook up this stuff, and the mothers pass it back and forth, and the kids just agree to it, or they spit out the wildest thing that comes into their heads, and that's how they get love and attention and bicycles and who knows what. They have no idea. No fucking idea!"

"Hey, keep it down," Ed said, glancing over his shoulder. "You'll get yourself in some real trouble with that kind of talk."

"They were supposed to all be naked sometimes," Terry continued in a ferocious stage whisper. "That was one of the allegations, that the teachers took all their clothes off, all fifty pupils that they had over there on an average day. They fucked 'em, pissed on 'em, rubbed rabbit blood all over their private parts, danced around in witches' outfits, shoved everything but the kitchen sink up the kids' asses. Then they got everybody cleaned up and dressed in their very same clothes, and so when the parents showed up—which they did throughout the day, in and out all day long, you understand—when the parents showed up, there wasn't any sign of any of it. Nothing! Isn't that amazing? And the kids were deliriously happy, despite the torments of hell. Ed, look—have you ever tried dressing a three-year-old?"

Ed shrugged uncertainly and glanced sideways again. "My niece. Once or twice."

"Well now imagine undressing fifty of them," he said, "throwing their clothes in a heap, and then getting them all dressed again. Not once, you understand, but on a regular basis. You see? You're doing this again and again, on a regular basis, yet not once—not one single solitary fucking time!—did one of those kids come home in somebody else's underwear or socks or shoes. Not a single article of clothing on the wrong kid. Do you understand what I'm saying to you here?"

Ed was silent. You could see the adrenaline pumping him up under his skin, changing his color as if you could see the minerals replacing the wood.

"Ed, there is no fucking force on earth that could accomplish that with fifty three- and four-year-olds. *It is a physical impossibility.*" Terry gulped from his beer glass. He kept his voice down, tried to seem more rational. "That's the least of it. Just the fucking least of it. It's all wrong, all of it, and I swallowed it hook, line, and sinker. I took a fake, Ed. I jumped so fucking high, I can't even see the earth below me."

"What about the medical evidence. Huh? The doctor found physical, medical evidence of abuse. Or don't you believe in science?"

"Oh, for God's sake, that guy Verdi wouldn't know abuse if it ran over him. I've seen his reports. He touches a kid on the anus with a Q-tip and if it opens he decides there was abuse. He's never examined a kid who really was abused. He has no fucking idea what it looks like. Do you know what a grown-up dick would do to the anus of a four-year-old?"

"I find it hard to believe that *nothing* happened at Alphabet Soup," his listener said coldly, inching away from Terry's touch. "That all this whole to-do arose out of thin air. But whatever it was, the school's closed, it's not gonna reopen, and Charlie Krieger is buying the place for the garage this town has needed for the past ten years."

"And you're happy about that."

"Why shouldn't I be?" Ed practically demanded. "We're invested in this company, we've put our money where our mouths and asses are. We own stock. I'm on the board, Terry. As head of this union, the livelihood of my members comes first. We can't just sit by while Rothwax closes the stores he doesn't like, maybe ours among them, for some concrete tilt-up that employs a tenth the workers at half the wages. How's it any different from the *Chronicle* wantin' Krieger's to stay viable and locally owned? Your livelihood depends on them too, which is why your wife is so involved in saving the company."

"A pact with the devil," Terry said in some wonder.

"I don't know about you, but I like to keep him where I can see him," Ed said. "And I can see him a lot clearer from the board than if he were down in Philadelphia, like Rothwax. Or in Tokyo, for that matter. Would you be happier if the Japanese got it?"

Terry took a long drink. The beer was warm now, and bitter.

"All this stuff," he said. "All this—crap. So fucking weird that more people around here believe in Satan than pay any attention to God. As if you could have the one without the other."

"The Stones had it right." Ed went for air guitar, thinking to lighten things up. " 'Can't always get what you want. But if you try sometimes, you get what you need.' "

Tramping home that night through Webster's darkened streets, the editor of the *Webster Chronicle* felt the calm that comes of clarity, and knowing that there are a few sweet anesthetized hours that are yours and yours alone—hours in which you are beyond the reach of your problems and numb even to your own sharpest reproaches. The wind was wet, and between the dripping trees he noticed a freezing rain was falling, adding to the treacherous footing along the well-worn sidewalks. Most of the lights in the old wood-frame houses that lined the street were out by now, their occupants asleep, but here and there signs of life persisted. Through a front window to his right, up beyond the porch, he could see a youngish couple on the sofa, necking tenderly in the way of couples just groping toward a relationship, and to his left, on another porch across the street, he could hear the wind chimes that would have driven him crazy if he lived next door. But he was just passing through. Alone, inebriated, a little used to the truth by now, he felt cosseted by the quiet streets, the mature trees rendering the sidewalks pleasingly undulant and making him feel enfolded by the great canopy of their branches overarching the roadway. The houses, all in a row for so many years, spoke of stability and comfort, parenthood and responsibility, the porches sheltered from the downpour and glowing yellow from dusty bulbs.

He hadn't particularly noticed the cold during his drunken ramble home from the bar, but as he mounted the icy wooden stairs to his front door, placing his big feet carefully to avoid slipping, he noticed that his face and ears were numb, his shoulders ached from hunching against the rain, and the joints in his hands were so stiff they seemed to need oiling. When he opened the door, he sensed an unfamiliar mass on the sofa, something that wasn't there when he'd left that morning, and he realized there was somebody in his apartment.

"I wanted to claw you," said a voice from the darkness. Terry made no move to turn on the light. "I was going to rake your cheeks, except I don't have fingernails. I was going to tell you how completely despicable I found your casual betrayal of what we had, and how as soon as you got tired of your girlfriend, you were willing to throw the kids to the wolves."

"Diana—"

"I fell asleep. I woke up in your awful apartment, on a couch surrounded by your newspapers and magazines and head shop paraphernalia. A place full of rented furniture I'd laugh at anywhere else. It seemed so silly, somehow. Pathetic. The anger I was feeling seemed so out of proportion. And I woke up wanting to fuck you—still! Can you believe it?"

"I feel the same way," he said. "What I was repudiating was a witch hunt, not a person."

"I've had doubts. I'm not immune, Terry. The wild allegations, the suspicion that seems to spread like a virus. People are afraid of kids, afraid of day care. Women who need this to be free. I worry that we're chaining them back to their babies. But the hysteria isn't my fault. It's your fault. It's their fault. I found child abuse, and I will stop at nothing to protect those children."

Terry was silent. For an instant, he thought to feign an outbreak of stuttering that prevented him from saying something heartfelt.

"We have stopped it. Don't you see, Terry? Those kids are safe now. They can start healing." She rose, and he saw her slide fluidly around the coffee table like a shadow. "If it helped that you and I were fucking, well then I'm doubly glad."

She put her arms around him beneath his open coat, tucking her fingers beneath his belt, and kissed him. Seduced by the pressure of her hands, he kissed her back. "What I need to know," she said softly, "is whether loving you is the mistake I think it was."

Her face was gorgeous in the dim light, her aroma sweet. Everything about her was so warm and inviting and sure. He wanted only to lose himself again in her well-remembered caresses.

"It's all a mistake," he whispered. He felt her hands slip gently out of his belt. "All of it, Diana. It needs to be undone somehow. Set right."

"This much—you and I—we can fix," she said, moving away from him and hugging herself again. He sensed that she was looking at him with great sadness. "But you're so wrong. So foolish and wrong about the rest. The children have been through hell, yet you can't believe in it even when it's staring you in the face."

"You and I, w-we're the architects of their hell," he said, still whispering. He felt the adrenaline rushing through his system, and he didn't want to stutter now. "But it's our hell too. It's everyone's hell."

"Not the children's, Terry."

"H-Help me demolish it. Help me make people see it's just a mirage, made of ego and prejudice and fear."

"I will always believe the children. Always."

"Do you believe they've flown in outer space?" he demanded. "Do you believe old ladies and clergymen and postal workers are Satan worshipers, impaling babies in front of four-year-olds?"

"You of all people should be able to distinguish symbolic truth from the literal expressions of these small children," Diana said. "If you can't—if your imagination is so bereft, and you're so naive about what goes on in the world around you—then I can't help you." She took her coat from an armchair and moved toward the door. "But don't expect me to abandon those kids, because it will never happen."

When the door closed behind Diana, Terry felt a brief rush of abandonment, and his first embarrassed thoughts were of Abigail. Later, sitting in the darkness, he wondered about the kids. If they really *believed* they had been molested by the adults they had previously trusted, wasn't that just as bad as having been molested? And weren't the people who planted these ideas the real molesters?

The consequences were horrifying. His own faith had helped destroy the lives of all the good people in prison—the preschool teachers, Albertson, Jesus. Bad as this was, it was just the epicenter of destruction, which moved outward in circular waves that swallowed up the school, vaporized individual reputations, sowed fear and suspicion throughout the community. All over Webster, parents were agonizing over the illusory sex lives of their four-year-olds, beating themselves up for leaving them in the finest preschool in the county, weeping before shrinks and begging off work, sex, and God knew what else so they could "work through" the heavy blows fate had rained on their children—except there were no such blows. Terry was filled with revulsion now to think he had eagerly broadcast these myths not just to every nook and cranny of Webster, but to the four corners of the globe. All over America, meanwhile, mothers worried not about traffic safety or education or what effect the shattered family could be having on our kids, but about whether people who devoted themselves to underpaid child care might, without a moment's privacy, be molesting the young. The guiltiest person in Webster isn't anyone in the Vanatee County Detention Center, he thought, the realization coming into focus now with chilling clarity. The guiltiest person is me.

Terry published the news that Krieger's was buying the former preschool site for a new parking garage—Pearl and Emily had sold it at fire-sale prices to raise money for legal fees—but the easing of the takeover battle gave him the opportunity to investigate how his hometown had fallen into the grip of a vast popular delusion. The monster that he and all the others had created in Webster—and turned loose on the entire country, where paranoia about child-care workers was spreading faster than car phones and VCRs—would not be slain in a single issue of the *Chronicle,* he knew. It would take time and effort, but the first step was to figure out what really happened, to gain some understanding. His disbelief, he knew, was not so different from the belief that had come before it. It was badly informed, contrary to common sense. Wasn't there a mountain of evidence against the accused? Were all the children of Webster lying? Why had one of the Alphabet Soup teachers confessed, if there was nothing to confess to?

Until he had a clearer picture of what was happening, he would go back to basics. Tartaglia's latest outburst was an obituary for his romance with Diana, and freed of that entanglement, he was both exiled from the core of the story and more able to be objective about it. Already he felt nostalgia for the woman he had lost. He remembered her lemony perfume and trilling laugh, the curve of her hip, her taut calves, all gone now and fading like an old Polaroid in his memory. At the same time, he felt refreshed and free, like someone who quits smoking and discovers the cravings aren't so bad after all.

Immediately, the tenor of the *Chronicle*'s Alphabet Soup coverage began to change. Terry made it sharply more skeptical at the same time he tried to tone things down, dampen the hysteria, persuade himself and his readers that this mysterious fever was not the central fact of the universe. And he bent over backwards to add balance to the story, taking pains to remove the obvious bias in favor of guilt that had pervaded the coverage before. He sought, without success, to visit some of the teachers in jail. And he finally got around to seeing Professor Edwin Meisner.

He was a stringy, avuncular man with a moppy cascade of chestnut-colored hair that should have been gray but somehow wasn't. Its length and color, coupled with oversized eyeglasses and the skin of a man over fifty, gave the professor the theatrical air of a bit player accustomed to providing comic relief. Yet his face, like his nondescript clothes, was a blank most of the time. Meisner's economy of movement and gesture spoke loudly of his seriousness. Terry sat with him watching videos in a windowless conference room of the drab brick Web State psychology building. Meisner had just popped open a Coke, which made Terry feel sticky and cold in the unventilated room.

On the screen, a little boy was saying in answer to Meisner's questioning that he had never been to a hospital, and his mother, a plump young woman with short red hair, was agreeing. "Other than when he was born, of course," she added. This was Session One. After a screen labeled Session Two, Terry saw Meisner alone with the boy, asking him if he didn't remember the time he'd fallen and cut his face. "No," the boy said suspiciously. "Are you sure you don't remember?" Meisner persisted. "Your mother had to rush you to the hospital. She had to call an ambulance, and the siren was blaring, and they rushed you to the hospital where they put some stitches in. I'm surprised you don't remember because it really hurt."

The boy insisted that no such thing had happened, but after a screen labeled Session Three, Meisner persisted, and the boy had begun to keep his doubts to himself, as if trying on the offered narrative for size. By Session Four, the boy was agreeing with this story about himself. He had been taken in an ambulance; there had been blood; it hurt! And by

Session Five, encouraged by his mother's sympathetic nodding, he was embellishing substantially. He remembered a long needle a nurse had given him, remembered the doctor preparing the needle and thread, remembered that they had inserted a zipper so they could look inside the wound while it healed. Meisner elicited these artful tropes with simple, open-ended inquiries. By now the questions weren't particularly leading. Someone seeing only the final session would assume the tale of the cut and the hospital had never been suggested to the boy.

"This is incredible," said Terry. "You brainwashed him as easily as you opened that Coke."

"It's as if I'd opened an empty can and made the Coke magically appear," Meisner corrected. "The point is, these kids are highly suggestible. That's why TV ads aimed at children are so insidious. It's also why children are of limited usefulness as witnesses unless they're handled with exquisite care to avoid tainting their recollections. See, they get so much of what they know about reality from grown-ups, and they want to please. Besides, adults tend to provide fairly reliable information. It's kind of like someone reading something in your newspaper. There's a presumption of reliability."

Meisner showed more videos. Almost effortlessly, kids were persuaded that there had been fires in their homes, that a giant frog had visited their classroom, that they had visited the Alps. It took shockingly little: no hugging from parents, no therapy sessions, no new bicycles or Krieger's toys.

"The amazing thing," Meisner said, "is that we've shown some of these films to dozens of students as well as faculty members from the psychology department, and if there are no plausibility clues—like doctors implanting zippers—nobody has any idea which kids are lying."

"I guess everybody wants to believe the children," Terry said.

"It's frightening, I know. But from what I read in the *Chronicle* lately, the evidence sounds awfully weak. I can't see how it would hold up. How can anyone say they have a reliable witness in any of these kids after all this hysteria?"

The problem, Terry knew, was that adults are suggestible too. The abuse mania that overtook Webster didn't just descend from outer space.

The town had been ready for it somehow, even eager, and he doubted the community was now suddenly ready to swallow the truth. Besides, it was hard for people to admit they were wrong. For Terry it meant days and nights of brooding at his desk, where he substituted tobacco for marijuana in mortification of his erring flesh. He knew he must act, must make amends, yet the burden of being wrong was so great that he could only stare into space with his feet on his desk. Everywhere he looked, he faced the carnage of his stupidity.

Oddly, the animosity generated by Tartaglia gave him strength. It helped the editor to see that he would find redemption only by publicly repudiating what had come before, and by making this repudiation under his own name. It was time for the Stammerer to drop his mask and stand exposed to his audience, in the hope that the sight would shock them back to some kind of sanity. And so it was done; he wrote a brief, signed editorial in which he said he had come to disbelieve everything that was alleged about the horrors supposedly visited on the children of Webster. "I want to emphasize that this is not a question of believing or doubting the children. The kids in this case are just mirrors reflecting back to us our own deepest fears. The stories they tell will change only when we change. Sad to say, the children are telling us a truth here. The rest of us just can't seem to recognize it."

"Have you taken leave of your senses?" his father demanded, throwing the printout onto Terry's desk in disgust. Maury was spending more time in Webster now, riding the Alphabet Soup story like a rocket to ever-higher ratings, and Terry had wanted him to see the editorial before it ran. "You're crazy. You're like Timon of Athens. First one extreme, then the other."

"Spare me the b-bard, Dad. This may not be c-convenient for you right now, but it's t-t-time to t-try and make amends. I've done a lot of damage. We all have."

"You don't have any idea what you're talking about," Maury said, shifting in his seat. His face was growing red. "You don't know what happened at that school. You can't usurp the role of the jurors in the trial of those teachers. Was your coverage biased in favor of the prosecution? That's for you to say and for you to fix. Work harder to be balanced. You publish this whole big thing exculpating the suspects, and what happens if they really are guilty? If they're convicted, for Chrissake?"

"If they're convicted, it'll be unjust. That's one reason I'm doing this."

"This is a generational thing, isn't it?" Maury said, shaking his head. "This notion that you're at the center of the universe, that the world revolves around you. You really think you matter that much? You've got to be kidding."

"If it doesn't matter, then why are you getting all bent out of shape? It's just a small-town newspaper!"

"You may not believe this, but I'm trying to help you here, son. I want to spare you the embarrassment you're about to cause yourself. Not to mention me."

"You s-s-solipsistic bastard, you're the one who can't see past his own petty problems. If Alphabet Soup is all about hysteria, the stories responsible for your comeback are a crock, aren't they? Just like you."

"The only crock here is the idea that these people are innocent," Maury said, rising angrily from his chair. "Your trouble is you bet the farm on a single source, and now you and she have had a falling out."

"Dad—"

"Listen to me, son. I've been in this business since before you were born, and I've been reporting this thing for weeks now, talking to people all over Webster, some of them folks I've known thirty years or more. If there's one thing I can say for sure, it's something awful happened at that preschool. If you got out there and did some more reporting, you'd see it too. Maybe now that you got your nose out from between that dame's legs, you can see for yourself what's happening in this town."

Terry was incredulous. "Dad, I can't think of anything funnier than a lecture from you on my love life. I'm afraid if I turn my back for five minutes, you'll be screwing Ariadne in the parking lot."

"Is she the blonde?" Maury said, glancing outward and lowering his voice.

"For Chrissake, give it a rest, will you? Your dick's already solved any problems with estate taxes I might have had to worry about. Why make things worse?"

"This isn't about money or sex," Maury said, his voice booming. Outside Terry's office, people looked. "It's about journalism, for which you never had much of a feel."

"You condescending prick," Terry said in wonder.

"I'm talking to you just the way I'd talk to anybody else in the business. I owe you that much respect at least. And what I'm telling you is, you can't run that editorial, not without making both of us into a national laughingstock."

"Is that what you're worried about?"

"Of course I'm worried about it. Terry, when this gets out, every paper in the country will marvel at how you've repudiated all the stuff you and I have been reporting on. You won't just be ruining yourself; you'll be cutting the legs out from under me. Do you appreciate what this means? You cast needless doubt on the Alphabet Soup prosecutions, and I could be out on my ass."

"Dad, we don't have to pretend here. This is all about what it means to Maury, right? You don't care about anyone in Webster. You never have."

"It's you I care about—can't you see that?" Maury shouted, jabbing the air with his finger. "You and me, pal. You're all I've got, and you never fail to disappoint. I keep hoping you've turned a corner, but your life is seamless, round, all of a piece. The only thing I can count on from you is trouble."

By the time his father left, Terry wanted to splash the article all over the front page, but Abigail persuaded him otherwise. "It's an exercise in maturity, I think, to do what some hated person wants when they happen to be right. The idea here is not to spite your father, remember."

They sat drinking martinis on the sagging sofa.

"Did you know that tabernacle and tavern have the same etymological root?" he said, holding his drink up to the light.

"Apropos of?"

"Albertson. He was a drunk and now he's a minister in something called the Tabernacle of the Resurrection. Tavern and tabernacle. They both come from the Latin *taberna*, which means 'hut.'"

"He's a good guy," Abigail said. "It'll all come out right."

"He won't post bail," Terry said. "It's only $25,000, meaning it only takes 10 percent for a bond, and he won't do it. Says he's no more or less guilty than Jesus Mendoza, so now he's sitting in jail. Won't let the congregation get him out either." Terry took a sip. "A regular Gandhi."

Abigail was right, Terry knew, and so he held the editorial. But he published a long story about Meisner's work on the suggestibility of young children, quoting other experts as well, and followed it up with a news analysis on the problem of prosecuting Satanic abusers selectively and with scant evidence beyond the testimony of three- and four-year-olds. Prosecution leaks no longer automatically turned into stories, and he worked to establish trust with the growing battery of defense attorneys. He was surprised when Julie agreed to meet with him and was even more surprised to find Chris with her when he got there. They gave him some herb tea, offered homemade fruit bars.

"They've offered me what my attorney is calling a very attractive deal," Julie said. "I plead to a single felony count, get sentenced to something like five years, serve eighteen months, get a lot of counseling."

"They promised her easier accommodations too," Chris said.

"I turned them down," Julie added, before Terry could ask. "I can't admit to something I didn't do. Not something like this. I can't be like Annette, and they don't have the same leverage with me. They can't take my child away, and I'm not rotting in prison in fear for my life every waking hour of the day."

Terry knew her parents had posted a bond to secure her release. It was rumored that they had done the same for Chris.

"They're already trying to take the thing that's most important to me," she continued. Terry noticed her squeeze her lover's hand.

"They won't succeed with that either," Chris said. "I'd barely been there ten minutes when all this abuse is supposed to have occurred. The vast bulk of the allegations were before my time."

"I really think they would have dropped the charges against her, but they're trying to use her to get to me. Just like they want to use me to get to the others."

"They even suggested they might go easy on me if you took the deal, remember?" Chris reminded.

"And they tried to suggest it would look bad in front of the jury otherwise. You know, everybody knows perverts like us abuse little kids."

"But you're both risking a lot, aren't you?" Terry asked. "If Julie is convicted, she could spend most of her life behind bars. And"—pointing at Chris—"who knows what will happen with your case?"

"We both understand the safe thing is to plead," said Julie. "Last week we were up all night talking about it, back and forth, back and forth. But I just can't. I refuse to believe the world is that way—that you have to claim you did something so horrible just to save yourself when you're innocent."

From Frank Joseph's mordant letters, Terry had some idea of what it was like for the others behind bars. In jail, Frank wrote a great deal. He also kept a journal. On receiving the news that Annette had pleaded guilty, he copied out a line from Erich Hoffer: "That which corrodes the souls of the persecuted is the monstrous inner agreement with the prevailing prejudice against them." This image of his own martyrdom, in conjunction with his certainty that sooner or later reason must prevail, gave him strength. He had long ago lost his material possessions and his good name, so he knew how little value they really had. For his own safety he was kept in isolation, as were his fellow defendants, since even murderous inmates feel entitled to prey upon child abusers behind bars. Although the solitary confinement was lonely at times, the seconds seeming to tick away with excruciating slowness, he had to admit that it suited him. The prison library was well stocked, and Melissa brought him whatever he asked for during her visits.

None of the others were as well adapted to their new environment. Emily struggled, not just with the destruction of her life by the outrageous allegations against her, but with the pain of her husband's betrayal and her mother's suffering. She was forbidden from seeing Pearl, who had various medical conditions related to her age, and these were made worse by her incarceration. Her censored letters, which made her daughter weep in sorrow and guilt—had she not insisted on taking in Tiffany?—spoke only of finding some comfortable end to her life, which was "such a bed of pain that no one would want it to go on any longer." An epidemic of accidents and medical problems had beset all the Alphabet Soup teachers, in fact. Sue suffered an agonizing outbreak of shingles that made it difficult for her to get comfortable in any position, and the prison doctors were stingy with painkillers. Despite their isolation, several of the imprisoned teachers came down with severe and persistent colds, and in Mary Maloney this blossomed into a case of pneumonia that required hospitalization. Annette was placed on medication.

The mere fact of imprisonment will take a toll on anyone; in this case, the individuals thrown into jail had never been there before and had to cope with not just the loss of freedom but separation from loved ones. They had to find a way to put on a brave face for their children, to participate in their defense, to withstand strip searches and the ill-fitting pariah's uniform of the inmate, with COUNTY JAIL emblazoned across the back. They got used to loneliness, bad food, and weight loss. Nearly all of them, sooner or later, turned to God, and so they also had to cope with the nagging fear that they were here because He wanted them here—that even He, at some level, agreed with their accusers. Even the Reverend Albertson, at times, had to wonder about this.

The man who shuffled into the visiting room was a wreck. His face was a mass of bruises, his left ear swollen beyond recognition, his nose flattened, and his hair, cut short by the prison barber, was missing in a patch where his head was bandaged. Instead of his customary aviator-style eyeglasses with the lenses that got dark in bright sunshine (but never seemed entirely clear), he wore a pair of plastic spectacles that were so goofy they achieved a kind of retro chic. In his orange prison jumpsuit, he was nearly unrecognizable.

"I must look a sight." Albertson smiled sheepishly, and Terry saw that there was something wrong with his teeth as well. Even the smallest movements made him wince. "Prison's a rough place sometimes. Hard crowd. Didn't believe I didn't do it."

Terry had never seen such a face. He said, "They were supposed to keep you safe."

"It's not their fault."

"God Almighty. I need to get your picture. The only way to put a stop to this is to get it into the newspaper."

"Please don't. The administration wanted to keep me separate, but I wouldn't do it. I thought I could minister to the inmates." He smiled wistfully, talking as if he had a mouthful of marbles. "Thought I had nothing to fear. You probably know I've been around the world a little bit. It was hubris. I thought I could take care of myself. Some tough odds in here though."

"Floyd, this is no time for martyrs. Look, I'll put up the paper, there's still some equity in the building. We can have you out of here in twenty-four hours. Next time, they'll kill you."

"No point closing the barn door now. I believe the good Lord wants me here at this particular moment, and his plan for me will work itself out. What I need from you right now is to know I can count on you for my family, when they need something."

"Whatever it is, just let me know. I've done wrong, Floyd. The only person who's been an instrument of Satan around here is me."

" 'The belief in a supernatural source of evil is not necessary,' " Albertson said. His split lip and damaged teeth made his speech hard to understand. He lisped. " 'Men alone are quite capable of every wickedness.' Conrad said that."

"You're right, of course. Satan's just a handy metaphor."

"A scapegoat."

"What's happened isn't his fault," Terry said. "It's mine."

"Don't give yourself too much credit," Albertson said, smiling faintly again.

"If it helps at all, the m-m-masters of irony that s-s-seem to control the universe are getting even. Now even I'm accused."

"You?" Albertson looked grave.

"The kids at the Y. Some of the same ones that accused you. Now they're saying that the basketball league was a hotbed of pederasty, that my wife threw me out 'cause of my taste for young boys."

"Terry, this is serious. They could bring Marty into this, even take him away. And if you ended up in here, what would happen to the *Chronicle*?"

"They'd be putting it out of its misery. But don't worry, the DA's Office isn't entertaining any more allegations. Otherwise they'd have to lock up the whole county. Half of Webster's been accused by now. There's no more midget basketball at the Y—too much liability. Lawyers made 'em shut down everything for kids under ten."

"It's incredible. A whole community gone mad."

"It seems obvious, doesn't it? Like people would wake up one morning and say, 'Whoa! What was *that* all about?' Everybody would be sheepish, but they'd realize the best thing would be to just cancel the whole business."

"Not gonna happen," Albertson mumbled.

"Nope. They seem b-b-bent on having a s-small herd of s-scapegoats, people they can s-saddle with all this crap and then s-send off into the wilderness."

"Aaron confessed his sins over that animal," Albertson reminded. "The goat wasn't guilty of anything, but the Israelites in that sense acknowledged their sins. Can't really have a scapegoat without first exposing the sins you plan to put on that creature."

"S-S-Sinning is in the eye of the b-beholder, no? I've been thinking about this. I think if you c-could peer into the s-souls of people, into the places they themselves are afraid to look, you'd discover that they consider themselves fallen. I think Webster s-sees its s-sins as child neglect, family dissolution, sexual obsession, lack of faith."

"Selfishness," Albertson said. "Too selfish even to believe in God. Too busy making money. Too arrogant to uphold the marriage contract."

"Tell me about it," Terry said ruefully. "So all of a s-sudden, we decide we've handed our kids over to the devil."

"Just exactly what we've done," Albertson said. "Ignore 'em. Let 'em sit in front of the TV day and night. Take away the social structure that was supposed to be their patrimony. They're the real scapegoats. We reveal our sins to them every day, right there in the home."

"Or it could also be something in the water. I don't know. I just know I did plenty to be sorry for, and I wanted to apologize to you. I hope you can forgive me."

"You don't need absolution from me. You've already figured out where you went wrong. Now go out and do what you can to make things right."

Late that night, in his office, Terry sat in the dark. He had far too great a hand in so much destruction and then had lacked the courage to stand up to his father and begin to set the wrongs right. It was as if his judgment had been discredited even to himself, so that having been so far wrong, he could not now trust himself to be right. Yet what courage was required? Wasn't everyone in Webster, if they looked into their hearts, sure that something was very wrong here?

Evidently not. Fishing around in his hard drive, he pulled up the editorial he had held out of the paper for fear he was going off the deep end in the other direction. He read through it once again, ran a spell check, and then got out the layouts for next week's editorial page, marking in the new editorial with his grease pencil. But the piece needed something, he felt, and so he found a quote from Pearl Buck to serve as a kind of epigraph: "Every great mistake has a halfway moment," he typed, "a split second when it can be recalled and perhaps remedied." Then, hoping and even praying that that instant had not passed him by, he removed an editorial meditating on the persistent cold and substituted the one about Alphabet Soup. That night, in his ramshackle apartment, he smoked nothing, drank nothing, and slept the sleep of the dead.

chapter SEVENTEEN

Terry never did go back to smoking dope. He threw away his stash, his papers, his favorite pipe. It seemed all crap to him now, childish sacrilege in the face of life's seriousness, Webster's tragedy. For it was obviously too late to undo the terrible events that had consumed so many innocent people—the accused, of course, but the children as well.

Webster itself was scarred by it. Terry had used to love that folks in his hometown always had time to talk, even when there was a line of people waiting to get to the counter where the chitchat was occurring. Now the loquacious majority seemed not friendly but lonely, their willingness to squeeze some small talk into every transaction not happy but sad. Post–Alphabet Soup, there was a quality of therapy about all this talk, a sympathetic squinting and nodding that you could elicit nowadays from almost anybody. "We've all been through a lot," it seemed to say, and this note of self-pity among a people Terry knew to be self-deluded made him cut short casual encounters that looked pregnant with idle chatter.

Maury, meanwhile, acted like a man watching from a distance as his son jumped off a cliff. There was much shouting and waving, an air of desperation, a long, nauseated look over the edge and then a turning away. It must have been like the look that Daedalus gave when Icarus disappeared at last into the sea.

"You go ahead, do what you think is best," Maury said when he heard about the apology, which ran on the front page. He adopted a familiar tone of resignation, the sound of parents everywhere finally throwing up their hands. "You'll excuse me if I'm not ready to share in your conversion experience. I just report the news, see. I don't sleep with my sources, and when I'm doing commentary everybody knows it."

Terry took much worse at first when he was in the post office, at the gas station, wherever he happened to encounter anybody with a strong opinion. To put people off, he got the barber to shave his head and cut off his beard. The brutality of the electric razor crawling across his scalp was cleansing. Wads of hair piled up around him like shards of ego. Partly he wanted to disappear, to disguise himself so as to pass unnoticed through the streets of Webster, yet notice was exactly what he wanted, for what else is the point of public penance? At the same time, he knew it would destroy his TV career. There was even something in his contract about radical changes to his appearance. Good. Good riddance.

"This proves desire is the root of all our troubles," Errol Jones said when they met the next day at the Y. "You had the desire for a shaved head, and now look at you."

Terry taped a stand-up in front of the county courthouse, but the network wouldn't use it.

"You've finally gone off the deep end, haven't you?" his father said.

"What if I were having c-c-chemotherapy?"

"You'd have cancer. But you don't have cancer. You just have a bad case of spite. At least you're consistent. You throw away absolutely every chance, don't you? Every single one."

In truth he looked frightening to himself, sometimes flaccid and bluish, a eunuch on a diet, other times thuggish and dim. Maintenance was a problem; he didn't want to shave his own head, so he spent a lot of time at the barber. And he worried that it wasn't helping his credibility in Webster, where he strove every week to persuade people not to believe the accusations. People would write him off as a weirdo, a nutcase, and dismiss his views about Alphabet Soup.

"I like you this way," Abigail insisted, feeling the soft skin of his round face. "It's kind of grown-up and boyish at the same time. The Yul Brynner look. And I'd forgotten what a dead ringer you are for your son."

They looked at Marty, playing peacefully with a set of miniature racing cars on the floor. Since Terry's move back home, Marty spent as much time around his father as possible, the way he liked to play near the woodstove during the coldest days of winter.

"The three of you," Abigail said. "Maury, Terry, and Marty. Is this one going to be a pundit also? Maybe it's genetic." She shook her head. "It's hard to believe that someday our baby will have crinkly white hair and three or four angry ex-wives."

"I don't have any angry ex-wives."

"You're not out of the woods yet, buster."

"Abby. You weren't really thinking of staying with Charlie, were you?!"

"Is it so ridiculous? I'll feel guilty giving him the heave-ho and keeping all those options that have suddenly made me so desirable to you."

"G-G-Give 'em back, and I'm g-gone like that," Terry said, snapping his fingers.

"It's nice at least to know where I stand."

Terry wrapped her in his arms.

"Yup," he whispered, a thickness rising in his throat. "Krieger's goes into the tank, and I'm out of here."

"You never did give a damn about money as long as you didn't have to worry too much about it. Your trouble is, you were meant to be rich. "

Now they both gave a damn, Abigail knew, and in the darkness that had descended on Webster like an unremitting snowfall, the prospect of this money from the Krieger's deal shone. Thanks in part to a change in law propelled through the state legislature on a wave of support from Krieger's employees, Webster residents, and the state's newspapers (including, of course, the *Chronicle*), Rothwax had thrown in the towel, selling his stake back to the company for a healthy profit and washing his hands of the whole thing. The victory gave everyone a lift, and Charles catered a huge party on the main floor of the flagship store, a festival that spilled out into the streets, which were closed to traffic for the occasion. Even the weather cooperated.

"That was such a great party," he said the next day. They sat in his office, where lunch had been brought in. "I only wish the parking structure was ready. I wanted to push the debris off to the side and let people just park amid the rubble, but the fucking lawyers won't let me."

"Now, Charles. Remember, I'm one."

"Yeah, but you can't say no." He took her by the wrist and kissed the inside of her forearm.

"Charles." She sighed. "Charles. I guess I need to surprise you."

And that was how she told him. It hurt her to do it, but she didn't love him and felt anxious to move on. He was an episode, she felt sure, and it was concluded now.

"Do you really think you'll be happy with your husband?"

"We're a family, Charles. Terry and the kids and I. I know he's a pain in the ass sometimes, but he looks too much like my son. I see Marty's face in his and I go all to pieces. It's a mother thing. Please understand."

She felt bad for him. During their time together, he had dropped the contrived face he put on for the world and shown her something like his unguarded self, but the mask was back now, and she felt guilty for betraying his tenderness. Other than that, she was surprised to discover later that letting go of Charles hadn't hurt her at all. What she hadn't let go of were the Krieger's options, which overnight became the financial bedrock of Abigail and Terry's lives. They began to look at them as money in the bank, and every day they checked the price of Krieger's stock in the newspaper. The options were already worth a fortune, but they were restricted, meaning in this case that Abigail couldn't exercise them for three years. Still, Terry spoke of how good it would feel to repay Maury finally, with interest.

In the interim, the Alphabet Soup scandal had increased the *Chronicle*'s circulation while the Krieger's story had produced an advertising windfall. Nowadays, though, instead of buying ads decrying the takeover bid, Krieger's advertised heavily to move merchandise. It had to; the company had piled on so much debt to buy out Rothwax that there was an urgent need to do more business. Krieger hired several new managers, all of them from New York or Boston, each more polished than the last, and they set about trying to "create a buzz" for the store. The Krieger's chain underwrote an exhibit of art deco furniture at the Webster Art Museum, and the store remade its ground floor with bent plywood furniture, period lighting and appliances, and retro clothing it hoped would make it young again.

Yet the *Chronicle* now had other troubles. Pickets positioned themselves outside the building five days a week to protest the paper's newly skeptical Alphabet Soup coverage, harassing anyone going in or out, and Abigail had to get a court order to keep them from blocking access to the building. Meanwhile she and Terry had to cope with a boycott that had recently sprung up, and Terry's new enemies were lobbying municipal officials to cut off the legal advertising that amounted to a public subsidy for the paper. The Krieger's options could not have come at a better time.

Webster had begun to thaw. Errol Jones noticed that his house was warm, even though the thermostat was set way down as usual, and on the way to work he began to spot the first harbingers of spring: campaign signs sprouting from snowy lawns like electoral crocuses. It was an important election year, and since Vanatee County had been overwhelmingly Democratic since the days of Woodrow Wilson, the Democratic primary was the race that counted. It was not lost on Errol that "Cal Hawthorne for District Attorney" signs outnumbered those of his opponent, Bob Varity, by perhaps two to one, and he knew that this wasn't just because Webster was Hawthorne territory. His boss was not especially personable, but his campaign chest was bulging and the Alphabet Soup prosecutions had helped him immeasurably all across the state, especially with women, narrowing the gender gap that was said by commentators to be his biggest weakness. Elliott Gordon, his reptilian media consultant, was at the office every day, and the district attorney was spending a lot of time with volunteer firefighters and at nursing homes and doing call-in radio shows, where the idea was to show his softer side. In response to callers who accused him of railroading innocent schoolteachers on sexual abuse charges, he was sorrowful more than angry, firm rather than dismissive. Sarcasm was banished from the district attorney's repertoire, leaving a gaping hole in his image that the voters, it was hoped, would fill with their own wishes.

These things mattered to Errol. Hawthorne's ambitions were larger than Vanatee County; assuming a victory in the primary, the election was a slam dunk, and he could be expected to run for statewide office before his term was out. Under the right circumstances, Errol Jones could hope to succeed him as district attorney. The first black district attorney in the county's history.

"You want to talk about it?" Hawthorne said when Errol got to his office. Gordon sat beside him, chin in hand, hunkered down behind the mask of innocence.

"The letter speaks for itself," Errol said. He wouldn't bother asking Gordon to leave. It no longer mattered. "I can't be a part of this anymore. It's crazy. I believe we're destroying innocent people. I won't do it."

"You have done it. You put them in this position. You pushed me to prosecute these cases."

"It was brilliant advice," Gordon said calmly. "That kind of insight is what makes this move so surprising."

Errol looked away from him, the patronizing little prick.

"Cal, it's a matter of conscience," he said.

"Personal reasons, in other words," Hawthorne prompted. "It's been a long run. You want to pursue other interests. Maybe even make a little money for change. Nobody will blame you."

"You *what?*" Terry said when Errol let drop, with studied casualness, that he had resigned. They were at the Y, and Terry held the ball, even though Errol had just sunk a jumper. They were shooting around, just playing, and by custom, hitting meant you were entitled to another.

"'Personal reasons,'" Errol said, signaling for the ball. "'Pursue other interests.' All the coded bullshit. Let people think I was fired or disgruntled or just greedy for a private-sector salary. I'll leave end of the month."

"But why?" Terry sent him a bounce pass and Errol took it, jumped, and hit another one. He was near his favorite spot, at the foul line but to the left.

"Because it's fucking evil, man! What the hell do you think? This whole thing is out of control."

"You think they're all innocent."

"I don't know, man. But I have to uphold the process, don't I? I have to believe in a certain system—otherwise I can't be a lawyer—and what we have here is a travesty of that system. The testimony is garbage, the investigation is almost the definition of a witch-hunt. They've even arrested witches."

"But there is a spell, don't you think?"

"There may even be witches; it makes no difference to the judicial process. I used to work on fraud—I know one when I see one. You need to write some more about Hawthorne. See if he has cloven hooves or a pointy tail. People looking high and low for Satan, and there he is, running for reelection, right here in Webster."

On election night, Terry was at Hawthorne's headquarters, where he scribbled down what he could of the candidate's banal victory speech. Hawthorne delivered it with his customary brio, mocking himself and his platitudes with his delivery.

"In short, it's been an eventful first term," he told the ballroom full of well-wishers. "With the help of my dedicated staff, we raised our conviction rates across the board, restructured the administration of the office, brought in new and diverse blood, and shattered a despicable ring of child abusers."

His wife was with him and had the same sharply chiseled features and thick-seeming skin. The devil's consort, Errol had taken to calling her. She was attractive but wary somehow. Terry recalled that she too was an athlete, a distance runner who could be seen on the roads around Webster no matter what the weather. Now and then she mustered the adoring smile expected of candidates' wives, but mostly she stared vacantly out at the audience.

"But we aren't going to rest on our laurels. We intend to convict every one of the individuals charged with abusing our precious children. Let the word go forth: you may worship Satan, but the devil himself won't save you if you're a child molester and Cal Hawthorne finds out about it!"

The room exploded in cheers. Hawthorne tried halfheartedly to suppress the ovation so he could continue, but people wouldn't stop clapping and whistling. All around, well-fed, sensible-looking people waved yellow handkerchiefs, a local semaphore of faith in the children. Fuzzy-headed and apostate, Terry felt himself a pariah among these believers, whose numbers astonished him.

Despite all the turmoil of the previous season, spring's rites went forward. The playgrounds filled with children, the sidewalks were at last cleared of snow, and young people stayed out later to take advantage of the lengthening days. Like the winter that seemed it would never go away, the child-abuse hysteria that had hovered over Webster for months suddenly and mysteriously lifted. The Webster Police made no further arrests, and most of those caught up in Jepson's sweeps were quietly released. While the District Attorney's Office said its investigation was ongoing, no new arrests were contemplated.

But despite the thaw, the initial Alphabet Soup defendants as well as a few others caught up in the case remained charged with crimes sufficient to send them to prison for the rest of their lives. While the rest of the town frolicked—the kids appearing in shorts and sandals the first day the temperature got past sixty—the former teachers, the minister and the janitor remained frozen in disgrace.

Terry's focus now was on freeing them. He turned more and more of his duties at the paper over to subordinates, obsessively covering and editorializing about the never-ending injustice of Alphabet Soup. The paper's new stance antagonized people, which cost circulation and revenue just as Krieger's for some reason began to advertise less as well. But he couldn't let go.

"Think of it as a marathon," Abigail said. "Like a marriage. It's not a sprint. You've got to pace yourself."

"Easy for you to say. Do you know what it's like in jail? You should have seen Albertson's face."

"You've done everything you could. You weren't on the grand jury that indicted those people."

"I advocated all this. Bought into the whole story."

"But you're turning the *Chronicle* into a weekly newsletter on the Alphabet Soup case. You're not going to be able to help anybody if circulation goes to hell and we lose all our business."

"What about all those Krieger's ads? They were going great guns for a while, then all of a sudden they've dried up."

"Just between seasons," Abigail said. "They'll be back."

Maybe it would be best if the Chronicle *finally did go under,* Terry thought yet again. They could be free of it and move on. Abigail could do something truly remunerative, and he could focus on getting the truth out to the larger world. When his father called to say the network was still interested in him, the timing seemed fortuitous.

"I told them you've grown your hair back, that the whole thing was kind of a Zen retreat. They're all really impressed by that sort of thing. You know, minimalism, detoxifying, all that crap. They eat it up in this business. Buddhists with BMWs, that's who runs these places. The executive VP even suggested some kind of talk show, taping a pilot for a test audience. You test really well among young and middle-aged women."

"G-G-Good timing. I'm w-w-working on something for PBS, a documentary. You'd be amazed what went on in the grand j-j-jury room. I'm focusing on Frank and Emily Joseph, because their case is probably the most egregious. There's a p-professor at Web State who's done some incredible work on the suggestibility of children. Maybe the n-n-network would be interested."

"Yesterday's news. Besides, everybody thinks these people are guilty, regardless. Child molesters belong in prison. You want to stop a conversation in this building, launch a defense of Satanic abuse. How about child labor next? Kiddy porn. Slavery. C'mon, son. Grow up."

"I'm trying, Dad."

That night, at dinner, Phoebe was uncharacteristically helpful, and Marty meanwhile could barely contain his glee at what his sister had taken to calling the Restoration. He was full of plans, wanting to lock his father into ball games and road trips and anything else that would prevent any further disappearance by his old man. *It can make you weep,* Terry thought, *the way kids need you.* He tucked both children in with hugs and kisses, even Phoebe, who seemed in some ways needier than Marty, more troubled by his return and less sure he would stay. She shocked him by asking that he read to her, and he did, from her girlhood favorite *My Ántonia,* until finally she couldn't keep her eyes open. She slept fitfully that night, worried because her grasp of the rhythm method had somehow been faulty, her body deceptive, and the next day Tim would drive her eighty-five miles to a clinic where she could get an abortion.

Phoebe didn't notice, but the day of her long, nervous drive was the anniversary of her grandmother Maria's death, and since anniversaries are important to journalists, Terry and his father made a pilgrimage of their own, albeit only to the cemetery behind the former church that now housed the *Chronicle.* It was Terry's idea; he knew Maury couldn't refuse him. The congregation had long since moved to the suburbs but still maintained this shady little Valhalla full of dead Puritans and modest tombstones in the heart of the community. Terry's mother was laid to rest there among her ancestors in the Weaver family section, with a marker bearing the name she was born with. Maria had kept her own name right through her marriage to Maury, even before it was fashionable for a married woman to do so, as if she knew the alliance was transient, and at a time when it made all sorts of trouble for Terry in school. She was buried with her parents and her older brother, no space left for a spouse, and it was this as much as anything that irked Maury, who couldn't abide her family yet whose deepest desires for belonging were thwarted in some ultimate way by these burial arrangements.

"Can you imagine not being laid to rest next to Abby?" he asked, shaking his head sadly. He looked sheepish, embarrassed at his role in the dead woman's life.

"No Dad. I c-can't."

But that was the trouble, Terry felt. There was something about being part of this old elite that felt like a hair shirt to restless Maury Mathers—

dusty and moribund and fake, like some joyless and perpetual Halloween. It crossed Terry's mind that he had avoided this mistake, and in this sense at least had exceeded his father.

"How's Diana?" Terry asked. It was a windy day, but the air smelled verdant.

"She asks about you," Maury said. "Kind of a doll, you know?"

Terry looked at him. "Not your type, Dad. Believe me."

"Look, it makes no difference. She's not interested right now. Still getting over you. Besides, she's had her hands full with that gorilla of a detective. Jetson, I think his name is. Guy practically tried to force himself on her. A borderline case, this close to attempted rape." He held thumb and forefinger an inch apart.

"Geez. She told you that?"

"I'm cultivating a source, which is something I'm reasonably good at. You know how that is."

Terry shook his head but said nothing. Finally he asked: "I wonder if she'll ever change her mind about all this. Do you think she'd tell you if she had any doubts?"

"Why would she have doubts?" Maury replied. "The evidence is overwhelming. One of them even admitted to it. Why do you persist in this messianic delusion of yours?"

"The t-t-truth is important, Dad."

"The truth! I just told you the truth. You've got nothing but the hypothesis of some thumb-sucking academic." Maury turned to him. "Is this really just the same old neurotic need of yours to pull me down?"

Terry barked a big laugh, an impropriety that infuriated his father.

"Well, you know it's all about you at some level, Dad. I'm trying to live up to some ideal of you that I've always h-held in my heart."

"Always the wise guy." Maury shook his head. "Even at your mother's grave."

"I'm not joking. I've really tried. You were such a big deal to me I resented the h-hell out of you for it. For casting such a long, crooked shadow."

"All I ever did was love you the best way I could."

"I know that. I guess I'm still trying to bring you back, still thinking I can make the world whole again. Probably that's why I brought you here. Just to have you and me and Mom again for a few minutes."

"Terry, I have cancer. I'll have plenty of time for cemeteries soon enough."

"Dad, please. This hypochondria is unseemly at your age."

"Do I have to show you the lab report?"

"What are you saying here?"

"I'm saying I have prostate cancer. I'm not making it up."

"What? Is it serious?"

"Well it's never funny."

"Are you b-being treated? What can I do?"

"You can relax. They got it early; it's treatable. The main thing is to make sure I don't come out a choirboy. They think they can keep the plumbing working—otherwise I wouldn't even go along with them. I wanted you to hear it from me."

"Where else would I hear it?"

"I'm doing a TV special. To raise awareness. 'One Man's Struggle.' We'll demystify proctology. Kind of a first in prime time, I think. New ground for me too."

chapter EIGHTEEN

It took months just for the Alphabet Soup trials to start, what with all the maneuvering on both sides beforehand, and during this time the defendants were imprisoned and reviled. The children's testimony was pivotal. In Frank's trial, which was first, they testified on videotape to spare them the trauma of doing so in open court. One of them said that Frank had taken him and several of the others on a trip into outer space aboard a rocketship, and that during this journey their private parts were bathed in the blood of dead rabbits.

"What kind of rocketship was it?" Frank's lawyer asked on cross-examination.

"Just a regular rocketship," the boy answered.

After the jury foreman read the first guilty verdict, the courtroom erupted in cheers, and though the judge quieted this with his gavel, there was a mounting sense of giddiness as each "guilty" was spoken. As Frank was led from the courthouse in handcuffs, Terry found himself amid a group of parents and little children dressed in Easter finery for the legal proceedings.

"There he is," said one father. "Now's the time!"

"Child molester!" his daughter shouted.

"I hope you rot in prison!" another child screamed.

"Dirty rapist, go back to jail where you belong."

"Good telling, Maggie!" her mother enthused. Frank had been hustled into a van that quickly drove away, but Maggie continued to rage on the sidewalk afterward.

"She's mourning her lost childhood," her mother volunteered to Terry. "Thank God she's willing to let it out."

He began to grow depressed. Each of the subsequent trials was a nightmare in its own way, and all of them ended in conviction. Frank, Emily and Pearl, as the ringleaders, were sentenced to decades in prison. Annette, who had pleaded guilty to lesser charges, got the lightest sentence, eight years. Julie, who had refused to plead, was treated more harshly and got twenty. So did Sue, who shrieked when the sentence was imposed. Chris was the only one to go free; prosecutors ultimately decided she hadn't worked at the school long enough and dropped the charges against her. Jesus wept when he was sentenced to ten years; Albertson told Terry the prison authorities had begun to sedate him because he had been crying all night, begging to be sent home to Mexico. Albertson himself, the only other person tried and convicted, got twenty years.

The civil suit, bolstered by the criminal jurors' findings of fact, went equally badly, although it mattered little to defendants who already were imprisoned and impoverished. Alphabet Soup's insurance company, however, had to pay out $12 million in damages to families claiming harm as a result of child abuse at the school. By the time the money was distributed, claims had been filed on behalf of most of the students who had ever spent time there. Lawyers' fees were held to a third of the settlement, with the lion's share going to Belinda Jackson's attorney, although all the lawyers' money was tied up in a dispute over apportionment. Belinda used her share to buy a new car, pay off her credit cards, and move away. She would serve out her probation in California.

Webster seemed to find the trials cathartic; they narrowed the suffering to the defendants and a small group of their family and friends, freeing everybody else to get on with life. Even most of the people who felt the teachers were wrongly accused didn't care enough to spend much time worrying about it, and so the few who stood by the convicted abusers were left to wage a lonely struggle against the weight of indifference and consistent legal findings. The Alphabet Soup mothers who had organized against the abuse, meanwhile, held a giant block party. They had formalized their organization, broadened it to advocate children's causes throughout Vanatee County, and put one of their own on the Webster City Council. There was talk she might run for county commissioner.

"It's important to move on," she told the *Chronicle.* "But it's also important not to forget. We'll never forget."

Terry knew this was no lie.

S urely He would understand if she could not wait. If He was the merciful and loving Son of God she had always believed in and recently rediscovered, it would be all right with Him. She wondered if this might even be an invitation. He must know what it's like, must have known when He sent her here. He had been through as much himself.

Annette lay on her bunk in the softness of the moonlight that poured into the room through the small window at the top of her cell. Beside her on the hard mattress lay the folded pages of a letter, small and inert. The catcalls of her fellow inmates still rang in her ears. The other women hurled curses at her as she was escorted to meals and exercise, to visiting hours and to meetings with Father O'Nan, the sad gray priest whose watery faith couldn't possibly sustain her.

"But sometimes we look to God and can't find the answers we hope to find," he said on her last visit. "Sometimes we have to look to ourselves."

"You think I'm guilty too, is that it?"

"I can't judge you, Mrs. Martini." She hated that name; it practically made her cringe. "Only God can do that."

"But I've been judged," she said. "Here on earth, I've been judged and found guilty and sent to prison. My family shuns me. I've been cast into Hell, and I don't know why."

"One of the biggest challenges in my work is getting people to own what they've done," Father O'Nan said. "You can't take the first step to salvation, not personal or spiritual, until then. If you want to see your little boy, you have to face whatever impulses brought you here in the first place and ask forgiveness. Ask it of the Lord and someday, when he's old enough to understand, of your son."

"Oh, my Lord," she said quietly, hand to mouth. How could she ever explain that it was her sinfulness with Frank that had caused all this?

"Mrs. Martini," said Father O'Nan, reaching for her arm.

She jerked away and began shaking. She was freezing. It was what she had expected Hell would be like. Hell was cold. The devil came cloaked in kindness.

"Mrs. Martini," said Father O'Nan, opening her file and peering at it through the little half-glasses that sat on his meaty nose. "I'm going to send you to see Dr. Alvarez. It says here you've seen him already, but I'll ask him to give you something."

"My faith is in my Redeemer," she said. "I don't need anything a psychiatrist has to offer."

"I'll write it up," said Father O'Nan. "He can help you rest."

She wouldn't see Dr. Alvarez again, with his dark beard and fierce eyebrows. The image of Satan, she thought when she first met him. Involuntarily, she looked at his feet, expecting cloven hooves. A seducer. Offering pharmaceutical candy to make you feel better, help you sleep. Anything but the truth, which he doesn't want to hear.

That morning's letter had come as a shock but not a surprise. She had expected something like this. She hadn't heard from Ray in weeks. He didn't answer her increasingly desperate letters, nor did her son. Now here was this letter telling about his plans to move away, to take Andy with him. "Please don't try to contact him. He wants no further part of a mother who could do such things."

She had seen her trials as a test at first, but no longer. Eating veal patties with her blunt fork, the only kind the inmates were allowed, the food felt alien in her mouth, a wad of cotton covered with tomato sauce and fake cheese. The minutes dragged as if life behind bars would go on forever, as if incarceration were the secret to immortality. She thought of a dripping sink, each droplet taking an eternity to form and fall, its successor just as slow, and an ocean to be emptied in this way. After dinner there was the noise of the rabble on both sides of the cell block, the cackles and taunts and foul language reverberating off the hard surfaces so that one was surrounded by them long after they were issued.

It felt good at least to lie down, even though she couldn't sleep. She hadn't slept in weeks. Months. Since all this started, since she was put on trial, since she was sent away. How can you sleep locked behind bars, caged among lepers, their loathing of your cleanliness in the air all around you? It was this isolation too. Hell was being utterly alone, somewhere so far away even Jesus couldn't seem to hear you.

Her cell was warm, but she huddled under the covers. It was almost like the first time she had taken a drink or had sex. Her heart pounded, but she'd done it so many times before in her mind that she knew just what to do now. Her cell, the night, the turn her life had taken—it was all like a dream. As she took off her shirt, she commenced shivering again, and shivered harder as she reached up to thread a sleeve through the bars across her window, trying not to think about her boy.

When Wayne Lyttle entered, Charles Krieger didn't even look up right away. The secretaries had gone home, and underlings tended to barge in.

"What's the news?" Krieger said, scribbling in the margins of a memo on his desk.

"Annette Martini was found hanging in her cell last night."

Krieger looked up.

"Who's Annette—"

"One of the Alphabet Soup teachers."

"Boo hoo," Krieger said. "I'll bet you're broken up about that."

Wayne looked out at the lights of Web State. It was late, and he resented his boss's unseemly nattiness at this dark hour. An expensive-looking clock ticked grandiosely in the corner. Krieger's richly appointed office filled him with disgust.

"Charlie, things are bad."

"Tell me something I don't know. Things have been bad for weeks."

"They just got worse. Word is out that we can't meet all our obligations from last Christmas—"

"Yet! Can't meet our obligations at this particular minute!"

"—and virtually all our major fashion suppliers have put us on a cash and carry basis."

He now had the other man's full attention.

"You're pulling my fucking leg."

Wayne said nothing. He had lost patience. The bleaker the future looked for Krieger's, the less reason he had to humor his boss or mask his contempt.

"Wayne. Tell me you're pulling my leg."

"If I were a dog, Charlie, I might be pulling your leg. I might sink my teeth all the way through. But I'm not a dog. I'm just an accountant. I'm just presenting the facts as I find them."

"What the fuck is that supposed to mean? Are you dissociating yourself from these facts? You had nothing to do with them?"

"Are you ready to discuss this seriously? 'Cause if you're not I don't have to be here."

Krieger rose and went to a cabinet, from which he retrieved glasses and a bottle. He gestured to Wayne.

"Might as well," he said, and Krieger handed him a drink.

"Tell me how much time we have," he said.

Wayne sipped. You could always count on Krieger to keep some obscure and ambrosial single-malt scotch on hand. He took another swallow, cherishing the combination of fire and ice.

"Charlie, we both know this is over. Whatever you've got in inventory, once the store starts getting that vacant look, it starts smelling like a corpse, and the customers will smell what the suppliers just got a whiff of."

"Look, I'm sure we can string this out three, four more weeks—just enough to come up with some alternative financing."

"Who's going to lend us money? We're already carrying so much debt we can't service it. In a couple of weeks, we're looking at a technical default on our bonds."

"An investor," Krieger said. "Not a lender. Someone to put in equity, which is what we need here."

"A fraction of a company this deep in the hole isn't worth anything to anybody, including you and me. The only possibility is somebody who buys the whole place outright, and we've been through that. That's how we got here tonight."

Krieger seemed distant, lost in some daydream of what might have been. Wayne drank some more and felt a little sympathy stirring within himself. He decided to be patient, have a heart.

"So we need a white knight," Krieger said.

"Doesn't matter what color he is," said Wayne, trying on a smile. "Just as long as he moves fast and his money's green."

"Really, how much time do you think?"

"Charlie, there's no time. Just before I came in here, I asked the lawyers to start drawing up Chapter 11 papers. You've tried everything. It's not your fault. Who knew the economy would pick now to go into recession?"

"Chapter 11. Wow. Well, it'll buy us time. We can find a buyer, somebody who wants to work with the management that already knows the business, and we'll come out again. Get a reorganization plan and come out stronger. It's just a rough patch we're going through."

Wayne took another drink and looked out the window, lest he say anything more. He was used to the idea by now that his options were worthless, and he had been smart enough to resist investing his retirement money in Krieger's shares. He was healthy, employable, not over the hill yet. He had been wanting to leave Webster anyway, ever since Jeffrey's troubles at Alphabet Soup. He took another, bigger sip. The ice felt good against his lips. Who was he kidding? He had wanted to leave long ago, leave Lucille behind, leave Charlie Krieger to his own sad delusions, and go someplace where people had a handle on reality. He'd been about to do it too, when Jeffrey's abuse came to light. The kid had never been the same; his behavior was still difficult, but now it was as if all that energy had turned inward, and instead of busting up the house he was chewing his cuticles bloody, screaming during the night, tearing at his hair. There were little bald spots around the front where he pulled most often. *We'll never know what happened,* Wayne thought bitterly. He loathed what had befallen his son, but found it hard to blame it all on the school. Lucille was out of hand, he knew. He would have to do something soon, would need a new job anyway. It was time to make a move. He wondered how on earth he would handle the children on his own.

R*outine is the essence of life in prison,* Emily wrote in her weekly letter to her cousin. *As I approach the fourth anniversary of my incarceration, as they like to call it here, I discover to my horror that I begin to be at home in this place. Not in any comfortable way; I wake up every morning as if from a nightmare that I can't leave behind in sleep. Imagine that: your worst dreams, and then you wake up and they're not dreams at all. No, what I mean by at home is just, well, changed—changed enough by the experience that the stamp of prison is on me. I have to work hard to remember freedom nowadays. It slips farther away every day, like the voice of a loved one who's died. You try to remember, but all you can hold onto is a hint of the thing. The other day one of the guards who's made a special project of me decided to search me, which she did very thoroughly and at length, and afterward I had to admit that beyond the humiliation I took a little pleasure in it. Isn't that sick? I enjoyed it. That's how badly I needed to be touched.*

They wouldn't even let me touch Mother. Did you know that? Just before she died, they brought me to her, but only at the very end, when there was no more hope and little in the way of comfort that I could give her. I want to tell you about this. You knew she had been sick for a while. Her heart problems were far along, and I was tormented by the fear that she wouldn't get out of here alive, wouldn't have me or you or anyone else to comfort her in her pain. Can you imagine dying in this place? I prayed in those days. I beseeched God to please just release my mother and let her rest. She is innocent, she is old, she is sick. How could anyone imagine that such a woman might abuse little children? God has been hard of hearing lately, I find. We are no longer on speaking terms.

Then one day they called me in and said "Your mother is dying." "I know that," I told them, but I knew what they really meant. They meant now. And so they took me to her. They put me in manacles with a chain around my waist, and another around my ankles, because a dangerous character like me has to be restrained anytime I go outside this wing of the prison. I hobbled this way to the hospital ward, and when I got there they wouldn't take all that stuff off of me. "It's a locked room," I told them. "What are you afraid of? What could I do in there?" I started to cry, but they said if I wanted to see her this was the best they could do. And so I went in, and there she was, wasted on the bed, with tubes running out of her arms and so forth and a band around her face delivering oxygen to her nostrils. I went to kiss her, and they wouldn't let me. I was speechless at the mindless cruelty of it. I just stared at the person who told me this, to see if I could make out any sense of shame, but all she said was, "You've got fifteen minutes. Don't waste them." So you see, they wouldn't let me touch my dying mother. I sat five feet away and tried to think what to say. I didn't want her to look at me, but suddenly she was speaking, and I leaned my head forward to hear.

She said she was glad, Melissa, and this broke my heart. You have to know that she was whispering. I could just make out the words. She could barely speak, she didn't have the strength. And this is what she said to me: that she was glad to be dying, because she had had a good life and had somehow fallen into a living hell from which she would now be delivered. "Don't give up," she said. "You and I will always know the truth."

I told her I loved her and would never give up until everyone knew we were all innocent, but after a while she couldn't talk anymore and then she seemed to go to sleep. I was so afraid at that instant, so afraid that she had died, and so I called out to her. I screamed, I guess. It was all happening outside of time, and I was covered with tears and my nose was running. I was incoherent, just raving. "Help her! Get a doctor, help her! Don't you see? She's innocent. My mother is innocent!"

Afterward I was furious at her for leaving me here—her ordeal was over and mine wasn't. And I realized what a good way out it might be to die. What difference did it make what people thought once you were gone? You wouldn't be around to mind. My mother's pain is over.

Emily put the pen down and stretched her right hand. She liked the image of being outside of time. That was what prison was like. Things went on in the outside world, the seasons changed, people had babies, moved away, aged, died, whatever, but inside it was always the same. Writing letters had become her main source of comfort. It was how she fought the sense of cosmic abandonment that she felt sometimes at night, when she heard the sounds of the others making love or masturbating or whatever it was they did in the dark. She felt like the man in that Poe story who gets walled up in the basement all by himself, except there was a little slot between the stones, a little opening, and she could send letters sailing out through it. These letters were often more satisfying than face-to-face visits, which somehow underscored her humiliation and left everyone feeling awkward and tongue-tied. Letter writing was different. After writing back and forth a few times, you really got to know somebody, and both parties expressed themselves in a way they never would have in person. She now saw that something had gone out of the world with the decline of old-fashioned correspondence, that maybe this was one reason for the thinness of contemporary relationships. Everyone was so inarticulate nowadays, and so frustrated by everyone else. What they needed was to write to one another, to sit down and think for a minute where it was quiet.

Thus she wrote to her son in Oregon, struggling in her letter not to seem emotionally greedy but shivering with joy and anguish when she thought once more of how he'd said in print how much he loved and believed in her. And of course, she wrote to Frank.

It's hard to know what to say sometimes, she wrote in her sharply leaning hand. *The everyday life we shared is all gone, except in our memories, and the daily experience of our lives now is too boring to dwell on. My work in the library passes the time, and today DeWanda showed me some new pictures of her little boy, which gave me a lump in my throat. Do you know what it means to have someone show me her child, instead of just assuming I am some kind of pedophile who can't even look at a picture without getting aroused? I have grown very fond of DeWanda; she actually seems to be learning to read, and the more she is able to tease sense from the printed word, the more hopeful she becomes for some kind of life once she gets out of here, although I know she tries not to let too much of this show around me. She and all the others assume I'll be here forever. Some news: this morning one of the appellate lawyers said they're all cautiously optimistic about this latest appeal they are hoping to have before the state Supreme Court in the next couple of months, and of course it's impossible not to get one's hopes up, even though I'm already fairly numb from going through this whole cycle of hope and despair 100 times before. Still, some judge, somewhere, has got to be distressed by the fact that a juror in my case brought a magazine article about child abuse into the jury room, and that she and the rest of them pored over the list of supposed characteristics of abusers to see if I fit the profile—which of course they decided I did when Dr. Brauner's records somehow came into evidence, and the whole world found out what my bastard uncle did to me. From that point, it was an open-and-shut case, in the small minds of the people in that small room: if I was abused, obviously I had grown up to become an abuser myself. After all, it was right there in the magazine.*

I am afraid I am feeling as cynical as you are about Cal Hawthorne's election as governor, although when I heard the news it came as a kind of anticlimax. It was clear all along he was likely to win, and I always thought that business about a gubernatorial pardon or commutation or whatever was some kind of pipe dream, although of course it certainly won't be forthcoming now. Personally I'm glad to have him out of Vanatee County. Even if we do succeed on appeal, the prosecution could decide to retry the cases. It's got to be easier for a new DA to let the whole thing go at long last, since it won't be a matter of defending his own record.

I'm sorry to hear about your never-ending colds, darling. I take comfort in your strength during this ordeal, and try to remind myself that you, more than any of us, can cope with solitude and confinement without becoming overwhelmed by shame.

She could sense from the waning light coming through the small, high window of the library that it was well into the afternoon, and she decided to see if she could catch a couple of her favorite soaps. She had acquired this habit in prison the way other inmates acquired drug habits, but it was clear that inmates were experts at killing time, and television was their most effective weapon. TV helped in forming a prison routine, which by blurring the distinction between days made the time go faster. Maybe this was why the inmates themselves embraced routine and fiercely protested departures from it.

"Julie," she said, taking a seat in the rec room with the usual crowd, next to some of the other better-educated women. "Your hair."

"I'd had enough; I wanted it real short." She ran her knobby fingers across her head, covered now with just a low nap of colorless fuzz. "You hate it, I know."

"No. I've thought of doing the same, but it's just something I hold on to. I can't give it up."

"It's a form of freedom, this way," Julie said. "I'm into renunciation lately. It grows back, anyway."

She stared at the TV, her jaw set, while Emily and some of the others stole glances at her. Short hair was supposed to make you look younger, but Emily felt it had aged her friend. It was her face too or maybe just the weight she had lost. She had used to glow, and there had been a downy fullness to her limbs, but all this was long gone. The shapeless prison garb hung wanly on her frame now, seemingly cut more for robots than for people, and the lack of makeup and jewelry, of color in her skin and a smile on her face, conspired to render Julie almost twice as old as she had been in happier days. This was a woman who had loved flowered dresses, Emily recalled, turning her attention finally back to the set mounted on the wall.

Afterward there was the news, which the women tended to ignore until a segment came on about overcrowded prisons. "Here in C-California, for instance," the reporter said, "a c-crackdown on drugs has resulted in an avalanche of convictions—and a state penal s-system that is bursting at the s-seams. Officials have t-taken to building new prisons in a m-m-modular design, so that additional hexagonal units can easily be added to accommodate growth."

"He's cute," one of the women said.

"You like him?!" one of others said. "He sounds like Porky Pig. You ever been with a white guy? They all pink that way. Little piggies, I don't care how clean."

The others laughed.

"Y'all wasting your time, 'cause he's Emily's boyfriend," a third woman said, stealing a glance at Emily to gauge the effect of this. She smiled.

"Whatever happened to that documentary he was supposed to be making?" Julie asked. "Have you heard anything more about that?"

Emily shook her head. He had visited several times, shooting miles of videotape, and had decided to make Emily the centerpiece of the project, which seemed to drag on for years. He'd seemed earnest and full of enthusiasm, but nothing ever came of it.

Cross-legged, Julie wiggled her foot as the women bickered over what to watch next. Emily put her hand on it to make it stop.

"Nerves," Julie said. "I can't sit still. I'm seeing Chrissie tomorrow."

"Is that what the short hair is about?"

"No! She liked it the other way. Thought it was sweet. Femme, as they say."

Emily watched her blush and then impulsively hugged her.

"I'm so happy for you. I know how hard you both had to fight for this."

Julie's eyes were damp when she emerged from the embrace. The state's policy on conjugal visits didn't grant them to same-sex couples or inmates held on charges of a sexual nature. Julie and Chris had become a cause célèbre for challenging the legality of the system. Governor Hawthorne had surprised everybody by ordering the change.

"I think he figured it was a low-cost way to soften up his image," Julie said. "And maybe he figured he had something to gain by emphasizing the lesbianism this way. Maybe he saw it as a chance to further stigmatize me. All of us, really. As perverts. Maybe stop all the appeals, all the agitation. Keep us all locked up."

"I'm not worried," Emily said. "The world can't stay this bad forever."

In Webster, things were not better for a long time. The national recession bit harder locally because two of the community's leading institutions, the Krieger's Department Store chain and the Webster *Chronicle,* failed. Krieger's never recovered from its Chapter 11 filing; it was eventually acquired by a friendly buyer who allowed Charles Krieger to remain chairman, although he had to give up the title of chief executive. That was reserved by the new owner (a real estate developer from Dallas) for his point man on such deals, who quickly liquidated the stores. Employees lost their jobs and, since the stockholders were wiped out in the bankruptcy, almost all their pension money as well. The plan was to redevelop the downtown Krieger's property into a multiscreen movie, shopping, and restaurant complex with an all-weather roller rink, but before this could happen the economy tanked and the project was halted. The store remained vacant for years thereafter, as did the spanking-new garage next door.

The *Chronicle* was reborn, with new owners and in less ambitious form. It was acquired for less than the value of its debts by a group of local investors headed by none other than Willie Niedleman, who became editor. It was filled now with flattering stories about advertisers and photos of smiling people at award ceremonies. The Tartaglia column was replaced by a popular horoscope feature. Circulation increased even though the paper still carried some bad news. People read in it, for example, about the death of Lucille Lyttle. Her downward spiral accelerated by divorce, she collapsed on her doorstep and was pronounced dead when she arrived at WebCare, the for-profit institution that used to be known as Webster Memorial Hospital. An autopsy gave advanced liver disease as the primary cause, along with congestive heart failure. But everyone knew she drank herself to death.

chapter NINETEEN

Jesus Mendoza, who learned a little English in prison but never stopped dreaming of his native Oaxaca, eventually died of AIDS.

The Reverend Floyd Albertson saw to his parishioner's funeral. It was sparsely attended, although that was no surprise, and Albertson was convinced this was not out of any disdain for Mendoza's supposed crimes, which most people had stopped believing in, but sheer embarrassment at the appalling episode that had led to his loss of life. It was a beautiful day, sunny and warm, the eighties over at last, and it made Albertson quake with anger that a decent and innocent man would no longer experience such days because of a virus—the virus not of AIDS, which Mendoza acquired as the result of a brutal prison assault, but of hysteria—which had left Jesus as one of its casualties. There were a few Mexicans, all of them standing shyly together off to the side, and the handful of others who might have been expected at such an event. Everybody seemed melancholy, but nobody was crying or leaning on anyone else, and this too seemed to Albertson horribly sad. It was as if Jesus had died long ago, on entering prison.

The coffin was already lowered into the open grave, and the idea popped into Albertson's head to have anybody who wished throw a shovelful of dirt onto the box. Terry Mathers, the only one for whom this concept wasn't alien, stepped forward, and the reverend was pleased. He felt that he would be honoring Jesus in this way, and the others stood by uncertainly as Terry jammed the shovel effortfully into the soil with his foot. The dirt and rocks made a hollow thumping sound as they landed on the plain pine box. Albertson had come to admire Terry despite his ambiguous role in the events that ultimately cost Jesus Mendoza his life and removed five years from Albertson's, to say nothing of the fortune in legal fees. Like the others who had survived the Alphabet Soup hysteria, Terry looked older, his cheeks lined and his closely cropped hair almost entirely gray.

"But even in death there is solace," the Reverend Albertson said, his voice booming into the breeze. "For this beloved young man, his suffering is at an end now."

An agnostic on the idea of an afterlife, Albertson knew from his own experience that redemption was possible—and even necessary—in the here and now. Terry was evidence of this proposition, having worked tirelessly to report the truth about Alphabet Soup after the convictions and even using the pulpit of television to preach about the injustice of it all. The tide was turned on appeal, the higher courts finding various flaws with the cases, including hopelessly tainted testimony from small children heavily influenced by their interrogators. Yet Albertson knew that these decisions do not happen in a vacuum, and just as the convictions arose from a society primed for them, exoneration could only arise from soil similarly prepared. As if on cue, a young Mexican in a dark shirt and pants took up the shovel and dug out some soil to throw onto the coffin. Afterward he nodded politely at Albertson who, with pain in his heart at having to say farewell, finally concluded the funeral.

Terry had more than prepared the soil. He had spent three years producing a devastating documentary that revealed some of the most egregious miscarriages in the case, including his and the *Chronicle's* role in fomenting a witch-hunt, and his interviews with jurors showed that many regretted their hasty verdicts. Jurors from the trial of Frank Joseph admitted that they hadn't understood the judge's instructions. One of them wept. The former assistant district attorney in charge of the prosecutions said on camera he thought innocent people had been sent to prison and asked Governor Hawthorne to issue pardons if all else failed. Thank God all else didn't fail, because Hawthorne remained immovable.

I t's a left up here," she said. "You just keep bearing left every time one of these little roads comes to an end."

Emily and Frank were on their way home from the funeral. They had been living in the house for two weeks now, but Frank still had trouble locating it among the vertiginous curves of the subdivision. Melissa Faircloth had found it for them; the owners wanted house-sitting while on a fellowship somewhere, and so all Emily and Frank had to do was look after the two cats. Emily was allergic, but she readily agreed anyway, since it was free and they had no money.

She was numb at first, but the taste of freedom now wouldn't go away, and sometimes, out of the blue, she'd feel the tears coming. They made her smile. She didn't care that they had lost everything, that they might face another trial, even that her mother had died in prison and would never know the joy she now felt. She would care about all these things soon enough, but meanwhile the air on her skin or her husband's embrace were enough to make her break down, make her giggle and cry at once like a crazy person.

"We can do anything," she said, turning to Frank in the driver's seat. "Eat or sleep or fuck. Anything we want."

"All those things sound good."

"Let's combine them."

"Or how about serially?" Frank said. "We'll have sex and eat and sleep."

"I didn't know how much I loved you," she said later, in his arms, and he agreed he felt the same. "So you see," he said, "there is some good that comes of this. It was something we had to take a hard road to learn."

It was conceivable they could be sent back, but not likely. The district attorney nowadays, appointed to fill out the term of Cal Hawthorne when the latter was elected governor, was Errol Jones, whose disillusionment with the Alphabet Soup cases was well known. Although he was said to be reviewing the evidence, hardly anyone believed he would want to retry the Josephs or anyone else associated with the matter. Even if he did believe in their guilt, it would be difficult after five years.

So for now they waited, just as they had before, for the other shoe to drop. Meanwhile they had their son looking around for them in Oregon. For a house, some kind of business opportunity. Something. He was quite successful for a young man, and they looked forward to moving west to join him there.

What the appeals court found, Emily wrote to him, *was that we were convicted on tainted evidence and deprived of due process. In other words, we were railroaded. During the appellate process they tried to get us to agree to some kind of extended probation in exchange for our release, I guess because they knew they were going to lose. It crossed my mind at one point to take it—just take it and get away from all this. Except then I'd be a released child sex offender. And so we said no. We'd come this far, and so we waited and worried and all of a sudden the lawyers called and said we won, that they couldn't say for sure but they thought it was over.*

The next thing we knew, we were out. It was like coming back from a long sea voyage, or from outer space; your father and I felt weightless, disoriented. It seemed hard just to walk. I somehow forgot how to drive in there or maybe developed a phobia about it.

Anyway, they give you a few dollars and send you on your way. The strange thing is that nobody ever says they're sorry about this—sorry about killing your mother and destroying your business and tarring you as a child molester in your community. On the contrary, there's this attitude that you got away with something, so the whole thing is grudging. You come out blinking in the light, a financial and emotional wreck, but you're so happy you don't care.

Your father and I haven't been apart more than a few minutes since our release. We feel like we've come back from the dead.

.   .   .

From almost any point in the sound stage, the set looked small and fake, a Potemkin village living room overwhelmed by the lights, microphones and cameras, the crisscross of wires and duct tape. The set consisted of a couple of bent chrome chairs and a little table holding a small carafe of water and a couple of glasses. In front of them stood a book, its cover clearly visible to the cameras. The title was *It Only Gets Better.*

"Sound check please," someone said. "Your plosives were popping just a little."

"Peter P-P-Piper picked a p-peck of pickled p-p-peppers," said the younger of two men on the set.

An older man occupied the other seat, a slightly sour expression on his face.

"Stand by," said one of the technicians.

The men in the chairs hardly moved. They had the air of people accustomed to being in front of the camera.

"Four, three, two, one . . ."

"We're back!" the younger man said. "If you're just joining us, w-w-welcome to *Terry Mathers Live.* We're happy to have you, and our guest today is none other than the legendary journalist and television personality Maury Mathers. And if you're wondering, yes, there is a relationship. We're brothers."

"Try to show a little respect, will you?" Maury said. Both men put up looks of comic exasperation.

"So Dad, let's talk about your new book. I understand it's about foreign policy in the post-nuclear age and postulates a new defense doctrine—wait a minute, that's not it. This one—this one's about sex?! Dad, people will be shocked! Is it really about sex?"

"Well I don't know if they'll be shocked, but what it's really about is sex after seventy, which is a time of life when most people think there's not a lot happening in that department."

"I for one will be relieved to hear otherwise."

And so it went, Terry clowning dryly and his father playing the put-upon straight man. During the next commercial break, Maury fidgeted uncomfortably.

"C'mon, Dad, it's not so bad."

"It's ghastly. I come out here flogging this pathetic book like some infomercial pitchman, except the act I follow is a guy who had a sex change operation and then had himself changed back again when he changed his mind."

"His l-l-lover was gay and w-wanted him to stay a man. It's a t-t-tragic story."

"It's beneath you."

"And you? What are you doing here?"

"Helping my son."

"Selling books!"

"You invited me. You said you wanted to give the show a little class."

"You're just jealous I got your old time slot."

"Abby's a sensible girl. What does she make of all this?"

"She doesn't watch. She's glad to be practicing law again, and Phoebe's finally starting to enjoy Wesleyan. You know all that. You talk to Abby more than you talk to me."

"Can you blame me? Women are so much more interesting than men."

"Stand by," said one of the technicians.

"They watch a lot of TV too," Terry whispered.

"Four, three, two, one . . ."

When they were back on the air, they took questions from the audience. People asked about the need to share men ("there are so few at that age"), about preventing transmission of disease, and of course about their own bizarre predicaments. One told of a man she suspected of bigamy. Another asked how young a man Maury thought she might be able to seduce. "The really old ones aren't any good. Let's face it."

A large woman in a pink sweatsuit, her hair a cloud of bluish gray, stood up way in back. A staff member rushed over with a microphone but didn't get there in time for her first few words.

"—be saying it's OK for old people to have sex, but I remember you both were on TV covering the case of that preschool where the teachers abused the kids, and one of those teachers was an old lady. Maybe some of these people don't have the self-control they should anymore about these things."

They got through it somehow. "Tomorrow," said Terry, "we'll have

Senator Richard Harrison, who'll talk about coping with the death of a spouse while raising two small children. Plus"—and here he held up an index card, reading aloud—"a man who slept with all three of his wife's sisters. Hmm. Evidently, we'll have the whole family on hand to confront the dirty dog."

Terry had learned to stop worrying. Not to stop caring, but to stop thinking of himself as the answer. He had been in the grip of a messianic complex, he now saw, and it was a relief to be cured. That's what youth was—a messianic complex. The world either ignored you or paid attention, and either way the disease went away.

Now that he was no longer young—a state of mind only loosely connected to the state of the body—and lived in a larger, more indifferent place once again, he had learned to love his scaled-down expectations, like some cherished and carefully pinned butterfly collection he could pore over with magnifying glass and tongs. With the *Chronicle* gone, Terry and Abigail were like people who had awakened from a coma; without the paper they felt alert, light-headed, free. Terry made vastly more money too, now that he had come to understand the human need for entertainment and to accept his work in this arena as God's own. In moments of grandiose self-pity, which still came over him now and again, he likened himself to the hero of the film *Sullivan's Travels,* who must suffer to learn the value of laughter. Preston Sturges instinctively understood the need to entertain, as do novelists, composers, even clergymen who are worth their salt. Why was twelve-tone music nobler somehow than *Terry Mathers Live?* How was it any different from Dostoyevsky, drawing on the lurid periodicals of his day, the early Russian tabloids, for his plots? At the end of every show, Terry went out into the audience for five minutes, asking what lessons might be drawn. He always led his viewers toward some moral, but they went there willingly. All men seek the good, said Aristotle, and women too. People strove for it even in the audience of a daytime television show. They tried to make sense of things, stood ready with forgiveness, wished for the guests to reconcile their grievances. The show reached 17 million people every day. Already, young people had never heard the name Maury Mathers, who did not live on in reruns or nostalgia but evaporated with the news he had delivered. Terry, on the other hand, was becoming famous everywhere.